D0989046

patchwork.

patchwork.

L. R. Walters

Patchwork

Copyright © 2023 L. R. Walters

All rights reserved. Without limiting the rights under copyright reserved alone, no part of this publication may be reproduced, stored in or introduced into a retrieval system, or transmitted in any form or by any means (electronic, mechanical, photocopying, recording, or otherwise) without the prior written permission of both the copyright owner and the above publisher of the book.

This is a work of fiction. Names, characters, places, brands, media, and incidents are either the product of the author's imagination or are used fictitiously. The author acknowledges the trademarked status and trademark owners of various products, bands, and/or restaurants referenced in this work of fiction, which have been used without permission. The publication/ use of these trademarks is not authorized, associated with, or sponsored by the trademark owners.

To my intrusive thoughts, for the inspiration.

And to my therapists over the years, for their help with that.

rules.

chapter 1.

I clutched the dishtowel to my right arm as I hurried up the stairs, finally finished with dinner. It was bleeding fast; I wondered in a dim, panicked way if she hadn't hit a major blood vessel, if I wasn't going to bleed out and die looking like a suicidal madman with a deep ragged stab wound where a clean, simple line with a razor would have sufficed.

"Good night, sweetie," sing-songed my mother's voice from behind me. I listened without turning to be sure it wasn't getting closer, then bolted for the bathroom as quietly as I could. It was five o'clock.

I'd wrapped a towel—*her* towel—around my arm so I wouldn't drip as I ran. Now, worrying about what might happen if she noticed it was gone, I fashioned it into a more passable bandage. She had stabbed me. Actually stabbed me. I was in the kitchen, preparing a dinner I would have no part in eating, as usual, and when I looked up from dicing chicken she had been standing there, asking if I was *done*, would I ever be *done*, was I capable of moving faster than one of those retards on the street corners or should she replace me with one instead?

I responded in kind (stupid), returning her glare and firing back "Great! I'll pack my bags."

And she had snatched the knife, grabbing and pinning my hand to the countertop at the same moment and as I plotted my next move, reminding myself to *shut up* and not get caught up in the next part of whatever game she was playing, she screamed something that sounded like "ungrateful little beeehhh." Maybe she had completed the thought, but I would never know because at this point she had plunged the knife straight into my arm and all I had heard was my own girlish, high-pitched screaming until she'd broken through with

"Oops. Hand must have slipped. Call me when dinner's ready!" And when I looked up, eyes wide with shock and glazed with pain (or vice versa, whatever), she'd already vanished back into the living room to finish her drink in front of a TV that hadn't shown anything more interesting than a blank black screen since I was a toddler. My mom was more of a reader, like me.

And now she was downstairs eating, having banished me with her words (good night, my ass) for the night, while I examined a wound that at the least required stitches and at the most would kill me by morning and worried that she would want her dishtowel back.

Once I decided it was probably nonfatal I knotted the towel around my arm. In the mirror, my hair hung limp and greasy. The face it framed appeared irritated by it, the way it dangled there, useless, annoying.

I met my own eyes. They were reddened still, from the pain, and too wide, but the same bright shade I could only hope looked some-what formidable when I was angry. Because I was always angry, and I wanted people to know it.

What "people"? You haven't seen "people" in ages besides Mom, and by the way, real good job scaring her with the angry eyes.

Doesn't count. I pushed the thought aside. My mother didn't count as a person. Besides, it hadn't been *ages*, probably no more than a week or so. And I actually looked scarier this way. I glared into the mirror for a long second more and then, deciding I was wasting valu-able being-in-my-room-and-feeling-not-much-but-a-little-safer time, bared my teeth into it and growled like a dog before leaving.

The nightly ritual was simple, pretty much just changing from what-ever I had worn that day—today, a pair of age-worn cargo shorts and some shirt from somewhere—into what I'd wear the next day, to save time—this time, a pair of age-worn cargo shorts and today's shirt again. I performed it in silence, in case my mother preferred to dine in peace tonight. Business as usual.

I was always a little shabbier than usual when I stayed in like this; I liked to give her something to complain about. It gave me a feeling of accomplishment, not that I never threw back an "it's not like we've been shopping lately" or anything. I wasn't *that* reckless.

Usually.

And I'd been dumb enough to think she was getting better, just because there were fewer people hanging around. On purpose or accident, my mother had a talent for keeping others at arms' length, meaning she hadn't had anyone as serious as a real friend here for as long as I could remember. Her relationships with others were transactions, short ones summed up by a name or word alone, depending on who was being used for what. And when it ended, whoever-it-was would disappear from her life as completely as if he, always he, had been imaginary.

Except me. Of course, I was still here. Different, though. If she didn't count as a person to me, I was even less to her. I was just stuff she was stuck with, the result of a transaction gone wrong. I made myself useful by maintaining the rest of her stuff, day after day from couches to walls to each individual plate, used or not, no margin of error allowed. As a result, the dishes had dulled and in places splotches of dingy gray surfaced through the paint—the place was starting to wear out from all the attention.

I could sympathize.

But since she'd stopped dating a few months ago—loud, opinionated, obnoxious men, the kind that screamed at her until she screamed at me, who would then go the kind of silent that made me feel their eyes on me as I entered the room, picked up the pieces of whatever had been broken, ran upstairs and wished I could lock my bedroom door—things at home had been better. Still the occasional one-sided "argument," the blatant refusal to treat me like a human being, the lectures about how much better her life had been before me (almost definitely lies), sure.

But this . . . I looked at my arm, relieved to see that the bleeding had slowed considerably. This was crazy. And worse, unexpected. Peter always said the worst thing about her wasn't that she was a complete sadist; plenty of people were. It was that she was unpredictable. With normal violent people, you can at least learn when to stay out of their way. With unpredictable ones, you never knew what might set them off, or how badly. One day singing and dancing in the kitchen the way Mom used to sometimes, the next cheerfully swinging at you with one of the kitchen knives. In my case, apparently, your own knife.

I looked out of the window for a moment, traced the shadows from my tree outside up the front of the small dresser across from my bed, trying to keep my mind blank, shut off the electricity before it was too late and . . . failing.

Great. He was in my head now. *Why do you do this?* I leaned against the wall and sighed, sliding soundlessly to the floor. He was always in my head, really. Like the imaginary friend and conscience from Hell, he wouldn't leave me alone. And if the days with my mother could be painful, I hated these nights even more, when he would jump front-and-center and I'd get stuck dredging up crap that was probably better off buried.

Peter had been my brother. Technically he still was. He was six years older, had too much chestnut-brown hair and my mother's deep brown eyes. Most days he was even my friend, kind of.

But that was before.

We hadn't exactly had a great start. It was bound to be that way, since back then it was still very much the Jacqueline and David show: two crazy dysfunctional kids raising two *more* crazy dysfunctional kids!

Main character David keeps his wife and kids in line with threats and violence . . . Though I didn't remember that part much, and what I did know I'd learned from Peter (meaning I'd pried what information I could from my brother, whose opinion of our father was less of an opinion than a wish both of us could forget we had one in the first place).

My father had once buried both fists in my hair and held me, dangling, off the ground for over a minute. That I could remember. Almost.

I could also almost remember the inexplicable feeling of loss I seem to remember right after David left. I guess when you're a little kid it doesn't matter *how* horrible they are, you want your parents around. Eventually I'd adopted a more appropriate attitude toward him, though.

And anyway, I'd had it better than Peter—David had done a real number on him.

Secondary character Jacqueline was a little harder to think about. For all that had happened since, I didn't like to imagine my mother then, only a little older than me, didn't like trying to figure out what she would have done if she'd known what I did, had seen the person my father would become.

Because what if she would have ended it, never given it all a chance to happen? That might mean she had just been some normal person, scared stupid at the wrong moment, long before I was born. I didn't think I could live with that.

But she didn't end it. So then there was Peter. And then me.

For the first few hazy years of my life I was sure he hated me— not that I knew why—and was terrified of him in turn. It was years before I learned why it was my father, not Peter, who I should have been worried about. All my brother really wanted was to be left alone. By everyone, not just me, and though he didn't have much of a violent streak he did whatever he could to make me keep my distance. Meaning sometimes I would simply look up to find him glaring daggers, and, not knowing any better, I *let* myself be scared.

If anything about my life could be called funny, my brother glaring at three-year-old me from one corner or another and my actually being frightened is one of them. But I didn't know that until later.

It was a strange time when my father left us—my mother took his absence much harder than anyone would expect, and took it out on us. Even stranger, for the first time I could remember, my brother began talking to me.

But at almost five years old, I wasn't dumb, and I didn't forget a lesson quickly. So I didn't make it easy for him to get close. Finally he learned to keep food on hand (meals were becoming a little irregular by then) and approach me only when he was sure I was hungry, so I would stuff myself and tolerate him a little longer before fleeing.

So it went. Peter got someone to talk to when he had almost no one else. I got proof that not everyone in the world was out to get me. And I guess I got someone to talk to myself, about everything from sixth-grade math to my favorite subject, why Mommy was so mad.

Peter was different than I'd thought. More serious than angry, more watchful than looming, my brother was more normal than was reasonable or wise in our situation. He followed each rule to the best of his ability, except when he was trying to stop me getting punishments I had technically earned—though he wasn't too nice to let me know how stupid I'd been in the first place. Yet, when he was treated no better than I was, he did this thing I never could: he forgave her. And me.

In most books—the good ones—this would be where I'd start explaining the weather, or the breakfast I remembered eating, on the unassuming morning of the day he died.

But Peter wasn't dead.

At least, I didn't think he was. And, most days, I hoped not. Other days, I thought I'd be better off knowing for sure, and on those days I hated myself almost as much as I wanted to hate him.

The last time I had seen my brother I was eleven, just over three years ago. As he approached eighteen Peter had become increasingly jumpy and paranoid, while our mother had somehow managed to grow less fond of him each day. Even so, when he'd confided in me that she might be planning something very final for him, and soon, I thought it was a joke. His next idea—that if he was right, he had to get out before it was too late—had been less funny (and to give what credit he deserved, he had shed a few tears himself). Less than a month later, he had woken me up in the middle of the night to say goodbye and promise he would be back soon; then he had climbed out of the window and down my tree for the last time, without me.

After the first month, I was still waiting. After the first year, I was worried. After the second, I'd come to terms with the fact that he had forgotten me, and was well on my way to wishing him dead.

Now that I was almost fifteen and the third year had come and gone, I was ready to kill him myself. Sometimes. Mostly, I was just glad at least one of us had escaped this place whole, and hoped if he was out there somewhere that he at least got frequent ear infections or something.

The only sure thing was that he had moved on, in one way or another, and life would get a lot easier for me if I'd do the same thing.

A hell of a lot easier to do the same if he died, though, I joked to myself, grinning inwardly.

Maybe that was too far. I finally rose, stretching awkwardly. It was almost eight; my mother would be in bed very soon, or at least passed out on the couch—gin made for pretty predictable bedtimes. Drained and lightheaded, I checked my makeshift bandage once more before falling (quietly) onto my bed and closing my eyes. Luckily, exhaustion beat the hot ache in my arm, and I was asleep before I could worry about it more.

"*Now!* Get out of my sight, *now!*" I raced to my bedroom in time to lose only a few strands of hair to the slamming door. I considered myself lucky when I turned and Mom wasn't in the room with me; not so much as the deadbolt *clunked* into place. Hard footsteps moved away, down the hall, the stairs, until I could barely hear them above the faucet sound of blood rushing in my head.

Looked like my day was over. And it had barely even started. Mom woke me up earliest when I wasn't going to school, but today had been later—I'd wondered, amused, if maybe she felt a little guilty about yesterday. So I seized the moment, asking when, exactly, she thought I'd be ready to go back to school. Even if it wasn't my favorite place, school was still somewhere to go and I hadn't in a while.

Looks like you have your answer. The semester would end soon, and it was starting to seem like I wouldn't make it back beforehand, which sucked. I hated summer.

The front door was the next one to slam as she took off, possibly to go to work somewhere near Cleveland, which she did some days. I couldn't remember what she did or where, but she often reminded no one in particular (me) how quickly we'd be out on the street if she didn't work so hard to support us. And we still hadn't lost the house in Hill Creek I'd lived in all my life, so she had to do something. Somewhere.

She might also be going out to meet "friends." I hoped it was work— I'd been dreading the possibility of her dating again.

Wherever she'd gone, she wouldn't be back for a while—tonight at the earliest, but maybe not for days. So here I was. I closed my eyes, willing a spinning room to be still. *Not good.*

Not much to do, though, except wait. In the meantime, I pulled a first aid kit from where it was buried in my closet and sat on the floor. It wasn't a great kit, nowhere near as well-stocked as the one my mom kept downstairs, really just good for little patchwork jobs. Unfortunately, an extremely short trial run revealed that clenching my hand into a fist was not only excruciating, but impossible. This was no small job. Even worse if it got infected, in which case pain would be the least of my worries (the greatest being when my mother would decide I needed a doctor). Part of me tried to reassure myself that it was nothing to worry about.

"Until it is," I replied.

chapter 2.

ONCE the room stabilized I glared at my bed, wishing to be tired enough to sleep off the rest of today and tonight. The adrenaline in my veins protested, but I tried to relax, lying down, attempting to ignore logistics like how long it had been since I'd had a drink of water and how long it would be before my stomach completely ate itself. It was fine. The scarred sky-blue walls were at their best at times like these, cool and relaxing. I stared into them and willed myself to take deep breaths. It was *fine*.

I must have been dreaming—I rolled over suddenly and nearly fell to the floor. The sun was gone; I didn't turn to look, but the moon was making patterns on my wall, which had gone from light blue to stark white in the darkness. My wish had come true. I had slept all day, but I was still tired.

Sitting, I fought a rolling wave of nausea, eyes closed against the dancing room. I could guess why I felt so sick, and tested myself, tentatively curling the fingers of my right hand toward my palm.

Liquid fire shot up my arm, followed by an even stronger wave of nausea. *Good guess,* I congratulated myself unnecessarily, shaking out my good elbow and staggering through the moonlight toward the single window. *Go toward the light*. I laughed, pleased with what I knew was a lame attempt at humor, and fumbled the window open, hoping the cool air would help keep this morning's meal down.

To be perfectly clear, I was preoccupied. Accustomed to being left to myself at night, I was still letting my mind wander as I sat on the windowsill, possibly remembering more history of the family Wilder, maybe more bad jokes to entertain myself. I was also pretending to ignore the pain in my arm at the same time as I attempted to lower my rising fever by sheer force of will.

I was distracted. That is the only reason why I didn't hear anything, or even open my eyes, until a rough hand clapped itself over my mouth and pulled me, headfirst, out of my window.

One second, I was absentmindedly examining the backs of my own eyelids; the next I was airborne, too suddenly to think of, let alone utter, a sound in response. I smashed through the first few branches—thin, too small to be of any help—before my left arm (lucky) finally found a more stable one (again, lucky). Still shocked silent, I let it absorb my weight, knowing I had more falling to do.

And fall I did, landing hard on my butt in the grass, shocked now for a different reason. This was apparently a lucky night—nothing *felt* broken, or even dislocated. *Well, there was an entire* tree *to break your fall. More importantly,* it finally occurred to me, looking up at the window with my mouth and eyes open idiotically wide, *what the hell was that?*

Nothing happened for so long that I started to wonder if, maybe, I'd imagined being pulled from the window—could I have fallen? But it must have only been a few seconds, judging by how quickly everything suddenly began to move.

There was a muttered swear (in my confusion, I believed momentarily it had come from the tree itself) and then a sound I knew well: the muted scrape of a shoe against bark.

I wasn't too disoriented to know what that meant.

Someone was coming down after me.

Even then, curiosity might normally have kept me rooted there for a little longer, long enough to come up with a coherent plan. But in the same second there was another sound. Dead twigs, leaves, crunching . . . Someone in the small wooded area behind the houses, coming closer. Which made for a much worse realization.

Whoever was coming down after me *wasn't alone.* And with this added bit of information coherence was no longer possible, so I didn't bother trying.

I scrambled to my feet, and I ran.

I'd like to say the pain and nausea were forgotten as I fled for my life through the strip of forest, heedless of the dangers the forest floor posed to my bare feet, sticking to what had become my own marked path over the last few years. They weren't. But I did my best to use them to my advantage. Every step brought a fresh jab of pain, every jab of pain brought on a wave of adrenaline, and I used each rush to propel me forward at what must have been record speed—or so I hoped.

A hand shot out of the darkness behind me, grabbing my right arm.

I screamed. I didn't mean to, it just happened and once it had there wasn't much I could do except cut it off as quickly as it began. Fortunately for me, the other thing that just happened was me clenching my free hand, swinging around, and throwing a punch in the general direction of my attacker. I was surprised, and oddly a little ashamed, when I felt it connect and heard another muffled oath, but more irritated than anything else when my attacker's grip didn't loosen enough for me to pull myself away.

If there's any other way, don't scream, I reprimanded myself, panicking even more (I hadn't realized that was possible) and scaling up from determined to frantic in my struggle against what felt like the grip of death itself. It worked. Painfully but silently, I wrenched my arm free and turned to finish running away.

No such luck; I rammed into another of my pursuers. *How many of them* are *there?* Both of my shoulders were suddenly locked in vises, but I used this to my advantage, too, picking up both feet and slamming my heels, hard, into this one's stomach. But my first attacker had already pulled both of my hands behind me, and was—horrifyingly—starting to tie them behind my back when the second let out a huge rush of air and dropped his hands, falling to the ground somewhere in front of me.

Too agitated to see, I aimed another kick at the fallen man as I was dragged away, and let out a wild-sounding growl (impressing myself, at least)—until I was lifted and tossed, again to my horror, over the first one's shoulder and carried away.

Bizarrely, my thoughts now became rational again. I rushed through my options: I wasn't gagged; I could scream my loudest one more time before anyone stopped me.

No. With my luck, I hadn't been gagged because these people— these *whatever* the hell they were just wanted an excuse to drug or kill me, one basically as bad as the other. Safer to stay quiet, be grateful I was still conscious.

My only other almost-option was to chew through the back of the man carrying me, hopefully forcing him to drop me. I did bite him once, as hard as I could, but even I had guessed it would hardly slow him down before we got to wherever we were headed.

He was walking by the time we emerged into a graveled playground parking lot; I didn't need the dim orange glow of the surrounding streetlights to know the lot was empty. *Mostly* empty.

My captor and I were both panting as he at last slowed to a stop. I sensed other people around, but wasn't sure how many until they started talking in hushed tones.

First: "Told you." A smug comment. If there were more than two, had this one stayed behind?

Then, a little louder: "What happened to you?" In response to this question the out-of-breath man carrying me seemed to shrug, though he was probably indicating me as the "what." I did look around now, but not at the people who belonged to the voices. *I used to walk home through this park when I missed the school bus.*

Finally, a voice that could have belonged to either of the first two speakers, or might have been new: "So, are we going? I mean, I heard that from here, have we got time to stop and chat?" I assumed "that" was me screaming before—so he was worried someone else might come to investigate. It sounded as if he were asking someone in charge. I steeled myself for the worst.

But nothing else was said. After a slight pause, I was carried to the open bed of a capped pickup truck that had, apparently, been there the whole time. "In you go, girl."

It's hard to say what happened when I heard that, and not only because my conscious mind went a weird shade of gray for a while afterward. The closest explanation is that he moved me toward that car, and something else moved—like a door slamming open—in me. And for maybe the first time, I actually *understood* what was happening, and-

Well, that's where everything gets fuzzy.

7, 13

TWO times fast, then three times slowly. The boy smiles as he pushes open the door down the hall; he has his own special knock, and using it is fun, like speaking in Morse code. Almost like being a spy, but he's too old for spy games. Just a cool feeling.

The little girl lies in bed, one sneaker poking out and the rest of her tangled up in the sheet. Her blanket is balled up on the floor beside her. No big deal, it isn't too cold, at least not inside. The boy is irritated, though, because he had told her to stay awake tonight until he came to get her. He rolls his eyes—it was stupid even to try—and shakes the girl's shoulder.

As usual, she wakes slowly, blinking around before resting her eyes on her brother.

"Are we going?"

"I told you not to fall asleep."

"I tried. Are we going or not?"

He sighs, nodding, and she grins back, abruptly and fully awake. She's been looking forward to it since he told her about his best idea ever weeks ago, but this is the first night that everything is just right for them to get away with it. Mom's been staying up late a lot lately, and even when she did go to bed early one of them has always been in trouble or something. But not tonight. Tonight, it's perfect.

She hops lightly from bed and tiptoes to where her brother is leaning out of the window.

"What?" she asks, afraid something is wrong. What if they can't go after all?

He says nothing, frowning at the ground below.

Now she laughs at him and climbs up to sit on the windowsill, shaking his hand off when he grabs her arm. "Come on, I'm not gonna fall. And you won't either," she adds, glancing back over her shoulder, "see, I can touch the branches from here." But she swallows as she leans out, catching a thick branch in one hand, and throws her whole body forward. There's a trick to it—she just moves too fast to let herself think about what she's doing.

She finds the first hand with the other; the branch bends a little, enough to let her land but not fall onto another under her feet. Easy. She does this over and over until the bottom branch, when she jumps the rest of the way to the ground, landing clumsily and falling to her rear end so hard she forgets how to breathe.

From above there are scraping and rustling sounds, and then a thud in front of her. She shakes her head and wheezes a little, then gets up. "What?" she challenges the boy's worried stare, annoyed.

He starts at the noise, looking around before answering. "Next time," he says seriously, "I go first."

She grins.

There are rules, like there always are for everything. She'd like it better if there weren't any, but from what she knows having and following rules usually means not being punished, and she doesn't want this to be the last time she ever gets to go into the city because she can't remember a few dumb things.

He quizzes her as they walk the miles to the bus stop. He came up with them on his own, but doesn't want her to know. His sister is stubborn; what if she gets angry and does something stupid just *to spite him? Better to let her believe there's some kind of law about this stuff.*

"Strangers?"

"Everyone is a stranger. Never talk to anyone, unless it's an emergency, and then just to make them go away. Especially don't talk to men."

He nods. "If someone grabs you?"

Part of a sweatshirt she hasn't quite grown into slips off one shoulder and she yanks it up again. "Then . . . try to get away, but don't do anything to make them too angry. Don't bite, don't scratch and don't scream, or they might panic and kill you or knock you out or something." She is quoting from memory, not really knowing what the words mean.

"If the police ask where your parents are?"

"I tell them I'm with my big brother, not my parents, and ask if we're supposed to go home, then we run away before anything else. You know, you could always–" He stops her with a look, and she sighs and keeps walking.

There's distracted silence for a while. The girl moves fast but in all the wrong directions, chasing the crunchiest-looking leaves and trying to jump on them mid-air while the wind blows them around. The boy steps on a big, curly one lying in front of him, satisfying himself with a single perfect crunch. *Then he asks, "What if you can't?"*

"Can't what?"

"Can't get away. If someone grabs you," he explains. There's no rule about this, he hadn't been able to think of one. He glances over, knowing he's thrown her off.

He has, but she looks determined to puzzle it out. A few minutes of thinking only gives her one answer she is pretty sure he won't like. But finally, she shrugs and goes for it. "Well, then I guess it doesn't matter, does it?"

She meets his eyes for a brief second, guessing his curiosity means she should go on. "I mean, the rules can't help me anymore, right? I'm kind of trapped either way? So I bite, scratch, scream and try to be as much trouble as I can, and maybe I'll get him worse than he gets me. Right?" She throws another uncertain look in her brother's direction.

He stares back. He is proud of her, which surprises him considering her answer is probably the exact opposite of what he would have said. She's not him, though. She is braver, stronger, and in this case, probably right. If that really did happen, he would definitely bet on his little sister before himself, though he hopes he never has to admit it.

So he just smiles. "Right."

They're just in time to catch the downtown line that stops out here so rarely this time of night. She hops up first and he steps in behind her, ignoring the driver's curious glance and suddenly weirdly conscious of his blackened left eye as he drops most of a handful of coins and bills into the fare box. Then he follows her to a seat near the back.

She plops down by the window and rubs at her runny nose a little, enjoying the rumbling of the bus under her and excited because even though she's been there before the city feels more special late at night. But the lights and the rumbling and the excitement even get repetitive after a while, and she slowly drifts off into the slumber she'd started earlier.

Feeling her head droop onto his shoulder, the boy laughs silently without looking down and gazes out the window instead, waiting for their stop.

chapter 3.

NO, no . . . This couldn't be happening. It wasn't. I wasn't letting it so it wasn't, and I would open my eyes in a minute and it would be a nightmare and it would be over and everything would be back to normal it would be back it *would*.

So do it! Open them.

God, this couldn't be happening.

No, it can't. But it is, isn't it?

No.

Of course it was. What it wasn't doing was going away, so there was only one other option. This was going to get worse.

And what, exactly, was *worse*? I didn't . . . I'd rather not have known.

So you have to be something other than paralyzed by the time you open your eyes.

Maybe I couldn't stop it getting worse, but I didn't have to *let* it.

Peter sat against the wall in the exam room, leaning back to relieve the pressure on his chest. He let out a sigh he hadn't felt building, winced, and leaned forward enough to rest his head against his fingertips. Tried to rest his eyes, too. Failed.

And this was only the beginning. He did not want to think about how bad this might get before it got better. He was going to have to keep a close eye—a closer eye—on her, which she was making difficult.

Though if what Doc had told him was true and nothing had changed, she wanted no one within a mile of her, which might mean she was feeling okay.

But something was starting to seem wrong. At first it had been easy enough to blame the girl's hostile, disoriented manner to the fever she had barely kicked days later. But now?

Either she wasn't recovering or something else, something more persistent than the fever, was making her act this way.

And if it had to be one of the two . . . he would rather it wasn't.

Because either way it was his fault.

Doc walked in and settled onto a stool in front of him with a small grin that only became real when he smiled back. "Well, you seem happy." She was a very direct person, which Peter appreciated even if he had a hard time getting used to it.

She reached toward him and he pulled back, then cursed himself. *Stupid.* Doctor Deleon was a friend, and a good one; if he expected his suspicious little sister to believe that, she'd need to see that he trusted Doc himself.

Doc (*Please, call me 'Lita*, he thought mundanely) looked up, squinting her glasses back up the too-narrow bridge of her nose to see him better. "To do what, exactly?"

He had been thinking out loud again. Peter groaned inwardly. *Why does that keep happening?* It bothered him, not knowing what he might accidentally say. "Nothing," he answered politely, and tried to smile again.

"I'm almost done with the ribs. Are you sure you haven't hit your head recently too?" She said it seriously, but then snorted a short laugh and went back to work.

There was more to say, but it was always awkward bringing it up. Doc and Peter had never so much as disagreed before, but once he'd explained the girl's condition, Doc had refused to waste one second on anyone else. He'd tried convincing her to waste a little more, saying they all needed a while to calm down (the "pickup" had been pretty hard on everyone involved). But Doc was insistent, even when he'd made it clear that using any sort of sedative on the poor kid would only make it worse.

And now, days later, they were both still pretty shaken from Doc's first encounter with his half-feral baby sister.

The doctor hid it better, though. Doc had rushed out of there right behind him, and though she usually loved to tell horror stories of her days "over in Vietnam," he hadn't heard one from her since.

But it wasn't her fault. The Drophouse had simply never seen the like of Alana Wilder before.

He was stalling again. Just like every day, after Doc checked his bruised ribs, after he declined a couple pills for the pain (it really wasn't so bad), once it was obvious what he should do next—here he sat, watching the doctor fiddle with supplies she barely needed and gnawing away at one of his few remaining fingernails.

Restocking cabinets and seemingly oblivious to his unease, Doc gave him a matronly look of disapproval. "If you're talking to me, you'll need to move your hand."

Peter sat up straight, grimacing, and let the hand fall. *Again?* "Apparently shutting my mouth seems to be a problem with me lately."

There was a pause. Peter tried not to think of anything at all. Doc, inspecting a bent tongue-depressor and spinning a box of bandages in her other hand, seemed to hear anyway.

"So how is Alana?" She asked casually.

He winced at the sound of her name, for two reasons. The first was that he did not like using names here. Real names were dangerous— they could be used against you. Doc was the only one here (aside from Peter and the girl herself) who knew Al's name and who she was, and only because of a certain business partner they had in common. He wondered if he should ask Doc to stop using it. But he wouldn't. There was no point; she used his, too.

The second reason was that he should, but didn't, know how to answer the question—he hadn't marshaled the nerve yet to see her today. Or yesterday.

Or the day before . . .

How is she? Nervously, groping for a believable lie or an allowable twist to the truth, he started back in on his thumb. "She's fine," he mumbled. Maybe Doc would let it drop.

No such luck. "Oh? And what are you basing that on?"

More silence, more guilt. This kept happening, him putting off seeing his sister, and he might be getting a little too good at it.

"It might be easier to control your thinking aloud if you sat down and talked to her, you know." Doc gazed sympathetically over her lenses.

Peter took in her concern quickly and looked away, annoyed at them both. He was headed to the door when she spoke again. "They say a family's love will forgive anything. You should keep that in mind." She poured cotton balls into a jar.

Peter blinked, trying to work that one out. Sure, if you do some trivial thing, your family is *supposed* to forgive you. Like scratch the car, or cheat in a class. You're supposed to go home and do the honest-and-repentant routine, maybe throw around some babyish nicknames for effect. And Mama, or Pop or whoever you're acting for does their part—rolls their eyes, pretends they aren't fooled, then uses words like "grounded" and "never again" before sending you to your room with a reminder that they're proud you told the truth, and they love you very much.

Peter sighed and left Doc to her inventory. He hadn't been raised on the old routine. He didn't expect to be let off easy for mistakes, no matter how small.

Which brought up another issue. If you backed Pop's car into the mailbox he might be pissed, sure, but it was a little thing, so easily fixed. *I wonder how forgiving Mama would be if you left her in a burning house for a while? Sure, Mama, I know the place was full of smoke, but I had to get outta there and I said I'd be back soon . . .*

Somehow, he got the feeling you would more likely end up in a locked cell than your own bedroom with *that* apology.

Unfortunately, it was also the closest thing he could give Alana to the apology she deserved.

He hadn't wanted to leave her. *As if that isn't the understatement of the past half-decade.* Leaving her had felt like ripping out a part of himself was closer. His sister had been his anchor to the real world for so long that learning to live without the indomitable kid's constant arguments had been like learning to do something fundamental all over again, like ride a bike.

Or talk.

He and Mom both had mixed emotions when they found out he was going to have a little brother. Things had been bad at home for a long time by then. He didn't know exactly why, but Mom and his father had been fighting a lot, and it was scary for a little kid. Lonely, too.

Back then Peter had thought they were perfectly normal, if unhappy. A mom at home, a dad at work, a kid who mostly stayed in his room of the little tan house on the edge of the woods, which was nearly identical to the ones on either side. Car in the driveway, junk in the garage. Quiet, during the day. Almost dull.

He didn't like thinking about that version of it anymore. He didn't like to think about his father at all.

The baby was supposed to change everything. Peter's father had always wanted a son just like him, right down to the name. A real son. So the new baby would be David Alan Wilder Jr., and when the original finally had his *good* son, he would surely be happy.

"Watch," Jacqueline had said to him—so many times that he now understood she was actually trying to convince herself, "it will be good again. You'll see." And then David would walk through the door, and

Peter would slip away and play too loud in his room as a distraction from the inevitable fight.

He didn't need to ask why the new baby would be David instead of him. David Sr. had always believed a boy was a man at birth, yelling and making demands of the nearest person (his mother, conveniently) to get what he needed, what he wanted. "A *man* makes himself heard. He doesn't need to be taught how," he would say, watching his son with contempt.

Peter hadn't known how, born pale and quiet with no more than a whimper to announce his arrival into the world—and technically, he'd proven David right, because five years later the one thing Peter had successfully done to announce himself was refuse to look like his father. Brazenly, as if to add insult to injury, much of his appearance had come from his mother's end of the gene pool: he had her dark eyes instead of his father's gray-blue ones, and her coarse, wavy hair—though the color was all his own. By David's astute measure, then, there was no way of being sure this dark, gentle boy was actually *his* at all.

Peter had always liked that idea.

David changed while they waited for the baby, became more the husband and father Peter thought he could almost remember from long ago. For the first time in a while his house was filled, if not with laughter, or peace, then not with yelling either, not with crying. So toward the end even Peter, who by then slipped away to play at distraction far less even with David around, was eager to meet him, waiting alone as his mother and father went off to the hospital with a promise that when they came back he would meet his new little man of a baby brother at last.

But when his parents finally came home it wasn't like he'd expected. It had been put down and left alone right away, so something was wrong. But what? Maybe baby David was deformed. Or sick? Another possibility tugged, innocent but insistent, at the back of his mind—maybe David made the same mistake as him. Had the new baby also whimpered its way into the world, daring to do not much more than look like someone else's kid? Had he come into the world without knowing the rules, too, accidentally proving he didn't deserve the highest honor his dad was willing to give—his own name? Innocuous at first, the idea grew, amplifying his curiosity beyond what any boy of six could be expected to handle. Peter knew a lot about being on David's bad side; if he had a small replica of a brother to look out for now, he had to find out.

Which was why not two hours after they returned from the hospital, and not five minutes after his first look at the new baby, Peter found himself fleeing from it, flinching away from David (the only David, apparently) to hide in his room. But even then, something stayed wrong, mixed up.

That noise. It filled the small bedroom and rolled in a wave down the hall, chasing him, a small but outraged squall the baby put his whole body into, which ended up lasting for hours. No question, this baby knew how to make himself heard. And for just a second, before he woke the sleeping probably-not-David, he had looked him over, noting his thatch of fuzzy, bright hair. What, exactly, was wrong with him?

He had told her all of this long before she could understand it. An abbreviated version, at least. He hadn't meant to. He was feeling the aftereffects of another late night—one of his father's unpredictable "companionable" moods, when he would wake his son and pump him full of as many beers as his small body could hold—and she had only been a toddler anyway. She was just standing there, waiting to see if he was going to stop hanging over the trash can and come downstairs for a grilled-cheese sandwich, when it spilled out. *If you'd been a boy like you were supposed to, they would still be happy.* Then, when she showed no sign of understanding, *all of this is your fault.*

Straightforward. Simple. It even made him feel less ill to say, and barely guilty at all. She was only a little kid, after all, and little kids forgot everything.

He had no idea what made the cruelest and most untrue thing he had ever said to her one of Alana's clearest memories from the days before their father finally did something good for their family—and left.

Once David was gone, the house was quiet for the first time in years. At last. He'd been wishing for it for years and here it was, one last chance to be happy.

It hadn't gone as he hoped.

He had only the barest hazy memories of his Mom as she used to be, and knew little about her life before him. Her parents were dead, and she didn't talk about them because she said she didn't miss them. (He was never curious about his father's family one way or the other.)

He remembered the Jacqueline Wilder of his childhood as always tired, but nice. Not always willing to play with or spend time around her son—who learned early to do things for himself to spare her the trouble—sometimes she would suddenly take it into her mind to have fun with him. And she could be plenty of fun. Cheesy science experiments for kids were her favorite. One of his earliest memories was staring hypnotized at a white ping pong ball bobbing in midair above the hairdryer he used to kill bad guys when he played by himself. He had tried to do it too, but his hands were too small and it bounced away every time.

Every new experiment would start the same way. She'd come find him and pause, smiling the tired but kind enough smile he almost never saw, and then lead him away to where she had set up her surprise. Only then would she speak, asking him a question that always had a "no" answer.

"Do you know what happens when you mix baking soda and vinegar?"

"No!"

"Watch this."

Sometimes the question was exciting because it was dangerous. "Do you know how to make a flamethrower?" He still answered no even if they had done it before because he understood by now that she liked him not to know. Then they would spend hours at the edge of the woods out back with a can of hairspray and a lighter, and he would laugh, even though it almost burned him sometimes, because Mom was laughing.

When they were done she would let him take the lighter inside while she took the hairspray and the bottle she'd been drinking from, and she would tell him, "remember, that's what I'll do to you if I ever catch you messing with this," and shake the bottle and grin, and Peter would grin back. She was kidding. She was better than her husband.

She had been, then. But that part of her had disappeared with David, and by the time Peter's father was finished with her it was too late for it to come back. The games ended; now she had a purpose, trying to satisfy something so dark, angry, and intense that it must have been there all along.

She experimented on herself, though, in a way, and as her outings became longer, Peter and his young sister were left to fend for themselves for days at a time. And then she would come home, sometimes tired and apathetic, others in a phony good humor he learned to dread far more. But he always reminded them both that it could be worse, back before he'd accepted how bad it was.

Because if there was anyone she cared for even less than herself, it was her children. More and more, Jacqueline found new standards her kids could fail to live up to, and since money was tight more often than not, she felt justified punishing even slight transgressions with a skipped meal—or two.

However, because no violation of her rules could ever *be* slight, she eventually needed no justification at all. Or she'd simply stopped making excuses.

chapter 4.

HE thought he understood her anger toward him. At least, part of him thought he did (not the part that saw his mother clearly, the part which, ultimately, had saved his life). She was wrong, though. He was nothing like his father.

The same childish piece of him also believed with time he could fix it, make his Mom see that David really was gone, that Peter would never become a monster like him.

It shut up in a hurry when he learned she was planning to kill him.

Peter had been sleeping. He wasn't sure if she spoke or if he was dreaming, but when he opened his eyes she was standing in the doorway.

She crooked a finger and he had been apprehensive right away but pretended to be calm, obediently following his Mom into one of his least favorite rooms in their house—the garage. It was freezing and damp, and he especially hated the angled gap beneath the door, which might allow any sort of vermin to squeeze inside. What did she want with him here? He froze on the threshold, trying to determine what he must have done wrong, but then she turned back.

"Shut the door."

Peter would never forget his mother's voice. It was sharp and cold, like the icicles that fell from buildings and impaled passers-by below. It had long since lost the warmer, soft quality of all those lifetimes ago.

He stepped into the chill and pulled the door closed, and then she'd smiled at him, an easy, genial smile. "Do you know what *culling* means?"

Peter's mind was working overtime, trying to figure out what game she was playing. He knew he'd done this before; through the haze of sleep, he studied her face, taking in that condescending, contented grin just long enough to guess his next move. Then he shook his head once, left to right. *Let her explain.*

"Of course you don't." The disgusted delight in her piercing voice told Peter he had made the right choice. He heaved a (purely mental) sigh of relief.

"Culling is how you keep mutant animals from spreading and making other little mutants like them." Peter felt his instant of contentment fall into the pit of his stomach, where it sat like a stone. "Can you guess how?"

He shook his head once more, forcing himself to move slowly, and froze again. *No sudden movements.* His hands clenched into fists slowly, independently, behind his back. He didn't want to hear the answer at all.

As if hearing him, Jacqueline turned and took something from the shelf behind her. The stone in his stomach seemed to stretch, crushing his lungs, his heart, as Peter recognized the small handgun his mother had purchased years ago to protect herself, should her ex-husband ever return. At least that's what she'd said.

He opened his mouth but shut it right away. He knew better.

She was turning the gun over in her hands now, thoughtful, so absorbed in it she might have forgotten her son. "They say people like your *father*," the word was a curse, and saying it fetched her attention back to the petrified boy, "run in families. They say it's genetic." And she smiled again, the same relaxed smile, while the night had ticked by—daring him to say out loud that it *wasn't true*, she *knew* it wasn't, Peter *wasn't him.* But he had kept his silence and eventually

Jacqueline had grown bored. She gave the gun another strangely tender glance, placed it at his feet and announced that she was going to bed.

Peter sat down on the spot and hadn't moved until the sun rose.

It could have been a nightmare, a bad one, horribly realistic but harmless enough. Unfortunately, though Peter had never exactly slept well, he had never been one to sleepwalk—and certainly not to dream himself into one of his least favorite places in the house, staring down his Mom's gun.

Still, he had barely believed it himself, until he told his then eleven year-old sister he had to leave. He'd only shared the barest details of that night, knowing she would have tried to "help"—she always did— and she couldn't get in Mom's way while she was like this. The poor kid had lashed out at him (very literally), and once he'd managed to calm her down somewhat she was already trying to convince him he'd made a mistake, he couldn't go . . . without her. Naïve as he was, though, Peter had known better.

He'd learned that lesson a long time ago. When he was barely a teenager, and she was honestly too small, they used to sneak out and take the late bus downtown, where the people were still awake and the restaurants still open. He'd tried to prepare her for the dangers of nights in the city, but the threats were minimal if they stayed together, and worth it for the simple fun of begging enough change for a cheeseburger each, fries, and a milkshake (it had to be a milkshake, or Al would throw a fit) to split by the lake as big as an ocean . . .

That's what he'd thought. Until one night he looked down and she wasn't there.

It was only a couple of minutes before he found her, nearby. She had wandered off the pier, probably chasing a seagull, and she was talking to someone—Peter came up in time to hear a man's voice, then Al describing who she was with and where they had been sitting.

She was asking for directions. For a single second Peter's hammering heart started to slow. Until the man glanced up and met Peter's eyes. "I know exactly where that is. How did you get so far away?"

She was only steps from the place she'd described as the man started to lead her away, further from the pier.

By then Peter's pulse was hurting his own ears. He had never before or since felt anything like the caustic white-hot rage that possessed him as he caught up to them and snatched the girl away, dragging her to the nearest bus stop without acknowledging any of the bewildered questions she had every right to ask.

He'd given her the rest of the milkshake on the ride home, but she'd been surly, too, aware he was angry but not sure she was okay with it.

He *was* angry at her. But mostly he was just angry—so angry it scared him, almost as much as what he had not seen in the eyes of the man on the pier.

That was the last time he took her downtown. It was also why he could never risk being out in the world, homeless, and with a little girl . . .

chapter 5.

AND now that she was here, and safe, and probably almost as scared as she was angry (and she had every reason to be angry) he was abandoning her all over again. He had to stop doing this to both of them. Yet, after that horrible day with Doc, he had only been to see her once. And Doc was wrong, not that he had the nerve to tell her. It hadn't helped.

It would have been easier if he could employ his old tricks. There was something he used to say to Alana when she got him into trouble with their mother (which, perhaps, was why she'd never learned to be as careful as she should). She would say it wasn't her fault—Mom should be better with kids since she was raising two of them—and Peter would answer that you could never raise a wild animal, only tame it.

She'd loved that. And it was true, once. Alana had only allowed him to approach her in the first place when he'd stopped treating her like a toddler and treated her like a skittish stray instead.

But something was wrong. This person was a different kind of animal, and the old trick clearly wouldn't work again.

And because she was acting strangely, so was he. Take the last visit, for example. Right at the end, when he'd shot to his feet to back away from what was starting to seem more and more like an uncolored drawing of his sister, he heard his own voice, though he hadn't known he'd been talking. ". . . anywhere, okay, I promise, not this time."

And then, despite what he'd (presumably) said, he had gone, and stayed that way. He tried to keep busy, had Doc check in for a while each day to make sure the girl was at least not getting any worse. But mostly, he waited. He was good at that.

Because it couldn't go on much longer. Once she'd had enough time, it would get better. One or two more days, maybe three. No more.

Peter had his own routines. Every day, after he checked in with Doc on her other patient, he ended up right here. The view was better from the roof, but the courtyard, recessed into the center of the building, was hidden, making it a more practical choice. A rare warm breeze stirred the air above him; he listened resentfully. *Careful always wins out in the end, doesn't it.*

Apparently "better" was not happening. A full week and little to no difference after his unfortunate only visit, Doc was starting to hint that perhaps there was something wrong with the girl that couldn't be waited out. Something else that, like her arm, he'd been too late to prevent and now just had to make the best of.

Peter had not addressed the hints yet, because Doc was wrong. That had to be the reason, because it was the best one. The only real reason, *not that it matters, because even if there was a chance it was true, even if I'd given up on her enough to believe that, even then . . .*

He would know how to handle it if so, he figured. He had been too late before.

(And insane.)

It was a cloudless, scorching day, almost as suffocating outside as in. It was becoming impossible to invent distractions for himself—there was simply nothing else to be done. Doc wouldn't let him spend whole days in her exam room forever. And, if he was going to handle anything, he couldn't do it from out here. Not anymore.

So he made his plodding way to the door he had been avoiding for days, trying to ignore his churning stomach, and he laid his hand on the doorknob and twisted.

Nothing happened.

After a couple of confused moments Peter remembered this particular door was locked from the outside. Remembering why, he grinned unsteadily—exactly what he needed to turn the key and step inside, after which the hint of good humor vanished, leaving him with a pat on the shoulder and a *you're on your own now, pal.*

The familiar rhythm of gasp-growl-repeat greeted him as he closed himself inside, inched up to the desk, and sat down. *No change*, just like Doc said. She didn't look at him.

As if summoned the walls of the small room started to inch, then race, inward. The tension in the air animated, taking on a semisolid, marshmallowy consistency that expanded from her corner to fill the room, forcing the air out. *Not now!* He glanced toward the door; defying logic, it flew backward, away, and he imagined he'd missed his chance to reach out, to open it, to escape before it was gone.

He shot upright and stood paralyzed for what had to be less time than it seemed, simultaneously fighting the attack and struggling not to suffocate in the spongy, elastic substance that had replaced the air. *No. No, it's not real.* One hand groped about until it found the chair and gripped it tight. Peter closed his eyes. *It's not the air, it's you. Breathe. Now.*

He tried to believe it, failed, and repeated the instruction. This attempt was better. By the time he opened his eyes again the walls were back where they started, and he sat down again, panting.

It didn't look like she'd seen him. She wasn't making any noise, though, now that he was sitting down, and that was a *kind* of change. Back to him, she faced off with the wall like she was trying to hold it back (he could sympathize). It was almost a good sign . . . Or it was exhaustion born of near-starvation: she was eating, but not enough. Not even close.

He moved a little, swept his shoe over the tile experimentally. She didn't turn but made it clear she had heard him. Starving herself or not, she was at least as alert as before. Maybe she really was improving. Could be that it was just taking a while. Which was better than *no change*, if nothing else. And, since she was *fine*, not—not sick, at least not like they were saying—she might even be using her strange behavior as a cover, stalling until she felt ready to come out of her shell.

Well, wishful thinking wouldn't hurt anyone.

She moved so fast, and Peter was so deep in his own head, that he almost missed it. One moment she was trying to disappear into the corner and then she was coming at him, *right* at him, clutching something small and unidentifiable in her good hand. It was pointed at him. And from the way she held it, he assumed it was dangerous.

Peter stood, trying to process the abrupt change in atmosphere. The girl lunged, jabbing at him. Forced to act before he could think he stepped aside, catching her wrist and grabbing at what turned out to be the broken and sharpened end of a plastic toothbrush. It bit deep into the fleshy part of his hand as he wrestled it away; he tossed it behind him, trying to ignore the pain. Distracted. Alana, disarmed and still trapped by her good wrist, wasted no time.

Three seconds later Peter was wheezing on the ground, clutching his bruised—and re-bruised—ribs. *One more time and she breaks them for sure.* The ache in his chest, familiar by now, flared to match his bleeding hand. Miles away a door slammed.

By the time he could manage small sips of air it had opened again, too nearby. There was only one door, and it was locked—she'd need to come after him for the key. Would she do it? Peter rolled onto his back. He looked up . . . and kept looking.

Whether it was Plan B or a sudden stroke of genius, Alana stood triumphant over him. In her hands was the heavy ceramic lid from the toilet's water tank, positioned above his head as though she meant to drop it. Hard. *Really* meant to.

Okay, now, calm down, put it down . . . "Uh, uh . . . uh." *Okay, good try,* but that probably wouldn't work and time was not exactly on his side. "Uh, ah. Aah-Al," he tried for her full name, but only the nickname made it out before his voice simply shut off, as quickly and completely as if by a flipped switch. Sprawled on the floor of his own building, thrashed by a teenager for the second time in less weeks, he fell back on an old habit, slowly raising one hand, palm out. He could not tear his eyes away from the shining white slab threatening to crush his skull.

After a long minute, it started to come down.

Peter threw both arms up, ineffective protection against the impact. But the impact didn't come. Finally—and against every instinct—he peered over his hands, still expecting the white flash and oblivion at any second.

The lid was in her hands but now she was backing away, giving him such a calculating look he couldn't help but be embarrassed by what he'd been thinking about her only moments before. When she saw him looking her mouth opened slightly, as if she were going to speak. She didn't. What she did do was shift her grip and, spinning in an awkward semi-circle, smash the lid into—and through—the room's single window.

Some of the glass flew outside, but most bounced off of the bars (yet another reason to hate those) and landed inside; the lid rebounded as well, breaking in two against the speckled tile with a single *crack* like a gunshot.

The girl crossed this jagged roomscape barefoot. After a beat, she wrapped her hands around the bars and, leaning through the shattered window, she *screamed.*

Oh no, no . . . Peter scrambled to his feet and lunged at her, pulling the resisting girl out into the hallway with a bloody hand clamped over her mouth. The next door stood open. He (they) fell through it into a room identical to the last, though more intact. And less bloody.

Fishing a zip tie from his pocket, he fastened the girl's hands to a bed-post and gave her a hard look before stalking away.

Odd. He hadn't realized he was angry. He shouldn't be—after all, hadn't he told himself he had no right to expect forgiveness?—but as the adrenaline wore off and the aches resurfaced, it was hard to avoid. He didn't look at her again as he removed the (evidently) more dangerous fixtures from this room and transplanted them next door. Perhaps he took more time replacing them than he needed, telling himself the kid needed a moment to calm down. As if she were the only one.

Eventually, though, he did have to go back in. When she saw him, Alana pushed herself away across the floor as far as she could, eyes wide. For a moment he was confused but, with a glance at the Swiss knife in his hand, he simply rolled his eyes, cut her loose and, without trying to look like he was *running*, exactly, left and locked the door behind him.

Sticking the heel of his hand into his mouth, Peter headed for the infirmary—yet again—tasting blood. It would have disturbed him deeply if he'd realized that rather than talking to himself, this time, he was smiling.

What did he say?

I blinked and twisted around, trying hard to take everything in. Ironic; I hadn't really bothered doing this yet, and now my eyes wouldn't work. The room dimmed, brightened, dimmed again. How long had it been since I'd slept?

And *what did he say?*

Not really the first time. Not . . . what he called me. More like how.

And the second thing, the gesture? *Stop.* That's what it meant. Simple, obvious. Anyone would've done the same thing.

But . . . I crawled forward, then up, and lay (okay, fell) down before I needed to worry about how tired I suddenly was. My right arm throbbed and itched. Though the first two may have been practically nothing, that last look had said something so clear I could actually hear it. I closed my eyes, at first to focus but they wouldn't open again.

And I had heard that look before.

chapter 6.

I woke to the strange (and not unpleasant) sensation of floating in cotton. I was pretty sure I was alive, but it took a little longer for me to figure out that I was not floating but lying on my back, between the bed where I'd fallen asleep yesterday and its soft, heavy blanket. *Yesterday,* my mind repeated lazily, recalling where I was, that day and the ones before it. *Well, there goes waking up calm and rested.* I mentally rolled my eyes (my real ones were still closed) and waited for fear to kick off.

And when it didn't, for anger.

And then for concern.

Okay, I reasoned, finally. *Don't panic or anything, as if you could, but I think you're paralyzed. Emotionally, at least.* I was mildly surprised to find myself a little amused by the idea, and wasn't surprised at all that the surprise was mild. *No need to jump to conclusions,* I answered. *Maybe I'm physically paralyzed, too. Does paralysis feel like floating?*

Yeah, like you're that lucky, I concluded, feeling a tiny tug at the corner of my mouth.

After a few leisurely minutes, I decided I liked this feeling. It was ridiculously serene, like being locked inside a soundproof, bulletproof room with a great view of all the people outside, looking at you like a hungry cat watches a canary in a cage. They yell, they scream. Hell, some of them even take a couple of cracks at the glass. But you can just sit back, relax, and laugh—because you know no one is getting through unless you choose to take the short walk to the door, unlock it, and let the world back in. Until then, you're untouchable.

Untouchable. That felt right. I was completely untouchable.

But now, I was also thinking about my arm. It had been cleaned and wrapped with very little civility and absolutely no permission; I might as well have been vaccinated and tagged at the same time. But I couldn't feel the cast anymore. Was it still there?

No, it disintegrated and you managed not to notice. What do you think?

I ignored the thought and tested the theory, lightly flexing my wrist. I was mildly surprised for the second time when my hand struck the cast and, instead of crashing waves of nausea, all I felt was plaster. *Huh.* I did it again, as hard as I could. Nothing more than muffled throbbing from inside the mold.

Good. Nightmarish as it had been to get the damn thing put on—a woman digging like some mad gardener through the open wound, someone I couldn't see holding an arm around my waist, *so I couldn't get away*—it had better be helping. And honestly, being able to move it at all was a major improvement. *I like this new optimism thing. We should do it more often.*

Had I just called myself "we"? I needed to *do* something—clearly I'd been lying here too long. Opening my eyes less than halfway, I scanned the area (what of it I could see, anyway). It seemed like I was alone . . . But people could hide, and might, so I opened my eyes a little wider and scanned again. Still no one. "Perfect," I murmured.

At least I tried to. What came out was a voice that could have been mine if I'd recently had the flu—and attempted to cure it by gargling coal dust. If I wasn't untouchable, I might have been upset to hear it. As it was, I just stretched myself upright and examined my arm again.

Dingy plaster covered the lower half of my hand. It felt hollow, light. Curious, I flexed my fingers, slowly bending them into as much of a fist as I could manage. They had only gone a little ways when a feeling—not painful but potent, like lightning beneath the skin—erupted from the center of my wrist, coursing through my hand all the way to my fingernails. Suddenly, so synchronized they might have been pulled by a string, every finger on my right hand hunched over, pulling down into a forced claw shape I couldn't relax away. After a few seconds it ended and the fingers straightened as if daring me to say something, say something, because no one was ever going to believe me.

Nerve damage aimed a rifle at the glass.

But the glass was bulletproof. The next time I bent my fingers they obeyed without incident, and the spasm slid from my mind as a more recognizable sensation sent me bolting for the bathroom on wobbly legs.

A few minutes later I was staring into the mirror, torn between dismay and perverse delight. Is this what I had looked like for the last few days? My face and arms could have belonged to an un-buried corpse, covered with dark brown dirt, blades of grass, and small, scabbed over scratches from catching trees when I ran. Here and there in the mess were smudged areas, muddy and thick—I must have rubbed my face a few times after the fall. And along my jaw was a long streak where grime had been replaced by a bright smear of blood.

But not my blood. I paused, trying to hold on to feelings and images that kept slipping by outside the bulletproof room. It was too hard, though, and eventually I gave up, settling back into untouchability.

But shock very nearly shattered the glass as I noticed what was behind me in the mirror.

Glass. Right. Bloody footprints marked the path I had taken, and they were getting bolder. Still, it took time to remember what had happened (the satisfying *crash*, the rush of fresh air, the immediate knowledge that I had no idea what to do next) and even then, I had to concentrate before I could start to feel the ache in the bottoms of my feet.

Crap. I didn't need feelings to know this wasn't good, and I worked quickly, the fingernails of both hands crusting with blood and grime but proving more than capable of removing the largest shards. They formed a wet, spiky pile on the floor, which I considered with far-away interest.

By the time my feet were relatively shard-free, I was winded and dizzy, but I couldn't resist—I was inescapably drawn back to the mirror, my bloody, muddy face. My hair was a nearly unrecognizable nest of snarls. It seemed to have made friends with a few trees; I could see where it had shaken hands with each, hello *and* goodbye.

Okay, upside—just imagine what Mom would say if she could see you. I grinned: definitely a plus of the new look.

But I actually kind of liked having hair . . . and I didn't exactly have anything better to do. So I grabbed a comb that had (*thoughtfully,* I supposed with disdain) been placed near the sink and went, painfully, to work. I started to look back up.

No. Not yet. It felt good to actually be *doing* something, so I had to do it right. Wetting a small towel, I wiped down my arms and legs, but I had to rinse it again, twice, before scrubbing at my face and neck and dragging it through my hair. *Crappy towel.*

This time I managed to face the mirror. *Not bad,* at least, not as bad as before. At any rate, I now looked more like live vermin than roadkill, though what was left of my hair still hung in mottled, muddy clumps.

As usual, I made eye contact with myself last. From the middle of an only slightly cleaner face, my eyes stared out, bright blue and familiar, regarding me with a cool wariness that was not without hostility, as if asking what, exactly, I was looking at. *Good to know not everything changes.* I smiled at me, then headed back toward the bed part of my room.

It was smaller than a hospital room, more like my bedroom at home. The window was smaller, though, and there was no closet or dresser, only a wardrobe that already had things inside. A twin-sized bed and a desk were shoved against the wall. Not a great place for hiding. It was also pretty dim—the fading light died near a lone skinny lamp by the door. *Where am I?*

Anxiety threw a rock at the glass as I realized I really didn't know. There were a few trees but no hills or landmarks outside, no signs or buildings to give me a clue. Of course only a map would help; I had never been more than a bus-ride away from home before. I squinted out into the evening, trying to find some difference in the trees. I might not even be in the same country as home.

For the first time since waking up, I began to actually feel something. And once I realized what it was, it seemed obvious that I'd been overwhelmed the entire time. I was being stretched tighter and tighter each second, with every new experience I hadn't asked for, and with the next the last fraying thread of me would probably snap. *Well don't let it, not over trees. Far too pathetic.* I squeezed my head between hand and cast, willing myself untouchable again, back into my bulletproof shelter, and was relieved when I managed it with no more than a slight worsening of my headache.

Calm again, I raked my good hand through my hair and leaned back against the wall to count the lost strands. I'd just pulled the first away with my teeth when I heard what immediately became my new least favorite noise—a turning doorknob.

Shit. What now? Dive back into bed? Lock myself in the bathroom? Find a weapon? Damn it, *why* did I fall asleep?

I settled for staying perfectly still, and forcing my face to do the same. Whoever controlled the rest of my body apparently decided to help; my blood seemed to cool about ten degrees as the door swung open, and without any coaching my eyelids shut halfway, turning my eyes to narrow slits. It occurred to me that I was now displaying some emotion I didn't feel. *Go with it.*

Peter (I flinched even *thinking* it) edged in and turned on the lamp, spotting me just as the room flooded with sad yellow light.

Right away he was on guard but tried to pretend otherwise, keeping between the door and me as he inched closer. Whoever was controlling my body had lost her nerve by now. I was putting so much into keeping my lip from curling, into holding back the defensive growl I felt building in my throat, into letting none of my sudden nervous energy through the glass, that I had to remind myself to take every second breath.

I was losing it, backsliding into the panic of the past few days all over again, and my focus was fading. The glass was warping dangerously. If he took one more step, it would break.

Maybe not. Because you know something new now, don't you? Who that is. Which means now there's another option. Right?

The glass was barely holding, but here I stood with a look of pure loathing on my face. Now I put every ounce of my nerve into making that rage real.

It took less effort than I expected. Turns out anger hadn't gone far.

Peter (wince) had frozen in place, staring at the ground. He looked up at me. And kept looking.

It's too quiet, my mind observed helpfully. So what was he waiting for? Did he expect me to say something? Because he had to know there was no way—

"Son of a bitch."

I blinked. A rasping, sheet-metal-on-stone voice spat the words, but they were mine. Though I couldn't remember deciding to say them. The next second lasted for an hour. Admittedly, I was kind of hoping for a reaction—that I'd shocked him as much as I had myself. I mean, I might not quite look like death anymore, but I sounded even worse. At least I could use that to my advantage.

Instead, a huge smile lit up my brother's face. "And I was starting to think you didn't recognize me."

At least, it went something like that. I barely heard. I had left the building. And now *all* my energy was focused on keeping my features under control, with no more allotted to breathing. What the hell was I seeing? He looked . . . okay. Better than before, and so different. His face was fuller, hair cropped neatly around his ears—but that wasn't it. And I'd seen him smile before, that wasn't it either. What it was, I realized as I glared point blank into that ridiculous grin, was that I had never seen him smile like *this*. And the difference was in his eyes.

Growing up I had learned to always look for hidden meanings, undercurrents, to everything a person said or did. It wasn't foolproof, but it was my way, and my way was better than listening to what people said. People lied.

Like in school, where the undercurrent had always been disgust. From teachers who always only blamed "the parents"—or so they said—it stood out like a bad aftertaste behind even the kindest gestures. And my classmates barely disguised their looks of distaste if I so much as walked too loudly between classes; of course, they probably wouldn't have hid anything at all if they weren't afraid of what I might do.

With Mom, it ranged from fear—which was hard to understand—to, sometimes, a pure, emotionless resolve. That one always scared me the most.

I mean it. Some kids imagine monsters' eyes made of shoes watching from their closets. Others don't need to imagine the eyes—they just need to see what's behind them.

Even with Peter, there had always been something. I should say especially with him. Sometimes it was all there *had* been; he'd used it to speak for him when he had no other choice. I caught myself before I shut my eyes on those memories.

It wasn't completely gone. I could see it, right where it had always been, so familiar that finding it was just like focusing in suddenly brighter light. But it wasn't saying anything. There was nothing to decode, no significance, and I could almost have sworn, if it was anyone I didn't know as well (a small part of my brain prodded *Do I? Do I know this person at all?*) that there was *laughter* under there. Shit, I couldn't breathe and he was smiling at me like he knew the funniest joke in the universe and I should hear it, too. And, *damn* him, he looked just fine.

Say it.

I did. *He's done pretty well without you.*

The thought put the decisive crack in my shelter of the past twenty or so short minutes, and it was gone. My peace was gone, and now I was heavy, and my feet hurt, and I was tired, and I wanted to go back to sleep and never wake up again.

It wouldn't happen soon. That insane painted-on-clown-grin was still floating in front of me. The unrecognizable person attached to it grew visibly upset when he realized I had finished my part of the script and, dimming a little, tried the classic "You clean up pretty good," and then, with an odd furtive look and a little desperation, "feel okay?"

I ignored him. *Just go away . . .* I tried to think something spiteful, but didn't have the energy for spite. Instead, I stared pointedly past the stranger. *Get it?*

He did, which didn't make me feel as good as I'd expected. "You should sit down," he stepped backward and away from the bed.

Well, no way was I sitting anywhere *now*. Instead I sidestepped into the far corner and leaned back, using the wall for support and trying to look as though it was the most comfortable place in the world. *No, I am definitely not feeling "okay."* And I was pretty sure I shouldn't be. Why wouldn't he leave? Couldn't we do this another time, when I could be as angry as I wanted without losing all of my standing-up energy?

Minutes, hours, weeks ticked by in silence. My hand twitched again, like before. I needed to move. My mind made itself up to go back to the bathroom—there had been a lock in there, I was pretty sure.

"Hungry?"

And I'd thought he sounded desperate before. The moment I'd started to turn, he'd gone for the last grenade in his arsenal.

He doesn't want you to leave. Nice idea. But memory served well enough to know that meant *this time. Not right now, not at the moment, however else you say it. So, what? "Glad you don't want to be rid of me any time soon, now you've had some time to yourself. Cool. Wanna see the pile of crap I just pulled out of my hair?"*

I don't think I can make myself work that way.

I argued with myself while watching him from the corner of my eye. He was holding out a styrofoam bowl my razor-sharp powers of observation had failed to detect like an offering, hanging back, not too close. I scrutinized the gesture and tried not to show it. It didn't mean anything, I didn't think—but I'd have sworn it looked familiar.

Suddenly and, for the sake of my dignity, I have to say for the first time in a *long* time, I felt my eyes go hot and prickly.

NO! I was not going to let this happen. I was *not* about to lose what little control I had over this situation by breaking down like a little girl who needed a hug, no matter how accurate the description might be at the moment.

Good, don't. I tried hard to pull myself back together. It wouldn't do any good, crying never did. It was a mystery to me why other people spent so much time doing it.

So knock it off. I clenched my jaw over the lump in my throat and looked away.

But now he was talking. When did he start doing that? I tuned in in time to catch the last few words.

". . . birthday, I guess."

He had my full focus now. "What the hell is that supposed to mean?"

Looking uncomfortable, he started to answer. But I wasn't done.

"You . . . You're . . . my-my *what*?" I stuttered in outrage. Words were genuinely not my friend right now. Maybe I should start over.

"My birthday. You cannot seriously be talking to me about my *birthday*." Better. Much better. The sandpaper started to work its way out of my throat, and too suddenly I couldn't stop. "Is that what this is to you? Pulling me out of my window in the middle of the night, having some of your good friends chase me through the *fucking* woods, leaving me to sit here for *five fucking days*" I made up a number so I wouldn't lose my momentum, "while I waited for something terrible to happen! Was this supposed to be some sort of a *birthday present*?

"Of course—it makes sense now! You disappear on me for three years and five months," a number I didn't have to guess, "and I'm thinking it must be because you're in prison, or dead, or . . . But no, it turns out you were just planning the perfect surprise party, and you had to take your time, right?

"Either that, or—stop me if I've got it this time—were you having doubts? Thought you were ready to say *hi* after some time to yourself, but maybe you needed a few more months before having to honor a promise you made to some fourteen-year-old girl!" I might actually have been spitting at this point.

"So what do you want now? How does the party end—with me telling you I'm fine?" I held up my bandaged arm, trying for a flippant smile and getting stuck at a grimace. "Do you just *need* to hear that, and, I don't know, a big thanks for finally showing your face while I'm at it? Fine! Thanks, and I'm great, and I guess I'll go back to waiting around here until my *birthday* is over—another week or so should do it—and your guilt can be gone and you can be done and you can send me back home. Because that is-is all you could possibly do for me at this point, is send me back now, before . . ."

I ran out of steam mid-sentence. I was next to the bathroom again; at some point during one of the longest speeches of my life, I had taken a walk. Spent, I looked back at my brother.

He was watching me back thoughtfully from the small chair. Apparently he had actually listened to the jumble of words I'd spewed at him—and now it looked like he was trying to sort it all out.

Well, so much for the cold shoulder.

Whatever. I had never been the quiet type. Anyway, I was curious to see what he would do with it all. I'd said some things I hadn't even known I was thinking. Worse, I'd realized something unimaginable.

I had no reason to, but I wanted to go home. I wanted to see the house from my path in the woods one more time, sit up in my window reading by moonlight, even if it was in a locked room.

It was crazy. But it was all I knew. And I still wasn't sure what this was supposed to be—if this whole thing really was some kind of trick, I would prefer the familiar any day.

I was expecting some pretty fancy excuses for it all, though. He owed me that much, even if he hadn't meant this nightmare to be some twisted "gift."

What I was not expecting was for him to apparently grow more and more confused until he simply shook his head, looked up at me, and said

"No."

chapter 7.

IT seemed unnecessary to say, so I just thought *What?* really hard, shutting my mouth over and over because it kept falling open. I was practically vibrating, but refused to show it. I could play it cool, too. So I stood up straight and calm as any soldier, took a deep, not-so-ragged breath and let it out. Then I spoke slowly. "No to what?"

His failure to get a rise out of me went unnoticed. Preoccupied, he stared at the floor and chewed his bottom lip for a few long seconds until finally, as if admitting defeat, "Pretty much . . . everything?" The last word was drawn out, each syllable treated as a word of its own, so "thing" was the only question. He seemed to have more difficulty meeting my eyes this time. "We clearly need to talk. Sit down." It was more an order than an offer, and he looked me up and down in a weirdly desperate way I didn't particularly like, pushing away from the bed to indicate it as a prime sitting area.

Again I ignored him, leaning back. *Yeah, you are the epitome of cool right now.* "You sure? In a few more years I was probably just going to pull the same disappearing act you did. Don't need you for that. Think about it before you say anything, it's a pretty good deal for you." Not just cool; I could bait, too.

He almost took it. It was pretty clear he wanted to, at least. But at the last second there was a change in his expression. Another look of consternation, then sadness, then a flash of what might have been panic all shot across his face in rapid succession. The rest of him didn't move. *Was it something I said?* No way he should have taken that last jab seriously (I never would have said it if I'd thought he might), but now he was worrying me a little.

Eventually he did remember that I had, technically, asked him a question. "Yeah, I am. Look," he ground the heel of one hand into his forehead and stared at his knees like he'd just remembered he left the stove on somewhere far away. "I meant to start from the beginning, but I can't remember where that was anymore . . . anyway, I kept trying to tell you." He'd started off muttering to himself, but now he was staring at me accusingly, like I really should be ashamed. I wasn't, though, and I also wasn't in the mood to help him make excuses. I waited.

"That night, in the woods. I kept trying. And you would have heard me if you'd slowed down enough to pay attention."

"Oh, quit whi-"

"And I'm sorry about the window, too. That . . . was not supposed to happen."

"Well I guess everything's all better, then."

He winced. "I mean it. You know I hate the idea of anyone falling from there."

True. When we were kids my tree was the only way to sneak in and out at night, and falling was one of those things, like small spaces (my brother was severely claustrophobic), that he was always freaking out about. But that only made it even worse, didn't it?

A small smile, not nearly as bright as the one earlier, had appeared on my brother's face, and now he turned it on me. I immediately turned up the volume on my withering glare, combating his joy with my wrath. "I didn't expect you to be asleep." He shook his head. "I should have known."

And then he just sat there, still staring at me as though, I don't know, he knew me from a long time ago or something. Which, of course, he did, but I didn't like it. The glare-volume turned up on its own now. Part of me laughed at my discomfort, and not the part that normally made snide comments and needled me unhelpfully. *Something might be wrong with you, Girl,* it said, and Girl was a name.

Noting but (hopefully) misinterpreting my hostility, Peter dropped the brotherly act and with it the dubious topic of the window.

"Of course, this is something we could've talked about any of the *thirteen*"—he drew it out, using his tone instead of words to tell me I was wrong—"days you've been here, because I did come and talk to you, even if it wasn't enough." All business now. I half expected him to stand up and tell me visiting hours were over for today, we'd have to pick up from here tomorrow.

"I think I'd remember that."

Instead of arguing, he stood and, without explanation or (you have to give him credit) any ceremony whatsoever, lifted the front of his shirt.

Instead of arguing, I—again—settled for keeping my mouth shut.

Spreading across my brother's abdomen was a giant, mottled purple-green bruise. *Oh*—I might have remembered something like that. "It used to be a little better, but . . ."

Crap. I tried hard to not feel terrible, to not even want to apologize and withdraw at least part of what I'd said before, and I hated myself for failing.

But he didn't look too satisfied to be winning. "And-and I know I haven't been here as much as I should. But you didn't- I'm sorry. I was . . . scared, I guess," he lifted a hand in front of his face, "obviously for a reason."

He sat down again, still moving slowly, cautiously. Because of me. *Okay, point made. Fine, oops, sorry. But, I mean, didn't he sort of deserve-*

Almost as if he didn't want me to finish, Peter broke in. "Even yesterday, which I don't think you could blame me for skipping," yesterday's *look* was back again, narrow and sharp, "since you'd tried to kill me—twice—the day before?"

"I did not." I was shaking my head hard, like a child. I hadn't even meant to say anything.

The too-fast slideshow of images that had rushed past the glass earlier slammed back into place all at once: the toothbrush, the tank lid, the not-my-blood on my face. It hadn't felt quite real then, but now, somehow, it was both *real* and *wrong* at the same time.

I tried to explain. "I wouldn't . . . I would nev- did not . . ." This was my day for long speeches, but now full sentences were tripping me up.

"Oh, you *wouldn't* try to kill me? Because for not trying you were pretty good at almost succeeding." I wasn't ready to hear him sound hurt. Not now, not yet.

"I . . . didn't know it was you," I said, though even I didn't fully understand what it meant. Maybe *now* I remembered the shadow-figure looming nearby as Peter, but who was it before? Could have been anyone. Could have been . . .

Quickly I tried to change the subject. "Anyway, that was yesterday. You should remember if it was so traumatic."

He dispatched my diversion quickly and without fanfare, like an annoying insect. "Two days ago. You've been asleep since then. Who did you *think* you were trying to kill, then?" he interrogated.

The problem was that I didn't know. The more I focused on it, the more the figure I was sure I'd seen turned into a blur. It was strange, but true, and I wasn't going to dwell on it to satisfy anyone's pointless curiosity. I shrugged instead. "I don't know. Not you."

More interesting was what he'd rushed through. Two whole days? That sort of thing only happened when people pricked their fingers on spinning wheels or bit poisoned apples or did other things that work in fairy tales but either slightly irritate real people or kill them outright. "Two days?"

He stared, not sure he was ready to let his line of questioning go.

Once it sunk in that *I* was done with it, though, he settled back and picked mine up. "Two days. It was creepy; I thought you were faking at first but I guess not. Actually, you probably shouldn't be up yet," he paused, evidently waiting for me to respond. I just watched the wall over his head and pointedly ignored being called "creepy." Eventually he went on.

"So. Eleven days, you tried to kill . . . *someone,* then you slept for two. Makes this day thirteen, doesn't it?" He smirked without quite smirking, and I glanced at him and away. I knew that look. I hated that look. *Fine, so it wasn't a very good guess.*

"Or did you just make something up because you didn't remember?" he asked, smugly echoing my thoughts. I hated that, too—at least right now. "Though maybe I should have played along. The shape you were in . . ." he shook his head. "I should have come back sooner."

You've stayed away longer, I thought but couldn't bring myself to say.

"Speaking of which, will you *please* sit down? It looks like a nightmare in here and you are literally standing in a puddle of your own blood. You *can* feel it, right? I don't know if you remember but there was a lot of glass-"

"I got most of it."

"Oh." He sounded taken aback and a little sad, so I knew he'd gotten my message: he wouldn't be allowed to fix this. "Okay. I left a first aid kit for the rest."

I kept my eyes level, finishing the thought—*and I've been much worse off.*

I must have lost myself trying to drown out a few less welcome notions, because I dropped away a little, barely but just enough to notice when the room swam back into focus. This time, though, I wasn't the only one.

My brother hadn't moved and looked like he might never get around to it, staring at a fixed point directly in front of his face. A muscle in his jaw twitched. He appeared to be puzzling something out, literally chewing it over. I hadn't even decided whether I cared what it was when he stood, crossed the small room in three quick steps, and wrapped both arms around me in what must have been the most earnest (and unexpected) crushing bear hug ever.

For the record, I am not a hug person. I tend to find them unnecessary, restrictive and even a little threatening—call me oversensitive—and this was definitely more rule than exception. So I did what came naturally: let every muscle in my body slowly clench to maximum tension and waited. And continued to wait, for what seemed like forever. He was really milking this minor triumph over my slow reflexes.

Or not. After what actually was nearly a minute (I started counting after a while), he broke the unbelievably awkward silence. "Three years, six months, eight days," he muttered very quietly over my head, like he would prefer I didn't hear. "Happy *belated* birthday. I did try not to miss it, but . . . it's May. I'm sorry."

I went slack. Not just on the outside; my organs liquefied, and I had to blink a few times, hard, to fix suddenly unfocusing eyes. *That's wrong*. Mid-blink air rushed back into my lungs, followed by the disturbingly final sound that is a door not slamming, but shutting quietly. He was gone.

I left my eyes closed. That couldn't be right. Okay, maybe not a lie or anything, but . . . what he said, it had to be wrong. *I* needed it to be wrong. I was fourteen, nearly fifteen, *nearly*, my birthday only about a week away. I would be fifteen on the seventeenth of April—party or no party, best wishes or not, like every year—and like every seventeenth of April for the past three, *three not four* birthdays, I would give myself the same gift and borrow one of Mom's sharpest kitchen knives to gouge a single mark down the outside of his bedroom door. She never chose to notice, though I kind of hoped she would.

It was a little ritual I'd started so I wouldn't forget my promise to my brother, who'd left the winter before I turned twelve, but it was something else now. Still, in part, a celebration: *Another year I'm still here.* But also a kind of petty reproach: *And I did it alone.* Part pride, part anger, though I'd probably earned neither.

I hadn't realized how much I had looked forward to that ritual, had held on to those feelings like an anchor.

Now I was fifteen. And I had missed it.

And I was gone—so I'd missed my chance, too. Permanently.

My liquid insides hardened and withered away, leaving me hollow. I had failed to play even my own game, with my own, easy rules. I faintly remembered believing when I was a kid that birthdays were stupid, wondering what was so important about knowing what day you were born, anyway?

Nothing I could remember thinking had ever felt a lifetime away before.

Now I was starting to fold, my empty body collapsing in on itself, and bent over I stumbled, blind, trying to find a spot where I could feel solid again. I wanted to go back to sleep; wanted to go back in time and know my own age; I wanted my brother to come back. I wanted Peter back, which was awful, because I didn't want him to know. Because if he did, because if I were wrapped again in a hug I would never say I needed, then I would want to be alone just as desperately.

Finding a small hollow behind the toilet I folded myself again, buried my face firmly into my knees, and held them hard until I could feel my heartbeat and my bad arm started to ache, curled up so tight that I barely shook with the first silent sobs.

8, 14

THE *girl's first clue something is wrong is when she walks into the house and finds her mother upstairs in her room throwing things into a little black bag.*

Actually, the bag itself is her second clue, and just in case that's not enough her mother looks up and gives her the third:

"Get in the car and wait for me."

"Where are we going?" She already knows. What she really wants to know is why, and Mom sometimes answers questions when she's busy like this.

"Just get in the car and be glad I'm not leaving you behind in the closet until I get back!" The girl goes. Her mother hadn't answered her, but she did say something useful and the girl figures the rest out herself.

The pantry, which her mother calls the closet even though it's in the kitchen and that's exactly why it isn't a closet, is empty. When she'd left for school this morning it hadn't been—her brother was inside. And if he's not there anymore and she doesn't see him anywhere else, it means something has happened to him and that is the why for why they are going to the hospital! She hops up into the back seat, proud of her detective work, at the same time remembering to hope he's okay.

Actually, she might kind of know what's wrong with him, too.

He's been acting weird for a while. It started a few months ago, right before the bus came to take them to school. He would stand there like always, and her too, but when the bus got where they could see it, he'd walk away from her. Not far, and then he would turn around and come back and turn right back around and do it over and over again. She'd thought he was pacing, but she asked him one day and the look he gave her back made her think maybe that wasn't the right word. But he was nervous, she could tell.

At first she'd thought he didn't want to go to school. He doesn't like it there—that's something else she's figured out. People ask him questions he isn't supposed to answer, and the other kids are mean to him sometimes. She knows that because the kids at her school are mean too, and some of them have brothers or sisters in High School like she does. It isn't only the school bus anymore, though. He still acts jumpy sometimes even if he's just riding in the car. She would ask why, but after that first time she hasn't wanted to again.

It's been getting worse and worse, too. It stopped only being buses and cars about a few weeks or so (or so was short for or something) ago, and she's started having to let him out of the pantry a lot when she gets home, even though usually they used to leave each other in there when Mom was coming back. She doesn't mind the pantry. It's dark and quiet, not that comfortable but almost never too cold, and while getting sent there is not fun it means whatever the trouble was about at first, it's over for now.

She guesses that's not what he thinks.

One time she had opened the door and almost didn't see him, he jumped out so fast, and then he ran upstairs before she could ask if he was okay. When she followed him her window was open and he was under it, sitting on one of the branches of her big tree and holding on to the trunk so hard it looked like he thought he was going to fall. He just looked shaky at first, but when she got closer she could see him doing something between gasping for air and sobbing it all out.

She didn't know what was wrong, but it was worse she didn't know what to do. She doesn't really freak out like that. But there was something he would do when she was scared or sad, and she hoped it might work for whatever this was too.

Leaning her whole top half out of the window, she had run the very tips of her fingers over the top of the boy's shaggy brown hair, and she had started to tell him it was okay or that it was going to be, but she couldn't because he had ducked his head, turned around and snapped at her to get back inside. So, pretending not to be kind of mad, she had.

When she asked later why he acted like that, he'd sighed and looked at her for a while. "Because men don't cry."

She was confused. "But you cry all the time."

And he'd told her to get out of his room and she'd laughed at him. She hopes he wasn't serious about that men stuff.

It looks like he is really serious about something, though. As her mother gets into the car and begins the drive to the children's hospital, she keeps muttering about him. "Only gone for . . . what am I supposed to think . . . normal people never . . ."

Those aren't usually the things she says when she has to take someone to the hospital. Usually she works on her story.

He's still kind of foggy when they get there, but the boy is nonetheless glad his sister is here. He feels bad when she's left alone for too long.

He moves his head a little. It still hurts, a lot honestly, but it's not like he's going to complain. And even if he could, there would be no point. He did this to himself.

He can't remember doing it, which he thinks might be normal since the doctors keep asking about his memory. Now they think he's partly unconscious, because he won't answer or look at them. But he knows he did it, because he can remember thinking about it when Mom put him in there.

For the past few days, he has been staying home—sick, apparently—after a scuffle at school left his clothes looking far too messy for Mom's standards. He doesn't think it was really about clothes, though. He thinks it was more likely about her "friend," who stopped coming around a little while ago.

Today she'd come into his room. He was reading for school and hadn't known what to do, so he waited until, with a heavy sigh, she plopped down on the bed next to him. "None of them is going to love me, are they?"

He stayed quiet, kind of knowing what she wanted to hear but sure he wasn't the person who was supposed to say the words. "Say something," she had almost pleaded.

But he could think of nothing to say.

They sat there for so long the silence almost became comfortable. And he had barely thought he could not remember the last time he'd felt something like related to Mom when she came back to herself with a vengeance, saying if he was going to be useless he might as well take up less space doing it, and she had dragged him downstairs to the kitchen.

That was when he had known he couldn't do it again. Ever. And when he'd tried pointlessly to tell his mother and gotten nowhere but stuck in that tiny airless black vault again, he'd known he meant it. Which had to be how he wound up with the concussion.

When they come in, his mother leaves almost immediately to speak to a doctor in the hall. The girl, undaunted as usual, bounces up next to the bed and takes a long look at him. He does not like for her to talk to him in public, and she doesn't want to upset him, so she doesn't ask everything she really wants to. Instead, she reaches out one hand, and he takes it, and she asks one question.

"Was it you?" Asking it might make him mad, but this whole day is so much weirder than usual. Might as well take the chance.

The answer is one quick squeeze from his hand to hers. Her eyes widen—one means yes. Needing to know more, she lets go and heads to the foot of his bed, picking up his chart and scanning it for the whole story. The boy watches the door nervously, but doesn't get a chance to warn her when it suddenly opens and Mom walks in, alone.

The girl starts, dropping the folder to the floor.

"What do you think you're doing?"

"I wanted to see what happened," the girl answers. It sounds okay to her.

"I told you what happened. Do you need to hear it again?" Her mother starts to head toward the chair where she left her purse and the girl looks at her brother uneasily, but only for a second. One thing she saw in the file was that he's been drugged, and anyway what could he do to help?

"You never actually said, so I wanted to see . . ." her brother would say she was digging a hole now, so she stops talking.

Her mother pulls a short wooden paddle out of the purse.

"I'm sorry, Mom." The girl had forgotten about the paddle. She is genuinely sorry, now. "I won't do it again."

"I know you won't, sweetie," her mother sighs, letting the paddle swing by her side. "Come here." She says here, but she pulls the white dividing curtain around the empty bed next to the boy and points there instead.

The girl looks briefly back at her brother, who strains to see what their mother is holding, then lets his head fall back onto the pillow with a loud sigh. He clenches his jaw and wills her not to make this worse.

She shakes her head, backing toward the door. But she doesn't run. It won't help. Someone will only find her and bring her back here, and then it would be not just bad, not like it already is, but Bad. Running away makes things from bad to Bad most times. So she does not put up as much of a fight as she wants to when Mom comes over and grabs her, dragging her over to the curtained part of the room. She just leans back, then rocks forward on her feet over and over, thinking about nothing as hard as she can.

"All I ever wanted were good children. Good, well-behaved children. Why don't I deserve that?" Her mother complains.

The girl is busy thinking about what color nothing would be, so she says the first thing that comes to mind. "Maybe we're all just Bad."

Her mother doesn't get it. "Don't lump me in with you," she spits. "Put your hands up." She indicates a small bedside table, and the girl does as she's told.

"Fingers spread," her mother instructs, and the girl again complies, swallowing with a suddenly dry throat. She watches her fingers, nails clean but irregular because she doesn't like to cut them, and feels more than sees her mother raise the paddle. Sometimes, there are more shelves in a pantry than a closet, she thinks, and then it comes down.

After Mom leaves, with a promise to be back tomorrow morning, the girl goes back over to the bed to see if her brother is still awake. She gingerly lays her hand on the bed at first, but draws it back with a quick, loud gasp when he takes it.

He lets go right away and turns apologetically to look at her. She looks okay, the defiant set of her jaw and shoulders the same as usual. Except that now instead of curiously rambling around the room, she glares holes into the floor, refusing to meet his gaze, a trail of snot down her chin shining in the light from the hall.

She's such a little kid. At least, some of the time, which is when it's his job to take care of her as much as he can.

Seemingly on the same train of thought, she steps close again and leans over against him. She is still shaking a little. He begins brushing a hand across the small tousled head and doesn't stop until she does.

chapter 8

THOSE days that followed are hard to describe. "Pretty damn scary" comes close, though, even if it was no one's fault but my own. It was a strange, restless time, filled with mindless actions meant to distract me from worse ones.

Like pacing. For hours I would pace tight circles around my room thinking vague, neutral thoughts when I suddenly, overwhelmingly, just *had* to chew on something. And before I could stop them my teeth would develop a hive-mind of their own, spiritedly sinking into a pillow from the bed or the pen I was holding or, once, the wood of the nearest doorjamb. Puzzled, I'd detach myself—once the teeth no longer felt the urge to turn on me instead—and begin pacing again, faster, all thoughts from before the episode erased from my mind.

Other times I would sit in the fetal position, like I had at first, on the chair or in my favorite corner and I would rock, holding my head tightly between my hands because even though it didn't hurt, I knew it wanted to explode.

I did not leave my room. I wasn't certain I would survive the trip.

But it was worse at night, when hundreds, *millions* of thoughts exploded through me like firecrackers too fast and loud to piece together, my mind thrashing in my skull like a wild animal that would tear us both to shreds trying to escape. These were the nights when I would lie down only to bolt right out of bed again, pace the length of my small room, and lean my head into the wall baring my teeth in agony that I didn't actually feel and couldn't explain, less often punching it hard enough to scrape knuckles raw. I wasn't brave enough to break a hand—though the distraction might have been worth the pain.

On those nights, just before I succumbed to exhaustion, I always wound up face to face with myself in the mirror, looking nothing like a stranger even though I was acting like one, asking myself

"What is wrong with you?"

Over and over, throwing in insults here and there when I admitted I didn't know.

Girl, the problem is staring you right in the fucking face.

Apparently it didn't end there, either; eventually I started to wake up stinging and bleeding, my arms, legs, stomach and neck covered in raised scratches and deeper cuts that went away in a few days but looked like hell meanwhile.

My brother helped as much as he could, "visiting" my self-made prison for at least half of each day. We spent some of the time fighting, a lot of it making idle conversation and skirting around the hundreds of questions we both clearly wanted to ask—questions have this tendency to multiply, and no one was ready for that yet—and most of the time the way we were used to, in a casual near-silence. Most of the time, it was nice to have him around.

But there were other times, when we were sitting together in that small room while the silence stretched just enough to become comfortable and I was thinking things were almost the way they used to be, when I would look up and see a question starting on his face. And then I would have to say or do something to make it stop, or him leave, or myself look even crazier than I was feeling. Usually that meant I ended up alone again, feeling like—*being*—the prisoner of the pissed off, confused me who seemed to hate myself even when I wasn't awake. Which wasn't great.

I wasn't even worried about him asking questions, not exactly. Questions are easy.

Answers, not so much.

chapter 9.

TROUBLED as he was by Alana's behavior, he should still worry more. He just couldn't bring himself to do it.

It wasn't tough love, nowhere near as conscious as that. It was just hard to worry about her when he knew where she was and that she was relatively safe (or at least that she was the most dangerous person in the room). And since they were talking now, Peter was more confident that his sister would come out of her self-destructive phase—and her room—any day now. He just had to be patient.

Anyway he had practically raised Alana, and he knew her well. Everything would settle down long before she actually did herself any harm.

Of course, he'd said that before.

I was a liar.

She would be *fine* with a little time. There was no reason to be worried.

It was fairly dull here lately. "Business" had slacked off and Peter had little to do during the day, except spend time with Al. She seemed exhausted lately—though she always said she slept fine—and as a result was an even more quick-tempered and overanxious version of her usual self, only cheered when she'd successfully engaged her brother in combat (at least now it was only the verbal kind). Most of their conversations followed a predictable pattern, so Peter was not at all surprised after the fifth knock on her door.

"Why do you bother knocking? It's not like I ever tell you to go away."

He rolled his eyes and let himself in. Almost immediately his cell buzzed and he winced, waiting for it to finish on its own. This was the second time today; he'd meant to silence the little pre-paid monster before coming in.

"Do you *ever* answer that thing?"

He grinned. "Not really."

Al was calmer today. She was cleaning her fingernails, and gave him a level gaze before refocusing on the task. She stared at a clean one from both sides and sighed, apparently disappointed. Then, disappointment intact, she chewed it down to level.

He watched, still thinking about the calls and how much longer he could keep avoiding them. He'd moved on to thinking about the person making them when she finished with her nails and turned to him, now biting the inside of her cheek.

After an uneasy silence, she sighed again. "That smile bothers me."

"What?"

"That smile. You know which one."

"What do you mean, bothers you?"

"I don't know, it's—"

She paused, brow furrowed. But silences could only last so long with Al. "It's different." She looked away.

"You're different too, you know. It has been a whi—"

"I know I'm different. I know. But you . . . aren't. Not really."

He thought for a moment, almost caught her meaning, lost it again. "I'm sorry, Al, you're going to have to explain."

"You haven't changed. I figured you would have, it has been a long time, like you said—"

"I didn't say a *long* time—"

"Whatever. But you still don't sleep, you're claustrophobic, you only call me Alana when you're mad, you still talk to yourself-"

Peter couldn't resist interrupting again. "I didn't talk to myself!"

"Yes, you did. Not often, maybe, and only when you were alone."

"Don't you mean when I *thought* I was alone?"

She shrugged. "I mean, some differences are good, I guess. I like that you talk more."

There wasn't much to say to that.

"And you're nicer. I'm not saying you weren't," she added quickly, "but I don't know, it's good to go ten minutes without you talking about what I can't do, or what I shouldn't have done, or giving me that look. The one you're giving me right now." Alana gave one small snort of laughter, with what might have been a little bit of a grin. Then, sighing, "I know that look."

"You can't pretend you were the most innocent little kid, Alana. I was there too, remember. And you know I—"

"You were right most of the time, yes, I know. Not the point. The point is I get where some of the changes came from.

"But you used to smile then, anyway, and it made sense . . . it was *yours*. You know?"

"I guess so," he said. Why was this suddenly feeling like an ambush?

"And now, you smile and it's like you know something I don't, like you learned something while you've been gone and you think it's really funny that I don't know."

"But I—"

"And it makes me think," Al shifted uncomfortably. "Well, I guess . . ."

His sister looked at him like she was asking for help and he saw what she was going to say in her eyes. He opened his mouth to contradict, to reassure, to do *anything* but let her get the words out, but she got her nerve up first.

"I guess I wonder if maybe you weren't better off without me."

And then, even worse, for the very first time since the night he left, she started to cry. She didn't sob or make any noise at all, but a few tears escaped her ironlike restraint to roll down her cheeks and her jaw locked firmly, trying to hold the rest back.

Peter sat next to her, at a loss. How were you supposed to reassure someone you'd abandoned that you wanted them around? How could you tell someone who already had a hard time with trust that you wouldn't let them down, when you already *had*? He opened his mouth, waited for words to come.

"Ally . . ." He didn't have anything else. So he reached out with one arm, pulled a suddenly stiff and unresponsive Alana into him and, smoothing down her hair with the same hand, he waited.

After a while, she let her head fall back onto his shoulder. He looked over, but she was staring at the far wall, composed, the battle with her emotions won.

A longer silence, and then she sat up. "I'm tired."

Peter was, too, but he wasn't sure if it was a good idea to leave her alone. She eventually asked him to, though, so he stood and started to head for the door.

She got up, too. "Hey-"

He turned, grabbing her shoulder hard. "Never, *never* think that. Ever. You are the *only* family I have left and no matter what you think, I love you, and I cannot be better off without you. Got it?"

She looked away and nodded one short time, embarrassed. When she looked up Peter gave her a quick kiss on the forehead, told her good night, and waited for her to close the door (without slamming, for once) before, scrubbing a hand across his eyes, he walked away.

He awoke a few midnights later to two huge, round, almost luminescent blue eyes boring into his own.

Peter bolted upright and away with a sound like a cat being stepped on, if one of the cat's parents had been part bullfrog. Al leaned against the bed for support, gasping between guffaws.

"What the hell are you doing?"

"I was in the neighborhood." She was panting almost as hard as him.

Irritated beyond words, Peter collapsed back onto the pillow and rolled over to give his sister another reproachful look—but instead asked, "Did you know you were out of your room?"

"Pretty sure I saw," she fired back, failing to hide a smile.

Apparently Al *had* been listening when he exhaustively, repeatedly described the condemned hotel that was his current home, and she'd located his door (at least *one* of his doors) from memory. But she was never up this late. "What's wrong?"

"I want my arm back."

The cast. That couldn't be all. "Now?" *That can not be all.*

"Now. It's starting to get on my nerves."

By the time he staggered upright, feeling for his phone in the darkness, he was thinking out loud again. "Yeah, I think I can sympathize."

"I don't know what you have against Doc. She likes you," he offered lamely.

"Just because *she* likes people she doesn't know *at all* does not mean I should." She glared at the floor. "Anyway, why should I trust some so-called doctor that lives in an abandoned hotel?"

"She doesn't. She's just . . . staying here for now."

"Like you."

"No," he laughed. "*I* live here. And I trust her, so that will have to be enough for now."

Dr. Deleon was a far better sport about being awakened before dawn. She smiled at them and squinted her glasses back onto her nose, and Peter tried to smile back, collapsing into the nearest chair.

This should be interesting.

"Good morning!" Doc chirped.

Alana tried to take a chair as well, but Peter pointed her toward the exam table. Then he observed as the doctor started asking questions. It was a strange thing to miss, but he'd missed watching his sister talk to people.

For all that (or, rather, because) she was so much more uninhibited than her brother, Al had a way of always having something at the ready any time she opened her mouth, whether flippant, funny, or sometimes downright cruel. She never stammered, never started speaking only to have her mouth slam shut again after a long silence. Peter, on the other hand . . .

He used to have a nickname. It was assigned in the prescribed pattern of all playground wars: a stolen turn, a few accidental-on-purpose shoves, then names and insults, fired like missiles before the final showdown. It was uncivilized and unreasonable, maybe, but so were children.

It went more quickly in this case. The name came early, and it stuck long after the first time another boy left him lying where he dropped. "Stay away from us, psycho."

The boy, Elijah, had been his friend once. Apparently he wasn't anymore. And Peter didn't have to look up at him—in fact he hadn't wanted to look anyone in the eye for a long time after that—to understand *us* meant everyone else, everyone who wasn't him. Elijah made it clear who he was. Not the kid who wrote stories and helped Mrs. Lin clean the chalkboard at the end of the day. Psycho. He wasn't one of them anymore.

It was a hard lesson, taught well. He'd kept his distance from his classmates, stopped acknowledging them at all. His teachers began to look at the air around him when they dubiously called his name.

He was given many labels then, maybe even now: retarded, disturbed, simply crazy. They'd always rolled over him, barely touching him at all—maybe because that first one had hit him so hard.

If I'm lucky, they don't even remember me anymore.

Tired and distracted as he was, it took longer than it should have for him to notice Doc wasn't the only one Al was talking to.

She was sitting on the table, visibly miserable and more than a little annoyed, but it wasn't in her face. While she held the encased hand up for inspection, the girl's left hand was hovering in an awkward position slightly above the table, fingers tapping rapidly against the metal. It looked like a tic born of nerves or irritation, which in a way it was.

The hand where he could see it was meant to get his attention; the tapping meant a question. Peter watched closely, but in the end he heard it instead of seeing.

After each brief answer to Doc's inquiries was a small sigh, hardly noticeable on its own but made obvious by the repetition. That same sound from him used to mean *trouble*. In this case, trouble brought about by answering questions.

Peter, should I be doing this?

He sat back. Nearly four years since they'd seen each other last, and she had slipped so seamlessly back into the bare-bones silent language they created together as kids. Of course, so had he.

It was meant for the times when one of the two (he) was not allowed to speak or communicate with anyone. They seemed like the same thing, but they weren't. Speech was communication, yes. But communication was much more as well. It was in the posture, the eyes, the hands, the chin. If he had been cut off from speech alone, this miniature "language" probably would not exist. But being cut off from communication was impossible, or so he assumed. He was lucky he'd never truly had to find out.

Though this was not one of those times, Al, not sure of what she was expected to share with the doctor, had lapsed into old habits. Doc—who really *did* like her, and knew her from stories probably better than Alana assumed—appeared not to notice, chatting pleasantly to the girl as she located the cast saw. It was a sad scene: Doc would be crushed if she knew how much anxiety she was causing. But Alana was obviously unable to imagine that the doctor's kindness might be sincere.

He went to his sister's side, patting the tapping hand twice with his own to answer her question, but when she didn't seem convinced he tried something else. "You don't need to do that, Al. We aren't hiding anything." She clenched her jaw at first, but then slowly began to relax, studying the cast as Doc prepared to take it off.

He lowered his voice to a whisper. "What?"

"Why do I have this?" She whispered back, even quieter.

"Have what? A hand?"

She gave him a look. "Ask her." He prompted, pointing.

Of course that didn't work, so Peter had to ask Doctor Deleon for her, enjoying the irony.

Doc hesitated, uncomfortable. Funny, since she'd been so oblivious seconds ago. "One of the bones in your arm was splintered when . . . and . . . well, we didn't want-"

"I was afraid you were going to rip out your stitches and finish breaking your arm, so I asked her to put a cast on it until you calmed down," Peter finished for her, with an embellished shrug. Close enough. Apparently she hadn't seen the few antibiotic beads the doctor had implanted in her arm while cleaning it, and if Doc was right and they would dissolve the rest of the way on their own, he certainly wasn't going to ruin their compromise by telling Al now. She could be very touchy about medicine.

Alana appeared to believe him, or at least she didn't say otherwise. But briefly, so briefly he might have imagined it, a shadow of sadness passed over her face, though she went back to looking bored and sullen a second later.

Peter pretended not to notice. So far she hadn't volunteered any information, let alone emotion, where Mom was concerned. As reserved as she usually was, he was stunned that Al would show even a hint of feeling in front of someone she apparently disliked so much. But there it was.

As he became more confident that she could handle the rest of the procedure without doing any harm to the doctor or herself, Peter finally rested his eyes.

chapter 10.

THESE halls were different at night. He did this sometimes when he couldn't sleep; it was nice. Like fun you weren't supposed to be having.

The first stop, as always, was the room Peter called his office. Slightly larger than the ones on the condemned hotel's higher floors, it was also the only room this far down to see any use. The first five floors—the little restaurant, the front desk and the rest of the larger rooms—were closed off, from the outside and the upper levels. At first Peter did not understand why he had to do this, but after the first marauding locals decided to pull off the secluded highway and go exploring he'd been glad. Visitors were dangerous. He still had the roof and the courtyard when fresh air and sun were needed, and plenty of stairs and long hallways for the nights when he couldn't lie down.

He'd never slept well. Bad memories tended to thrive on darkness and silence, and Peter's were particularly obnoxious.

Sometimes it's hard being a coward.

Not that being the family scaredy-cat was all bad. Worriers thought things through. He would never have survived on his own if he hadn't worried—constantly—about the worst case scenario. That, at least, was a positive.

Usually a nice long walk did the trick, but tonight it looked like Peter was up for good. Which meant it was best to keep moving, keep wandering. And after a while, without a sun or anything happening on the horizon, he was not only moderately more clear-headed—he was bored.

Why couldn't Al have picked tonight for her little adventure? Of course she would choose this night to be in bed, sleeping like a very heavy log in a very quiet swamp while he paced the halls, weary and edgy.

And he couldn't do what she had done to him. For one thing, she wouldn't be particularly easy to wake (she was more of an extremely heavy log in a graveyard). But she also needed the rest. She was more at ease since she'd started exploring, but she still had ill-tempered days that he certainly recognized. He was the expert, after all.

So he wouldn't wake her. He had some other things he could do, maybe—a few sets of pushups and a book sometimes wore him out when a walk couldn't. He would let her sleep.

Even if she hadn't done the same for him.

Minutes later there he was, stock-still and alert outside her room. He wasn't tired anymore, had forgotten about being bored. All was quiet now, but a moment ago, just when he'd decided to call it a night— maybe he *was* ready to lie down—he'd heard a small, quavering sound from behind the door.

She's talking in her sleep. Peter yawned, starting to turn away when he heard it again, higher and still too quiet to make out. *She's fine*, he tried again lamely, but a second later he gave in, pushed the door open with a single whispery creak and crept through. "Al?" he whispered, "Are you-"

Then he looked up and the words evaporated.

Al didn't wake when he opened the door, or look around when he spoke. Of course, he'd expected her to be asleep, so that wasn't odd in itself.

She was sitting straight up in bed.

Peter started, stepped back before he understood what he was seeing. She was up, but she *was* asleep, and slowly the shock faded, giving way to a type of relief that approached amusement. He stayed quiet.

Another thing he was wrong about: she wasn't sleep-talking. Up close, the sounds were no more distinct than they were from outside. Alana was whimpering quietly, the pitch rising and falling at odd intervals and broken up by random, quick breaths. It almost sounded like she was crying. She wasn't, though. Determined, twisting and kicking out at the end of the small bed, she grimly fought something he couldn't see. The desk chair was against the far wall. He gently moved it and sat.

Alana still didn't see him. She looked nowhere and everywhere, waving her head madly. As he watched, her right arm shot out to strike the wall. Peter winced as the clenched fist struck, expecting her to jolt awake. But she did not seem bothered.

Al brought her arm back to cross the other one and lay down again, and the show was apparently over. Peter wondered whether he should be more concerned for her or the wall. The plaster *was* a little worn. But could she have injured herself even without waking?

Unlikely. Still, he glanced back down—and gasped.

In the dim room, black blood welled around the fingernails she'd buried in her shoulder.

Still foggy, he could only gape as her fist tightened, carving short but deep furrows in the skin. Al's eyes were screwed shut in concentration, her jaw set and locked as she attacked again, plainly out for more blood.

"What the-?" The bemused curiosity was melting away, making room for something else. Alana usually wore long sleeves regardless of the weather, and he didn't question her about it—not even in the middle of a Missouri summer. He had barely remarked on her apparently sleepless nights or moody days, either, but a lot was falling into place tonight. As he connected those symptoms with this horror show, his worry was rapidly replaced by a sort of indignant fury. Barely thinking, Peter laid a hand heavily on his sister's shoulder.

Her eyes sprung open. She bolted upright. She *screamed.*

She didn't stop.

Peter was surprised, but too furious to be sorry—even when the screaming reached such impressive volumes he was sure it could be heard outside the building, maybe even on the nearby highway . . .

"Shut up, shut up-" Finally he planted a hand across her mouth. She lashed out, and he pushed her backward, pinning her to the wall as well.

Almost at the same time she went still, and her eyes closed. Asleep, again. *If she ever was.* A symphony of crickets swelled outside; the sound filled his ears painfully and Peter began to wonder if he hadn't imagined the entire surreal episode when, with the air of one waking up from a light nap, Alana blinked.

She tried to flex an immobilized shoulder. Couldn't, blinked, tried again. She started to inspect it, but couldn't move that way either.

There was a beat in which she certainly *appeared* confused. Then she woke up fast, shoving both feet out and striking at him with her free hand, fighting hard. Peter, wisely placed to one side (he had learned that lesson slowly, but effectively), waited for her to calm down.

Once she recognized him Alana settled back, tangible waves of indignant fury rolling off her in the near-darkness, glaring hellfire. Peter scowled steadily back. He didn't trust her not to start again as soon as he let go, so he didn't—though he wasn't sure which worried him more, the self-mutilation or the blood-curdling screaming.

He did, however, let his guard down, and a second later yanked his hand away. "Ow!"

Alana was not one to waste time, or mince words. "What in the *fuck* are you doing here?"

Her voice was cold and quiet, shaking with rage, shockingly famil-iar. *Wonderful. Next time I miss Mom all I have to do is piss Al off.* "I could ask you the same thing."

She was incredulous—or faked it well. "What am *I* doing here. In my own bed. At night. Ly-" she broke off, looked down, then amended, "*probably* lying down. Correct me if I'm wrong, but signs point to, I don't know, *sleeping*?"

The cricket song had died down, but a heavy drone still filled his head. "You were doing more than sleeping and you know it."

Another dubious look. She knew what he was talking about. She *must* know. How could she not?

She considered him for a while, asking nothing but clearly looking for an answer. Whatever she found she must not have liked, though, so instead she made a show of changing the subject, indicating her immobilized shoulder. "I'm not going anywhere, you know."

"I want to know what you were doing. Now." Peter willed the crick-ets in his head quiet. When they finally obliged, he was still angry. Good. If she was going to lie, he was allowed to be angry.

She squinted at him, looked like she might argue again, didn't. "Okay, I give up. What am I supposed to have done?"

He released her then; stalking to the bathroom, he snapped on the light and tried not to wince, crossing his arms. She trudged after him, her nose wrinkled. "Why do you get to be the cranky one when you wake *me* up in the middle of the night—I mean, you got to be cranky when *I* woke *you* up, too . . ."

Peter steered her around to the mirror and yanked up her sleeve, cutting in.

"Hey!"

He knew without having to ask that Al's relationship with Mom had gone even further south after he left. So he barely registered any surprise at the other scars he noticed—deeper, older ones that pocked

her arms from the elbows as far up as he could see in the bright fluorescent light.

Instead, he directed her attention to the mirror, to the freshest of
the dozen or so red interwoven scratches on her upper arm. She had
been hiding this for a while. How could he not have noticed?

Alana's face became slowly blank, unreadable. She hesitated,
started to say something, hesitated again. Turned away from the mirror to stare at nothing instead.

Finally, she spoke. "Oh."

Peter knew better than to ask. She gulped and gave him a
searching look.

"So then, that really *is* me, I guess?"

"What do you mean, *that*?" Peter was becoming more nervous
than furious again, and worked hard not to let her hear it.

"I . . . don't exactly know." Al read his response and squared her
shoulders. "I mean it. This has happened before, I guess, but I don't
know *why*. I mean, don't you think if I did . . . ?"

He watched rather than listened, not sure if she was lying. The
adrenaline was wearing off, all of the room's edges were starting to
soften, and the buzzing was picking up again. It happened sometimes,
paradoxically being shocked into lethargy. Alana, who appeared almost as upset as he was, agreed immediately when he suggested with
a badly-concealed yawn that maybe they should drop it for now, get
some sleep and talk again in the morning.

"And I'll stay here tonight," Peter added reasonably.

She scowled. Her hands clenched to fists at her sides, but just when
it looked like she might raise them, or her voice at least, she shrugged
instead. "Fine."

Peter shrugged back. "Fine."

Al tossed and stirred noisily on the bed, keeping them both up. He lay
with his head on his arm, trying to ignore her, passably comfortable on

the cool tile. He could sleep almost anywhere if he was tired enough, and it had been a very long night. He began to drift, the hard floor and shuffling noises fading away . . .

"Look, if you're going to hang around all night keeping me up, could you at least do something useful?"

Peter jolted and gave his sister a long, withering glare she couldn't see. "Like what?"

"Could you just talk?"

She sounded different this time, and he softened a bit. "About?"

"I don't care," came the quiet response, "anything."

He thought. "You like cats, right? Well, a while back I was-" (a hopefully undetectable pause,) "spending most of my time in this park. I fell asleep outside one day, and when I woke up there was this big gray cat sitting on my-"

"Can I have a cat?" He felt Al's eyes on him.

"Um . . . not here."

"Where, then?" It was a sarcastic question, but Peter smiled.

"Anyway, the cat had one eye, so for some reason I decided to call him Jack."

Peter awoke the next morning feeling terrifically clearheaded. Sleep was always a success, but last night's misadventures made this a special case.

The thick blanket fell to a heap as he sat up. It hadn't been there last night. A sharp glance, however, showed that Al was soundly asleep. He tossed the blanket over her again and checked the wall for new marks. *Looks like I'm not the only one with sleep problems anymore.*

But why?

chapter 11.

APPARENTLY he was destined to keep wondering. Though she never denied what she had done, Alana still couldn't—or wouldn't—explain what happened during those nights when she hurt herself. Peter, who admittedly asked a little too often over the next few weeks, only ever got one (unsatisfying) answer: it was new, and it was related to some dream she had. But she swore she couldn't remember what the dream was about.

Peter would pretend to accept this answer. Then he would ask again. Eventually he was forced (by her) to admit that talking in circles all day wouldn't do her any good at night.

Which was how the running started.

Based on what he knew about how frequently Al had the nightmare, Peter surmised that they were growing worse, possibly because his sister was not getting out enough of the anxious energy she displayed during the day. It was just an idea, but he was caught off-guard by how seriously she took it. On a particularly brave day she'd gone exploring and found some leftover exercise equipment that still worked, and though she ran only with her brother nearby, she soon reported with obvious relief that she didn't think she was having the nightmare at all anymore. That wasn't quite true—there were still mornings when Peter found his sister shaken and wiping smears of blood from her neck and arms—but the bad nights were rarer, the damage less severe than that awful first night.

Peter moved a treadmill down to his office so he could keep Al company when he worked, and it quickly became a daily routine. Her appetite improved, she wasn't as tired, and less fighting meant the two of them were actually talking. Altogether, things were much as Peter had hoped they would be from the beginning—excluding, of course, the constant hum of the treadmill.

"Oh, I thought of something." Al yelled, breathless but social nonetheless.

Peter didn't look up from the newspaper he was browsing. "Go for it."

"So I'm sent to the principal's office in eighth grade, and when I get there," she paused, either for effect or to catch her breath, "he's already on the phone with her. Or so I-"

"Why?" Now he did look up. He often asked her about the years he'd been gone, and Al didn't seem to mind sharing stories, but she wasn't always upfront about the details.

"Well, he was talking to *someone*, so I assumed-"

"Why were you in the principal's office?"

She gave him a sharp glance, shook her head.

He shook his back. "Really, Al?" Of course, it was ridiculous to be surprised—this was one mistake she seemed determined not to learn from. "Fighting? Again?"

Grinning, she turned her palms up to the ceiling in a pseudo-shrug.

"And here I was hoping you might have even made some friends while I was, um . . ."

She exhaled, one short, fast burst—the running equivalent of laugher. "When have I ever needed friends?" She was still smiling, but there was a strange, absent look about it.

"Not counting me?" He pretended to contemplate. "I guess you have a point."

Another short outward breath.

It was a good point. Al hadn't made many friends since she was very little, and there was only one reason the streak would have con-tinued. He smiled sympathetically. "As I recall, Mom was never ex-actly big on the idea of either of us getting too close to people."

She ran a few more paces and then came to a sudden stop; the treadmill key disconnected and it halted as well. In the abrupt quiet she stepped down and sagged, silent, onto the tartan couch.

Damn it. She was understandably sensitive where Mom was con-cerned—he knew that. "Don't . . . don't stop running," Peter tried, sounding even less authoritative than he felt. His sister stared at the floor. He sighed. "Okay, um, I promise I'll stop talking. Won't say a thing. Promise."

She flicked a glance in his direction, then stood and made her way back to the dejected-looking machine without a word. While she re-inserted the key and worked her way up to a fast jog, he continued to berate himself. It was all still so fresh for her. He should know to tread lightly.

Still . . . as long as there was no mood to kill (*anymore, idiot*), he had another question it was almost definitely too soon to ask. "Al, your arm, y-you never . . . I mean, I never asked how . . . um, why, before-"

Mercifully, she cut him off. "I said the exact wrong thing at the worst possible time, like always. And she didn't take it well, like always."

He nodded, but couldn't help thinking that it made no sense. Peter had known his mother for longer than Al had, and this was just not right. She should have been taken to a doctor. She could have lost her *hand*. How could Mom not realize that? His grip tightened on the fragile pages, and he thought he could feel the corners of the room shrinking inward.

"Peter snap out of it," Alana barked, back up to full speed. She had a talent for checking panic attacks before they were out of control. "I was holding a knife, I mouthed off, I should have seen it a mile away. Okay?"

Peter breathed himself calm, then glanced up. He hadn't forgotten that shadow of sadness during their night adventure with Doc. But he'd blundered enough for today. "Okay. Look, I'm sorry. About wh-what I brought up, before."

Al ran, staring coolly ahead, and Peter returned a little miserably to his newspaper. A little while later the treadmill began to die again, dwindling back into silence. Peter looked up.

She was staring back. She looked serious, but as he watched she stretched both arms above her and tilted her head. "Make it up to me."

Raising an eyebrow, he gave a single nod.

She hopped down from the treadmill too fast, nearly falling as she hurried to take the swivel chair behind the desk. Peter watched warily from one of the more comfortable ones on its other side. "Tell me about all of this." She didn't gesture or look around, but as usual he knew what she meant anyway. He sighed heavily, looking away.

"Come on, you never tell me anything about when you were gone. You ask about me and Mom, but if I ask you anything you change the subject or stop talking until I give up." She continued to stare and he continued to avoid her eyes. "So? Tell me—what's the worst that could happen?"

"It's . . . I just don't like to talk about it."

"But it has something to do with how you brought me here." She wasn't dropping it this time. Worse, she wasn't wrong.

"You used to be dumber."

"You kidnap people."

He winced. "N-No!"

She sat back.

"Okay, not exactly. Mostly they come from . . . somewhere else. We get them settled, get documents together, find out if they have family nearby."

"You're talking about trafficking." Al sounded disturbed.

He nodded. "'Smuggling' is technically more correct. I prefer 'importing,' personally." Peter didn't mind mincing words once in a while. "But there's more to it than that."

Much more. They didn't sell the people they brought in, or force them to work for their freedom. Most of their "imports" were Alana's age or younger, kids hoping to be reunited with long-lost family in the States. And, with an extremely low profit margin, that was what they did.

He was not ashamed of the "Drophouse," but the less said about it the better. Talk wasn't completely harmless. There were ears everywhere.

The thin description was met with skepticism. "I can't help thinking you could have told me this beforehand . . ."

"I tried. I waited days before I realized you weren't coming out."

"Hm."

"And I tried again, that night. It didn't go well."

"Fine. But . . ."

"But?"

"But, you've run this place for years." The question was implied, and suggested another would follow.

"Not that long. Why?"

She watched him, but didn't ask.

He nodded anyway. There was only one question left, and he happened to be staring the answer in the face right now. "Had to keep this place up and running for as long as possible." She could handle it, but he didn't tell Al she was the reason the Drophouse had ceased operations. She was scared enough of the several unnamed coyotes who drifted in and out; she didn't need to know what could happen if their bosses learned that she was here. "Any risk of getting caught could have shut us down. The first step went okay—we could have gotten caught, um, picking you up from Mom's. But then we had to hope she wouldn't try too hard to find you . . ."

"And?"

Peter slid the *Plain Dealer* he'd been looking over across the desk. Eight inches high, Alana gazed out at them in black and white, smiling an unmistakably forced school-picture smile. Under her neatly folded hands was the capitalized, underlined print:

HAVE YOU SEEN ME?

Al (the three-dimensional one) grimaced at her likeness, and Peter shook his head. "What do you think?"

chapter 12.

DI had high expectations for herself. Not that she held herself in higher regard than she did others, obviously, and she didn't waste her energy dwelling on other people's failings. That would be foolish, and she was not, so she tried not to expect anyone to live by her standards. Still, other people could be tremendously frustrating.

Of course, she wasn't a person people made a habit of frustrating—with some exceptions.

Lifting her chin, she rounded on a young woman who was following her.

"Dominique-"

"No, that's not me. Bye!" She smiled brightly, but did not turn to leave.

The other woman looked thrown, but persisted. "I have a messa-"

"You have a job." Di held her smile. Then, taking a step down toward the young woman, "And I think you should probably be doing it right now. Deliveries, right? That's a few floors down."

Her new friend did not follow the next time she walked away.

Di liked to think of herself as a woman of many talents and many names, and though the former was arguable the latter was certainly not. She had an alias for every occasion—and enough occasions for a lifetime. The moniker "Di" was as close as she used to a real name in her business, and it was working fine so far.

Sometimes she liked to treat these multiple aliases as a necessity, but she knew otherwise. Since childhood, Chaka's classic hit "I'm Every Woman" had been a solid favorite. And now, though of course there was no way to ever be *all* of them, she was unquestionably a good deal *more* women than most.

The question her therapist would undoubtedly one day ask was *why*—from the outside, many would probably call her pathological. It would be easy to simply attribute the numerous identities of the only child of a somewhat busy mother and extremely busy father to deep-seated loneliness, haunted by hordes of childhood imaginary friends. But it would also be wholly inaccurate. Charming and confident, she had grown up with the ever-present nanny and a very strong personality but never had any problem maintaining a close circle of *real* friends.

Back then, Di—long before "Di" existed—was Elizabeth, a self-proclaimed daddy's girl. Her father, the well-known Anderson Karras, spent his days overseeing a national chain of hotels and resorts and investing the profits into ventures all over New England, constantly strengthening the network of fronts for the smuggling operations he handled for the then-infamous *Oikogéneia*'s American wing. It sounded like the world's most stereotypical television show. Maybe, after all, it was that. But the family was the most important front of all. Anderson made sure it ran smoothly so as not to arouse any suspicions, and arousing no suspicions it was allowed to run smoothly—though there were exceptions for the only child and heir of the mobster, who enjoyed many "take your daughter to work" days.

She'd learned quickly, and well, about the business that was eventually meant to be her own; by fifth grade she was knowledgeable enough to be entrusted with investing a paltry million of her father's profits. Publicly, the stunt had been a failure, though in reality Di had never had to live on a salary even before inheriting her father's estate.

But there was more to it than money. She'd long understood—better than any child should—that the shipping side of her father's business could be ugly, but back then, even the sight of such ugliness was not enough to turn her against him. She loved him too much. If she hadn't found out what was in some of those shipments, she never would have turned at all.

Some of them were legitimate, he'd tried to explain, as if he had any right to decide. Some were here to find family, or get an education, and some had escaped horrible things and were just buying their way to freedom.

The next answer was so easy, too smooth not to be rehearsed, so that Di had regretted her question immediately. Those who had to would work to pay their fare, that was all. And when they had done well enough to pay off every dollar, they would be on to better things, like everyone else. He answered it with the same wide, comforting smile as when she had fallen at the skating rink at four years old and he'd told her it was okay, to give it a go again. He'd known she would learn this eventually. He'd meant for her to *accept* it.

And when she realized that, Di had been forced to admit the doting father she thought she adored was only one face of a man she might not know at all.

Her father had schooled her well in business, however. "Take everything in, give nothing back. That is how you become successful while those around fall to ruin." And hadn't she he put that advice to good use! From the day of her vile discovery until he died, Di kept her silence, continuing to learn from and spend time with her father but simply resigned to his company, rather than enjoying it. Under other circumstances it might have been a sad thing: Anderson, unaware of or perhaps not fully comprehending the reason for this rejection, continuing to lavish gifts and affection upon his unresponsive daughter for years before realizing his efforts were futile.

His associates were more suspicious. Once they sensed Karras' inability to hold his heir's respect, their apparent devotion to him faded away far quicker than the man himself. So, despite her lack of ill—or good—will toward her father, she had ruined him after all. He wouldn't be happy with the way she'd rebuilt his empire, if he knew. But she was.

Except for one little mistake that hadn't stayed little for long. Young as she was when her father passed away, she'd been overzealous in her attempt to right his wrongs. His fingers had pulled so many different strings; she had immediately detached herself from—among others— the business of smuggling people, determined to have one less person involved in such a horrific trade. Atonement for Anderson's legacy.

She was still so naïve. With her father gone and the *Oikogéneia* in the hands of an apparently incompetent heir, others had stepped up in droves to take up the dropped reins. Years later she was still doing damage control, putting herself back into the open as a representative of the reclusive heir to the Karras family. She'd even put together a small team to take care of the lighter side of things while she did pest control on the worst of the rodents. Meanwhile she stayed some variation of "Di" to those who didn't know better, and it suited her fine— she was doing her job so well that Elizabeth Karras was becoming too big a trademark to carry around.

Di rounded the corner, checking the numbered door to be sure she was going the right way. She knew she was, but it was still fun to check. It used to be necessary, back when the building was an unfamiliar, unwelcoming labyrinth. Now she liked the sense of perspective that came from remembering what it felt like those first times, lost at this very spot. She smiled, continuing down the corridor.

This unused building was itself part of the "lighter side," a new approach to atonement that was more effective than the last, under the right circumstances. It was nice to visit; she only had two employees here, but she considered them both friends. In fact, she never would have come up with the idea if she hadn't been doing a favor for a friend.

A favor like this one required others in turn, however, chief among them being the lack of questions as to why a place so long abandoned was still there at all. It had never seen much use in the middle of nowhere, Missouri (though the lovely people of Lebanon would probably disagree) and wasn't likely to reopen for business. In fact, it had been marked "condemned" now for as long as she had been using it, but due to a plague of implausible clerical errors and "forgetfulness," the demolition was forever being rescheduled.

Judging by her new admirer on the stairs, however, forever might be coming to an end. Shame.

After rejecting her father she had steeled herself to be independent, survive forever without the support of her family. But Damara Karras had immediately forgotten Elizabeth's years of aloofness the moment she came home one day and buried her tear-streaked face in her mother's two thousand dollar dress, had just wrapped her arms around her daughter as she cried and hadn't said a word.

Her mother had been both anchor and role model, wiser than Di had ever expected and with a strength that—unlike her father's—she didn't think could be taught. But she had tried to learn, and of the many people Di pretended to be, Damara was always the one she hoped to be most like.

Di finally paused at another door. There was a brief hesitation, just a second to tug, tease and pat her dark mane back into shape, then she pushed open the door with the faded 612 stuck on.

She was momentarily thrown for a loop by a small inconsistency, so casually bizarre it was shocking—a treadmill, of all things, in the middle of the room. And next to it, another unfamiliar and even more arresting sight: an absolutely beautiful girl, looking as though she was simultaneously trying to disappear and intimidate. A river of hair the color of bright honey spilled from her ponytail, and the damp ring around the neck of her blue T-shirt suggested that the beautiful girl and the treadmill had some history in common. Her body mixed the lanky thin-limbed look of a child with a hint of the more age-appropriate qualities of a young woman and a sort of unrealized strength, like it knew it did not quite fit the mind of the person it belonged to and was steadily working to change that. Di stared, enchanted.

Apparently the girl disapproved. She grimaced strangely and her hands clenched into fists, one resting on the treadmill, the other at her side.

Still charmed but not wanting to be rude Di focused on another face, more familiar but to her no less beautiful. *As a matter of fact . . .* this face even held an expression similar to the girl's, if relatively muted. Di smiled back and forth at them, amused—they clearly had no idea how alike they looked. For a second she felt the familiar twinge of regret that her parents hadn't had more children.

Di had been attracted to him the first time she met him—not as soon as she saw him, but one second later, when he looked up and moved out of her way and she saw his eyes for the first time. Something in them seemed to bear more investigation, and he had been more than worth the considerable effort. Much more. Undoing her own unwitting damage was a process she needed a whole team's help with, and he had taken risk upon risk to help her begin to heal what she and Anderson had broken.

And when she'd finally gotten him to admit that he could use some help himself, he had only asked for two things: some privacy and a little time. Obviously that was far too easy, so she'd flatly refused to help him unless he asked for a better deal.

It was rare to get a smile from him, but she did that day.

Her friend wasn't smiling now. His soulful dark eyes regarded her with an exasperation she didn't think she had seen on him before, his mouth was set disapprovingly. But she saw something else, too. Was she imagining it, or did he for once appear—she struggled to place the concept—alive? Engaged?

No, she realized. Or—rather, yes, it was both. He was watching her along with his sister, just watching, evenly, not once breaking eye contact. He looked *present*, and all the more alive for it.

She was glad for him, but she was also eager to start breaking the ice before this peculiar introduction grew any more awkward. So before she could agonize over what to say, Di gave her friend a small version of her most winning smile. "Been a while."

"I thought we agreed you weren't going to come by until we had a chance to talk about it."

His voice was quiet, but serious, and held a tinge of strain. As far as she knew this was how he always sounded. It was the same as when they'd spoken for the first time, if a little slower—a trick she'd taught him to help control his stuttering. Sometimes, however, something else crept in, a bit of a hard edge lying underneath. His "dead" serious tone, which he was trying to use on her now.

The winning smile turned into a smirk. "Seems like you've had plenty of chances, don't you think?" Di retorted sweetly, referring to her frequent calls.

Peter seemed about to reply. Then he sighed deeply, the exasperated look melting away, and shook his head. Di took this as an admission of defeat and, bleeding the triumph while she could, turned her attention back to the silent girl. "And you must be Alana," she said warmly, extending a hand and starting toward her.

The next few seconds happened very quickly. Di was starting to add that she had heard many wonderful things about her friend's younger sister when the girl, teeth still bared, uttered a strange guttural sound and moved forward, matching Di step for step.

Peter snapped back to attention. "*Stay where you are!*" His voice was all edge and no quiet. The girl halted.

He'd spoken so affectionately of her, and so frequently; Di was shocked to hear him speak to her this way. "How *dare* you yell at her?" She half-shouted herself, outraged.

And now for the first time the teenager spoke, in a low voice that matched her posture in its thinly veiled violence. "Who the hell do you think you are," she spat each word separately as she again began to advance.

"I said *freeze!*" Peter yelled again, bringing the girl to a slow stop once more and neatly rounding off the scene.

For a moment the three of them simply stood there regarding each other, sharing but trying to ignore the awareness that this could almost be funny, if not for the one person from whom they felt they had to protect the other.

Di did not understand what was wrong, but Peter knew. *This* was why he had not wanted Di to meet his sister yet—he was hoping for a slight improvement in Alana's tendency to lash out at people she did not already know (so far him and, most of the time, Doc). She hadn't heard a thing about Di yet and, considering his own tense reaction to the other woman's unexpected arrival, her lashing out this time was almost reasonable. Still, this did not mean he was willing to subject the equally dangerous but otherwise completely opposite women to each other under the wrong circumstances.

So, with an eye firmly trained on his sister, he spoke first to his friend. "You probably want to leave her alone for a little while." He gave his sister a look that meant the same thing, but with a different inflection. She kept glaring at Di.

"He really shouldn't talk to you like that, honey," Di told Alana soothingly.

Alana, who really preferred not to be called anything other than her name, narrowed her eyes further.

Clearly no one was planning to listen to him. Peter changed tactics—maybe he could just make this shorter instead of less painful. Like ripping off a bandage, *and not knowing what's underneath.* "Okay, yes, this is Alana. Di knows a lot about you. Not everything, apparently . . ." he realized he was speaking to his sister and turned toward her, waiting for eye contact before he fumbled on.

"And Alana. This is," he paused, "um . . ." Stumped, he turned and shrugged at Di.

A shrug was more invitation than she needed. "Dionne, and it's so good to finally *meet* you!" She hesitated, seeming to realize she was gushing. But she could not be stifled for long, so with a conspiring smile and a decidedly coquettish tilt of the head she added, "Do you like it?"

Alana opened her mouth—undoubtedly to give her opinion not only of Di's name, but of where she could put it and then go afterward—but Peter cut in first.

"What's the story?" This was his usual question when she changed her alias, which normally meant he wanted to know why she picked it but which she also understood now as a plea not to talk to the girl as much as she perhaps wanted to.

Di smiled brightly, and was pleasantly surprised when he grinned back. "It's Greek. Dionne is the mother of Aphrodite, or a Titaness, or sometimes a prophetess. At least, those are the definitions I like best."

"Getting back to your roots?"

She laughed, making a sweeping gesture down the olive-colored arm emerging from her *maize* blouse. "Sweetie, my roots never get *away* from me."

Peter smiled at her a moment longer. As disastrous as this meeting was, and though most of his attention was focused on sending "chill out" vibes to a suddenly feral Al, he was happy to see Di again. She was the best friend he could have asked for after leaving home, and though now she was sometimes his partner, sometimes his boss, she always made an effort to let him know she was still his friend. This was not insignificant. Peter knew about Di's (Elizabeth's) family, and he was aware that in some very real way she was using him—and Doc, who she'd also met in rough circumstances and helped get back on her feet—to right some karmic injustice her father had done. He didn't hold that against her; it was something they had in common.

She was a sort of energy source. Whenever she walked into a room, every person and thing in it seemed to orient around her, putting her at the center no matter where she was standing. *Like a magnet,* he mused. Yes, she was magnetic, and being so at ease with this quality without having to rely on it—she was also a widely respected investment guru—made her indispensable as a business partner.

And again, a good friend to have.

A sudden movement startled the two out of their conversation, paused though it was. Al was unusually grim as she passed between her brother and Di, dead-set on a quick getaway.

"Wait!" Peter would never be unwise enough to expect her to *welcome* a sudden visitor, but he did want Di and Al to get to know each other. He knew Di would like his sister; she was able to get along with almost anyone and had always wanted a sister herself (and, later, a daughter—she had two foster sons instead). And he hoped Alana would eventually be able get along with Di, too. "Di is a friend of mine, and she's been looking forward to meeting you for a long time now. Stay?" He added the last part with a smile, asking her to trust him.

To her credit—and although she did fix him with the look one gives a person who forgets how to pronounce his own name—Al did pause for a second, steps away from freedom, to consider the invitation. With tortured slowness she turned her head back in Di's direction, though her eyes shied away from the stranger to refocus on the door with increased longing.

"You said she was cute, Peter, but she is actually very pretty, isn't she?" Di offered.

She was honestly trying, but that clinched it: the grim face was back in half a second, and in the next Alana was gone.

For a moment they silently watched the empty doorway.

"You know I was only trying to be nice . . . ?"

"I know. It—isn't really how she works."

Another long pause.

"So I guess I wouldn't be able to bribe her calm with soup and a sandwich."

"Unlike some of us." Peter half-laughed at the empty space. Slowly he returned to the present, then started as he finally realized this wasn't just any friend visiting. "Wait, did you really come to–"

"Has anyone seen her?"

He shook his head but didn't elaborate, watching her with such naked concern that she felt compelled to cushion the blow.

"I came because I have been *dying* to meet this infamous sister of yours. But . . . I got bad news today. Looks like my work has been linked to this location. Be ready."

"What kind of ready?" It was asked with a sort of quiet resignation. This was bad news, but he'd been prepared. Privacy, and especially time, always came with limits.

"The 'for anything' kind."

10, 16

THERE'S knocking at the front door. She has been pretending to do homework for the last half hour, but the sound brings the girl tip-toeing out to the top of the staircase. This is too exciting to ignore. No one ever comes here!

Okay, well, that isn't true. People come sometimes, but she never even gets to see any of them—they're always with Mom, they're not around to talk to her.

Okay, so these people aren't really here to talk to her now. But she thinks they will if she does first. Should she?

Her mother walks them inside. One is wearing a big jacket and one has a vest, but they don't look like police, not real ones. Truant officers must not be police, then, like she thought they were.

Her mother calls upstairs for the boy, and she doesn't realize until he pushes by that she's already halfway down the stairs, craning her neck to try and see into the kitchen. Of course that's impossible; she chews on her lip thoughtfully for a second trying, really trying, to talk herself into going back to her room. She has more homework. She was having trouble with the Spanish. There's a new library book in her backpack.

But no one ever comes here.

That must be good enough, because she's already springing down the rest of the stairs, neatly dodging past her mother into the kitchen.

She even feels bold enough to snatch a bunch of green grapes from a bowl that has appeared on the kitchen counter as she goes in. She pops one into her mouth as she slides down against the refrigerator, where she can see all of them at the table at once.

The boy seems far away, arms loose at his sides, leaning back in his chair, but as she settles in and starts on her second grape his eyes roll upward to stare at the ceiling for a split second and he sighs, just a little, but she hears it. She pretends she didn't see or hear; he can't make her leave, and she wants to be here too.

Her Mom wants her out, though. She knows that even before the grownups stop talking and her mother puts on her Mommy voice to talk to the girl, but as she's starting to do what she's told and go back upstairs she gets exactly what she was hoping for.

"Actually ma'am, your daughter's school says she's getting close to the limit, too. It might be helpful to talk to her while we're here, if it's okay." Then her mother says yes, of course she can stay, but the girl doesn't meet her eyes as she leaves the four of them alone.

Pretty soon it becomes obvious that this whole thing would be way more boring if it were happening anywhere but her own kitchen. They start asking questions, but no one is talking to her so none of them get answered. She knows how this goes—eventually they always give up on him and move on. Why not help them along?

"You know he's not gonna talk to you," she says scornfully, checking the next grape for brown spots.

They look at her until it starts to feel like maybe she shouldn't have said anything after all. She keeps checking the grape. After forever one of the truant officers says, "He won't talk anywhere? Not even at home?"

The boy yawns big. The girl looks up for a fraction of a second and then down again, irritated. Like she was dumb enough to tell them the truth anyway. She wishes she could tell him to butt out, she knows what she's doing and he needs to just let her handle it. But he probably doesn't think of it that way. He probably thinks he is in charge right now, so she'll be nice and won't ruin it for him. Anyway she can't say anything to him now.

"He never talks anywhere. Not in forever." She shrugs and eats the grape. She feels better when she's telling the right kind of lie. It feels like a game that way, one she's winning. She sometimes feels bad about it later, but it is the smart thing to do and at least it's not hard.

So they give her the boy's lecture instead of him, and the boy watches them out of the corner of his eye, writing an essay in his head that started as an assignment for history, but is now too off-topic to hand in. He still kind of wants to write it anyway, though. She's giving them some story about how she's supposed to get him up in the morning when their Mom works long hours, and she forgets. It's an obvious lie, but sounds nice, so they'll pretend to buy it. Smart.

The story reminds him of something though, and he wonders if it's for his benefit, if she's trying to remind him of the time she left him on the bus a week ago. (Or maybe two, or only a couple of days?)

He doesn't actually need her to get him, he obviously knows where the stop is. He could get himself off the bus easily.

It's just . . . well, they've been riding the same bus for so long, and she usually walks by and grabs his hand so he knows to get off.

No, so it looks like she's telling him to get off. It's not real, only something she started doing a while ago, and so this time he wasn't paying attention, so he didn't notice, that's all. Because he's so used to pretending.

He's so used to pretending that he really can't get himself off the bus anymore.

She must have thought it was funny, because she's refusing to apologize. Or maybe she knew exactly what she was doing and just isn't sorry.

This is getting boring. The boy fidgets. He doesn't want to do this anymore, wants them gone. Having two more people sit in a room with him and pretend he doesn't exist is not his idea of exciting; he would rather be up in his room alone, pretending he does exist. He considers signaling the girl to wrap it up, but she wouldn't do it so he doesn't try. She has all the power in situations like this, and more and more she knows it. Not that he minds exactly—she does okay usually, like she is now—but he still tries to steer her one way or another when he can. It's the closest he gets to being part of a conversation.

With other people, at least. And the other two are still pretending he isn't there, so diligently that he can study them for a long minute as they sit across from him, engrossed in his sister's stories.

The older one's jacket has letters stitched on it: CMSD, which must mean they're here with the school system, and not officers like his Mom said or social workers like he thought. They probably aren't even official, just volunteers. The "make a difference" type, here to give a pep talk to a teen who thinks he is literally too cool for school.

And instead they're getting snowed by a fifth-grader. Excellent. Bored again, the boy zones back out. He taps a finger on his knee for a bit, then flexes his right hand, open and closed. Taps again, opens and closes.

The girl is busy defending herself from her own version of the speech meant for him. The movement almost distracts her, but she isn't a bad student, and she doesn't like being called one. "It isn't fair. I do all my work," the girl mutters angrily, punctuating each thought with a grape, this time thrown across the kitchen. They bounce off the boy and fall to the floor and the truant officers look shocked for a moment and stare at the boy like they think he's going to explode or something, but he just reaches down without looking and picks them up. He bites the first one in half and the lady with the jacket stares at her weirdly, saying she shouldn't throw things.

The girl gives her a look. Wimp. It was only grapes. But she tries to apologize politely and agrees when they tell her something about class being just as important as homework and someday doesn't she want to go to college? And become a doctor, or a lawyer . . .

Or a ballerina, or an astronaut, *she continues in her head, nodding. Satisfied, the truant officers turn back to her brother, and so does she. This time when they start talking at him he doesn't even look like he knows they're here, and she wonders if he's doing it again. Forgetting he's supposed to be faking it. Like before, on the bus.*

When she looks back at the truant officers, they're talking to each other and shuffling stuff around like they're getting ready to go. But they can't, they just got here, and . . .

"Wanna see a trick?" *She blurts before she can think.* "I can throw this super high and catch it in my mouth midair, want me to show you?" *But she can't do that, at least most of the time she can't and once she remembers she's too embarrassed to actually try it, but not enough to give up yet.*

"Or, I bet if you open your mouth I can make it too, even from here! Try it!" *That's not much better, especially for the lady who's afraid of flying grapes, but they barely even got to talk yet. And once they leave, it will go back to normal. To no one ever coming here.*

She is vaguely aware that she doesn't even really like them, and they don't seem to like her too much either, but they're pretending to be nice as they stand up and head for the doorway. "Your teachers say your work can be very insightful, they would simply like to see— and, honestly, hear—more of that in school. Try not to fall behind, and I'll bet people will be lining up to hear what's going on up there someday," *the woman in the vest says to the boy, who is pretty sure no one ever will.*

"Okay, I don't know how, but you could teach me, though! You don't have to leave yet!" *Even she knows she should shut up now, but the girl can't help herself, almost following them from the room until she hears her mother's voice on the other side of the wall saying sorry, she's kind of an attention whore sometimes, and the grownups start talking again. Then the girl backs up a little and just looks at where they were.*

Her heart is pounding hard and after a second she guesses why. This room she's still in, the kitchen, it's too quiet. It's silent, and soon the rest of the house will be again too. She forgets all the time how much she hates the quiet until it goes away and comes back, and every time it comes back it feels like it'll never go away again. Or it never left in the first place, like it lives in the whole house with the rest of them.

But most likely she'll wish she'd been quieter later. She was doing such a good job at first, too, handling the truant officers, and then she had to ruin it even though she didn't even like them. Stupid!

"What was that?"

She can barely hear it but does, and really does not feel like being made fun of so she spins around, aiming her anger at him instead. "What did you say?" She snaps back, just loud enough for someone to possibly hear her talking to him. He stops and looks away.

Great, now she's scared him. She rocks back on her heels. Damn it, she was doing so good!

There's a long, bad moment. Finally, pulling a couple more grapes from the bunch—she should put the rest back—she approaches her brother. She doesn't know what to say exactly so she just holds them out.

He reaches up but doesn't take them, folding her hand back around them instead. The boy is at least looking at her now, even though he looks more like he thinks she's an idiot than like he's actually worried about her. He looks up again, only since no one else is here now he also tilts his head toward the doorway.

She sighs. So he thinks she ruined everything, too. But it's still not going to do any good to go back to her room now. Might as well stay and deal with it. She shakes her head once, hesitates, then shakes it again. He smiles back, but he actually looks very serious, and very worried. It's not a real smile. He wants her to trust him.

That's a favor for him, though, not her, the girl thinks, staring back. She's the one who should be in trouble, and it's not fair for her to leave so he's the only one here when the truant officers are gone. The right thing is for her to stay, but he wants her to do the wrong thing and he'll get mad if she doesn't. He might not talk to her for days. And there's already so much quiet filling up this house.

chapter 13.

CLUTCHING my head between fists I knotted onto the bed, knees drawn into my chest as far as they'd go, eyes screwed shut, jaw, toes and everything in between clenched. I didn't know what I was thinking—or more accurately, I didn't know which thought was loudest and as I sorted through them I tried to force myself to go more and more limp, relaxing my body to set an example for my mind. *Okay, simple, keep it simple.*

I sat up, pretending to be calm. Right.

One. I was having an extremely unusual, but in itself also perfectly normal, day.

Two. A strange woman showed up.

Three. Peter started acting weird, but I didn't know why.

Four. Then I had to leave.

Did you?

Then I *had* to leave.

Why did the simple world I was trying to build myself have to keep making itself more complicated? All I wanted was to know what was going to happen next, it wasn't too much to ask. Just wanted to know what was coming, so I could avoid it. It was only practical—I had long since decided that people were the most reliable when they had no idea you existed.

Doesn't seem like that's possible, with your whole family babbling about you and putting pictures of you all over the place.

You think? Who *was* she, even—I opened my eyes to stare down a cup with DAMON'S written in blaze-red letters along the side—he didn't even know her name. He didn't know her name! He said she was a close friend, but when he started to introduce her he couldn't even do it, Damon, he had to ask her who she . . .

A little of the old crazy was bubbling up. I turned away from the cup, taking deep breaths to settle myself.

She knew him all right, though. I would have known that if no one had said a word, just from the look of her as she breezed in wearing a pale yellow sleeveless shirt with a pair of sunglasses hung on the front and a skirt in a shade of green that I honestly had *no* idea was available in cloth form, a crinkled scarf wrapped around her neck the way people in old stories, riding cross-country in convertibles after killing their millionaire husbands, might wear them. And as I noticed how the cream-colored heels matched her scarf and that her toenails were painted the exact same yellow as her shirt, I hadn't been able to help it. I stared at her, and I grabbed a fistful of the damp blue t-shirt hanging over my sweatpants, and I hoped she wouldn't see me. And not just in the regular way.

That bitch. I flinched a little at the thought's vehemence before springing to my own defense. *She deserves it. She* does.

It didn't work. I was pacing the room in long strides; I hadn't gotten to finish my run.

She hadn't said anything about it, though, hadn't commented on my appearance at all. Except that one thing at the end, like she could manipulate me with some generic little compliment. She was like a toddler at a playground: I like your dress. Will you be my friend?

My blood began to boil at that, and I was relieved—anger was easier than guilt. But when my thoughts began to swim again I knew this time I was the one scrambling them, trying and failing to stop them in their tracks. *Yeah, she definitely knows him.*

It was the look, the one that had passed between them when they were talking in circles and above my head before. They were talking, and then they weren't. And by the time I noticed it had been there, not all the way but there enough to hit me before I could dodge it: he knew *her*, too.

The thing was, *is*, there are people. And then there is me. There is family. And then there are me and Peter. And there are looks. And this was the look that cracked something inside of me like very brittle glass.

Because there was my brother, grown from seventeen to twenty-one since I had last seen him, and a world different than I remembered him already . . .

I tried not even to let the mattress creak as I lay back down, stiff, a grimace I could do nothing about plastered across my rigid face. My fingers dug into my sides, and I felt like I should blink but my eyes would only close part of the way. It was a charley horse of the mind, and as it faded I felt my body go slack, so devoid of energy that I couldn't even look around. It was okay; the sheet under my head made good enough scenery.

I don't think I can handle this. Finally aware enough to start berating some resolve into myself, I sat up again, swaying. Beating around the bush wasn't going to fix anything—I needed to make a decision.

"I can't handle this," I decided, though it came out sounding strange, choked. I wasn't ready to think of Peter that way, as . . .

What, a man?

Maybe so, but that seemed fair. I didn't exactly have a great track record with those.

Sitting under the window at end of my room, I looked up, wishing pathetically for the crooked shadows of my oak tree catching the sunlight, remembering the horrible sound the branches made against the glass, like fingernails down a chalkboard. I slept with my window open a lot when I was a little older. At first it was because of that sound, but eventually I grew to like the way the branches stretched about an inch through the open window and made me feel like I lived in a tree house. Still, I always pretended it was the noise, even though no one ever asked me to explain.

I'd moved on to missing the shadows my tree made in the moonlight when I noticed the knocking. *How long has that been going on?* I invited him in as sullenly as I could. *He'd better be planning to explain his old "friend."*

Apparently, my invitation should have been more specific. Instead of my brother ambling in and taking a seat on pretty much anything like I expected, it was her, the brightly-colored woman with the name he had to ask for, who sashayed in, moved the chair obstructively into the doorway of the bathroom and sat down, looking for all the world like she chose the spot because that's just where chairs went.

I waited for Peter to follow, pissed at him for using her to corner me like this. I looked pointedly past her to the door and waited. I clenched my hands into fists and waited.

The door closed.

The air turned solid, lodged in my lungs. I held it almost long enough to choke. For one long moment, then another, I stood frozen in near panic (I may or may not have jumped to my feet when What's-Her-Name walked in), more and more conscious that she was staring at me from barely a few feet away. Too close.

What I wanted to do was call Peter. He had to be right there, on the other side of the door. It couldn't close by itself. So he was there, and if I called he might come in.

He won't.

There was my daily dose of reality. I sucked in a lungful of air anyway, but it ended up as nothing but a rush of air on the way out too, over and over until I realized that if I could hear my own heavy breathing, the strange woman could hear it, too.

Strangers—everyone is a stranger.

Woah. Where had *that* come from? It was one of Peter's fake rules from when I was little and we used to sneak out to catch the late bus downtown, where we'd stay all night begging for change and using it to buy junk food. He made them up for me, to keep me safe even when he wasn't nearby. Basically, it was the standard warning about talking to strangers—but my brother, being himself, had warped it, prescribing a set of responses to some of the most terrible scenarios he could imagine.

It was weird, though, because I didn't still *use* them. I hadn't even thought about them in ages. They were his rules, and regardless of who they were made for, they were very much *him* and very little *me*. I didn't look at unfamiliar people the way he did, like they would just as soon slaughter as look at me.

You're kidding, right? I glanced over at the neon-clad woman, glaring as I contemplated escaping past her into the hallway. There was no point, I already knew that: the door would be locked, or Peter would be standing on the other side, holding it closed. *You're exactly as bad as he is,* the voice in my head concluded, *you just have a different way of showing it.*

So that was it, then. I carefully kept the resignation off of my face and hoped Peter could feel through the door how much he was going to pay for this.

"I've known your brother for a long time," Crayon-Box Barbie ventured, almost emotionless compared to fifteen minutes ago.

I groaned inwardly. *Kill me now. Stray bullet, meteor, lightning strike, I don't care as long as it gets the job done.*

"Obviously, of course, not as long as you have . . ."

So obviously, in fact, that maybe you could have just not said it at all.

". . . but, well, he has told me a ton about you. It almost makes me feel like I know you, sometimes."

Look, no-name. Even my brother doesn't know me as well as you both seem to think anymore. And you. Do not. Know me. I looked over at her, pointedly directing my furious gaze right at her left ear. *At. All.*

Was it impossible to make this woman uncomfortable? She returned my off-center gaze with a direct one of her own, level, clear, as though she could easily look straight into my mind but was kindly waiting for an invitation.

"However." That was a whole sentence according to her clipped tone, which reminded me of the way my principals used to sound when they called my mother to the school. I wondered if the next words would be *there's been an incident.* "That does not give me the right to act like I *do* know you, especially since I'm sure you have no idea who I am."

Damn right I don't.

"So I wanted to let you know I'm sorry, if I upset you before. I get a little excited sometimes, you might have noticed," one of the corners of her mouth pulled up, "but I'll try to hold it back a little from now on."

Hold it wherever you want, just get it out of here.

I guess she was done because she finally fell silent, her too-attentive eyes fixed on me as I shuffled backwards. She'd said "from now on." Now *on*, which meant there was a *later* somewhere, at least in her head. And the fact that Peter was right outside eavesdropping (less a guess than simple fact) suggested that he most likely agreed.

"You know, when I met—"

"I'm not him, you know," I snapped.

Crayon Barbie watched me, interested.

I watched her too, cautiously, trying to guess whether my outburst would have any other effect on her. Like, I don't know, maybe causing her to grow a set of fangs, double in size and try to chew one of my arms off. Or something. I hadn't chosen to be here with her, and I wasn't going to be a stand-in; if she wanted to impress my brother, she could go talk to *him*. Honestly, she was more than welcome. To go away.

And if she expected to get some big heart-to-heart speech out of

me that was a shame, too, because I'd used up all of my nerve interrupting her. She kept waiting, for longer than I would have thought
her physically capable, but I simply could not find it in myself to say
another word.

"I'd like to find out who you are," Crayon Barbie coaxed.

I refused to look at her, but it was too hard to stand up anymore.
Back against the wall, I slid to the floor. It felt strange; aside from
principals' offices, doctors' offices and other places where you aren't
supposed to stand, I couldn't remember the last time I'd ever just sat
down with anyone who was not my brother. I shot the woman a look,
trying not to seem curious, but she was still staring at me so I looked
away again.

Okay, I give, I mentally yelled through the door, *whatever it takes
to get the Neon Demon out of my face. You want me to talk to her?
Fine, I'll fucking talk to her.* I could still feel the weight of her patient,
nauseatingly friendly gaze and turned toward the source. "When are
you going to leave?"

I said I'd talk. I didn't have to be polite.

She seemed ecstatic to have me say anything at all; straightening
up—and no doubt barely keeping her butt in my chair—she rewarded
my good behavior with honesty. "I really don't know yet, sweetheart.
Your big brother and I were both hoping you and I could get to know
each other a little. So, after that?" She cocked her head and widened her grin.

Sweetheart.

My eyes were narrow slits, but it took me a while to notice, to even
recognize what word was bothering me. *Sweetheart.* One of the things
my mother called me, when she was trying to lure me into some trap,
when she had decided she was done Putting Up With Me and sent me
away to make myself look "presentable" for tomorrow, when she was
about to tell me to outright lie to any number of concerned citizens
who dared to question her about me . . . and then again, after. That

was one of *her* names. And how *dare* this bitch come in here and use it, talk down to me with *her* words like she has some sort of *right,* like she *owns* me . . .

"I *have.* A name." The words came out harsh and chewed up, unrecognizable. But I was somewhat mollified to see that frank gaze waver a bit as she registered their ferocity.

"Well . . ." I wondered if she was going to stutter like Peter did when he got nervous, but she bounced back quickly, if cautiously. "Of course you do. A beautiful name, Alana. I know that," she added quietly, still staring but now wearing a look more like you'd expect from a person who is begging another to put the gun down.

Another pause. I was getting sick of these long silences, even sicker of talking to this . . . person. *Crap, I'm even getting sick of insulting her,* I tried to joke with myself. But I was not in the mood for jokes—and I was not in the mood to play my brother's stupid game anymore. She needed to leave.

Whatever-her-name-was, however, had decided to try again, retreating to where she felt the conversation had gone wrong. "It's just, you know, I only know what he's told me about you, and I-"

"There's one thing I can tell you," I sighed, staring straight ahead, "that we don't have in common."

She was delighted. "Really? Well, tha-"

"Yeah," I cut her off again, "I'm not too interested in what's up your skirt to notice how obvious you are about advertising it."

She fell silent.

Who said that? For a few years, at least, the world went still. Eventually, the floor decayed and dropped away a few hundred feet and my hand twitched and the only sound I could hear was a sudden rushing in my ears and my own panicky brain coaching my heart to *keep going, keep going, keep going . . .*

What must I look like right now, frozen in a corner looking like I'd been punched in the stomach? And *why did I just say that?*

A few people, who I prefer to leave unnamed, tell me I have a tendency to speak without thinking. And that, sometimes, the things I say have certain effects on others—like, for instance, making them start to wish I was . . . perhaps . . . not alive, anymore. *And here we are, plenty of time to practice keeping my mouth shut, and I go and say something to one of the first friends of his I meet that even I think is horrible? Great. Really excellent.* And all because I hadn't known she was coming.

I gulped. *How much can he hear out there?* I mean, I wasn't scared or anything, that would be ridiculous. He was the mildest person I knew, almost impossible to provoke. But he was not an admirer of this particular talent of mine; he didn't like people to get "hurt"—I mentally rolled my eyes—and if he ever did manage to get worked up, he could be . . . marginally *less* mild. To put it mildly.

"Don't worry, I don't think he heard you. Old doors are thick. Anyway, so what if he did? You have every right to say what you want, it can't be easy meeting someone your brother's never talked about and having her be as, well," she paused at the last word, apparently at a loss, and then made a vague gesture around the side of her head.

I valiantly defeated the urge to volunteer my own adjectives, even in my mind. *Is there any chance that maybe you could have not heard it, either?* I thought instead, scowling.

Apparently she had, unfortunately, because she went on. "But, hon- Alana," she corrected quickly, "you should know it's just not like that. I've known Peter for a while, yes. And we *are* friends. He's a good person, I'm glad to know him. But to tell you the truth," she transformed the opinion into a conspiracy, "beyond that, he barely knows I exist."

If I could have come up with a sound to make there's no way it would have been words, so I let her go on.

"So let me get to the point, then. I want you to like me. Partly because of your brother, yes," she gave me a beseeching glance, wanting credit for her honesty. I stared back. Wasn't she tired of this yet? "But also because just from his stories, I already know I'd be glad to know you, too, and—although I'm sure there's no chance of you believing me right now—I truly hope we can be friends."

Who knew? You did get one right, I wearily (and not, really) responded.

"So here's what I have to offer. If you give me a trial run, I will tell you anything, *anything* you want to know about your brother from the day we met until right now. I can even tell you a little from before. My information is yours, if you'll only try me out." She awaited my answer with babyish enthusiasm.

Why did she keep talking about herself like a used car? *Maybe she doesn't know I can't drive yet,* I mused. Trial run a person? Let someone try to force friendship on me because she had a crush on my *brother?* This was immature and ridiculous, and there was no way I was getting dragged into it.

Except . . .

"Condition." I said, trying not glare for a moment.

She didn't hesitate for a second. "Name it."

I caught myself starting to look away and drew my gaze back toward her with difficulty. She waited while I corralled the words. "Don't . . . tell him. What I said." I looked up again, my eyes having wandered as I spoke.

Absurd smile plastered across her face, she was already nodding.

She talked more, then left. Afterward, Peter did the same. He called Crayon Barbie "Di," said the name she gave earlier was a fake one— I stopped paying attention once I was sure he hadn't heard the awful thing I'd said to her. My thoughts had gone back to one innocuous word from before, and I'd gone with them.

I thought we said we were going to work on your handwriting, sweetheart.

No big deal, it's an A minus assignment—decent enough. *My pencil broke halfway through, no one had a spare.* No need to mention I hadn't exactly asked.

Broke in half? She doesn't sound too interested. Neither am I.

Yeah—s. Wouldn't want to sound disrespectful.

Quiet on all fronts for a minute. Then: What the fuck were you doing?

I weigh answering against silence and choose wrong, as usual. *Nothing. It just happened.*

No, it didn't. It's not that easy. She looks at me self-righteously. It's not that easy to do.

I'm still not concerned until I see the way she's holding the pencil. Even then I'm resigned, silent, giving her the reproachful look that she doesn't know is actually me begging her to stop here, it was only a little thing and I'm the only family she has left so just put it *down—*

Or maybe she does know, because she senses the weakness and is on me like a snake on a slow rat. Sweetie, I know what I'm talking about. Come here. She smiles at me and I think maybe she's bleached her teeth. They're so white. Especially the fake ones, further back, where the real ones were knocked out.

Mom, I

I don't get a chance to finish. Come here and sit down.

And I hate myself because I do. I was always going to.

I'm going to need you to be more careful.

It takes her a while to make her point.

I'll be more careful, I say to no one later, working at my thigh with a pair of tweezers. It's meant to be sarcastic, but I'm whimpering like a kicked dog and when I speak the words come out as a promise. For punishment, I bite my tongue and drive the tweezers much deeper the next time.

I had been thinking about my mother a lot in the past few days. And not just her—my room with its sparse furniture and many hiding places, the house I knew top to bottom, front to back with my eyes closed (because sometimes I got bored), the yard, my tree. For days now they'd been on my mind and, truthfully, I had not the slightest idea why. And Peter always seemed to want to talk about her. Like before, when he'd brought up her thing about us having friends . . . I was sad, I guess. But a different kind of sad. Probably because I was already thinking about her so much.

I rolled my head against the cool, solid wall and gnawed my thumb mindlessly. As I was examining the tooth prints left behind it occurred to me: it was the same sort of sadness I used to feel when my mother used her "maternal" look. It kind of reminded me of every teenage-girl book I'd ever read, where they would always follow that look with some line about how "Mom thinks she knows everything, but she's like a million years old."

Problem was, I still had no idea what it meant.

Well that was useful exactly not at all, thanks. Somehow, the sarcasm made me smile. I returned a jaunty *you're welcome* (to myself, I know) and finally got up from the corner, heading for the bathroom and a nice, hot shower.

And, of course, found myself slumped onto the bed a few steps later.

I wonder if she still hates me. Peter would say that wasn't ever true, she had never hated him *or* me, she just didn't—couldn't, or refused to—really love anyone, either. *Yeah, right.* It was a cute theory, but the evidence proved it was wrong. She hated me, all right—whether because I never knew when to shut up, or because I resembled a man I barely remembered, or because I just wasn't a very good daughter, I don't know.

Or care, I had to prompt myself. The bathroom was five steps away—so far. *Right, or care.* If I believed for a second that I needed *her* approval, I was obviously even closer to crazy than I'd guessed.

"Well, where do the signs point?" I muttered, lying back, no longer interested in showering. The bite marks were still fading, pink to tan, from either side of my thumb.

You know, the odds are she didn't come here just to talk to you. She's probably still hanging around somewhere, and if she's not too busy flirting with your brother, I bet she thinks you're hiding from her.

This is what it took for me to stop ignoring the trapped energy crawling up and down my legs and head out to finish my disrupted workout with a walk.

"No one's hiding," I replied to myself, throwing open the door and striding out into the hallway. Only a moment's hesitation, then I was on my way, up to the roof or one floor down, to the courtyard or even outside. Anywhere but where I'd usually go.

Because really, it wasn't about finishing my workout. I rushed down, skipping steps in an embarrassingly transparent pretense of playfulness. *No. It's about not letting her chase you up into your room, letting her corner you. Right? Can't let her think if she shows up, my whole day is over, right? I wanted to exercise this afternoon, and even if I don't have my treadmill I still have plenty of space, so I can and I will. Right? It's not like I need permission. I can do whatever I–*

Thunk, whoosh.

The *thunk* was me running into the old woman who didn't live here, but always seemed to be around. The *whoosh*, a flurry of papers exploding from her arms like birds whose chance at freedom had been a long time coming. It felt like ages before their flight finally turned to slow, lazy descent.

By then I was already on the floor, grabbing some, waiting for others. *Oh shit. Oh shit. Oh shit. Oh shit.*

Normally I would have been hugging the corners, following the wall, eyes trained on the ground three feet in front of me—to avoid, as if it isn't obvious, this *exact* kind of situation. Normally I wouldn't even be here, not alone. But today I had to be cocky, I had to come here even though I *knew* she spent most of her time on this floor, I just *had* to not look where I was going and ram into her and now I was frantically shoving papers back into something imitating a pile, careful not to crease any of them, trying not to whisper as I repeated the words "Oh shit oh shit oh shit oh shit" out loud so she would know I was sorry and realizing suddenly, too suddenly, that I had been thinking about my mother so much because I *missed her,* I missed my Mom and that was the sickest thing I had ever done or could do to myself but it was *true* . . .

"Alana." I felt a hand on my shoulder and jerked backward so hard that I went from kneeling in the middle of the mess to sitting a foot away from it. Staring at the pile, I took one more shaky breath and then crawled back over, silently gathering the rest of it. By the time I stood, I was able to meet the old woman's eyes with, if not confidence, then no expression in my own. My hand, reaching out to offer the dropped papers, did not even shake.

She took them, but continued to watch me. I could see her mulling over what she'd seen, turning it around and around in her brain, wondering how—or if—she should respond. I, in turn, stood still and did not slink away to throw myself down an elevator shaft.

Her eyes, I'd never had reason to notice before, were dark hazel behind her tortoiseshell frames. What was her name? I only knew my brother called her "Doc" even though she didn't want him to, asked him to use some other name that may or may not have been her real one. Had I ever heard it? I considered the possibility as we studied each other and decided that no, I had not.

So Doc, then, wore her graying black hair in a predictably neat bun, a clean white coat cinched precisely at her waist over a flannel shirt and khakis. The horn-rimmed glasses gave her a grandmotherly appearance, and the prim, concerned gaze she had fixed on me now only intensified it. She looked sixtyish, if I was any kind of judge, and when she opened her mouth I always expected to hear a creaky old-lady voice, the one adults always faked in Little Red Riding Hood (*The better to see you with, my dear*). But when she talked it was clear and loud, concise. She spoke like a good doctor who knew what she was doing.

Regardless of my feelings for Doc herself, I did like her voice.

You certainly have come a long way, haven't you, I teased myself, and chalked it up to time. I had known Doc for longer, had time to get used to her, so now that a new person had shown up I was switching over, finding reasons to like Doc instead. That was all.

"I won't keep you. But you know where to find me, should you want to talk." Doc smiled a little, still concerned, squinting through her lenses as she turned away. I'm not sure what it was—the biting, the nightmares, the collision, (missing my mother) or Di's sudden appearance. Or even none of the above. Maybe, for a moment, I actually did want to talk. No conversations, of course, nothing as taxing as that. But I had been proud of myself before, and maybe I kind of wanted the feeling back. Maybe that's what made me say

"What kind of doctor are you?"

Doc turned, blinked, squinted again. "Emergency physician. Broken bones, infections, diseases. Why do you ask?" She wasn't exactly distracted, but after answering she unfocused a little, not quite looking at me.

This was not the answer I'd been hoping for. "So you don't . . . you aren't . . . a shrink, too?" I tried to be offhand, but there it was.

"Oh." She didn't seem surprised or like she was judging me at all, just sort of like she wished she could have answered differently. "Sorry, no. I . . ."

Doc cocked her head to the side, a weirdly youthful gesture that, weirdly, didn't make her look any younger. Then she snapped her fingers. "But your brother and I do have a friend with a degree in psychology. Among others," she chuckled.

My stomach sank, but I let her finish.

"I'm sure you'll meet her soon; honestly, it's strange you haven't yet. It's hard not to think of her as Dierdre—first impressions—but last I heard, it was . . . Dharma? Maybe Deanna . . ."

I stared.

Di. Dee? He hadn't spelled it, had he.

So it might have just been the *letter* "D."

Of course.

chapter 14.

OVER the next weeks Di devoted herself to proving she was capable of nothing so much as keeping a promise. Except for talking, maybe. She was very good at that.

She upheld both her ends of the bargain, keeping my part of our first conversation to herself (or at least convincing my brother to pretend *extremely* well), and of course telling me everything she knew about Peter's life before she met me. Everything.

Once, as the three of us sat in his office doing nothing in particular—a concept I still found strange (and probably always would)—Di had turned to me with a look I'd learned to recognize as the precursor to a lecture the likes of which would probably have put me to sleep if I weren't the considerate and attentive person I am. Before I could signal her to save her breath (by shoving my face deeper into my book, striking up a less taxing conversation with Peter or, my favorite, simply standing up and walking away) she had launched into a one-sided interrogation about how Peter used to only eat things with *tomatoes* in them. His favorite food had to be *tomatoes*. At least he must like them a lot, right? Because . . .

At least nine hours into this "conversation" I gave up trying to stare her mute; instead, I glanced at my brother for help. He was looking away by then, combing through newspapers for more "missing" ads— but as I watched, a slow smile spread over his face, and soon he was unable to hold back a few seconds of silent laughter even with me looking right at him.

I'd never noticed how many tomatoes were in the food Doc brought us from town. I started picking them out of anything I ate.

Honoring my own end of the agreement was harder than I expected—when Di said she could tell me things that Peter might not want to, I didn't realize I'd also be obligated to listen to every *other* insignificant thought she had. But to be fair, as exhausting as she was, she really did know a lot. She answered my questions gladly, and she was always willing to distract me when Peter was busy—though I did still savor the silence after she was gone.

Whenever she was around, she was talking, which is how I learned over a remarkably short time that Peter had travelled a full two states south of home after running away. That he spent the first few months nearby, actually, looking for work and a place to live.

And that it hadn't gone well.

So he tried again, kept moving from town to town trying to be an adult even though he hadn't so much as introduced himself in nearly a decade. How he managed to live this way for over two years was beyond Di *and* me, but he'd made a considerable journey by the time he crossed paths with Dorothy (the then-alias of Elizabeth Karras, wealthy heiress and investment wiz by day, organized criminal by night). She was in town on not-entirely-legitimate business—her words: she'd finally explained her multiple personalities to me after dramatically unveiling her true identity, which was apparently some sort of big deal—my brother was living in a city park. She practically stumbled over him one day while he was halfheartedly playing with a cat in the grass.

Apparently, the person she met then was very different from how he was now. He hadn't so much as smiled for months after their first conversation. "Even when he did, you could see how miserable he still was. And there was nothing you could do. It just broke your heart to look at him sometimes."

I didn't like hearing that. Sure, I had wished many terrible things upon my brother over the years out of hurt and anger. I'd even almost—almost—wished he was dead sometimes. But I had never, not once, actually wanted him to be unhappy.

Though it wasn't easy to admit, knowing he had been actually made me a little *glad* Di existed. It was good that he had someone to help him back then.

And it turned out "helping" was possibly the understatement of the decade. Reluctant at first, Peter had found steady work and a new friend in Di. She'd even handed over part of her personal project, which she called the Drophouse and Peter—insisting no good could come of naming places that were never supposed to have existed— called nothing. Except, in a way, home.

As promised, Di told me far more than Peter liked about how learning her own family's secrets had led her to create what was somewhere between a halfway-house and a hostel, in hopes of making good on what she called "thousands of promises those people went back on, time and again."

Once I did a miracle by complete accident and shut her up simply by joking about whether her little project had ever made her any supervillain-style enemies.

It was almost nice to see-but-not-hear her for once, but for some reason I couldn't enjoy it.

She was exactly the type to misinterpret our deal as mutual. Not that she ever acted hurt when I sat back and did none of the talking, perish the thought. But the deal I recalled required me to tolerate her presence, only *tolerate* it, in return for information. So I kept to my part.

Come on. She may not be your favorite person, but at least she's trying. Honestly? You might even owe *her a little.*

I glanced over the picnic table, the overgrown wreckage of the courtyard rising up all around. I liked it here—it was all scraggly saplings that would never survive, giant vines that would never die, trapped dirt and exposed pipes. And the one picnic table, of course.

I was rarely allowed into the courtyard anymore, and never alone. It used to be fine, but a while ago I'd found a small pile of ash and a pile of cut vines. Local kids, probably. Peter didn't take it well—among other things, he'd agonized, there was no sprinkler system; what if the place had caught fire? But Di and I still came here often for her to talk, sitting on either side of the splintering table.

She was quiet but thinking hard, wracking her brain for any piece of information or anecdote she hadn't already shared—something to fill the silence I placed between us so often. There was a time, and it didn't seem so long ago, when I would have given anything to meet someone who would bother to be nice to my brother. And here she was, literally that person, and he was the farthest thing from a bother, to hear her talk about him. And I couldn't even say two words to her.

Yeah, the words "thank" and "you" come to mind.

Fine. Di seemed like the sort of person who liked to talk about feelings and all, so I tried to ease in. It took effort to get the words past my suddenly clenched jaw, but I did it. "He probably would have said something about you soon, you know."

"I know he would have." She looked like she meant it. "And I'm sorry there is so much I can't explain, but I want you to know he *did* tell me about you. Even when he didn't say much. It was so sweet to see him with that look on his face talking about you like you were his own little girl, I-"

I was leaned over the table, screaming before I'd even opened my mouth. "No! *No I am not-*"

Stop it!

Di gaped.

I stared back. I was bleeding, but I couldn't stop biting my tongue. *Shut up. Just shut up, don't make it worse.*

Of course, she recovered first. "I didn't mean . . . well . . ."

I placed my hands on the table and stood up.

"Alana?"

No longer in the mood for conversation, I turned and forced my legs and feet to walk—*walk not run*—across the courtyard and back inside.

chapter 15.

"I mean, she's nice enough," I answered Peter later, casually flipping pages in the center of his bed. Two more books lay on the edge; Peter was out of sight behind a tower of boxes, trying to find more. "Nice isn't the issue. It's just . . . well, she's a bit of an *airhead*, isn't she?"

He rummaged around a little more and then emerged with an armload of paperbacks for my inspection. Dumping it untidily by the bed, he sat down and looked back at me. "Come here." He held out a hand. I scooted down, and he grasped the front of my shirt, slowly pulling me in until he was squinting directly into my eyes. I scrutinized him back, trying not to give anything away. *What did she tell you?*

In the next second Peter sat back and lifted his other hand. A small but sharp pain suddenly exploded between my eyes.

"*Ow!*"

I yanked back, but Peter was still holding onto my shirt collar. He leaned in again. "Be nice."

"Did you just *flick* me?"

"Not the point. Be nice to Di. She's a good person and she's incredibly smart, no matter what you think. And since *somehow* she never has a bad thing to say about you, the least you can do is not call her names." He still didn't let go, just stared condescendingly. *Does he think I'm going to apologize or something?*

Eventually, though, I did drop my eyes. "You're messing up your shirt," I muttered, rubbing a knuckle over the bridge of my nose.

He looked down, confused. Then, heaving an angry sigh, he rolled his eyes and went back to his search. His shoulders and jaw were set in a peculiar way—had that jab at Di actually gotten to him? I suppressed a grin.

We were both silent for a while, then Peter dumped another load of books next to me and started picking up the rest. "Why can't you wear your own clothes?"

I didn't answer, just idly tried to calculate how many long, wakeful nights it would take to require this much reading material and watched *him* try to start a fight for a change.

"There's nothing wrong with them. I get it, you're used to hand-me-downs, but my stuff keeps going missing and I think I'm going crazy or something-"

No way was I setting foot in that minefield. "Nice try," I cut in, "but I know she picked out my clothes." I didn't even bother waiting for the next question. "I can't even *look* at half those colors without shielding my eyes, I'm pretty sure you know me better than that."

Peter tried to answer with a disapproving look and I rolled my eyes, but we just ended up laughing over the neglected pile of books. Still, I hadn't forgotten why I'd started us talking about Di in the first place, and it looked like I had my answer.

To be clear, lying was not something I made a habit of doing—not when I had a choice. What was the point? The truth might not always be pretty, but it was easier to remember. And normally, lying to Peter was something I would never even give a moment's consideration.

But when it came to my somewhat-more-frequent-than-I-care d-to-admit dreams, which roughly half the time resulted in the cuts and scratches my brother worried about so much and the other half only woke me up in a cold sweat, shaking and sometimes in tears, I just couldn't bring myself to tell the truth. He wasn't the only one who was freaked out by them, no matter what he thought—of course I was. Maybe not as much as him, maybe not enough. That might have been why, ever since the first time he'd grabbed my bleeding shoulders and *demanded* that if I remembered this dream I *had* to tell him, I couldn't do it.

But I felt better, running myself into oblivion during the day to get some peace at night—and if it kept working he might never need to know I'd lied at all. Not about something as stupid as a dream.

I wish I could just go to sleep. And I know I should, because it's late at night and I'll have to start my chores in the morning whether I'm tired or not. But there's someone right behind me, *right* behind me, and if I do fall asleep, something terrible might happen. *Will* happen.

As always I start in bed, lying down. But at the realization that someone is there, I find myself standing, forehead against the wall. I try to take a step forward but something reaches out, a humanoid paw or a hand with the callouses and claws of an animal, and drags me back to where I was before. The paw traces a path up my leg lightly, too lightly; where the claws make contact my dream-skin crawls and itches. I resist the urge to scratch as it traces up and down my arms, my other leg, my neck. Soon I close my eyes. Crickets chirp outside— *shhhh, shhh.* I am no longer worried about getting to sleep.

The thing behind me shifts and suddenly I am sitting, staring out the window across the room. The branches are striking as if trying to break the glass, but when they scrape they don't make any sound at all.

Something terrible. I open my mouth. I see my own eyes, stretching open wide, but everything else is dark. Something is wrong, something is going wrong. My elbow is braced against me, holding something away. My mouth is still open, but as always, my dream self makes no sound. The tree silently thrashes against the window.

Something terrible.

And suddenly I'm suffocating. I sit up but am quickly slammed back—I'm trying to look around, but can only see the window. My feet and fists flail in all directions, striking out at the nothing around me, the nothing fighting back with the many limbs of an octopus or spider. My mouth and nose are glued shut and there is no air, there is *no air* and I can't move but I am moving and the window is closing up with gray and the gray is coming toward me as I fall and I can still hear the *shh, shhh, shhhhh–*

Wake up.

I wish I could go to sleep.

Please wake up.

Something's wrong.

"Ally, come on."

"NO!" The word came out garbled and unrecognizable, my mouth stubbornly refusing to open. Still rooted in the dream I gasped for air anyway, rolling and twisting to both sides to free my arms, to save myself.

It would *end* this time, I resolved myself. I would fight through it, and for once *I* would end it. I yanked even harder and opened my eyes when I'd nearly freed one arm, to get a clearer shot at . . .

Although I was already lying down I managed to flinch even further back. Horrified, I looked him in the eye for a long while before I regained my grip on reality and the nightmare finally began to fade away. At almost the same moment Peter released his grip on my wrists. He was more cautious about taking his other hand off my mouth, however.

"Are you sure you're awake?" He asked, emphasizing the word "sure," as though I might be somehow faking consciousness.

In response I violently shook my head in what I like to think of as the universal sign for *get the fuck off me.*

He did, and I leapt past him, locking myself into the bathroom. The air was stale. I turned the sink and bathtub faucets on full blast, listened to the hollow rushing noise as the sink filled with cold water.

Both eyes stayed firmly closed; I didn't want to look at myself—my face in the mirror or the rest of my body beneath me.

I'm getting good at this, I thought bitterly, recognizing the sound of a nearly full sink and reaching for the knob again. Then I held my breath and plunged my face into the water.

The sensation, which slammed my eyes and mouth shut while flooding the rest of my body with fresh adrenaline, was (as always) successful in driving out the last vestiges of the dream. Those thoughts emptied through the back of my head as though I'd pulled a trigger into my mouth and my brain warred with itself instead, telling me first to gasp against the cold and then to hold my breath so I wouldn't drown.

I stayed under until my instincts had calmed and then some more, ears full of running-water white-noise. Finally a clear idea surfaced: *If I stay here, maybe when I come out he'll be gone.*

Then: *If I stay* here, *I'm pretty sure coming out will stop being an option soon.* I pulled myself out of the water and half-grimaced, feeling less refreshed by my first gulp of oxygen than I'd felt without it. Before I dried my face I opened my eyes to the mirror, my vision blurred by the few drops that trickled in, stinging lightly.

He was trying to help, I knew that. He was worried about me, didn't want me to hurt myself. I understood, which was why I'd tried several times, and very graciously (for me), to tell him not to wake me up like that.

Yeah, right. *"I have this random nightmare I 'don't remember,' and I'd prefer if you'd be so kind as to stay out of it, please, so I can keep carving myself up like a bathroom stall? Thanks."* I groaned softly into the towel, then smashed it against my face hard before shutting off the faucet. How much water had I wasted on nights like these?

It was still dark, so when the door opened, pale light and my irritated glare flooded the room. Tense, coffee-clear eyes met my own for a long moment, and I went to sit next to Peter on the bed again.

"So, you still can't rem-"

"What are you doing here?"

A quiet sigh.

If I'd been feeling particularly curious, I may have turned the investigation back onto Peter, whose own sleep problems had plagued him at least for my whole life. I, however, was never the type to go prying into the nocturnal lives of other people.

"Ally, I'm sorry I scared you." A pause between each word. His voice was low, pitched as if someone in the otherwise empty room might be eavesdropping.

I placed my palms over my eyes so none of the light from the bathroom got through and tried to remember. Where in the dream did I start scratching myself? Why? Slowly, something started to surface, something solid and memorylike—but before I could make it out it changed, blurring into something more defensive, less definite.

If he stopped bothering me about it, I don't think I'd even care this much. His overanxiety must be rubbing off on me.

Peter had already started his own ritual, rambling in the same quiet monotone he'd used to tell me stories when I was sick as a kid. He'd keep it up, talking about nothing in particular, until I quit trying to wait him out and fell asleep. Sliding to the floor, he grabbed a handful of the tangles my hair liked to rest in and tugged twice, quickly, letting go before I could pull away.

". . . the first couple of times I tried talking to people without—you know—it was basically impossible, but now it's almost completely under control. But Di always wanted to be a psychologist, so I guess she's sort of disappointed when it does happen. By the way, I think you would like Devontae, he's a foster kid who's been with her for a few years. When I met him . . ."

chapter 16.

DI was just storming out as I approached Peter's bedroom. Dodging past her, I raised an eyebrow. "Which one of you did what this time?"

"What do you want?"

The irritation in the room was palpable; they'd been fighting, and I was glad I'd missed out. It had taken time (and some cajoling, and a few outright threats) for me to stop jumping in to defend my brother and, even though it was rarely too serious, the yelling matches were still hard to watch. Instead of answering I nudged a box out of the cardboard wall and started rifling through it. Peter dropped down next to me.

"I take that to mean it was you," I said, annoying him for the sheer joy of it. I mean, it's nice and all, and I know I'm lucky to have him, but anyone who can't enjoy jumping rope with someone's last nerve when you know they eventually *have* to forgive you is both an only child and a pitifully boring person. Peter shot me a look, and I grinned.

"What are you looking for?"

"Nothing." I liked digging through the collected pieces of my brother's last few years. I never knew what I'd find—usually it was boring things like toothpaste or clothes, but once I'd found a stack of newspaper articles and though most had been signed "Anonymous," a couple were initialed

P.C.W.

I finished disemboweling the first box and reached for another, but Peter grabbed it before I could dig in. The fight appeared forgotten as he rooted through it, then pulled something out and stuffed it into a box that had already been emptied and reorganized.

I leaned over. "What was that?"

"Work stuff. Off limits."

I rolled my eyes, but didn't ask again. Di would probably get around to it.

Peter was pushing the box back to me with a strange expression that may have been a small smile or a grimace. He slid it the last few inches with his foot and waited, chewing his lip.

It was mostly empty; all that was left were a few crumpled and re-smoothed papers. At first I thought they might be more articles, but these were more weathered, mostly handwritten pages . . . and the typed ones said things like "Rubric" and "Syllabus."

I stared at my full hands like I had no idea how they'd gotten that way and then shook off my momentary confusion literally, like a dog shaking off water. "What-"

"I may or may not have a degree in journalism." He refused to look at me.

There was no need to worry, though—actually I was impressed. "You have a degree?" Maybe a little too much emphasis on the *you*, but it did seem like a fair question.

"I said may or *may not*. I've taken almost all of the classes, I even went to graduation. I just . . . wasn't . . ."

I was laughing before I even realized I'd caught on. "You," I wheezed, "did remember to *enroll* in the college beforehand, right?"

"Colleg*es*," Peter corrected a little forcefully, then smiled himself. "And, well . . . no. I did not. But all things considered I think I did okay, don't you?"

Before I could decide how to answer, Di strode back up, walking in these long-legged strides that made it seem like she was wearing high heels although—today at least—she was not.

Crap. They weren't going to start fighting again, were they?

She asked Peter to step outside, and then I was alone.

I thumbed through some of the crinkled papers. There were notes, a syllabus or two. Even a couple of term papers. Why had he saved all of these?

Not just these; whatever he had pulled out before was in a box nearby.

I cocked my head. Only scraps of conversation from outside. *Should I?*

No. I didn't pry into "work stuff." Anyway, there were tons of boxes I hadn't gone through yet. Plenty of books I hadn't read. The stack of papers in my hands. The fact that I *didn't pry* into *work* stuff.

But . . .

I scurried over. They were barely hidden in a box of paperbacks—envelopes, thick ones, no stamps or addresses. Each was stuffed with sheets of paper, some yellow, some white.

The talking stopped. *Hurry!* Despite the disorienting urgency I quickly grabbed two envelopes. Would he miss two?

Maybe not, but still . . . I picked one, put it back. *There, that seems right.* Darting away, I picked up the bound stack of term papers and shoved the envelope deep into the middle, trying to calm the hot flush from my ears and face.

Just in time. But when they came back, neither seemed curious about what I'd been up to while they were gone.

chapter 17.

LAUGHTER created a creepy echo in the stairwell, but I couldn't stop. I was pretending not to be nervous, and anyway, it *was* a little funny, my brother shepherding me around like an especially self-important, especially grim hall monitor.

I saw the humor, anyway.

"Can you shut up?" Laugh twenty-seven or -eight.

"Can you chill out?"

"When you're around. Honest answer?"

I didn't have a comeback for that. I tried to think of one, but as we reached the top floor all of my energy sort of fell away, leaving only nerves behind.

The weird laughter was better. The stack of papers, with the envelope stashed inside, was clutched in my good (meaning non-spazzing) hand; hopefully sweating palms wouldn't smudge the pages.

They were here. Now. The They even *Di* refused to talk about.

Peter opened the door and I stared at the thin line where hall and room met, some of the tiles cut to fit the doorway. *Ookay.* I sighed mentally, then physically and looked up, imagining the same boundary in the air—a force field between there and here. "Will they come upstairs?"

His head snapped up, over-attentive but muddled, like I was a movie he'd missed an important part of. "No. They've never been here before, so." He sounded subdued, reassuring, like when he talked me down after one of my nightmares. Watching him watch me back like that was familiar, but not in the kind of way I'd want to mention.

I nodded instead. Then sighed again. "But you're still going to . . ."

He was already nodding.

Well, all right then. "All right." I echoed myself, stepping over the mutilated tiles. I shouldn't even have bothered asking. When I was small and Mom was dating for the first time (of many), he'd always locked me in my room when she had "company." I didn't mind. I don't suffer from panic attacks like my brother, and I was okay spending time by myself. That was when I taught myself to read, and learned to enjoy it. Books never said to pay attention to that sound downstairs. There was never a page that told you yes, that was shouting, and yes, that was a crash, and you won't know who made it until it's already too late to do anything, you useless little baby.

The best ones took you away from it all, pulled you in so it felt like you could never leave, even when you closed them, put them away for months. The lives of the people in the story became your life; they were better sometimes and worse others, but even if you didn't want to live them it didn't matter because at some point it wasn't about you anymore. There was a piece of you in the book, stuck to the binding. And it would stay there forever.

I had some books already and now the papers, too—at least a few hours of entertainment. *All things considered,* I told myself, *not a bad afternoon.*

"Try not to smash any windows while I'm gone," Peter said this hoping for a smile so I gave him a quick one, then made sure to catch his gaze before he turned away. From across the room I examined him for signs my brother might know something he wasn't saying. He'd always been on the other side of the door. *Do I need to be worried about you?*

Peter straightened a little and gave me a slight double-nod. "Al, I'm with Di, remember? I'm fine."

I nodded once, relieved to find I actually believed him.

As always, a shower helped. By the time the water started to cool, the perfectly almost-too-hot robe of water had turned the volume on my thoughts back down to a manageable level.

He was already back, lying on my bed, by the time I grudgingly stepped out of the bathroom. Luckily I'd already pulled on a pair of jeans and a long pink shirt in the bathroom—I was trying to be brave, but it was aggressively cheerful, already getting on my nerves—still, Peter thoughtfully faced the wall. He didn't move when I walked in, and his voice held no emotion.

"Hi."

"Uh . . . huh." I raised an eyebrow when he finally sat up. He seemed off, not in a way I could understand even, just . . . blank. "You okay?"

He faced me, silent. I watched him, hoping for an excuse to shrug the odd behavior off, when I saw the stack of papers with its stolen cargo sitting on the pillow right next to him.

Crap. I moved to grab them, but as I passed by Peter reached out and ran a hand over my damp hair. As he shook it dry, I abandoned my stolen goods to give him another look.

There was a trace of a smile on his face. "It gets cold out at night," was all he said.

"Like I ever *go* out," I shot back. Then I shook my head hard, spraying every surface in the room. A few strands of hair took offense, clinging to my face reproachfully, and when I wiped them away from my eyes I was a little relieved to see that Peter—though he'd shrunk back and was frantically scrubbing his face against his shoulder—seemed to have relaxed a little bit.

"So how did it go?"

He stopped scrubbing at that. In fact, he didn't move at all. For a long time he just sat there frozen, eyes locked onto nothing like he'd stepped out of himself for a moment, hoping he wouldn't have to decide what to say.

My head suddenly ached, and realized I was clenching my jaw. Opened my hands and realized I'd been clenching those too. "Look, if you're going to lie then you might as well forget I asked," I snapped at last.

Finally, he brought his eyes up to meet mine.

I glared back.

And no one said a thing.

Not a week later I walked up to Doc's infirmary door looking for him and heard them talking.

"She's fine." Peter sounded severe, even hostile. Odd. He was usually so deferential with the doctor.

"I am not saying she isn't. All I mean is that you did not see what I saw. And what I saw was not what *I* would call fine, *per se*."

Damn it. They were talking about me, how I freaked out when I ran into Doc that time. But I'd been so careful to be normal, composed, the total *opposite* of that every time I'd seen her since. Hadn't she noticed? I hung back, out of sight.

But they'd moved on to other topics. "So, what's next?"

Doc mentioned something about a niece she'd been exchanging letters with, and I stepped out, trying to act fine, *per se*.

Doc and my brother went quiet. Doc was perched on a little stool. Balanced across her knees was a small box with a word stenciled along the side: FRAGILE.

The two of them stared out at me from the sterile-smelling exam room, and I considered going in to join them. They always found so much to talk about, and for a second I thought it might be interesting to go in, take a seat, and try my hand at a real conversation for once.

But this was not the time. They'd been talking about me; if I tried to speak to Doc right now, I would probably end up looking crazy again, and I really didn't want her thinking of me that way.

I planned to wait for another day to sit down and talk to her. One that felt more "right."

I should have just gone in.

4, 11

SHE *knows she must be in trouble, but not why. And Mommy never said, either, just woke her up from her nap early and told her to go downstairs and get into the little closet in the kitchen until Mommy got back. She didn't sound angry, so maybe she isn't in trouble but that's even more confusing. The little girl plays with the light beneath the door and hopes she won't need to go potty before Mommy gets back.*

She's lucky. A little while later the car rumbles up the driveway again, and she barely has to pee at all by the time the door starts to open. It's so soon that now she knows *she's not in trouble, and she starts bouncing up and down, peeking through the crack to make a face at—*

Wait. *Even though she really wants to be able to come out now, even if it means going right back to bed for being Too Hyper (her Mommy says that sometimes), the girl actually pushes herself back into the closet even more when she sees it wasn't Mommy who opened it. And she doesn't even know which is scarier, that the boy is* there, *right outside—or how he is looking at her.*

He doesn't know why the first thing he did when they got home was open the pantry. He figured he'd tell the girl to run, maybe even give her a reason if she didn't move fast enough, but now that he's standing here all he does is stare, and shake.

How did he make Mom so angry? Actually, he knows what he did . . . but he doesn't understand why it was so wrong.

All he knows is, according to Mom, he's been having a hard time dealing with his father's disappearance. The boy doesn't think so; in fact, he thinks he feels pretty okay about it. But Mom has kept insisting and insisting, to his teachers, other kids' parents, anyone who would listen. He was a little relieved when she finally told the principal that she would be putting him in therapy for his "behavior issues." At least now whatever was wrong with him might get better.

It had made a lot less sense a couple hours ago, though, when Mom had locked the girl into the pantry instead of taking her with them. And then, in the car. He had been watching the road through the window, looking for trucks—if you moved your arm like you were blowing a horn, sometimes they would blow theirs for real and it was amazing, almost as loud as a train. But before he saw any she called his name and through the rearview mirror she fixed him with a look and told him that no matter what anyone said to him in the doctor's office (he didn't know it was a doctor, he thought it was just like going to a school counselor), he was not to say one thing, not one word back.

That wasn't what he expected therapy to be like. On TV people would sometimes lay down on couches or sit up or whatever, but everyone always did a lot of talking. Still, when she asked if he understood she had been so serious that he nodded anyway.

And he almost did it, too, to the puzzlement of the doctor, who had talked to Mom for a very long time afterward. The nice receptionist had seemed a little upset too, but that hadn't mattered much to him. It was enough to have done what his mother asked. He was so proud of himself for following directions, in fact, that he'd accidentally let his guard down by the time Mom was saying her goodbyes, when the receptionist had asked him to at least try and be good for his Mommy until the next time they saw each other.

"Okay."

The moment he said it he knew it was a mistake. The achievement that meant so much seconds ago was worthless now—he had ruined everything. And from her stony silence and the screeching of tires as she sped home it seemed clear that Mom would be less than forgiving about it.

Mom stayed in the front room while he was opening the pantry, but now she's calling him back. He makes his meandering, stumbling way back to her, and her voice freezes him from the inside out but still holds enough feeling to shake as she speaks. "What was the one, simple, little thing that I asked you to do?" *She waits.*

Like a frozen volcano, the boy thinks.

"Well?"

Or an earthquake on a glacier. He swallows.

"Did you hear me?"

"You said-" *the boy is cut off before he can finish, and by the time his vision stops swimming the only sound he's making is a low moaning that seems like it must be coming from farther away than just the floor of the front room . . .*

Mom kneels beside him. She's leaning on something he slowly recognizes as the heavy wooden baseball bat from the big ceramic vase by the front door. She used to say it was there in case someone dangerous tried to get inside the house, and the boy wonders when that stopped being all it was for. She waits patiently for his senses to return, then asks more quietly, "What did I ask you to do?"

This time he answers right away, thinking the previous blow was punishment for hesitating. "To not-"

This time she brings the bat down on his outstretched arm. He screams, as much from pain as from the alarming crunching sound made by the wood, or the bone. Immediately it comes down again, slamming into his ribs as he curls around his injured arm. A blast of air explodes from his nose and mouth, but there is still enough left for him to whisper at nothing, "Mom? Stop, Mom . . ."

But she brings down the bat again, and again, raining blows on his legs, back, and shoulders as she screams "SHUT UP! SHUT UP! SHUT YOUR FUCKING MOUTH!"

The screaming continues, both from the boy and from his mother, until she seems to forget the bat and begins lashing out at him with her feet instead. By this time the girl has joined in; she does not understand what is happening but her own shrieks grow even more frantic when the boy does fall abruptly silent and her Mommy still picks up her foot like she is going to kick him again. Hiccups start interrupting the girl's screams, and her mother carefully places her foot back down.

Then she kneels next to the boy again, and although he is not moving she must still know he is listening because she is real quiet when she talks again. "You speak. When I tell. You to. I hope to God that for your sake you understand now." And she reaches down to ruffle his hair. Then she goes back to her bedroom, pausing to yell that the girl had better get up to her room right now if she doesn't want something to cry about.

The little girl gets quiet right away. She's quick, too, and nearly knocks over the end table and a whole vase of fake flowers on her way to the stairs before she changes her mind, drops to hands and knees, and silently makes her way back to the boy, who is lying still in front of the door. She's scared to make noise, but even more scared to touch him, so in the end she whispers "Hey," and pokes the boy in the shoulder at the same time.

He is awake, but barely. He winces as a small finger hits the exact spot where, moments ago, the bat did, and the girl shrinks back. But she stays, still hiccupping a little, and tries to figure out what she is supposed to do. He let her out of the closet. Why? She can't figure out if that was being nice.

But he made Mommy mad, maybe she should just leave him here and let him get what he gets. Anyway that's probably what he would do if she was in trouble.

Her mind's nearly made up when she hears noises from the back bedroom. Making a split second choice the girl touches him again, this time ignoring his small movement. "Get up. Come on," she whines, trying the baby voice that sometimes worked on Daddy when she wanted to get her way.

But it doesn't work, and the noise from Mommy's room is getting even louder and she's going to be so mad if she comes back and the girl's still here so she just quits thinking and jumps up, kicking the boy, hard, in the chest.

That makes him move a little more, but he doesn't make even a little noise. Good, thinks the girl, and whispers at him again to get up. He doesn't look like he will, but when she picks her foot up again he finally rolls over and, keeping one of his arms off the ground, gets himself into a good crawling position.

After a lot of pushing, pulling, lifting, and threatening the girl manages to get the boy far enough into his room to close the door. She can't get him up on the bed, she's too little, but at least maybe Mommy will stop being mad sooner if he isn't still lying there when she comes back. She leans against the wall, as far from the boy as she can get, and tries to catch her breath. From here she can see his face, and on it she sees that he was crying. Either Mommy made him cry or her, while she was getting him up the stairs. She hopes Mommy.

The little girl doesn't have many words for her thoughts as she watches him, but the boy does, and his are fairly similar. He wonders if the girl remembers all the things he used to say to her, or the things he did, like knock her down or pull her hair to make her cry when he was angry at their father. He wonders if she remembers him heating up her bottles because she wouldn't drink them cold, or dropping her in her crib when Mom and David fought so she wouldn't have to see. Most likely she only remembers the worst stuff and nothing from *when she was a baby, he guesses, because she never likes it when he talks to her or gets too close.*

Except for this time. He looks at her closely again.

"You okay?" She whispers, like she hadn't just kicked him up a flight of stairs and shoved him into his room.

He opens his mouth, but then his eyes go wide and when he tries to shake his head the pain just makes him start sobbing all over again. When he glances back at her she is giving him a strange look. He thinks she might be standing a little closer, too. Not knowing why, he starts to lift a hand in her direction.

"Okay, bye." The girl looks away, speaking very quickly. She has to pee bad, and now she remembers she was supposed to finish her nap. She skirts around his open hand and is gone a moment later, leaving the boy staring after her.

Eventually he looks down, and the stray hand comes back to wrap itself tightly around him.

collateral.

chapter 18.

WAS it excitement or nervousness? On the one hand, perhaps it was the prospect of finally moving on that had tied his stomach into a knot so tight he worried about it pinching apart, his heart and brain racing almost too fast for his body to keep up. The feeling was not totally unpleasant, although he kept nearly tripping over his own feet and tumbling down to the next landing. On the other hand . . .

He stifled a series of coughs that would only have further irritated his burning throat. Resisted the urge to swipe at watering eyes.

Nerves would make more than a little sense, too.

At least the abrupt end of the former Drophouse—easier to name now that it would soon be less than a memory—hadn't come as a total surprise. Di had understood from the beginning that being known for disregarding even the criteria of the other criminals that protected it meant the Drophouse had little chance of ending well.

Not that this was a particularly *ordinary* method of shutting down. *It could be worse.*

No kidding.

He might be the one fleeing it, but at least this furnace was not meant for him; he wasn't important enough for that.

Di was a good employer, and Peter knew this firsthand (a complicated story, starting when he considered himself lucky not to be kicked off his Booker Park bench at night and ending with a substantial investment account she'd started with his past earnings). But she was a reckless businesswoman, especially when her heart was in the right place.

Of course he could never be ashamed of the work they'd done, re-uniting lost children with parents who had come to this country to provide for them only to be told, once they'd "paid their debts," that their son or daughter was lost, or had died. He had even made his peace sharing the hotel with merchandise she had . . . imported along with the live cargo.

But powerful people made powerful enemies. Which, in this case, would be lucky for him.

As long as he got out of here alive.

"Put. Me. Down."

Peter lost his balance, stumbling on the last landing. *So close.* He didn't answer.

"Put me down, *now!*"

"No," was all he could say.

On his feet and running before he was even fully awake, he'd been halfway upstairs by the time he even thought about the emergency supplies he'd left behind. So while he barely escaped with a pair of shoes for himself, he had made time to stuff plenty into the spare bag he kept in Al's room while she hardly stirred—and then had pulled the blanket over her head and grabbed *her* as well. It was the opposite of an idea; he hadn't really been thinking at all. He'd been reacting.

He blinked hard and swallowed, resisting the urge to cough. *Almost there . . .*

Not there yet, though, and with Alana now fully awake and tensed to continue the fight, she felt even heavier than she was. By the time he reached the ground floor exit, it was only his forward momentum that carried them through door and into the sunny, if smoky, morning outside.

Al, with a yelp, was first to hit the ground. Peter crumpled and was working through a nightmarish fit of hacking coughs by the time his sister sprung back to her feet in a fit of a different sort.

"What the *hell* do you think . . ." His eyes were squeezed shut and wouldn't open, but when she fell silent he knew she'd finally seen it. "Peter. Hey. Pax? Are you okay?"

Not that again. It wasn't as cute as it sounded—when she was learning to read, Al had once mistaken the name Paxil for his on a bottle. Still, she sounded panicked and he tried to say he was fine, which only instigated another round of coughing.

A loud *crack* came from the burning building, and something landed on him a moment later. He started.

"Relax," Al said critically, pounding his back. Eventually the coughing subsided, and then Peter could open his eyes to watch the show.

The first three floors were completely engulfed in flames. Smoke poured from the building's upper levels, either through broken windows or random cracks in the structure itself. It had gone up so fast. That, or they had done an extremely thorough job. And the secluded escape and empty parking lot made it pretty clear who "they" were.

He tried to locate what for years had been his window, his room, always half-packed in case he had to leave in a hurry. He hadn't gotten a single box out, and now all of it—his clothes, his phone, every page he'd ever written—was literally going up in flames. And after all this time, he'd lost the letters, too.

All that was left were a few of his shirts and old class assignments that Al insisted she had to read. And he wouldn't even have those if his sister didn't amuse herself by raiding his things whenever she could.

Well, there's my silver lining, he thought, watching everything burn.

Alana was watching the flames too, her hand resting on his shoulder—but her gaze flicked from the building to her brother, up at the fire and then past him and away. Peter followed the pattern until he understood what she was doing, though if the door hadn't opened yet it certainly wouldn't now.

"Doc. We need Doc, but I don't see her."

Peter didn't know if she was more concerned for him or the doctor. But the way she looked at him suggested that it was a bad idea to chance another coughing spell by trying to answer out loud. Instead he pulled himself into a sitting position and lifted a finger in the direction of the jagged parking lot.

She followed his point, then shook her head. "No, she couldn't have gotten out yet, Peter, is she-?"

He shook his head emphatically two times, swallowed a cough and made an imprecise winding gesture.

She paused for a while. Finally she said, "Oh. She just—already—she just left?" Apparently, despite what she might have said, his sister really had cared for Doc—or at least liked her a little.

He coughed again to clear his throat. "She said,"—he choked a little on the words and had to take a break, but at least he sounded mostly like himself—"she said to tell you her name is Adelita."

Al nodded, thoughtful. Peter caught a ghost of a smile before she became sober again. "So, are you going to be okay without her?"

He nodded, grinning before he could stop himself.

"Don't laugh. You really scared me."

He grimaced. He hadn't meant to make fun of her, but he couldn't help being charmed when the girl he had practically raised showed a little of her own protective side—as long as it was only a little.

Of course, he didn't dare say that to her face. He cleared his throat. "Wasn't laugh-"

"And shut up! You're making it worse."

He gave her a withering look.

"*What?*"

Never mind. Shaking his head, Peter struggled to his feet. *Well, that's it, then. Show's over. So . . . where did I park?*

"Perfect," he muttered, casting around helplessly for the old Ford Aerostar that had been meant to carry much more than two people and a duffel bag. It was an ancient, beat-up van, and it wasn't much, wasn't even *his*, but it was something they would need if they were planning to get past the edge of the blacktop before the fire trucks showed up. Sense of urgency restored, he started off to search in earnest.

A moment later he was back. Al was still sitting there, arms wrapped around her knees as she watched the fire. Confused, he stuck one foot out, nudging the girl gently in the ribs.

Her face turned toward him, but Alana kept her gaze trained on the burning hotel. "So . . . I take it we can't stay here anymore," she turned away again, rested her chin on her knees, "can we?"

Oh. Peter found himself staring at the building with her. He hadn't considered this part from her point of view. Sure, he hated to lose all the things he'd kept there; he was even a little put out to find himself evicted so abruptly after almost two years. But this wasn't Al's head-quarters. She hadn't agreed to the condition that she could be forced, violently, to leave at any time. To her the Drophouse had been home, and she didn't seem prepared to say goodbye.

For a few minutes he watched with her and pictured it as she must have—the hallways at night, the one crumbling picnic table in the courtyard—and tried to imagine it that way, as something to be missed.

A crash sounded from inside. He gave up trying. To Alana: "Nah," he reached down and caught a handful of sunlit honey-colored hair, drawing her head back until she met his eyes, "but we can do better. Let's go."

For once, she didn't ask any questions.

chapter 19.

THE gas station was so empty it looked haunted in the dark, and the convenience store (Kwik-Mart, was the misspelling supposed to be charming?) was small, but lit—still open. He coasted in, *deep breath*, and opened the door. "*Don't, Al.*"

She snatched her hand from her own door handle, then shot him an irritated look. "There's no one here."

"Still." He couldn't know if there were cameras, and either way he would be less conspicuous on his own.

The van didn't look great, a few dings, blue paint hidden under a thick coat of grime, but it probably wouldn't attract attention here. There were three gas cans left in the back; the tank had been siphoned and the fourth one stolen, so he was filling up a little earlier than expected. Lifting the cans out and closing the hatch, he alternated between scanning the parking lot and watching the passenger door in case the passenger took off running into the night. Not that he couldn't understand the impulse.

Headlights blazed by. Peter ducked behind the car awkwardly, trying to watch the passer-by at the same time. The car was nearly out of sight. Still, from a distance, it looked a lot like the same long, beige sedan he'd seen two times this evening. Maybe he was just being paranoid, but his heart was pounding as he sidled away from the car.

Inside, he grabbed a few bottles of water and some junk food, unremarkably unwholesome road-trip fare. The drowsy-looking young cashier eyed him as he approached the register—Peter needed to look calm, but he was suddenly moving through a deepening tunnel that tilted around him, and it was getting warmer and now his hand was shaking, barely holding onto a rattling bag of chips and the air was turning thick but *don't say you can't breathe, you're fine, don't say it don't even* think *it-*

He didn't remember holding anything out, but the cashier took his money without comment and handed back a full paper sack. Peter nodded and did his best to walk all the way back to the van.

This had been a long day, but the night amplified things. He heard an engine idling in the dark and watched for the lights again—but none appeared.

The pumps were more modern than the rest of the Kwik-Mart, the drone of GoTV News washing over him as he filled the tank and cans. Al was still in the car. Already, she was getting restless. Maybe it was best not to say how much time they had ahead of them.

Not that he knew, either, not yet. There was only one safe place for them, but he couldn't go there now. The people who had ordered the Drophouse burned had been going after Di, and for now he was still too easy to trace back to her. They'd made a plan for this. But the (ironically named) burner had been stolen as well, and without a phone he was stranded.

The second can was almost full. He started loading up again, but he must have been listening for longer than he thought because when he turned back his eyes flew directly to the little screen.

It showed a building on fire. Not the oversized tinderbox he barely escaped this morning; this was smaller, its shape obscured by a column of smoke.

". . . none of the part-time residences were occupied at the time. However, authorities have not yet reached the owner of the three properties . . ."

That was it, what he'd barely heard before. Owner. One owner, four homes. Three of which were now on fire, just like the Drophouse. Arson to make a point.

Peter climbed in again while Alana dug into the snacks. The thing was, Di didn't care much for vacation homes—there was no chance she would ever own three.

So she'd found out. And it looked like she was making a point of her own.

Which meant he knew what to do next.

chapter 20.

THE rest of the first night passed in relative quiet. Peter didn't mind; now that he knew the plan was basically intact he felt much calmer, and he wasn't uncomfortable with silence. Al was alternatively comatose or fidgety, and when she was awake he had to keep telling her to stay out of sight. In the confined, stale space he kept it together by scanning the road—not only for potential shadows now.

And, after his third northward trip along the Kentucky border, he found it. Some traffic barrels and cones left behind from a cleanup or construction project—he'd seen them before. But now they had been rearranged, two cones and a dingy orange barrel clustered away from the rest. A deceptively simple signal: there were three, and three was how many miles were left before he met up with Trevon.

"Is something wrong?"

Peter found the second mile marker and tilted his head momentarily, too focused to look over. "No. Why?"

"You're talking to yourself. I think. Either that or speak up," She said, formally, making fun of them both.

Of course I am. "Ignore me."

"And . . ." Al propped herself up on her elbows to verify, "you're slowing down. A lot."

Peter started to ask how *else* he was supposed to stop, but suddenly remembered forgetting and grimaced instead, asking himself if he had learned *nothing* from the other times he'd introduced a new person unexpectedly into his sister's very exclusive social circle (sure, Di still thought of their meeting as a funny story; Doc had practically gone into shock after her first encounter with the girl). Was it too late for damage control?

"Uh-um," he began inadequately, pulling onto the shoulder at the last marker, "we . . ."—he cast around for signs of the mechanic, saw none—"are meeting someone. Okay?" he finished slowly, a trick to keep himself from tripping over syllables even when he was on edge.

She was immediately on her guard. "What? *Now?* Why? Do you know this-"

Peter cut her off. She had covered most of the five W's; perhaps he could introduce some sanity before *where* and *how*. He was too hasty this time. "Yes. Now. L-loo . . . look, just don't-"

It was his turn to be interrupted; a car horn suddenly blared behind them, close and loud enough to send the siblings out of their seats momentarily, testing the old van's seatbelts (Peter's failed, and he caught the edge of the doorframe).

A bronze Mazda minivan had pulled up behind them. It was bulky still but sleeker than their own, with a luggage rack on top—another mockery of Peter's botched plan to escape with more than just their lives and the one bag. Leaving a still-panicked Al asking what, don't *what?* he grabbed it and massaged his bruised forehead, stepping out of the Ford at the same time as another man, with close-cropped hair and a dark gray jean jacket, leapt from the Mazda.

"Tray!"

"Hey, man," came the response, warm enough considering he had next to no clue what was going on. Trevon—Tray, for short—had lent Peter the Aerostar about a year back, in exchange for a promise that if he could swap it back again at some point he would make it worth the mechanic's while.

They chatted good-naturedly for a minute, trying in the awkward way old friends do to find the things about each other that have con-cretely changed or stayed exactly the same without asking too many questions or embarrassing themselves with long-winded answers. It was harder than it should have been. Tray had been, and remained, a man of relatively few words—depending on who he was compared to, of course. More than anything, this was why the two had become friends back when Peter was making his way through West Virginia and took it into his mind to attend college whether he'd been accepted or not. His grades had been good enough. It wasn't right for his edu-cation to suffer simply because he was unable to provide things like transcripts, or proof of identity . . .

Tray's path to the tiny community college where they met was un-usual in its own right. He'd grown up with a pre-determined future: his great-grandparents' garage, handed down through the genera-tions, which Tray was next in line to run. Knowledgeable about cars and good with his hands, Tray was happy to oblige. But he did not see why he shouldn't be able to broaden his horizons a little in what he al-ways referred to as "the meantime."

"So I just said to 'em, man," he would say as he copied notes after a day's absence working on a motorcycle or sedan, "you know I have your back in the shop. I'm always here for the big jobs, right? But I de-serve my own life, you know, in the meantime." And he would look up at Peter, who would nod, and then go back to writing.

Still, despite their proximity and due in large part to their simi-lar personalities, Peter and Tray never learned very much about each other. The short, polite questions about families had been met—on both sides—with little more than stony silence at first. Tray, the more talkative of the two, was first to open up, starting with his family's shop and even sharing details about some friction with a grandmother following his then-recent coming out. Still, he had been quietly ac-cepting of Peter's own unwillingness to utter a word on the subject. So when Trevon startled Peter out of another long silence with "Hey,

Petey, man this really *is* like old times, isn't it?" Peter's smile and laugh were genuine even though he hated that nickname.

Sentimental or not, though, he couldn't enjoy this for long. With a warm handshake, Peter excused himself to take a closer look at the Mazda, tossing in the few belongings he and Al had left. He knew little about automobiles, though, and found himself simply walking around the minivan a couple of times afterward, nodding politely for his friend's benefit.

"So who's that?" Tray materialized at Peter's side, tilting his head toward the Aerostar.

Peter smiled again, feeling badly for leaving his sister alone in the car. *Maybe it will calm her down,* he reasoned tardily, then attempted to force the thought into the past. He tried to sound casual. "Oh yeah, she's a relative. She's . . . shy."

"I'll say, man. Not even a 'hi.' Hell, I even tried telling her I was about as gay's they come. Tough audience."

That was another thing about Tray. He wasn't just gay, he was gay as they came, or gay as hell, or sometimes gayer *than* Hell itself. He and Peter had only been classmates for one semester before Peter, spooked by one thing or another, moved on, so he'd never mustered the courage to ask the mechanic exactly how the scale worked.

Now did not seem like the time, either. Alana was still firmly planted in her seat when they got back to the Aerostar, glaring at Tray through the open window. Peter rolled his eyes. You would almost think she'd had the twenty-four hours *he* had—escaped a burning building, driven for tense hours in a cramped cage, lost nearly everything she owned—all on a couple short hours' sleep.

None of which is her fault.

No. It was his. Was that supposed to make him feel better?

As Tray made another futile effort to charm the girl by accusing her of "barking up the wrong tree," Peter glared back at his sister and tried to stifle a yawn. Tray lapsed into bemused silence.

"This," Peter spoke up, nearly adding her name. Suddenly the sunlight was harsh, hurting his eyes. He shaded them briefly with his hand. "Don't do *this*. Get out of the car."

Yes, maybe it came out a bit sharper than he meant, and no, nothing that had gone wrong yesterday was her fault. It was just so *bright* out here.

And for her part, after years of causing them Al was all but impervious to his bad moods. She climbed out and slunk away, moving quickly to the far side of the Mazda. Peter thanked her silently for remembering to stay out of sight and turned to the mechanic once again. "There's a key in an envelope underneath the floor mat on the second row," he began, then shrugged. "I don't know much about cars, you know that. But this really means a lot to me—to us-"

"You and the blonde over there, or the one who called me today?" Trevon replied, curiosity finally overcoming courtesy. He looked away immediately. "Not that I'm trying to get nosy or anything, man, it's just they're both pretty scary ladies, is all." And he laughed at his own joke, clearing Peter to ignore the question.

Peter smiled. It was true, and he said as much. But this needed to be explained precisely, or one of the scary ladies would have his head for it. "Well the person who called you knows more about these things than me. So I don't know exactly what it looks like, but I do know . . . she gave you the name, right?" The mechanic nodded, fascinated. Peter had insisted Di pull every complicated maneuver possible to keep Tray from putting himself at risk, becoming too involved. He was, or at least could have been, a friend, after all.

"Good. There's a number written in the envelope—an impound lot south of here. Get there as soon as you can, give them the name, and the car's yours once you put that key in the ignition. Okay?" This time they both nodded, one in agreement and the other for reassurance. "I don't know," he said again, "but I've heard it's rare."

Tray nodded. "She said to wish you a good long weekend."

"Is it the weekend?"

"Not yet."

"Ah. Good to know."

Tray grimaced a little and ran the tip of his tongue over his teeth. Closed his mouth, then did it again—almost, but not quite, biting his tongue.

Apparently it didn't work. "Look, man. I, uh, if this isn't something I should be asking you, you let me know. But . . . that girl over there. I've seen some stories on the news, in papers." He stopped.

Peter's heart stuttered and he didn't feel it start again. He just watched Tray, trying hard not to look panicked as the silence grew from awkward to terrifying. Just as the ground tilted Tray broke it again, with a sigh. "In the van. There's a cooler in the passenger seat. That's for you, didn't know if you'd been taking care of yourself in the meantime, you know, since I saw you last."

Peter smiled, partly from relief and partly at the familiar phrase, nodding his thanks. Tray, with the same strange look, nodded back, heading for the Aerostar. But a few steps from the van he turned. "Hey, man."

Peter clenched his jaw, looked over. "Yeah?"

"Just wondering if I need to be worried about you."

Peter glanced over his shoulder, making sure Al was still where she'd been standing fifteen seconds ago. She was checking up on him as well, and they met eyes for a second. She didn't gesture, didn't move, but he had the feeling she was asking a question nonetheless. He nodded, and she turned away again. "We're okay. Really."

Tray pointed at the van. "It's an MPV. Old-fashioned, but I rebuilt the engine myself. It'll run for a long time, and you'll blend in with the soccer-mom crowd no problem." Watching Alana again, he hesitated for a second longer, then shrugged. "You know, forget it. She don't look anything like that girl." He gave his old friend one more long look, climbed into the Aerostar and, with another startling honk, pulled back into the lazy late-morning traffic. Peter watched him disappear around a curve with an unexpected pang. He hadn't made many friends, and he couldn't help worrying that he had just seen his first one for the last time.

Al was looking out over the drop-off. Her eyes narrowed as he walked up, and he couldn't blame her. This wasn't going smoothly for her so far.

"We should-"

"No."

"Seriously-"

"Shut up and go to sleep already."

He caught himself chewing on his lower lip and stopped.

"I mean it. You've been an asshole since yesterday, it's getting on my nerves." She flopped down onto the grass and leaned against the Mazda's front tire.

"Language, Alana." But she had a point, and even an hour would make a world of difference, considering how far they had to go. Still . . . "I don't thi-"

"If you're worried about whoever you think is following us, I can keep watch."

Sometimes he didn't give her enough credit; of course she'd noticed. But he doubted Al fully understood the situation. "There could be-"

"Then I'll stay out of sight and keep watch."

He closed his eyes and took one deep breath, then another. "I don't think so, Al. We need to keep going." Then again, the far-too-recognizable Aerostar wasn't a problem anymore. And Di's message about the weekend . . . Well, he couldn't wait that long to get some sleep, and the mulish look on his sister's face said it might as well be now.

"I'm not moving."

He was already climbing through the open rear door, so he spoke at the same time. "Stay behind the van, there's food, it's in . . . in the front. Be . . ."

He was asleep before he could say the rest.

A rustling sound startled him awake, too soon, as Al fished a jacket from the duffel bag. The wind was picking up, and through the open door at his feet Peter saw no sun, only large, gray-white clouds that had drifted in while he slept. He'd been having a strange dream, but he couldn't quite remember it.

Al was sitting in the grass a few yards away. He dropped heavily next to her, enjoying the chilly breeze, the blowing leaves. It seemed worth commenting on, but his sputtering train of thought was interrupted before he could say anything.

"Only a couple hours. Ish. Still tired?"

He shook his head, twice, grinding the heel of one hand into his eye.

"Sure?"

He rested his forehead in the same hand, shaking his head once more.

"Then can I ask you something?"

He grunted more than encouraged.

"I guess I was just wondering."

Still looking down, "About?"

There was a pause, and then the answer came rapid-fire. "Jack. The cat? I was wondering what happened, you know, to him."

Peter gave his sister a long look. *Sure, you were.* He wondered how long it would be before she said what was *really* on her mind.

Still, the world started sharpening into reluctant focus. He hadn't thought about Jack in a while.

"Jack was gone before I left. He liked me and all, but I never gave him much more than a scrap of food every now and again. He probably found someone who fed him better and moved on."

It was the first thing that came to mind, but it wasn't true. The cat *was* gone—he had been since just before Peter permanently moved out of Booker Memorial Park. Jack was good company; he followed Peter everywhere and was actually the first "person" to hear him speak without stuttering for over seven years, present company excluded, of course. Jack only left his side when Peter had settled in for the night, but always returned to his preferred spot on Peter's chest or back by morning. He was street-smart and independent by nature, so Peter never fully understood why Jack chose to spend all of his free time with any human—particularly one who had never been especially fond of cats.

Peter didn't tell his sister the sad truth, whether out of consideration for her feelings or his, he did not know.

One early morning he woke with the cat weighing oddly on his chest. It was par for the course with this particular roommate, and normally when he would shift or roll over during the night the cat would leap to the ground, reproving him noisily until both of them got comfortable again. This time, still half asleep, he rubbed his eyes and sat up.

The cat slid to the ground in a heap, leaving a large, gluey, rapidly chilling slick down the front of Peter's shirt.

It had been a dog, probably, or a coyote. Bites and tears covering the cat's body from head to awkwardly twisted tail proved it was some larger animal. Jack was torn to shreds—he must have been attacked at least a hundred yards away, must have fought hard for there to be any of him left at all. And still, he came back.

This was the part Peter could not understand. Why? Had he come looking for help? The cat had not made a sound; Peter, ever the light sleeper, would have been on alert immediately. No. More likely Jack had predicted the inevitable after the fight, and had faced a question simple enough for any living creature to answer: Die alone, or with a friend?

Strangely, Peter had always felt . . . flattered somehow by Jack's decision, even honored.

But Al didn't need to know that.

"You don't look very awake. You know, if we need to keep going *I* could always drive . . ."

"Like hell you could," he grinned, shook himself and climbed to somewhat steady feet. Al, smiling her unashamed smile, readily abandoned the brittle grass braid she was making to follow.

They went through the passenger door, one, then the other, to avoid being seen from the road. The MPV sprang to life with a discontented roar but turned back toward the thickening late-afternoon rush agreeably enough. Alana shoved her seat back and lay staring up at the ceiling, and while he waited for space to pull out onto the road, Peter was perplexed to find himself still thinking of Jack's winking, scarred face, his last choice. *Honored. By a cat.*

Unbelievable.

chapter 21.

"NOT to be materialistic, but if I'd known I was signing up to live in a van . . ." I muttered, mostly to myself but sort of hoping Peter was listening.

"What?" he called back, twisting in my direction without taking his eyes off the road.

"Nothing," I said more loudly, this time talking to him but not really caring if he heard. In my head I shot back something more scornful, kicking idly at the plastic-paneled wall, stretched out in the backseat. I wasn't getting much exercise. My muscles screamed for a run, even a light jog, even a long walk, and all I could do was kick the walls of the van, or the doors, or sometimes the ceiling, and wonder what my cabin fever was in comparison to claustrophobia.

It was going to be another boring night. A long one, too, if I was reading it right—we were both exhausted, but refusing to sleep for reasons of our own.

In my case, it was working. Though getting less sleep than normal was emphatically *not* helping the boredom situation, the nightmares were more important, and now that I wasn't running I was positive they would get worse again. There hadn't been any yet, whether it was the increasing tension of being on the move, or how tired I was, or they were just biding their time, I wasn't ready to learn.

Peter seemed to be doing okay too, considering the circumstances.

He was irritable at times (normal), always tired (normal), and extremely paranoid (normal). He had also suffered far fewer panic attacks than expected, only one after the first day, and I'd caught him
smiling oddly at nothing more than once. The last time I'd apparently
screwed up by asking what the smiling was about, factor Irritable At
Times had reared its head, and now here I was in the back seat of the
van, pretending not to still be angry at my brother for snapping at me
an hour ago. Aside from him driving, it could have been five years
ago, and I could have been ten. *Apparently some things always feel
exactly the same.*

It had been almost five days since the Drophouse burned. And
yes, some things did always feel the same: already, I had it filed away
with my first home, my tree, all the other things I would never see
again. Actually, in some ways the place had been more like home than
home ever had. Oddly enough I had genuinely felt, or thought I'd felt,
something like safe there—I mean, if safe is the ability to worry about
things you *don't* know instead of things you *do*.

Like that makes any sense.

It did to me. And so to me, what I felt there was safe.

That's what made the day so shitty. Not the fire itself—Peter was so
nonchalant about leaving, and Doc was gone before it started—not the
loss of the crumbling courtyard or most of my books, which were really my brother's anyway. It happened after I stood up and finally saw
what we'd escaped—flames slowly but steadily consuming my safe
place, Peter choking on the ground beside me. Everyone and everything, gone. I'd turned away and there it was: an inescapably bright,
cheerful sky, assaulting me with its cloudless blue warmth.

It may be trivial, but in stories when something awful happens the
weather has the decency to show a little solidarity. A blizzard, a sudden downpour, some cloud cover. At the very least it's night, and the
narrator gets to make note of it to prove there's a little order to the
universe because misery loves company or whatever.

So maybe, with everything that was going on, I was a little too sensitive to the apathetically pretty morning, perfect for an early run through a neighborhood park with a dog at your heel. Not too cold and not too warm, no haze mingling with the rising smoke. It just wasn't right.

It was harder to feel safe in the van, with Peter constantly on guard for . . . everyone, apparently, on our way to . . . somewhere, hopefully. I didn't even know where we were going, and so far I'd been too chicken to ask.

But I couldn't stop wondering, and during most of my ample staring-at-treetops time (or maybe because of it) I thought about nothing else. Peter had grabbed me a paperback at our last pit stop, and I was keeping a close eye on the rubber-banded stack of term papers that had survived the fire with us, but I was too tense to read. It put less stress on my brother for me to go with it so that's what I was trying to do, but with the days dragging on and no end in sight, five hours of sleep at a time and not even always at *night*, my legs begging me for a little exercise and the knowledge that the nightmares wouldn't hold out forever-

"Where are we going?"

Oh. Okay, then. Apparently I was done waiting. I started to scold myself but decided I didn't care and sat up, trying not to look too self-conscious (or eager, for that matter).

I should have expected it. The psychic's smile, the knowing glance in the rearview mirror, the smug tone. "That's been eating you alive, hasn't it?"

Should have, but didn't. So, instead, I was again treated to the exasperating feeling of being last across the finish line. I rolled my eyes, angry at both of us. "Only because you never bothered to say anything. Please tell me we're at least going *somewhere*. Not that I don't love the idea of wandering the continent aimlessly for the rest of my life, you know . . ."

"You're exaggerating."

"Brilliant deduction. See? *Now* I'm exaggerating."

"Jerk."

"Where are we going?"

"East."

"And *I'm* a jerk?"

"We're going to Di's. Eventually."

Oh. Well that definitely explained what all the grinning was about. My mind grappled with itself for a moment, weighing the inherent awkwardness of the idea against a morsel of relief at being amongst— well, even though she was only one, *sort* of amongst—friends. That last part was a little hard to admit, but there'd honestly been a moment when I was worried she was gone forever, too. "For how long?"

He hesitated. "That's . . . kind of a hard one, Al. I guess, until we're sure the whole thing's really blown over?" It was the kind of question that was phrased as a statement to be more reassuring. But the furrowed brow and halting speech didn't seem very sure.

"How will you know when it has?"

"That's what makes it a hard question."

Fair enough. "Fair enough. But what happens then?"

Another cryptic smile. But the only response was, "Don't get ahead of yourself, Al."

"What the hell is *that* supposed to mean?"

"It means you'll see." He had a particular talent for being just frustrating enough to make me stop asking without being informative enough that I could stop wondering.

I scrutinized the ceiling, eventually deciding he wasn't only pretending to have a plan. Still, for good measure I rolled clumsily off the seat and crept to the front of the van. Grabbing a package of beef jerky as a lame attempt at nonchalance, I studied my brother, and although he did not look over I could tell he was studying me back.

"Think you'll be okay with this?"

Excellent question. But weirdly enough it seemed like maybe there was more than a slight chance that *perhaps . . .* I might be. Okay. I mean, maybe not stellar or anything, and I couldn't promise I would be any less annoyed with her in her own home than I'd been in mine, but consider the facts. Di lived in an as yet Undisclosed Location—I was getting pretty familiar with that place—apparently well below her means. Rumor had it she had two kids, foster sons, one pretty close to my own age.

Peter had good reason to be worried. This did seem like the sort of thing that would usually spell disaster with me, which made *maybe okay* seem so extraordinary that I rebelled against it, panicking senselessly for just long enough that my next thought caught me off guard. *I wonder what it looks like.*

Well, it was *Di.* Most likely she would have a lot of expensive-looking things, the kind you only turned over once in your hands while you heard their history, then never touched again, the kind of furniture that needed to be vacuumed every three days, or dusted every week, or laundered every month. Colors like royal purple or crimson or sea green, the kind that could be guessed even by the most uncultured people (or so I hoped). Probably pretty clean, not grimy or dusty at all, but lived in, a little clutter and some dishes in the sink most of the time because of the kids.

I'd always wondered what a lived-in feel actually felt like. Clutter made me paranoid, like someone might be hiding in it, watching me. A big inexplicable ditto for the lifeless, washed-out cleanness of my old house. I wondered if, then decided that Di's was the kind of place where stains had stories—a red spot on the countertop from a spilled soda, a few hairs caught in the carpet from the last time one of the kids had a friend over. A place you could leave a mark on, just something small that proved you'd been there, made it the kind of place I could go back to.

Isn't that why cats and dogs pee on things? I ignored myself.

I knew less about Di's sons themselves, but if I stuck with Peter and Di most of the time I (hopefully) wouldn't have to worry much about them. Of course the boys wouldn't know her as Di—not in her real life—they would call her Elizabeth, or Beth, or Liz or Mom and so would I, with the exception of the last one obviously.

A thought hit me like a ton of bricks, or a tidal wave, or an avalanche, or falling out of a window in the middle of the night. "Peter, I'm not going to have to change my name, am I?"

He hesitated, possibly because I hadn't answered his last question yet and I'd done that thing I do where my question sounded like a challenge. *Oh well.* "That one is entirely up to you, Al, but . . ." he said the words slowly, gently, like he'd just run my puppy over and was breaking the bad news. "Well, it wouldn't hurt to consider a nickname you could live with for the next three-ish years."

Good point. Three years wasn't such a long time, and my real name *was* a bit of a liability right now. I would only need the one name (unlike some people I could mention) but still, it seemed like a gigantic decision. If I decided to do it, anyway.

Glad for something to finally do, I rummaged through my mind, trying to imagine what kind of name a person would have—a character in one of my favorite books, for instance—who had no parents, and lived with her brother, and could ask personal favors of Elizabeth Karras, the famous multimillionaire.

6, 12

HE'S only been up for an hour, but he's tired of being alone. All the responsible stuff is done, he's raided the cabinets and fashioned the only thing he could find—a box of cornmeal—into a sort of porridge that looks like yellow mud in bowls. He had to use a match to light the stove, which was fun but not easy, so now they are out of matches along with pretty much everything else. They like milk in their oatmeal, and the yellow stuff is kind of like oatmeal, so it might not be very good. But there is sugar, so it's sweet, so she'll eat it. And it's there, so he will, too.

He thought he was in a good mood today, but he's grumbling quietly by the time he starts scrubbing out the pot. And it's only another minute before it's dried and put away and the only thing left to do is stare at the twin pillars of steam rising from the table and be lonely.

It's not fair. If she'd woken up first, she wouldn't still be sitting down here by herself—she wouldn't have made breakfast, either. She's too little to use the stove.

He waits another minute, and then one more, then heads upstairs. The hall clock is battery-operated, and it's only nine-thirty. Even so, he throws open the door to her room without knocking and pretends to be even more irritated than he actually is. "Are you planning to sleep all day?"

The girl squeezes her eyes shut even harder. Maybe he really *will let her sleep all day if she pretends he isn't there. And after a few more moments of pretending, she can't hear him anymore. It worked! Except that when she opens her eyes he's moved right up next to her. "Boo."*

She gasps, but then recovers enough to get mad right away. "No fair."

The boy smiles back anyway. She's always like this when she wakes up—and for the rest of the day, too. But conversation is still conversation even if it's with a cranky little kid. "C'mon. Breakfast."

Downstairs, they sit at the table and the boy raises the blinds on the window to let the sun in. The power went out a couple of days ago, but that's okay, the oven still works well enough and the refrigerator was easy to clean out—kind of fun, too, while it lasted.

"Can I put milk in this?" The girl uses her spoon to jab at the contents of her bowl.

The boy rolls his eyes and swallows his first bite. Not bad. "We don't have any, remember?"

She does now, so she tries to make it seem like she never forgot. "Yeah, I just meant if we did *have some, could I." Then she shrugs so he knows it doesn't matter, swallows a few fast bites, and hops down from her chair. "Thanks, I'm done."*

"No you're not," replies the boy, concerned. He doesn't know enough yet to distinguish his own dietary needs from those of a six-year-old girl. All he knows is that, while he gets hungrier and hungrier each day, she seems to be perfectly content with only a bite or two of food every couple of hours. He convinces her to take two more bites, but when he tries for another two she turns stubborn and before long he's by himself again, carefully pouring half of her leftovers into his bowl. No point wasting it.

The girl sits at the top of the stairs, watching the front door. The house is nice when it's calm like this. But it can't be this way all the time, and she knows why. The lights are out and so is the little clock beside her bed which she doesn't mind during the day but it gets creepy at night. And the kitchen is almost out of food. And what if something bad happens but Mommy can't tell them because the phone won't work? She has to leave sometimes, the girl knows that, because it drives her crazy being around them every day, but she's been gone this time for almost a week.

Eventually the boy comes up to sit by her, wrapping an arm around her shoulders. He doesn't bother to ask what's troubling her; he's been thinking about the same thing. "Don't worry, she'll be back before you know it. You'll see." He thinks for a moment longer and then, to reassure both of them, adds, "She's fine."

The girl buries her face in her knees so he won't see it. He would be mad at her if she told him maybe it isn't Mommy they should worry about.

After a couple hours the boy gets nervous and makes her wash the rest of her uneaten breakfast down the sink. The girl hopes that means he has another idea for dinner, but probably he just wants the bowl to be clean. He's always so worried about getting in trouble that he never seems to think about anything else. Especially at home or at school, when they're around other people. Sometimes when it's only the two of them he looks happy, and sometimes when she catches him sitting alone, like before the school bus comes. But mostly he's just jumpy, like he's waiting for something to happen. Like that time Mommy told him to make her a drink and by the time he came back with it she was asleep.

He was letting her do his long division problems before then, so the girl had come out quietly, to get away from all the numbers. He did something weird when she didn't wake up. But it was only weird because he didn't do anything at all, just kept standing there. She had to kind of squint her eyes to see—at first she thought Mom was telling him something she couldn't hear. And he looked like he couldn't really hear it either, because his head was kind of tilted and he was squinting too, like her. But he still wasn't moving after a long, long time, and Mommy was asleep so she didn't move either, so actually no one had moved at all until later the boy had kind of sniffed and wiped his face, and then covered Mommy with a blanket and poured her drink into the sink.

The girl guesses he must have been waiting for Mommy to wake up, or maybe to talk in her sleep like some people do. Whatever it was, it didn't happen then but it's not hard to tell he's going to keep waiting and waiting until it does.

When she comes back the sun is just starting to dip behind the trees in the backyard. It's pretty early to get dark, but the girl is having fun watching the mostly-bare branch shadows creep down the walls like a curtain when she hears keys in the lock. She lets out a giant relieved sigh and then sucks it all back in and the boy is at her door, motioning for her to follow to the top of the staircase where they can both watch Mommy stumble in, holding the side of her head like her hair might fall off. Maybe it will; usually Mommy's hair is dark and golden, like the chocolate candies wrapped in foil but not the regular ones, the gross ones with nuts. But now it's so dark it's more like the candy itself, and the girl wonders if it's a wig at the same time as she can't help thinking the chocolate hair looks kind of cool.

Their Mom looks around for a moment with that hand still on her head. Her hair is different, but the boy's more trained eye travels to her face first. There's a stain traveling up one side of her face that could either be a bruise or smeared makeup. Same for the grayish circles under her eyes. She painted her fingernails before she left, and those are still in nearly perfect condition—he chooses to take that as a good sign. Hopeful, he takes one step down, then turns and gives his sister a long look.

The girl hesitates, but finally tries. "Mommy." The lack of enthusiasm in her voice makes the boy spin around again and glare at her with a force that actually causes the girl to flinch. She starts again. "Hi!" But she already feels a lump working its way up her throat. It's like she's barely there at all. Sometimes home is loneliest when everyone's here.

Well, *she thinks in the quietest, most secret way she ever could,* everyone but Daddy.

Mom looks around for a little longer. When her gaze locks on the two children it muddies even more, like she sees what they are but isn't quite sure how they've gotten into her house. Then she smiles sheepishly. "Oh, hi, um . . . hi." Her hand is over her face, and she laughs into it. "Oh no. Wait. Wait. Wait there!" At first, thinking she's talking to herself, the boy continues down the stairs, but she is flapping her hand and her voice gets louder and louder as she runs away toward her room, so he quickly backtracks and does as she says.

The sound of water running in the back corner of the house is followed by such a long silence that he starts thinking maybe she forgot them and fell asleep. She did *look tired. He exchanges a few looks with the girl, who is as confused as he but much less patient and is beginning to squirm a bit. He pokes her lightly in the ribs and she jumps, then gives him a look of pure childish outrage and sticks out her tongue. He starts to grin a little, then wipes all expression from his face as Mom lurches back into the entryway, made up and in new clothes but looking no more refreshed than when she first came in. "So," she begins, smoothing down her new chocolate-brown hair with one hand, "what do you think?"*

The girl opens her mouth to answer that she likes it, because she does, but Mom is looking at the boy, not her, and he speaks up faster. "Really, really p . . . retty, M-mom," he struggles. The girl's head nods along, but she's chewing her lip.

Mom gives him a funny look that keeps getting funnier, and the girl holds her breath again. Then the look goes away and she grins at them. "Well, okay. Who wants McDonalds?" and then there are grins all around.

chapter 22.

I didn't need to wake up.

Obviously not. Because nothing was wrong.

The car hit some tiny thing in the road—not a bump or pothole exactly, more like somebody else's flattened possum—and I screwed my eyes even more tightly shut. To keep from waking up, that is.

Because there was no need to do that.

This is embarrassing. Just look around for one second and you can go back to sleep.

My breaths sounded strange—slow and loud, odd for a reason I couldn't place. My inner voice switched tactics.

Aw, did you have a bad dweam?

Even from myself, that was a low blow.

Whatever. Wake up.

No.

"I know you're awake."

Amazingly, I did not jump. The words were the only sound from the driver's side, which, it finally dawned on me, was why my breathing sounded odd. I was the only one doing it.

"Okay, keep your eyes closed. That's probably-" a slight pause, which my overloaded, *not-panicking* brain stretched like a rubber band . . . "better anyway. I need you to listen, though, because I have two things to tell you.

The first one is that I love you, because it's true and because you don't break promises to people you love. And I made you one, months ago, which I won't repeat because I don't think I ever actually meant to make it, and you remember everything I don't mean to say."

I tried not to smile, but couldn't hold it back and hold my eyes shut at the same time. So I smiled anyway. I thought I did remember, in a hazy way not a little tainted by fever and fear and pain, the same way a stray remembers a bit of lunchmeat offered to it on its first day at the pound, and I'd given it about as much thought. *No matter what happens I'm not going anywhere. Not this time.* That was what he meant.

He must have looked over. "Good. And you know I'd never . . . I mean nothing . . ." He let out a short frustrated groan. "Just remember I made that promise, and know I plan to keep it. Okay? I need you to say it."

"Okay." He was breathing now—somehow not reassuring. I turned toward him, cracked my eyes open, but apparently I'd had it right before.

"Not yet! I need *you* to promise *me* something."

"No."

"Listen."

"*No,*" I persisted, suddenly and absolutely sure something terrible was going to happen but thinking maybe, if I could stop this, prolong the part where I didn't know what . . .

"Just *shut up and listen!*" He shouted. "The Drophouse. It's gone, it never existed, and nothing needs to be said about it ever again. Not to anyone, not Di, not even me. Ever. Got it?"

Everything was intense and unfamiliar, and he was talking so *fast,* and suddenly I was inexplicably hesitant even to agree to something I'd sensed on my own, months ago. "Yeah."

"Promise."

"I promise." I hadn't realized how tightly I was curled in the seat; now my hand twitched and I knotted up even tighter. My back and

legs ached but I couldn't relax. The long silence grew, gained substance—I couldn't see it, but I felt it looming over me, more and more
threatening. Someone had to end it, so I mumbled the first thing that
crossed my mind. "I love you too."

And for a fraction of a second, I looked—windshield, side mirror,
window—just long enough to confirm the bad feeling I'd had all along.

They were all around the van. Another, more popular way of saying that: they had us surrounded. My brother and I were locked into
a convoy of police cars, all keeping pace as he slowed down, sped up,
then slowed again, inviting them to leave him behind.

I slammed back down into the seat and stared at the dash. A few
questions bubbled up in my mind. Maybe I asked them. If I did they
went unanswered, which was just as well since my brain had taken
the easy exit, simply packed up and dropped away though the floor-
board, letting me continue on at sixty miles an hour without any instructions for what to do should this kind of situation occur. I could
barely even turn my head, though my peripheral vision was filled with
a wild-eyed gaze that cut molten laser-tracks right though the asphalt
in front of us and shot over the horizon. Peter's brain had taken the
opposite route.

There almost seemed to be something clever in that, a joke to
lighten the mood. I was Scarecrow, it passed me by. Peter's hand was
there, too, on the wheel—was it closer than before? It occurred to me
that I should reach out and grab it. I didn't.

And those were the moments when there was still *hope*. Dim and
flickering, hope sat between us like we were trapped survivors of a car
crash, waiting to see what happened next. We might be okay. Maybe
they would get bored and leave us alone. Maybe they would decide
they'd found the wrong car-

When the first siren came on my brother made a loud sobbing
sound, then squeezed his eyes shut as the other three simultaneously
shrieked to life. After that I stopped looking at things. My eyelids,

suddenly heavy again, drooped on their own, my body resumed the slightly fetal posture of sleep, I breathed in and out, in and out . . .

"It's fine. It's fine, just . . . just don't say anything-" it started out controlled but Peter paused for some reason before he could finish, "-stupid, it'll be fine."

Which one of us was he talking to? I kept inhaling, exhaling— couldn't feel it but kept going nonetheless.

Finally, through the haze of a mild stress coma, I heard a knock on the far window.

Voice (male, seemingly enjoying itself): "Late to be out, isn't it?"

Peter (shockingly calm): "It is, a, a little. I was actually on my way home now."

Voice: "Still, looks like your . . . um . . ."

Peter: "M-my cousin . . . s-sir."

Voice (still amused): "Oh? Looks like your cousin there's had a pretty long night. She lives with you?"

Peter: "I'm, um. In, in, in t-town visiting my aunt."

Voice: "And figured you'd take your young cousin out 'til two in the morning on a school night?"

Peter: silence.

Voice: "Honestly, I'm surprised you didn't try taking off on us there. Wouldn't have made it far, but with a story like that it almost would of served you better, so you know."

Peter: silence.

Voice: "Call came out from a sweet old lady a little while ago. Said this car was missing off her lot. Probably only kids joyriding, but best to call it in, just in case. Not something I'd normally worry about, but imagine my surprise when the cameras caught more than just your plates!"

Peter: silence.

Voice (sounding bored): "Maryland State Police. Step out of the car."

This was apparently the cue for another, hopefully less talkative, officer to tap on my window. I didn't want to, and therefore did not, look up. The door opened anyway and I sat up, doing my best to look groggy and confused as another cop—a younger, baby-faced model this time—reached for me. "Hi there. Are you Alana Wilder?" He spoke to me like I was a frightened fucking five-year-old.

"No?" I asked, trying to be convincing in the role of Anyone But Myself, though I deserved an award for being able to answer at all. The chatty first cop repeated himself and I threw a glance at Peter, still staring through an open window at the officer. Slowly, he turned to face me, and of all the things I read in his expression by far the most disturbing was resignation. He stared at me like he was trying to commit me to memory and I stared at him like he was insane, shaking my head, because I could easily remember the last time I saw that look and he *was not* going to leave me again. Hands came from nowhere and tried to drag me away and I fought them, clinging to anything I could, and said no, no, no over and over because he'd *promised* and he was looking at me like he was already gone and I wasn't—I *was not*—going to let him leave me again.

Not again.

Peter looked as if he were about to speak; he stretched a hand toward me. And all of a sudden, somewhere under the din that was mostly me and the baby-faced cop talking over each other, there was another sound that instantly took priority: a low, metallic click.

"I think it'd be best for you to keep your hands to yourself, son."

Peter froze, arm out. My heart had stepped out to meet my brain.

The earth ground to a halt on its axis. For the second time that night, I was certain that as long as no one moved, this terrible moment would last forever and whatever was about to make it even worse would never get a chance to happen.

There was no air in my lungs but I still managed to make a high-pitched moaning sound for the two seconds it took for me to be pulled from the car and then wrench myself away from Baby-Face. I wasn't thinking any concrete thoughts, but my head was threatening to explode, free the silent screams that built and built on each other as I dashed around to the driver's side. But—like a true heroine—my brain reconsidered deserting me, finally caught up and slammed back into my skull, stopping me stock-still about a foot away from the aging officer who still held his revolver a couple of inches from the side of my brother's head.

What are you doing? Usually I'd prefer a course of action that involved . . . well, *action.* A lot of it, and fast. But I'd gone to the school assemblies, I'd read the horror stories and seen the short film, and I had something approaching an ounce of common sense—which right now was very clearly saying that guns and sudden movements did not mix well. So tackling Officer Friendly and taking the gun was out. Same for loud noises, so no screaming. At least not out loud—the noise in my mind had passed hysterical already.

Officer Friendly's lips were moving. Finally my legs made the executive decision, and I found myself slowly, slowly—more slowly than I'd ever imagined I *could* move until then—inching up to him. I caught a hitching breath that shocked me as much as a gunshot itself considering I hadn't realized I was crying and kept my voice low and quiet, but let it tremble as much as it wanted.

"Please," (*get the fuck away from my brother!*) "please don't-" (*you dare hurt him or I swear I will put the next bullet right between your eyes*) "-kill him?" I tried something new, choosing my words carefully, using my tears and obvious distress to my advantage. I could feel other pairs of eyes watching and tried to use those as well—hung my head and wrapped my arms around myself and even tried to cry a little harder, not giving a second's thought to how humiliating this all was because that's honestly just how good a person I am.

A millennium of moments ticked by before Officer Friendly finally lowered his gun. Then my brother was also pulled from the van and immediately treated to the traditional welcome of being slammed into the next nearest vehicle and handcuffed while one of the other cops explained that he was under arrest for kidnapping. There was no expression on his face at all.

"You have the right to remain silent . . ."

And he might. I hoped not, I really did. But something in the tone of his expression made me think my brother may not have overcome the old habit as completely as he said. That might not be a bad thing, though. They wouldn't know how to read my brother, only I could pull that off reliably. So the officers would need me close, at least, and they'd figure that out for themselves soon enough. I started to follow as two of them propelled Peter toward their shared vehicle but was cut off by Baby-Face and his partner—a pair no doubt assembled to put me at ease, the police-boy and a woman who could have been his mother—who told me in the same dumbed-down, infantile tone as before that I got to go with them now.

"No, I . . . um . . ." *Swing and a miss.* But if Peter was allowed to completely check out, a little mumbling on my part was fair, too. Instead of trying again I gestured vigorously toward my disappearing brother.

"No, honey, you don't have to go with him. Not anymore." The matronly cop gave me a pitying look and tried to place a guiding arm around me while Baby-Face, mimicking her concern, started to lead the way back to their squad car.

I shook her off and backed away; shouting (or maybe whining, I'm not sure) even more emphatically I stalked off down the shoulder, to the car that held my brother. They couldn't take him away from me. He was *mine.* He was my whole family, pretty much my only friend. He had practically raised me. No one else could help me sleep when I had nightmares. And he wouldn't protect himself, he never did—so he needed me, too. It wouldn't be right just to stand there and let him go.

Baby-Face and his mom caught up with me before I was halfway there. "It's okay, you're *safe* now." Either one of them could have said it as they grabbed my arms and started dragging me back to where I'd run from. I refused to move—or tried not to—fixing that car to the spot with my eyes, praying if I didn't look away, didn't blink, it wouldn't be able to move.

The engine rumbled to life. The lights flashed on. *Oh no, no, no, no* . . . I struggled to get to it as it began to roll away.

"Poor thing, I'm so sorry. But we all have to take our own cars to the station. We wouldn't put you in there with . . . him, honey."

Screw you. Original, I know. But the other thing she'd said was what eventually caught a flying fragment of my attention. Apparently they were taking us to a police station. Operative word: *us.* Why hadn't she said so?

I practically led the twosome past our blank and somewhat confused-looking van, let them load their unwilling cargo into the back of the cop car without any more resistance. The Boy Wonder and Grandma made a few over-the-shoulder appeals toward my seat as the car crept along. I pulled my knees into my chest and stared at nothing.

They might be lying. There was no car in front of the one I was in, but my brother's had left first and honestly, I could only see about ten feet ahead of me before the world went seriously blurry. The drive turned long.

I should have grabbed his hand. I didn't like thinking like this. He was not dead and there would be another chance. I just had to . . . to . . .

But that was the problem—I had no idea what to do. Normally I would look to Peter, but all I had to go on were the last words my brother said to me, along with the crippling notion of them being the last ones he ever would (of course not, *moron*). "Don't say anything stupid."

And what in hell did that even mean, anyway? Did he think we could talk ourselves out of this?

Somehow, that seems unlikely. I closed my eyes.

professionals.

chapter 23.

SOL sat extremely still. Sudden movements scared her, and they were having a hard enough time already.

Carrie, a young clerk from the day shift, stood nearby, doing her best to look both authoritative and encouraging. The only reason she'd been called in at all was because she was the only woman here near this girl's age, which they had thought might make her more comfortable. Something similar had been tried before, at the scene of the arrest. However, the girl had never shown the slightest preference for either the younger male officer or the more mature—not *older*, Sol knew better—woman.

And he could see now that combining the two elements was no more than another desperate, failed move. It was more obvious every minute that she wasn't comfortable with anyone.

Hell, though, what a sorry sight. Sol wondered what her favorite color might be. Purple, he figured, or yellow. Maybe one of those poetic colors like midnight blue. Colors for the carefree kid she should be, instead of the grass-stained gray shirt and sagging jeans that looked about as dejected as she did. His nose picked out the faint savory tang of smoke. Kids her age, that usually meant a bonfire. His gut said not this time.

Break over, Sol repeated his usual bland entreaty. "My name is

Solomon Lucass. I am a detective, and I am here to help you. But first, I would like to know your name. Can you tell me your first or last name?" He couldn't help using a toned-down version of the voice he used to ask the dogs if they wanted a cookie or to go outside: Go ahead, agree with me, good things will happen!

Her mouth opened sharply, and Sol leaned forward in his chair, ears pricked, but he was too late. As she bit down on her answer Sol saw a flash of something rush to hide behind her eyes before they resumed their former baleful, glazed stare. He knew what would come next—the closest thing to an answer she ever gave.

"I want to see my brother."

She said it every time, and it was the only thing she ever said, delivered in a near-whisper that always tugged at his heartstrings. Clearly the abductor had done a number on the poor girl if she still didn't feel safe even speaking to the people trying to protect her.

She was still helping herself and the detectives in a way, though. She asked to see her brother, *brother* specifically, which narrowed down the number of missing child cases to the one Cleveland police had given up on months ago. She could have been buried in the bureaucracy for days or even weeks, but her words—what few there were—had convinced them within hours that they were, in fact, looking at the missing teenaged daughter of Jaqueline Wilder, presumed kidnapped by a severely disturbed older brother.

The girl's refusal to leave the station where her brother was being held had helped, too—though even the sergeant had taken some convincing on that point. Having her here gave them more chances to speak with her, use her name, try to shape the beginnings of the bond she might otherwise form with some inexperienced or, worse, uncaring foster parent. Sure, Sol had been licensed himself, in case of emergency—but he'd been fortunate enough to avoid emergencies so far. Of course, once they knew she could understand what was going on they'd place her. But for now he would only ruin all this hard work if

he sent her away somewhere when she did not want to go, and hadn't
Alana had enough of that already?

He tried once more. "Just tell me, yes or no. Are you Alana Wilder?"
Alana didn't answer.

Sol stood, slowly, reminding himself that this wasn't her fault. As
he reached the door it came back at him like a strange echo. "I want
to see my brother." Alana choked on the words, barely forcing them
out, and his stomach turned in sympathy. He had to say something to
the poor kid.

"Maybe you can. How about you ask again when your Mom gets in,
she might even want to go with you." She didn't say anything else and
so, with a sad good-night smile for the lost girl, he motioned Carrie to
follow him out. But something had struck him, and as he headed for
his car and a morning full of the rest he'd missed out on last night, Sol
puzzled it out.

Years ago, Sol and Ashley—and Tania, her best friend who he joked
had plans to steal his wife right from under his nose—had gone away
together to Virginia Beach for the weekend (together in the sense that
all three of them had been there, though he supposed the girls would
barely have noticed if he'd floated away on a parasail). Never having
gotten around to kids of their own, he and Ashley compromised with
four of nature's absolute best alternative, and this time they'd left the
pack under the care of a neighborhood teen with instructions to feed
them, water them, and try to run them into a placid stupor by the time
their "parents" came home.

The sitter, all self-importance and good intentions, had taken the
job to heart and met her match in Milo, a six-months-old Border collie
mix with a passion for the chase. Neither Sol nor Ashley remembered
the whole story anymore—*Milo slipped his collar, or yanked his leash,
to chase a squirrel-rabbit-bird, and a big something-or-other came
barreling down the road and nearly took his nose right off!*

They did remember the battle over the next few months, persuading

Milo to go back and walk along that road again. It was exasperating, days and days of who's-a-good-boy and come-on-buddies, until finally Milo slunk along beside them, nervous but willing to try.

Every time, though, as soon as his stride lengthened from a creep to a comfortable lope, the inevitable happened: a car rushed by. And like a shot, Milo would slip his collar and take off racing for home. And the next time they pushed him to go back the puppy would hunker down again, ears pinned, licking his chops and using his eyes to tell his Mom and Dad how afraid he was of the big bad thing that didn't scare them at all.

Yes. That was it. Obviously, the body language wasn't the same—she couldn't exactly pin her ears. But when he said Alana might see her kidnapper once Jacqueline Wilder arrived, he imagined he'd caught that same look, finally a glimpse of what he knew she must be feeling.

chapter 24.

I made a mental note to add water to the list of things this place was starting to make me hate. Normally I enjoyed a long, scorching shower—perfect for a minute, or an hour, to rest and think, or hide. If I concentrated hard I could practically feel the steamy water at the Drophouse surrounding me like a garment. It *was* cold (my jacket was still in the van), but I was also sick of being watched all the time, so when Detective Grandma half-kindly suggested I take a "nice" shower I'd seized my chance.

But no, no warm draft-free robes of water here. The tepid water trickling down my legs actually felt more like taking an accidental piss in the woods on a chilly day.

You don't know how that feels, my thoughts accused.

"Yeah, I do. Like this." Even talking to myself, I was sullen. Two and a half days of not being able to speak to anyone was really wearing on my mood—how had Peter lived like this? *Although he didn't technically say not to* speak, *just not to say anything "stupid."*

Yes, but if someone could identify the "stupid" things to say, she wouldn't need the advice at all, now, would she? I'd come up with this argument about three hours ago and was using it on myself pretty much constantly, it being my only source of (fake) conversation and all. And anyway I was sort of talking, a little, even if it was just the same thing over and over.

But it was still hard. That long first night, shoved into a room with no one but the man who had nearly shot Peter and some living furniture in the form of a woman Di's age who might as well have had I'M A HUMAN ACCESSORY painted across her shirt, grilled for hours about my own *name*, was hardest. Detective Solomon Lucass—I should have known his name, he only said it about sixty times—suddenly reeking of sympathy and talking at me like he hadn't pointed a loaded gun at my brother (anybody really, it was a crappy thing to do) was worst. He acted like I was too stupid to comprehend simple English even though he pretended not to understand me *every time*; if anything broke my silence, it would be his greasy, condescending tone.

I swallowed a few mouthfuls of water, then shut it off and re-dressed in my same clothes without drying, one eye on the bathroom door in case any of my entourage decided to come "check" on me. When nobody did I decided to wait, drip-drying in the empty room and eavesdropping on the talk outside.

"-on the couches."

"Why not? She's the one under arrest now? It's not like she's a . . ."

"-don't know what he's been doing to her, she might try to hurt herself . . ."

Enough. I strode out of the empty locker room shoulder first, glaring at no one in particular, arms crossed awkwardly. This was the second time today I'd wished for long sleeves, but I couldn't ask about my jacket.

The conversation hushed immediately, like it always did when they talked about my brother around me. Maybe they felt guilty about the things they said.

Yeah. Sure.

After the probably-not-guilt wore off, though, the conversation picked up again, and by the time it died down I understood that they'd decided to find me a private place to sleep. It was probably supposed to be considerate, and I was probably supposed to give them credit for that. But there was one flaw in the idea—I was not sleeping any time soon. Being shuffled around so much, no more than one or two hours on each couch or desk or chair, was not the reason I was still awake. It was just helping me stay that way.

Still, I let them melodramatically lead me to a not-quite-private storage room far from the holding cells, where my brother was being kept. It was cluttered and dim. Old Officer Friendly asked if I was hungry or thirsty, then turned away when I told him for what had to be at least the hundredth time exactly what I wanted. Leaning back into a dark corner, I waited to be left alone, trying to hide the slowly growing awareness that the two men and old woman had me cornered and outnumbered in this small, dark space.

They were all looking at me. Actually one of them must have been talking, giving instructions or asking a question. *No, look normal, look normal.* I couldn't, felt myself flattening against the wall, melting back while they looked at me like they wanted something. One of the men stepped closer. *Shh, quiet, that's my good girl . . .*

What? I never talked to myself like that. Even so, I screwed my eyes shut and swore at whoever could hear to leave me alone. Every muscle tensed and relaxed in turn in a sort of full-body dry heave, and I held my breath, ready to vomit—but they were gone when I opened my eyes again.

So I was alone, crushing my fists against the side of my head until the unpleasant episode was mostly forgotten. Then I waited. It had been a rough few days; I was due for more tears.

They didn't come. My chest felt tight, and my throat ached—on the inside it still felt like I was screaming at the top of my lungs. But outwardly, I'd apparently passed the point of crying.

Fine. It wouldn't have helped anyway. I took a mental inventory: my brother was imprisoned somewhere I couldn't get to by people who, judging by how they talked, seemed to really hate him. I couldn't bring myself to eat anything and was terrified of falling asleep without him around. And, whether I said it or not, these people knew who I was. And that meant she was coming.

These were the things that were happening. Nothing I could do to fix them. But I couldn't stand here, screaming inside, saying nothing, barely even *thinking*—this was worse than doing nothing at all.

So, do something else. The thought made me feel calm for the first time in days. I hadn't *done* anything in a while.

The world stayed upside down, but spun a little slower. The closet was tiny and dim, but the walls (beneath the scuff marks) were a tan the single bulb turned gold. The piles and stacks of papers, former evidence and, apparently, recycling were cleared to form a path between the door and a cot, where some dry, warm-looking clothes waited for me. Quiet, cozy, and practical. The cops had done a decent job.

Hopefully, this was my last night here.

Still . . . it had been a long walk from the desks. If I *did* have a nightmare, there was little chance of anyone hearing me before I eventually woke myself up. No one to hear me scream, so to speak. And I was *so* tired, I probably wouldn't dream anyway.

Just a couple hours, I thought, heading for the cot.

Just a couple hours, and I'll be ready to figure out what I'm getting ready to do.

Every ten minutes or so Peter opened his eyes for exactly one second. Checking whether the walls had receded or the door magically opened, he supposed. Just because it hadn't happened yet didn't mean it never would.

His palms meandered over the cold metal table, finding Room 3's telltale groove with a thumb like last time and the time before that. He was actually starting to enjoy coming here. There was nothing to do in his own personal Hell, the cinderblock cell where he spent most of his time. Room 3 might only be one cramped space swapped for another, but at least it was variety.

He'd been waiting for some time, but someone would come soon. It was an interrogation room, after all, and cops didn't waste their own time. Soon, one of the few he saw most often would stomp in and face him across the table. And then he'd have a chance to ask his questions or answer theirs. Which had not gone well so far, no. But it would this time. He'd spent years trying to avoid this possible outcome, but also preparing for it. And tired and scared as he was, he still knew how to handle this.

The only thing left was to unfreeze his throat, activate his tongue, and actually *do* what had seemed so easy back when he had the freedom to walk away.

Someone was approaching. Peter opened his eyes, sitting taller. *Just start with something simple, like "okay." "Okay." It's easy.*

This detective was new to him. Peter knew the trigger-happy one who had nearly given him a heart attack, he knew Vargas, he knew McCowan. This one was new, and in a rush. Stepping into the room, he shoved the second chair aside and slammed his hands onto the table, inches from where Peter's had been moments before.

The chair overturned, clattered to the floor. Peter watched it and stood slowly. *Scare tactics,* he reminded himself. Though this was a new one.

He stared down and was stared down by the new officer for a couple of seconds. "So. Here's the big man."

Okay . . .

"I was expecting a little more." He started around the table. "I've got a cousin in grade school—she's about your size."

Peter tried to hold his ground.

"No matter, though, I still have the honor of a little one-on-one with the celebrity."

That does not sound good. The door was off to one side. If he was fast enough-

The officer saw where he was looking and moved, blocking his path. "You're not getting edgy from a little taste of your own medicine, are you?" A muscle near his jaw bunched and relaxed in time with the next two steps. "Tough shit. Until this little pact you've got going with that girl ends I'm your new best friend. *You* can die without saying another word, for all I care, but you're letting her out of it."

Peter had controlled the impulse long enough—he took two steps backward, wondering if his confusion showed on his face. *You're making no sense. What do you mean, pact?*

Oh. Wait—he remembered thinking something over and over, right before they pulled him out of the car, trying to keep himself calm. *It's fine, just don't say anything stupid, don't say anything stupid, everything will be fine . . .*

He didn't *think* he'd said that out loud.

The officer seized the small triumph, advancing faster. "You hear me? I hope so, but I'm not convinced."

Peter tried to move back again, but collided with the concrete wall almost immediately.

Scare tactics. Right.

He took it back, shutting his eyes as the officer moved again, closing the gap, and the wall stubbornly refused to move any further away.

Variety could screw itself; he would kill to be back in his cell.

chapter 25.

IT wasn't late enough to be sure everyone was back in their cell (or closet-slash-room, in my case) for the night. I skulked around another corner, working on my mental map of the station. Finding Peter would have to wait.

I hadn't slept for as long as I'd wanted. This part was going more according to plan, but then maybe that was only because the "plan" was vague at best: find the exits, find my brother. Figure it out from there.

Better than no plan at all. That was true enough. And it was easier than I'd expected—either I was free to roam as I pleased, or the police here made ironically terrible guards. I barely saw anyone in the hallways at all, and since I was making sure no one saw me my mapping project was coming along nicely. In my mind the station was a sort of three-sided horseshoe, the holding cells furthest from the main entrance and sealed off by large metal doors that looked heavy, but did not have a lock. The opposite side of the horseshoe, the entry, held lots of breakrooms, bathrooms, couches and storage. That's where my roomcloset was, too far from the cells to sneak all the way there and back to the front door and therefore completely worthless. I needed an escape route that covered less distance.

Interrogation rooms and offices lined the middle of the horseshoe, the double-wide, divided hallway that connected the other two. This was probably my best bet. Counting doors, I passed the offices, each with a hall-view window exactly like the interrogation room windows, though the blinds added some extra dignity.

But there were so many doors. It would be too easy to get trapped in a dead-end, like the basement, for instance, or any of the interrogation rooms—which I was passing now-

I stopped in my tracks when I saw him. The top of his head, at least. He was taking a first-grade style siesta on a big metal table and I nearly shouted; by dumb luck, I had managed to stumble, unsupervised, across my brother while he was also alone. And it was unlocked! The dopey smile couldn't have been slapped from my face as I skipped in, past an overturned chair, and waited with a child's dramatic flair for him to look up. Which, unfortunately, he did.

Peter is extremely claustrophobic, and shy, too, for all his talk about certain other people being bad with strangers. So it wasn't surprising if he didn't exactly look *good*—kind of pale, a little zombieish around the eyes. Not great, but to be expected.

This was worse than that. My joy immediately dissolved into hot, acid anger as I took in the bruised cheekbone, the bloodied nose. Peter watched me back, radiating anxiety but somehow managing to smile relief.

Well, you said you missed his old smile. Congratulations—there it is. I could've been remorseful but was paralyzed with rage instead, actually glaring across the table at my brother as if he'd done this to himself. Which of course he hadn't. I'd wanted to ask him something but in those seconds it was lost, buried under a rockslide of sadness, confusion and the requisite protective surge anyone should feel when they see someone they care about looking the way my brother did right then.

Something startled him out of our staring match. He looked up and away, but I didn't stop watching him until the moment he whispered

"Get behind the door."

He said it so quickly, and I was still so shocked, that I stepped back immediately. Lucky I did, because about a second later the door opened again. It neatly boxed me into the corner and bounced shut, showing me the back half of someone I'd last seen a few hours ago, when he was speculating (practically to my face, even if he didn't know it) about me hurting myself. Unlike the Boy Wonder, Granny, and Officer Friendly, I had no nickname—or real name—for this one. I didn't see him much, and he hadn't made much of an impression. I'd certainly never noticed the pent-up-serial-killer vibe I heard when he spoke now.

"Make up your mind yet? I wouldn't mind ending this conversation right here, but we can always try again."

Peter threw a microsecond's glance my way. Then, almost unconsciously, he winced and shook his head at the man who I right away decided to call Bad Cop. The look said *lie*—that Bad Cop had made a mistake by telling the truth. I saw it, but to the untrained eye it could just as easily have meant *sorry, it's not happening.*

I didn't wait for Bad Cop to pick his favorite interpretation—I knew what I had to do already. The chair was still lying on the floor. I held my breath for exactly three seconds before stepping toward it. That was the only moment of hesitation I gave myself, so that by the time I lifted the chair by its thick back posts and made the last not-so-quiet move into the center of the room, my head was clear except for one word pulled from Bad Cop's own short speech, which my brain had somehow turned into a question.

Again?

chapter 26.

WITH the excitement of the past few days dying down, they were dropping like flies all around. The ones who could had already returned to their own homes and beds, children's plays and field days; the rest were settling for long naps in their cars and something hot, greasy and fast. It was funny, Sol thought, how getting back to normal could mean so many different things.

His old definition of normal was why he and Ashley had struck a deal just the week before: for every missed dinner, Sol would relieve his wife of one week of yard pick-up duty. Miraculously, he'd made it home for two of the past three nights. If he could finish up before six tonight—which looked hopeful—it would be three out of four.

Jingling his keys, Sol made a mental note to ask Ashley about adding a reward system into the bargain.

He hadn't even opened the caryard door when a sharp *crack* sounded from down the hall. With a bad feeling and a clairvoyant apology to Ashley, Sol turned back. He hadn't realized how unstaffed this relaxed atmosphere had left them.

Quick for his age, Sol followed the noise and was in Interview 3 in a flash. Though his eyes flew straight to the kidnapper, who looked a little more banged-up than this morning, the criminal was only just rising from his seat.

What in hell was going on?

The din was growing; the few folks left on-duty came running up, but all, like Solomon, froze just before they went inside. In front of them was an impossible scene, and he expected they were still watching the criminal, not truly seeing it yet.

Felix Daniels—good enough guy, but clearly watched too many cop dramas—was curled on the floor, arms up over his ears. Perched on the fallen man, one knee on either shoulder, was the girl whose favorite color was probably purple or midnight blue. Her right hand moved like a piston, pummeling Daniels' face and neck forcefully and tirelessly. She was shouting, a blow punctuating each word, but Sol only caught a few.

"Go . . . near . . . my . . ."

It was not what he'd have expected to hear. Even less did he expect the kidnapper to cut in, shouting at her to stop until finally he lifted the girl bodily away from Daniels, dragged her away, and jammed her against the far wall, still kicking and swearing like a sailor.

Not good. Now they had gotten themselves shocked into a tight spot. Not only had the kidnapper placed himself between them and the girl, but they had been specifically warned not to allow him ever to communicate with her. And now he was gripping the girl's shoulders, leaning down and speaking quietly into her ear before anyone could think how to get her away. This could go badly.

But she barely seemed to hear him. Daniels had regained his feet to join the rest of the gawkers, and the sight of her prey in motion started the girl shrieking around her captor at top volume again, doubling her efforts to free herself.

"If you touch him again, I swear I will-"

Strange, mused Sol. He never would have thought of the girl as a predator before.

The kid had started making a strange guttural noise reminiscent of Milo when he thought he was in danger of losing a prime chew-toy when, out of nowhere, abductor and abductee, wanted criminal and lost girl, were hugging, embracing just like a brother and sister. Sol's cop side sounded the alarm. Jacqueline Wilder had barely made time to be relieved over the phone before warning them about her son.

He was a somewhat sickly and difficult boy who had grown into a disturbed and dangerous man. He said little, but was extremely manipulative—in his youth he'd amused himself by turning his baby sister against her mother, isolating her in a cycle of abuse that had ended only when Jacqueline finally kicked him out of the family home at seventeen.

The cop in him wanted to heed that warning. But Sol's other side—the one he liked to think was pure Ashley after all their years together—was starting to wonder how hard it must be to break the will of a girl who attacked trained police officers three times her size.

Either way, the situation had gone from shocking to stalemate. The patrol officers and Sol's new partner Jude McCowan hovered near the threshold, exchanging looks, frowns, and shakes of the head as they assessed how impossible it was to extract the girl without risking an ugly scene like the one at the arrest. Drawing a loaded weapon on a violent criminal was one thing. No one was willing to take chances with a child at the other end of the barrel.

But Sol hadn't been a detective for fifteen years without learning a little about stalemates—and the value of faking what you didn't know. He gambled, turning to his workmates. "All right, fellas. Why don't you go on and give us some space while I straighten this out." As the arresting officer, Sol had dedicated the most time to this case. It might as well be him, then, who resolved this strange standoff.

Alana first. He put out a hand and edged forward. "Sweetheart, how about you walk toward me now," he tried.

The girl's lips tightened over her teeth as though pulled by a drawstring. She stayed put.

This couldn't go sideways on him. He spoke to both Wilders next time. "All right," he repeated, floundering, "I'm going to have my friends leave us alone so we can talk just the three of us, okay?"

The crowd had mostly dissipated when he turned back. Daniels remained, but with a look and a nod from Sol he, too, departed. Sol made a mental note to try that again next time the other man was getting full of himself.

Finally the three of them stood sizing each other up in the interrogation room. Hoping it was the right move, Sol righted the overturned chair and set himself up at the table. "Why don't we all have a seat?"

The wheels kept spinning while he waited. What now? Somehow he had to get the girl out of here, put the prisoner back in his cell, and try to figure out why he'd been out in the first place—that was what everyone would expect when Sol walked out of this room.

On the other hand . . . the girl who refused to admit she was Alana Wilder had finally gotten what she asked for, and now they'd heard more out of them both in five minutes than the previous three days combined. And as far as what he needed to accomplish, he didn't exactly have any time limit, did he?

By the time the girl had cautiously seated herself—on the radiator beneath the window instead of the chair—Solomon had an idea. He just hoped he wasn't next to wind up on the floor.

It took a stern repetition to get the other one to the table, and then he took a friendlier tone. "That's better. Now, so you know, I'm-"

"Solomon Lucass, the detective who's here to help me." The girl interrupted him with a bored paraphrase of the greeting he'd extended so many times. "But you want something first."

The kidnapper glanced from her to Sol, silent.

This was surprising, but any talking was better than none. "Well, actually-"

"Before you help me, you want to know my name. Because you're really only here to help me if my name is Alana Wilder, and fine, it is. I'm Alana Wilder, not that you didn't know already, and it'd be *helpful* if you stopped talking to me like I'm stupid." She looked like she would keep going, but instead exchanged a look with her brother and shook her head. The silence returned.

She was already overwhelmed, and she'd just begun to cooperate. Maybe he should focus on the other one, the inmate, who seemed to have trouble maintaining eye contact. Not surprising. "And you?" He couldn't help if some contempt showed through, but it was definitely not his job to aid a criminal in any way—that would be left to whatever sap public defender drew the short straw. He was curious, though, about what the silent man had to say.

He said nothing.

"I know you have a right to remain silent, son, but it's in your best interest to defend yourself some. You're looking at an awful lot of prison time here."

The other man stopped chewing his lip, opened his mouth . . . and closed it again, looking almost apologetic. Turning toward Alana, he gave her a second's glance.

She started up again. "This is Peter. He's my brother, which you also know. And he won't talk because he's afraid of you."

The younger man's eyes widened and he wrenched around. "*Hey.*"

Not much of a contribution, but it was something.

Alana all but ignored him. "What? Shouldn't he be? I mean, person-ally, I just don't like you. But then, you didn't aim a gun at *my* head."

Sol didn't want to engage in any kind of combat with a teenage girl—about half the reason why he was pretty content without human children—but something made him defend himself. "To be fair, young lady, I was concerned for your safety at the time."

The girl glared. "And why exactly was that?"

Sol was incredulous. "Aside from the fact that this deranged man kidnapped you half a year ago, and for most of that time you were pre-sumed dead?" This was crazy. He had never meant to say anything so frank to the poor kid. There was just something about her that made him forget to hold back. He softened his tone. "What about that big scar on your arm?"

All expression disappeared from Alana's face. She squeezed her right hand into a fist and tucked it further into the sweater they had given her, but it was no use. Of course they had noticed the network of scars crissing and crossing the otherwise youthfully smooth skin of her wrists, and that one was newer and more jagged than the rest.

"De-dera-, um, deranged is a kind of, a, kind of s-strong word." The kidnapper had spoken up at last, and Sol was less surprised at the words themselves than the quiet, measured tone in which they were offered. He seemed to wait for Sol's full attention. "I think I mi . . . uh, I might know where you heard that. Bu-but it's not true. And-and-and I did not do *that*."

He spoke slowly, apparently to keep his stuttering under control. Mrs. Wilder had never mentioned a speech impediment, though—he might be faking it for sympathy.

Looked like the girl's turn to clam up. And though she did briefly agree with the kidnapper, it lacked the vehemence of anything else she'd said so far.

Something was off. Solomon wasn't falling for this new twist in the story, and said as much. The criminal looked concerned, opening his mouth to no doubt make another labored argument, but a hand fell on his shoulder as Alana, again, interjected.

To him: "Wait a minute." To Sol: "I want to get something clear before it's too late." Her gaze was shrewd, yet cautious, and did not waver. "I don't talk unless he's with me." The possessive grip made it abundantly clear who she meant.

Now Sol went blank, wracking his brain for the diplomatic way to tell her that couldn't happen. The reasons were obvious, even if the police department did intend to build a reputation for acquiescing to the demands of teenagers.

"Same for me." Again that slow, quiet voice—if Sol hadn't been here only moments ago, he would have sworn this bastard was dead calm.

He couldn't resist poking a hole in Wilder's undeserved confidence. "Believe me, we don't need to hear your story to see you spend the next quarter of a century behind bars."

"Oh believe *me*, you'll want it." Alana spoke with authority far beyond her years. She could have been his wife's age, where a moment ago she'd been a snotty grade-schooler.

Of course Ashley would say, "You can't find the nugget of truth if you only hear one side." She thought *any* story was worth hearing— even a fake one.

Sol figured she wanted life to be more like her favorite crime dramas. But in this case, something stuck. So, although even having this conversation meant bending the rules nearly beyond recognition, Sol nibbled at the bait. "Hm. So say I were to agree to your terms-" he bowed his head with ironic deference to the young negotiator "-and I'm not saying I will, or even could if I wanted to. But if I did agree, what reason can you give me to believe your story is anything but some lie *he* concocted-" a less deferential nod to the chair opposite him "-to keep himself out of prison?"

There was a momentary pause. The kidnapper shot his sister another look. She was still watching Sol, mouth set in a grim but rather triumphant grin. "How could he do that? He could barely even tell you his name."

Now the brother turned all the way around in his seat to look up at the girl and gave two very deliberate shakes of his head (everything about this guy seemed unusually deliberate when you paid attention).

Alana watched him coldly. "She's on her way, you know. What do you think she'll do when she finds out who you've been talking to?"

Nothing much happened. "Look, Miss, I don't know what-"

"All this to avoid her, and it *failed*," the girl spat, "what do you think happens to you now? Well? You're supposed to be telling *me* what to say. Say something!"

The kidnapper turned and stared past Sol, silent. This time, nothing the detective said could get his attention again.

When Alana spoke next it was not to her brother. "It's kind of an old habit. Easier than I thought, actually." She shrugged at the floor.

Sol caught the hint—he was meant to play a role in this little act. "What old habit, exactly?"

She almost looked grateful.

"Well, when my dad left, Mom wasn't working. We didn't have any money. So if she didn't want to lose the house, she had to get creative . . ."

chapter 27.

I didn't tell him everything. Honestly, even I tried to tune myself out from the beginning, so maybe I had only babbled nonsense. But it felt like I talked for days.

It felt like I told him *everything*.

It was like I'd always expected, him looking at me like he thought I was a liar. Once or twice he looked away and shook his head, which made me nervous, so I stopped talking but then realized that probably made me seem even *more* like a liar so when I started again I was going faster than even I could follow and without knowing what I was saying or how much . . .

Eventually he put a palm out to stop me and said to hold on for a moment before continuing my story (like I was reading him a fairytale) because he would need to talk to someone outside about this, and then Officer Friendly shook his head again, turned his back on both of us, and left the room.

If he had been less incredulous he probably would have remembered to convey some sort of veiled threat to Peter about what would happen if we started plotting against him while he was out there. But it wouldn't have been necessary anyway.

The space had quickly filled with silence as the door closed, and not the normal kind. There wasn't even eye contact, and though Peter sat barely a foot in front of me, he didn't say anything—out loud or otherwise. Neither did I; even if I could have opened my mouth I'd already said enough (too much) to last me another decade at least.

What have you done? This was *wrong*. Friendly said Mom was on her way here, and I had just broken her most important rule.

And then there was Peter, who had obviously spent years trying to conquer a problem that went far deeper than he could say. He had always loved our Mom in a way that involved too much forgiveness and too little reality, as far as I was concerned. It was part of the reason she hated me—and why she'd singled him out over me for years of near-isolation.

I'd never have dreamed of using it against him that way.

But I did.

Right in front of the man who had threatened to kill him.

Which is why, though I didn't know what to do next, though I wanted so badly to ask and for him to tell me, though I figured I owed him about six months' worth of apologies and wanted to get started right away, I just kept staring at my knees, left, then right, then left . . .

I was afraid, genuinely afraid that if I looked up at him he wouldn't look back. And then I'd be alone.

He'd said she was coming three days ago, but my mother still wasn't here. Three nights and halfway through a fourth without so much as a phone call, and I was starting to feel a little insulted.

So what if I wasn't exactly excited about seeing her, or if the anticipation was causing an unpleasant sort of clawing, ripping sensation in my abdomen—wasn't she supposed to dash in straight from the airport, no time for makeup or a clean shirt, tearfully demanding to be taken to her daughter *this minute*?

I grinned into the darkness. Even for her that would be dramatic. But it would still be more normal than whatever she was doing now, and my mother was usually an expert at acting normal.

I tried to clean under a thumbnail with a tooth, bit it off instead and pulled my knees to my chin, looking out over the edge of my cot. The line of light beneath the roomcloset door had been bright and uninterrupted for a while now—it had been some time since the last check-in. *Should have stolen Bad Cop's watch, too.*

"Not funny."

Agree to disagree. But if my babysitters really were gone for the night, it was go time.

Stealthy even inside my closetroom, I repeated my performance from earlier, peeking around the door and creeping into the empty hallway. Though the sitters were taking themselves a little more seriously, it was very late. Anyone still hanging around would be making excuses to lie down and snatch a couple hours' sleep, figuring I was doing the same.

Eventually someone had realized Officer Friendly's mistake and come back to separate us. I was still studying the tops of my knees, but I shook my head hard when Baby Face tried to coax me out and away so they could "talk to us by ourselves for a moment, just a moment." He tried the same spiel on Peter, failed again, and then just settled back into a corner and waited.

Officer Friendly had used words like *highly unusual* and *unique* when laying out our options. Or, actually, our option, take it or leave it. The good news: they would let us be present for each other's interrogations, in effect to be questioned together. The catch: we had to follow their rules. If, for instance, one of us refused to answer a question, or disagreed, or answered for the other, or even *hesitated* too long (for shit's sake), we would be split up and have to continue alone until they were satisfied with our answers. If they weren't pleased even then, that was it, game over. No more tandem interviews. Possibly no seeing each other at all.

It made sense. They could have sent me away to a home by now, pulling me off the shelf when they wanted something and then putting me back again. I'd tried to make it clear how badly I didn't want that.

Apparently I'd succeeded—and handed Detective Solomon Lucass the perfect weapon to use against me.

I agreed. And so, a second later, did Peter. But when Baby Face and Friendly had taken the table with that Let's Begin look, we hadn't been able to. Begin. I was still too horrified at myself to speak, and when I finally dared to sneak a glance at my brother he'd been giving the door such a greedy look that Baby Face had kindly suggested we all give each other a day to adjust or rest up or something else helpful and overeager.

For a second I slowed, suddenly wanting to sink to the floor where it met the long wall and curl into a ball. He'd never wanted to get away from me so badly before.

Almost never.

Didn't count. He wasn't trying to get away from *me* then.

Maybe not. But it's still what he did.

The white, almost day-bright hall nearly reminded me of a hospital—minus the colors and pictures meant to make you feel like life was *worth* living, and except for all the bars. But I wasn't complaining. They made it a lot easier to see where my brother was not.

It was wide but not very long, just five cells on each side. At the moment only one was occupied.

Peter was combatting his claustrophobia, sitting with his head pressed against the bars of the cell door—which I had assumed he would—so all he had to do was look up to watch me approaching—which he didn't.

"You," he said.

"You." I swallowed a slight lump and sank to the floor opposite him.

"You're not supposed to be here." Not a question, so I didn't answer.

He didn't say anything else. Instead he turned away and shifted so it looked like he might get up, might move away.

"You're mad at me?" I hadn't meant to ask, I'd meant to tell him.

At least my voice was steady. I wouldn't guilt him into pretending he was over what I'd done today; he'd forgive me on his own or not at all.

His eyes flicked to mine—I was watching him like a hungry hawk for no particular reason—and down. "Yeah."

Somehow, that was not what I'd expected. Still.

Okay, I thought miserably. "Okay," I said miserably.

He reached for me and I ducked back. When I looked up he was watching me, disdainfully, hand still out. *Fine.* I inched closer and Peter took hold of my shirt collar, pulling until our heads touched between the bars. Then he just sat there breathing, like he'd fallen asleep. I relaxed, too, realizing yet again how tired I was. Oddly enough, even at this awkward angle I hadn't felt so comfortable since the Drophouse burned.

I didn't realize he'd moved until what felt like a tiny missile suddenly exploded between my eyes. Ow. *Ow.*

"What the . . ." I started to protest, but the look on Peter's face stopped me cold.

"*What* did you think you were *doing*?" he hissed, less than an inch from my face. Surprised again and a little confused, too, I resisted the urge to rub my forehead and drew back as far as the cotton band would allow. Sure I was sorry, but this particular brand of mad was not at all what I'd meant when I asked the question.

"You promised me."

My brain immediately flew into overtime, replaying the events of the past few days. I hadn't said a word about the Drophouse to anyone, nothing about the time I'd been missing at all, what was he talking about? My head shook itself as I insisted that "I never said anyth-"

"Years ago. You made a promise."

I blinked, just on the verge of understanding.

"And then you broke it. Right away, Alana. Days later, you broke it. And you didn't learn anything. *Nothing.*"

My eyes opened wide and kept opening. I was mistaken, thinking the horrible thing I'd done today was—what? Actually help us both by exposing my Mom's side job as a dealer of uppers, downers, stimulants and anything else she could supply with my brother's many "illnesses"? *Embarrassed* him by demonstrating how she kept him playing along for years?

Not even close. This was something completely different, and yes, he was Mad and I should have known why much earlier.

My heart started playing racquetball with itself as the ball and I shrunk down to about half my normal size. My voice sounded exactly like I remembered it seven years ago—so I was nearly half my age, too. "I didn't want to."

Peter laughed quietly and not in a good way. I tried to twist away, but not very hard. A half-slice of pizza I'd barely forced down was doing frantic backflips in my gut and I gave up the moment he told me to stop.

"What would you have done? If it was me?"

"Something. But nothing that stupid." He shook his head.

I tried to grin. "Well, you told me not to *say* anything stupid, not-" He yanked me forward again. "Okay, okay, okay okay."

"What if-if it's like last time, Alana? Did you bother to think about that?"

No, I didn't think about it because I didn't want to think about it *and I wouldn't think about it* and it was gone. Gone.

Except it couldn't be, because a fucking six-foot reminder of what had happened last time I tried to stand up for my brother literally had me by the throat and wasn't going away. "Let go." I really tried not to beg.

"Did you?" The grip tightened.

"Let *go* . . ."

Tightened again.

I started to shake and couldn't stop, tried to ignore it, but couldn't do that either—it spilled out in my babyish don't-be-mad-at-me whine. "I was trying to help."

Peter loosened his grip but still didn't let me go. "Don't." He almost whispered. There was a faint line of blood crusting beneath his nose, which looked swollen and painful. "It's not your job. You need to understand that."

I sagged. That was something I could not do. My brother had been protecting me since the day I was born, maybe the day after. Even now, he was in a tiny cell risking his sanity *and* safety all because he'd been looking out for me.

Though there must be some sort of logic at play there, I could never understand how it wasn't my personal obligation to watch over him the exact same way.

Trying not to let my expression betray me, I pictured it. Walking into the interrogation room, Peter looking like he did, standing behind the door, Bad Cop swaggering in (he said *again*, how else were you supposed to take that?). Standing aside, silent, doing nothing as he pulled one fist back and . . .

Something in me reacted to that, something visceral and imperative. I *would* do it again. As far as I was concerned there was no other option, and I would gladly break that promise to let my brother fight his own battles over and over again if it would keep him safe.

And of all the Officer Friendlies in the world, not a single one will lift a finger to help you at the hearing.

True, but for now there was only the one Friendly to worry about. So I would just have to lay low for now and try not to get into any more trouble, or figure it out when I did.

And I would also have to hope the worst-case scenario wouldn't happen twice.

Of course I couldn't exactly say that right this moment, so I kept my head down. "Fine." It was too close to an outright lie for comfort, so I followed it up with some truth. "I figured it was about, you know, what I made you do earlier."

"Oh. Right." Finally the death-grip released and I turned away to straighten my collar with still-shaking hands. "Yeah, I guess I'm mad about that too."

I lay on the floor and closed my eyes.

"But, still, I—it's—it's fine," he kept pausing, like he didn't know how to finish. I wished he wouldn't. "You were always . . . I couldn't have . . ." At last he gave up.

"Okay. Night," I said shortly, throwing an arm over my eyes to block out the worst of the light.

The answer was some shuffling on the other side of the bars and silence. And then more silence.

The light seemed to be growing brighter. I closed my eyes tighter by degrees, a little more every few seconds, until they rebelled and sprang open and I was staring at the five thin white lines graffiting the inside of my forearm instead. Well, six, now. My hands were clenched, my toes were curled and I had an absurd urge to sit up and rock, fists to my temples. I was pretty sure if I did get up, I would start shaking again.

8, 15

IT isn't as big a deal as everyone's making it is all she can think. And she doesn't care if she should look sorry and sad like they keep telling her, either, because she isn't.

Every year during Welcome Week after summer vacation the counselor comes in and talks to her class about bullies. Bullies are people who don't understand the Golden Rule (be nice to others because you'd want them to be nice to you) or just don't care. The girl likes the Golden Rule, but she believes it would be a lot better of a rule if everybody actually followed it.

She doesn't know if she never listened to the talk before or if she was too little to understand it, but this year she's started to realize there are a lot of them in school. Even in High School, with the bigger kids. Even grownups are bullies sometimes, but there isn't much you can do about that.

In school, the counselor says what you should do is Stand Up. He says it that way, like it's another rule, you Stand Up to bullies by sticking up for yourself and for others, but the way he says it works isn't right. He doesn't get that when you tell grownups on them it doesn't make them sorry, bullies just get angrier and come after you again, but worse. But the girl gets it. Because if you get pushed down the stairs and the bully just has to go to the principal's office and be talked at and get out of class, then that isn't the Golden Rule at all *because they don't get hurt even if you did. Since she started to Stand Up the right way bullies in her school know the Golden Rule applies to them too now, and they leave her alone.*

But only in her school, and the ones in the High School have always been worse anyway, which is partly because they don't follow the Golden Rule but also because he doesn't know how to Stand Up. And the one named Avery used to be the worst, the one who got her in trouble three times because he wouldn't stop beating the girl's brother up and stealing his stuff.

She doesn't usually like to ask when she thinks there's been trouble with bullies in school because he won't say anything when she does, or even look at her. They could be sitting right in front of each other at the table or doing homework and if she asked he would just sort of start looking right through her like he wasn't even thinking anything for a long time. She doesn't like being ignored, at least not like that, like the way he ignores other people, so she doesn't bother asking usually.

But it's way, way beyond against the rules to come home without your shoes and Mom had been right there at home after school when he did. And she was not happy. So the girl got a chance to ask when she snuck into the garage later to turn on the light for him, and this time he had finally told her the bully's name was Avery because he was so busy making sure there were no rats around to bite him and give him a disease or something (which she thinks is funny, but he doesn't) that he forgot to ignore her.

"Well I'm going to find him tomorrow and make him stop."

He looked up but wasn't paying attention because of worrying about rats so he kind of squinted and tilted his head, asking what she meant.

"I'm gonna tell him to leave you alone or else."

That made him give her a different look and he shook his head hard, two times. "No you will not." He said it all mean and serious to show he meant it, but she meant what she'd said more so she crossed her arms and nodded back, one time, real slowly.

"No you won't because it isn't your problem. It's mine, and I'll handle it how I want to."

He didn't normally talk this much when Mom was in the house. But she did. "Well it's my problem too, 'cause now you're in trouble at home because of him so now I have to take care of you." Wait that's not right, she remembers thinking right after she said it.

The boy tried to look like he wasn't angry but he glared at her anyway. She started to look away but he did first, staring out in front of him at the garage door. "I'm sorry that's so hard for you," this time he didn't sound mean or anything but she knew he was serious anyway. She rocked back and forth on her feet, toes to heels.

"That's not what I-"

"I don't care." But he did. Even though he sounded like he didn't care about anything. And she didn't know what else to say, so it got quiet enough to hear the crickets outside and she kept rocking, toes to heels, toes to heels.

"Before you go I want you to do something."

"I'm not going."

"Doesn't matter. Promise me you'll drop it."

She went back to her heels and balanced there.

"Now."

She went front to back again, chewing her lip.

"You don't even know Avery, so leave him alone. Say it."

She wished she hadn't accidentally hurt his feelings before, because she felt like she had to. "I'll drop it."

"Say you promise."

"I promise." He might have made her shake on it if he could move his hands. Even if he didn't always, it was still supposed to be part of a promise. So only kind of is what she thought, but she did mostly promise.

And even though she'd stayed the whole night instead of only a little while it still counts as the first time Avery the bully got her in trouble, because she still feels pretty bad about it.

She is puzzled and amused at the same time to see her principal here, outside of school. It makes sitting in this big room with the judges even weirder and makes it harder not to look around. The judges might be called judges or they might not; she guesses they are because of the principal telling her mother about an attorney before, and they're basically the same as lawyers and lawyers work in courts with judges. But there isn't an attorney or a lawyer here today, and when she asked Mom why she didn't have one the only answer was a kind of fake laugh and "That's all I need."

So no lawyers, a principal not in school, five judges who might not be and her family in the very back. Her brother would probably know the real reason why she doesn't have an attorney, but he hasn't spoken to her for days.

The next time Avery had tried to steal shoes had gotten her in trouble again. This time the boy had come off of the bus all scraped and dirty, with a splotchy red mark on his cheek.

When the girl saw him the first thing she did was look down at his feet. But the new shoes were still there, the shoes he hadn't even had for a whole week yet. Mom would have gotten to Bad real fast if he lost those too, and that's what the girl said when she looked up and smiled at her brother.

When he didn't smile back at first she just figured maybe his face was hurting, or he was worried about Mom seeing him looking like crap. It took her a while to see it for herself. "Hey. Where's your backpack?"

The very next day she'd rushed home by herself and run inside, past the living room, up the stairs and all the way to her room at the end of the hall. She didn't hear anyone as she ran, but she kept listening as hard as she could, even after the door was closed. Especially after the door was closed, because that's when she opened her backpack, took out the two smallish shoes, and shoved them under the chest of drawers where she kept her stash of candy bars and stuff that didn't fit anywhere else.

The rule was you had to not look sick or marked-up to be allowed to go to school, so it was another week almost before the boy went back. But that day, he left looking okay and came back home all bloody and definitely-not-okay again. He ran right off the bus and past her to the house so fast she couldn't catch up until he was in her room on his hands and knees, looking under the bed and the nightstand and inside the closet.

"Get out of my room!" She shouted, mostly to scare him into not looking anymore. They could have both gotten into trouble for her being so loud.

But it hadn't worked—he just looked up for a second. "Idiot!" He whispered harshly.

The girl stepped back but didn't say anything.

"Where are they?"

"That's my business, not yours." She crossed her arms and glared. She wasn't telling him anything, especially if he was going to call her names.

Then he got up and started walking, too fast, toward her. She started rocking but stopped herself because she wasn't wrong, an idiot would be wrong and that's not what she was.

He read her mind. "Idiot is what I think you are," he whispered again. "You want to know what Avery called you?" He leaned down real close and waited for the girl to look him in the eye. "Psycho." After a minute, "You said you would drop it. You promised."

Kind of, she thought. Plus, this way she hadn't fought with

somebody she didn't know, and she left Avery alone, like he said. She told the boy so.

"So you just decided to go pick on his little brother instead!"

"It's the Golden Rule. My brother got in trouble, and now his did too." She had come up with it back when she found out one of the second graders she had lunch with was Avery's brother. She hoped when Avery saw Justin at home, he would learn not to beat people up and take their things.

Her brother's bottom lip was bleeding all the way down to his chin. She didn't understand why, but she could tell it hadn't worked. "What did he ever do to you?"

He was giving her that look she hated because it meant he was disappointed, which was kind of angry and surprised that you had to be angry and sad that you had to be surprised or angry in the first place. She stared back, and it dawned on her how she had gotten it wrong. No, the little kid in the grade below hers hadn't done any-thing to get pushed down and have his shoes stolen, but then nei-ther had her brother. But if the Golden Rule was be nice to people so they're nice to you, then being mean to the little kid Justin made her the same as Avery the bully! Maybe even a little psycho like Avery said, though that was way meaner to call someone than bully or even idiot.

Next time the boy asked her where the shoes were, she went and got them without saying anything. But he didn't take them. She had to put them in her backpack and give them back to Justin tomorrow, he said. And say she was sorry, like she meant it even if she didn't. And then he'd gone away and closed her door behind him.

She was sorry, she remembers, because she hadn't meant to turn into a bully when she was actually trying to stop one. But she was glad, too, because she knew how to fix it for good now. She didn't like to see her brother coming home with bruises and dirt and blood, especially when Mom saw and then it was just the same thing all over again, like it was after the backpack with the iron, and him saying nothing the whole time no matter what. She thought it made her disappointed for a moment, except surprised wasn't really part of it, but scared was, so she was whatever disappointed was with that instead.

So she was sorry, but also glad he was gone because to fix it she would have to go back on her promise, which was only a kind-of promise anyway because they didn't shake on it, and he would probably get Madder than ever because she'd never done that before.

Still, she was tired of being sad-mad-scared and not being allowed to help. And now all she needed was to ask a second-grader to take a message when she gave him his shoes back tomorrow. Maybe she would wait to say sorry too, so she could be sure he'd do it.

And now here she is, in trouble again for wanting to help. Another woman walks in, all rushed and tired, with two other grownups. The girl doesn't know who the tired lady is, but she can pretty much tell from the way the other man and woman look at her they must be Avery and Justin's mom and dad. If she was sorry like they tell her to be she would look down or say something nice, but instead she just looks back in front of her to the other door and wonders what they had to do to make a kid as mean as the one they have.

She already told the principal her side of the story with Mom before. He liked to listen to people's sides of things, so he nodded and even looked like he understood sometimes until she finished talking. Then she got distracted trying to make sure she hadn't forgotten anything, so all she heard afterward was a lot of stuff about when she had been Standing Up for herself. Only he didn't call it Standing Up, he called it fighting like it was a bad thing and like she didn't know fighting was against the rules. Also he used the word "expel" a couple of times, which she didn't like, because getting expelled was not something she wanted. That day was when she heard the word attorney that she asked her Mom about later.

Then she got to tell it to a bored looking stranger who told her she could tell him the truth because he was here to help her as long as she was honest. He asked her a lot about fighting, too, but he didn't look like he got it when she tried to explain the Golden Rule thing to him. But because she was being honest she did tell him she was sorry about taking the shoes. When he asked why only the shoes, she didn't know what he meant. "Well I didn't need anything else," she had said. That made him look confused. And when he asked her about things at home she remembered the most important rule of all and said it was good and wouldn't talk to him anymore, although she did say he should shut up when he didn't quit asking.

All she wants is for people to leave them alone. Why is that so bad it could get her expelled? It isn't like she started this, and they sure didn't make it stop. And if her brother had taken his own advice and let her fight her own battle with Avery, maybe it would have been okay.

The girl doesn't cross her arms now but doesn't look down either as the middle judge stands up to start talking, even though she's madder at them than any of them are at her. Still, at least she can be pretty sure Avery will leave her brother alone from now on.

chapter 28.

IT may have been pitch black outside still, or faint gray with barely-visible traces of pink, or even the pale white-blue of late early-morning. But in the windowless, white hallway outside the cells time stood still, so for me there could have been less than two seconds between closing my eyes and being shaken awake to a quiet but insistent murmur saying to go back to my bed before they came. The light was still as blinding as before, the floor as unpleasantly hard.

Groggy, uncomprehending, I went. Sleep makes me more a creature of instinct than flesh and bone; I barely knew why I went, or where to go, but sleep took me there. Sleep is quiet: I moved toward quiet. Sleep is dark: I moved toward dark. Sleep is warm, or soft. I didn't need both.

I was back in my roomcloset, reliably buried under the blanket, when they came to get me for the first interview.

It really wasn't bad. We were together, at least. For now.

Not that we should be, it was almost never done, possibly even illegal, like they'd said about a million times. Still, they were *happy* to help, since it was so important to us—with some strings attached.

I imagined the two detectives as a large, amorphous sort of "Them" when they weren't around, but in person Friendly and his trusty side-kick were always a little . . . life-sized. Like they might drink coffee in the mornings, or pay bills. It was kind of unsatisfying.

(On the other hand, *They* made my brother give up his lawyer so he could sit next to me and say things that at best neither of them be-lieved and at worst were outright lies, so perhaps we weren't very sat-isfying either.)

We told and retold it so many times that I started to enjoy reciting The Tale of the Night of My Disappearance. The title needed some work, though.

It was easy enough. There had been only one person outside that night. I swapped being pulled out of the window for going out to in-vestigate a noise in the woods. Peter skipped the bruised ribs and ulti-mately placed us in a condemned apartment building in rural Virginia, where we squatted for months and where several people were likely to have (said they had) seen us—another courtesy of Di's. Otherwise, we more or less stuck to the truth.

After each telling I had to remind myself not to smile or stand for applause. I mean, I had practice lying, and plenty of it. But this was the Big Leagues and here I was, holding my own. We weren't just good liars. We were professionals.

"So you did not plan to leave home that night," McCowan—Boy Wonder's human name—said-rather-than-asked.

"Well . . . not exactly." I admitted. For authenticity's sake I had left in some details about the first time I saw Peter—not that they needed to know how long it took for me to really *see* him. Or that I'd nearly smashed in his skull before I did.

"But you were forcibly removed anyway."

Peter winced a little. I stared at the Boy Wonder. He was differ-ent in questioning than I'd expected, touchy, quicker to strike at the smallest divergences between my story and the one he preferred.

"No." It was what he wanted to be true—and it was—so I needed to be firm. "I decided to leave on my own. But that didn't make me any less angry at him."

Lucass had also taken a surprising role. For a man who would pull a gun on an unarmed kid, practically, Lucass' passive, observant manner actually paralleled Peter very well. He nodded coolly. "And when did you notice the wound on your sister's arm?"

Fixated on that again, are we? Even though I'd explained how my arm had been sliced open long before Peter's arrival.

Peter paused—but not for long. By all appearances he could have been trying to pinpoint the exact moment. "Just after getting out of the truck the first time."

"Before you arrived at the apartment."

Peter nodded.

"And I assume when you say 'getting out' you mean letting her out of the back, also."

He grimaced slightly, just enough to show teeth, then sighed. *Lie to them/you'll get in trouble,* they meant: in this case, *I wish you'd told them something else.* "Yeah."

But I'd had to leave it in. It was the clearest thing I remembered from those first few days: moving toward the back hatch of the small truck and having that first moment of realization that something was happening, something terrible I'd been waiting for . . .

It was too real to pretend otherwise. And sometimes being a professional also meant knowing which kernels of truth made your lie more believable.

Lucass and Peter were still talking. I tuned back in just in time to hear

"-by yourself with a needle, thread, and no pain medication, she just sat there and let you?"

No kidding. Peter answered and I barely listened, trying not to roll my eyes.

Lucass turned to me. "And you support that claim." Not very specific. I shrugged politely anyway.

"He's been doing stuff like that for as long as I can remember. I would have done it myself, eventually."

"Doing what—sewing you up?"

"Patchwork . . . like on old clothing." Sewing was almost never necessary, but burns, cuts, even pneumonia once . . . we could take care of most things by ourselves.

"Mr. Wilder, I'd appreciate if you'd let your sister answer for herself."

I looked over at Lucass, confused, and Peter tilted his head. But a split second before I opened my mouth to ask what the hell he was talking about I realized I hadn't answered that last question yet. And since it was exactly what I was thinking, I didn't even notice when Peter, also oblivious, spoke up instead.

He mumbled an apology, and I couldn't help grinning a little.

It is getting easier. It was. The walls stayed put longer, he breathed easier. And when panic was keeping its distance and tiredness was still a long way off, there was . . . nothing. About as much of it as he could stand, and then some. Monotony so oppressive it didn't allow him to think of anything else. Anything at all.

The walls were starting to creep in when the one guaranteed cure for crippling boredom strolled up.

"What are you doing here?"

"What does it look like?" She dug into her shoe and held up her hand with a flourish, the thing in it gleaming dully. "Voila`."

She had a damned *key*! He spluttered a few disbelieving syllables and naturally she ignored him, utterly delighted with this latest dig at law, order, and common sense. By the time she let herself in he'd finally managed to ask how she got it.

"Bad cop," she replied unhelpfully, slipping the key back into its hiding spot. "I kept waiting for someone to notice I took his keys when . . ." She trailed off. "Anyway, this one looked different. I took it and put the rest back, and I guess it turned out to-" this time she stopped more abruptly, noticing for the first time the hungry way her brother was watching the open door.

Four steps. Four to this door, another ten or so to the next, and then . . . where? Could he find his way outside? It might be cold and windy this late, but it would be worth the chill to breathe outside air, to look at something other than walls.

Somewhere, in the corners of his mind not filled with the primal urge to escape, he wondered if, once faced with freedom and the choice of whether to keep it, he would choose to return. Could he do that?

The open door answered him. *Does it matter?*

"Um."

He was startled, but nonetheless turned very slowly—and very slightly—toward the small sound.

Alana took an uncertain step backward, placing herself between him and the door. "Hey, I'm—I mean, I didn't—well . . ." A speechless Al was rare enough that Peter stopped focusing on the doorway to watch her struggle to finish. And the second he did, the illusion shattered.

It was ridiculous, thinking he could escape this place. Even if he did manage to slip outside, there would be at most one or two seconds of freedom in total. In the chaos, and only a few yards from rows of empty cruisers (and maybe even his own car), no one was likely to believe he *did* plan to return.

I might get myself shot for real, this time.

Al fought on. "I'm just . . . not . . ."

He held up a hand. "I know." He didn't mean to snap, only to stop her from saying it out loud. After one last long look, Peter wrenched away and with tremendous effort took two short steps further into the cell. "You should c-" he choked on a word rather than stuttering for once, "close the door."

She did, and then remained awkwardly near it. "I was *planning* to mention the key last night but, as I recall, within fifteen seconds I was busy getting chewed out. Figured I'd wait until you calmed down."

Peter refused to acknowledge that, dropping onto the lower bunk. The prongs supporting the thin mattress emitted a series of shrill pops and groans under him. "What about them?" He gestured vaguely.

Al glanced behind her, then took a few quick steps and pulled herself neatly into the top bunk. "They didn't catch me last time," she said, "so I guess we hope."

She burrowed into the mattress above his head.

They both knew why she was back. He'd tried to drop it before, because the nightmares were still a sensitive topic for her, but he didn't stop thinking about them any more than she did. She wasn't completely honest about them, though. He'd suspected it at first, then banished the idea of her lying until a cryptic remark from Di ("is that what she told you, or what you heard?") brought it back. Peter settled in, too, still wide awake. He wished he could banish it now. The thought, like the blanket, was uncomfortable. It scratched.

"Pax, I'm sorry," his sister interrupted.

He blinked, waited. "For what?"

"That I prefer this to you being gone," she whispered, almost inaudibly.

Oh, was all he could think. Staring at his side of the depression that had formed around Al, Peter fumbled for something to say. In the end, apologizing back seemed like insultingly little. He said nothing instead.

Alana must have misunderstood the silence. "I'm really sorry."

chapter 29.

"NOW, son, I don't want you to think I'm calling you a liar," Peter resisted the urge to remind Lucass that he was not, in fact, his son, and to tell him it was perfectly obvious neither of the detectives wanted to believe a word he said, "but I don't think you understand. What we've got here is you and your mother accusing each other of the same things.

"However, unlike you, she and your former psychiatrist—you've warned us to be skeptical, but he is still an expert in his field, remember—have provided some basic evidence. And though your sister does appear to support your version," at the word *appear* Al's eyes narrowed dangerously, "if you think showing us a scar and putting your own spin on how it happened is enough to prove that you've never laid a hand on your sister, you should understand that can cut both ways."

In fact, Sol was not sure he *didn't* believe their story. Compared to the self-possessed and cautious brother, hotheaded Alana seemed more likely to commit a felony. And the more time passed, the clearer it became that if this was an act, it wasn't the kind he'd expected. He hadn't shared his feelings with McCowan or even Ashley yet, though; he had not come this far by broadcasting every unpopular conclusion he'd ever come to.

But something had just changed in the atmosphere of this small group, and Sol had *also* not gotten this far without learning how to tell when something he said raised hackles. His detective side positioned itself to pounce, but his wife's voice warned him to ease in.

"'Course my wife has a sister, and the two of them managed to get into some knock-down-drag-outs you wouldn't believe, so it's not like sisters and brothers don't terrorize each other all the time."

There. It was faint, but the atmosphere lifted a touch as they waited for him to move on. Of course, that wasn't the plan—Ashley was an only child. Sol had stumbled upon a brittle spot, and he was going to put some pressure on it. He sat forward. "Sometimes, you know, even when they don't want to."

Now he'd got his finger on it. This time he caught the exact second they both looked away. He pressed a little more, keeping casual. "Heard it happens all the time, in some families. No real choice. You understand what I mean?"

He was watching the older one so intently—glazed over, no longer up to looking anyone in the eye—that he almost didn't see the girl nodding.

"Not often, though. And you can stop staring at him, it was . . . I mostly did-" She stopped abruptly, but when Sol shifted his shocked gaze to her she was glaring back. Then she answered the question he hadn't figured out how to ask. "I was smaller. Figure it out." She paused again, but couldn't check herself for long. "*He* did."

Sol was dumbfounded as much by the statement as by the fury behind it. But McCowan—a rookie who, as they all did for some reason, came in his first day thinking he was already up for a promotion—was surprisingly unfazed. He nudged the other detective, bringing Sol's attention back to the brother.

He was scowling at her in a way that clearly said whatever came next, it was nothing new. "Let it go, Alana."

She met the warning with a snarl and even more venom. "Screw you."

"I was a kid, too! I thought I was-"

"All you were thinking about was protecting yourself!"

"What was I *supposed* to *do*?"

In sudden silence, Peter and the girl faced off.

Well, this was different. Though Sol had seen this side of her—as much as any other, actually—he didn't know what to make of the brother, who until now had seemed immune to Alana's singular talent for fire-starting. And it went without saying that they would not be sitting together today if the man across from him had been the one he'd met at first. The restrained manner was gone, but the stutter hadn't returned; by the end of the exchange he was nearly shouting at her. For her part Alana backed down not at all.

They glared until Peter broke the silence. "Anyway, if it makes us *even*," he'd gone quiet as usual again. "You could explain why you almost-"

"*Shut.* Up." And Sol thought she'd sounded ferocious before. Even her brother shrank back a little.

McCowan was haughty, but it could be a time-saver. He picked up Lucass' line of questioning and took off as if it were his own, possibly thinking it was. "So at least once, it was you who hurt her, then?" He had been waiting for this break since day one, and to his credit he tried to moderate his obvious excitement. "Even if you were forced to, I mean."

"*No.*" She was spitting.

"Yeah."

The girl watched them for longer than her brother, rocking a tad in her chair, then looked sideways. When Peter stretched one hand toward her, she flinched—a tiny angry twitch, but that's definitely what it was—and he withdrew.

"Finally," the young detective muttered under his breath. "Does anyone care to elaborate?"

More silence. McCowan beamed, preparing to invoke one of the many conditions the Wilders had been forced to accept.

"It was my fault."

"Alana, it wasn't. Don't say that."

She stared at her hands and drew a slow breath, a gesture which made her seem more like a tired old woman than an ornery teenage girl. "He hit me because I tried to kill myself."

"No," before Sol could react, Wilder answered. "No, you can't do that. You mean you tried to kill yourself because I-"

Alana shook her head, hard. "I *don't* want to talk about-"

"It's true!"

She shook her head again.

Baffled, Sol gratefully allowed McCowan to jump in again. "Sounds like a disagreement to me!" He practically clapped his hands. "So I guess we'll be hearing from you individually today. As they say, ladies-"

The door slammed, cutting the detective short; Alana had fled the room.

Both confused now, McCowan and Lucass silently watched their dismayed suspect.

But how do you start when you never want anyone to hear what you're about to say? Peter had never even told Di what happened to— and after—Avery.

Like writing. Just get it out. Stutters and all. "None of it should have happened," he began shakily. Then, running into no resistance (if no encouragement, either) from his audience, he picked up. "A couple of things that went wrong and kept escalating, spiraling more and more out of control until . . . but it started at school.

"I got picked on a lot as a kid. With the way things, um, were, it was par for the course, I guess. Honestly, I don't get why this one—Avery, Avery something—set her off. I mean, he got me in trouble with our mom once or twice, that might have been it." Peter glanced up. "Alana has always been kind of overprotective. She didn't like to see me get picked on," he explained, for a moment forgetting they knew this particular fact very well.

"Anyway, I made her promise she would leave it alone. Let me handle it—or not. But she couldn't let it go. She started going after his little brother at her school, sending him home with threats.

"To his credit Avery did his best not to engage her. He did try to make *me* call her off once or twice, but she was laser focused. After every fight, she got angrier and more difficult until even I was avoiding her. She's always been headstrong, but this was extreme.

"Finally, she got sick of being ignored. She sent messages home with the little boy saying she would fight him herself, setting times and places. He never showed up. So she came to my school looking for him.

"She found him. I don't know, but my guess is he refused to fight, and she refused to back down, and . . . Anyway, he shoved her. Hard enough to make her fall. I saw that part, I was headed to my bus and I saw him move and her go down and I just started running. I was— honestly, I don't know *what* I was thinking.

"But I hit him shoulder-level at the same time as she got her feet back under her and launched herself at his other side . . .

"It shouldn't have happened. If I had been there thirty seconds later, one minute earlier, if he'd been inside at his locker-" If she had kept her damned *promise* . . .

Peter closed his eyes. They had hit him from different angles at the same moment. He still recalled the sucking and popping sounds perfectly, sickening and fast and quiet, and the far-too-easy crumpling of the screaming boy on the sidewalk like a dropped puppet with perversely flailing arms. He couldn't forget it.

Either Lucass or McCowan cleared his throat. Peter took the hint and went on. "Avery was paralyzed. Not permanently, but he was in a wheelchair for almost a year, on crutches for a long time afterward.

"There was a hearing. Not for me; even if I was crazy, no one could blame me for trying to defend my little sister. But there was the intimidation of the little boy, going to someone else's school to threaten a student she had never met—of course they didn't use those words. Assault, stalking, harassment . . . she'd barely touched the kid—hopefully—and I got her to make it right and apologize to him, but they went after that, too. He was a witness, and so were the principals of both schools, a counselor, Avery's doctor. Witnesses against an eight-year-old. Avery wasn't, his parents kept him out of it, and I . . . guess I was kept out of it, too.

"They gave us—gave Mom—three options. She could be expelled, which the other boy's parents were pushing for. They could have suspended her with counseling for a few weeks, then assigned her an 'individual monitor,' which was basically the school's version of a parole officer." He had liked that idea, personally. Maybe more one-on-one attention from an adult might mellow her out, at least until she grew out of the strange, angry phase he'd (incorrectly) assumed could only last for so long. And maybe he was right, "but that would never have happened, it couldn't, Al would have slipped-" he caught himself and moved on, trying to blink himself comfortable.

"The third option was to have her evaluated by a psychiatrist, placed on medication if necessary—which they had already decided it was—and sent back to school in a week."

He stopped talking, but Sol was sure this was nowhere near the end. The elder Wilder suddenly seemed very young. "Go on, son," he prompted the boy, "your mother took the third option?"

The answer was sharp and brittle as flint. "Well, it made the most sense, didn't it? It was *convenient*. Remember, I'd been seeing a psychiatrist under Mom's direction for . . . almost five years, then. She would tell me how to act when I saw him, or tell him about something I'd supposedly done, and as long as I didn't say anything they were—he was willing to believe it all. So in five years, I'd had as many disorders and illnesses as she could think up, whatever she could "treat" with drugs someone else might be willing to buy. All she had to do was look through what hadn't sold, what nobody else wanted. That turned out to be the lithium. Bipolar disorder hadn't been very lucrative.

The actual evaluation she skipped altogether. Why bother? The schools already had what they wanted—they'd punished a problem student—and they were done. We never heard from them about it again.

"What she didn't know—didn't think about—maybe even what she liked was that doctors had stopped giving Alana strong *painkillers* by then because of how much she hated them. Lithium is an antipsychotic. She was eight, almost nine and small for her age, about half my size. I was supposed to take half a pill twice per day on a full stomach." What did he look like to them, accused of felony upon felony and complaining about childhood traumas as if he couldn't have done anything then, as if they could now? He stared, pleading. "She started her with one the next morning.

"The first day, Alana protested. The second, she screamed. The third, she tried to sneak out of the house before Mom woke up. But the drugs were working, and she tripped on the last step.

"The punishment was always the same: one extra pill, usually at night. I didn't help, then, but it would have felt wrong to leave. So I stayed, watching or holding Alana's hand while my mother held her down on the kitchen floor and forced pills down her throat. But Al was not the type to give up, so it went on that way until one morning when she stood up and stuck her finger down her own throat.

"By the time I got up Mom was already on top of her, she was on the ground but Mom was still hitting her, screaming . . ."

Once he'd pulled her away Mom had opened the bottle again, shaken three of the tablets out and stuffed them all down the throat of the unconscious girl. But when she finally acknowledged her son, she was terrifyingly calm.

"Your sister needs medicine, and I am sick of her insolent attitude about it. So, from now on, she will be right here-" she pointed, "-*every* morning, *when* I call her. And there will be no more . . ." she indicated the mess on the floor, her face a caricature of disgust. "Otherwise, we will have another morning like this, only we'll see how she does with more. Okay?" The longer she spoke, the more cheery her voice became—his arms had erupted in gooseflesh (and now, in the interrogation room, did again). Mom smiled, wide and bright enough to show all of her teeth, even the false ones near the back.

She was bluffing. He looked for a sign, a tell, anything to prove she wasn't serious. Then he wished he could be surprised at what he found instead. "You'll kill her," he whispered, in case Al could hear them.

The chipper smile became small and brittle. "Well," a counterfeit chirp, "then she'd better not be late, *hm*?"

The first seizure had happened later that day.

"By the time she went back to school, it was two each morning. And she wasn't. Late. Ever. She still hid from our mother, but it didn't work anymore, because . . ." *say it, it's bad enough what you did, you don't get to bow out of it now you spineless little shit . . .*

"Because she couldn't hide from me." Peter tasted bile, swallowed again and again. "I knew every place she would go. So I would find her myself and take her to my mother. I had to hold her down, too . . . during and after Mom gave her both of them, or three, if she felt Alana deserved it.

"Whether she got two or three usually determined if she sobbed or screamed when she saw me coming. She did those things a lot, then.

"She turned nine at some point. During the day, Alana wouldn't speak. She tried sometimes, but she slurred so badly, and she tended to forget what she was saying. Worse, she sometimes got these spasms, twitches, even from the strain of *trying* to remember. She started walking slower, watching the ground before each foot touched down like she thought it might shift under her.

"The seizures didn't happen that often, but she was trembling all the time, head to toe, and she was so scared she might have one in the wrong place. She avoided strange things, strange because they were so common—the curb, the bathtub, stairs—she could have been killed if she'd seized near those places. Nights were her most lucid time, so she stayed awake then; she slept through school."

And I kept doing it to her. Me, more than Mom, because I'd spent years convincing her to trust me, and she was too trapped to realize she should stop. Every time—*every* morning—when he inevitably found a relatively coherent Al curled up behind a bed or in the back of a closet, yes, she would cry or scream, but *what* she would cry or scream was that he wasn't going to, was he, not this time, he didn't have to, he could just say he hadn't found her, that was all he had to do so would he please, *would he just say he couldn't find her, please* . . .

And he would sit down with her, and hold her until the pleading had faded back into wordless sobs and tell her it was okay, Ally would be all right (because he was a liar) and then he would pick her up and carry her down the stairs, because he *did* have to, and she would let him because she had nowhere else to turn.

"I was a liar," he said, not knowing if he was repeating himself, "it wasn't going to be all right, it was getting worse. I told myself she would get a break soon, Mom would take one of her overnight trips sooner or later—but she didn't. Mom had never spent more than a couple of weeks straight at home and now she went two months, and Alana was getting worse all the time. She kept dropping things, she didn't know her way around the house anymore. She had to crawl up the staircase because she didn't trust her legs to pull her up.

"I wasn't entirely surprised when she told me she thought she was going to die.

"It was dark, she said, everything was dark and fuzzy around the edges, the world kept tilting and didn't right itself for hours. She was trying to eat at night because she knew she should, but everything tasted the same and she was tired of it. Tired of *eating*.

"I told her she was going to be fine and not to even think that way.

She stared at me. She knew and I knew this couldn't go on forever: her prediction was practical, mine was a wish.

"Then she asked if we were upstairs or downstairs, and I got her a glass of water and went to bed.

"The next day I had some appointment—I can't remember anymore what kind—and on the way home I told Mom I was done helping her. I said she was going to kill her daughter, and if she did I would tell everyone, my psychiatrist, the police and anyone else I could think of what she had done, and she couldn't stop me."

He gave a sudden bizarre gasp of laughter, surprising all of them. "For the first time in years I truly stood up to my mother, and do you know what she said? She looked at me in the rearview mirror and *laughed* and told me to relax. She said the prescription was about to run out anyway, and by then, Alana would have learned her lesson, wouldn't she?

"Just like that. She laughed it off and then said she really would give her the rest all at once if I didn't keep doing my *job*."

The pleading look was back as Peter once again remembered his audience. "And I didn't say anything but I swear, I meant it. I never would have helped her again." They had not said much but now Peter suddenly felt a weight of accusation in the stares of the detectives, and he answered it *I hope, I hope . . .*

When the front door swung open, something in the air had rushed out with a message: *something's wrong*. Maybe his mother felt it, too, because she was right behind him as he mounted the steps, heading for Al's room in case something had-

"Blood . . . was . . . it was dripping down the side of the tub." He swallowed between each word. His heart was beating in his throat, the color draining from his face, just like it had then. "It was full, of water and—and—the water was red." He couldn't bring himself to say it, say why. It was still, so calm. And she was under it, fully clothed and sleeping—it looked like sleeping—underneath a floating web of hair, lying even more still than the water, tinted by it. He could see part of one arm, the wrist crosshatched with darker, even more crimson lines.

His mother said something and then turned and walked out. He didn't hear—or had she told him to clean this up? Yes, she must have because that was what he started doing, edging into the bright room which normally smelled of bleach and now was filled with the humid smell of hot water, heavy with the mineral tinge of blood.

She was dead, she was dead, *she was already dead* . . . Peter tried with limited success to bring himself back to the present. "I thought . . . when I pulled her out she was limp, both wrists slashed open. I spoke to her, shook her . . . she turned blue, once she was out of the water."

He'd recoiled instinctively, shoved himself as far away as he could though his feet slipped in the bloody water spreading around the body and sat, shivering but not sobbing—unable to even cry— against the tub.

Eventually he'd stood, mechanically, and unstopped it. While the water drained, he scrubbed the darker tributaries and the small puddles they formed on the floor. They left behind stains, which had to be soaked, bleached, they would never come out otherwise, and as he was looking for it he realized *this is the last time I'll ever clean up after Al* and he was burying his face in his wet, bloody hands when she coughed.

He turned around and she did it again, coughed and gasped and then started up more violently, twitching in the pool on the floor and retching up volumes of the same bloody water. How long he had stood there staring, he didn't know.

"But she was bleeding, and I went to get her off of the floor, to . . . I don't know. I don't know.

"But when I tried, she started talking. To me, though I didn't understand at first—telling me to leave, to let her get back into the tub, to let her go—let her die, she meant.

"I hit her. With-" Unable to say it, he made a fist with his right hand and brought the flat side haphazardly against his own temple. He would have to trust his listeners to understand. He was still too disturbed by that abrupt rage to like probing too deeply into it—whether it was shock, or confused grief (or the pain of knowing this was all his fault).

"And then she was flailing around, scrabbling at the floor to get away, but she bled more the more she moved, and it . . . she had already lost so much. I hit her again—harder," he flinched himself, "and yelled. Something. Then she stopped, went completely limp again, so I could pick her up.

"She hadn't known how . . . which direction to . . . cut, so—because she was still only a little kid—she did both. Cut her left wrist one way, her right the other. It slowed down the loss of blood, so her head stayed above water for a few minutes longer. She saved her own life.

"Anyway, I bandaged her up and put her to bed, which is where she stayed, for the most part, until she was able to get around on her own again."

Wilder calmed somewhat once he was done. He sniffed and wiped at his eyes with the backs of his thumbs, and Sol fleetingly saw the person portrayed by the story, a frightened boy trying to do the right thing.

"Your sister is out in the hall right now," he reminded Wilder in a peculiar, fatherly tone that was as shocking to him as it was insignificant to the other two. He tried something more formal. "You may return to your cell until we are done speaking with her." Sol didn't like that any better.

chapter 30.

"I don't remember any of that," I lied again. McCowan gave me a look.

"We need you to tell us what you do remember, then," he coaxed.

I looked down. I was making them lead me. It was a fair sort of compromise, I figured, since I didn't want to say anything and they wanted to know everything, to answer only the questions they asked. But they would have to ask.

Lucass caught on first. "If you don't remember anything before, could you tell us what about that day you can remember most clearly? Before your, um." He didn't finish.

I saw my hands and looked away from myself in disgust. "The water," my voice broke and I stopped, startled.

"What about it, Alana?"

"It was hot. Not too hot, but hot."

If I hadn't been such a pathetic liar I would have said, *that day* is as clear as a bell in my memory. The rest of them are a hazy and nightmarish sort of blur, but not this one. This is what I remember: I was on the floor, lying down. Waking up. I didn't know if I'd been asleep or had a seizure, but my pants were wet and the carpet was damp behind my nightstand, under me. I remember it wasn't the first time, but I don't know how I kept anyone from finding out. That time, I crawled to the bathroom for a towel. And I realized I was tired.

I couldn't sleep behind the nightstand anymore. And I was in the bathroom now, leaning against the closet door, but what was outside? Was it night? Was there someone waiting out there? Was it—please, no—morning already? I could go out and look, but there was nowhere safe. As a matter of fact the only place I hadn't tried hiding yet was right in front of me. With its high, hard, skull-cracking sides and faucets, the bathtub was one of my Danger places—probably no one would think to look for me here for a long time. I stared at it for a few minutes longer, thinking faster than I had in weeks, grinning at the idea slowly weaving itself together in my deteriorating mind. Yeah, I could rest here for a long time.

But it was still too hard and cold, too, so I plugged it and turned on the hot water before I took back a towel to clean up my mess.

It seemed to take a long time to clean up, maybe because I became obsessed. Every few blots at the carpet I was compelled to creep back to the bathtub and check the temperature of the water: it couldn't be too hot or I couldn't get in, not hot enough and it would get cold too quickly. Then I'd go back to my task, unhurried, still tired but deriving a good deal of comfort from knowing that soon, so soon, so *very* soon I would get to rest.

Lucass asked if I had been thinking for a long time about killing myself. Didn't say "killing yourself," but skirted around it in a weird, considerate way. I said no, just about dying. It was coming—I knew that.

I thought maybe I could see it coming, and I thought probably it wouldn't be fun. It would be like everything was becoming these days; scary and painful and dark and filled with this high-pitched sound I didn't realize sometimes was me. But it had to happen, and soon, because if I didn't die it would keep going. For the first time in my life I understood that. If the pills didn't kill me, if they somehow stopped working and I wasn't even scared of them anymore, she would find something I *was* scared of and she would use that. And then something even worse, over and over.

She didn't want me to be good. She didn't want me to be polite or get good grades. *This* is what she wanted.

So this was my life, if I lived.

My nine-year-old self knew I wouldn't. But this way, it was just as much my decision as hers. And I decided to go out warm.

"So in the beginning you'd only planned to take a warm bath, but you got the idea somewhere to cut your wrists, as well." McCowan was trying to urge me on.

So they knew. Of course they did. I looked up to nod, caught sight of myself in the one-way glass and closed my eyes, swallowing. It was another lie, but a small one. Once the water had been the perfect temperature I'd stared into it, captivated. I wanted to get in, wanted to curl up on the bottom and let out one long, contented sigh. But it wouldn't work. I wouldn't fall asleep, no matter how tired I was. I'd choke. That was no good. I needed to be mostly asleep already, so by the time I was underwater I wouldn't care at all. My choices, as I saw them, were more pills—my mother had mine with her so I couldn't hide them—or one of the knives from the kitchen.

No choice I would ever make in my life would be so easy.

Since my pants and shirt were still dirty and I didn't want anyone to find out I had wet myself like a baby, I left them on, easing in. I should, but can't, want to forget that feeling. The just-barely-too-hot water squeezing, then relaxing every muscle. The ticklish lapping of the water against my neck, the only part of me sticking out of it.

The hardest part had been making myself bleed. It took several tries before I realized if I held my hands and the knife underwater, I barely felt the smallest sting as it sliced right through the skin. I only had to cut once on my left arm and got more blood than I did out of a bunch of crisscrossed ones on the right, then I leaned over and threw the wet knife across the bathroom floor. It slid far, into the darkness under a closed door.

I should not, and never will, tell anyone how proud of myself, how content I was in that moment. Most people had to wait their entire lives for this kind of peace, I kept thinking. And I was only nine years old.

"And your brother came home and pulled you from the tub? What do you remember about that?"

"It was cold." My voice sounded like a computerized recording of itself. Too calm, not quiet enough. Strange.

"You were cold, okay. Can you tell us what happened, though?"

I shook my head but didn't look. I wanted to glare up like my normal self and explain in a pissed-off human voice that no, I was not *just* cold. The cold was the first thing, yes—a thick, deep chill I could see and taste—but there was so much more. There was the ache in my throat and the burning in my ribs, like I had been up all night coughing, there was the heavy, corrosive feeling of water in my lungs. Still, I believed I'd succeeded, even when my body began convulsing. Which was when I'd begun thinking about Hell.

I hadn't done much research, but from what I gathered Hell was some sort of unending fiery torture, or else the most horrible thing you could imagine. Possibly both. The more I coughed, the more the burning sensation spread through my body, and finally panic set in. I shouldn't be in Hell! I couldn't! Bizarrely, because this underworld still felt like my old bathroom, I suddenly became absolutely certain that my only shot at a second chance was to get back to the tub, into the water. I wouldn't be so cold anymore, for one thing, and if I could get all the way to the bottom again maybe this time I'd come up in the right place, where I should have gone the first time . . .

But the more I coughed, the more my head and body ached and burned, and yet the colder I felt. I couldn't get back unless it stopped.

I was waiting for it to end when a face like my old older brother's swam into my field of vision, and for the first time in longer than my muddy memory could reach I was a little relieved to see it. I tried to explain to the phantom-Peter that he needed to get me back, put me back into the tub, and at first he seemed ready to help. I kept en-couraging him.

Then pain exploded across my face like a gunshot and I did not un-derstand at first where it had come from. I just saw the flash behind my eyes and tried desperately with disobedient and suddenly painful hands to pull myself back toward the bathtub, thinking that nowhere, not even here, not in Hell itself would he ever do something like-

Once it happened again I began to realize I was wrong. He rasped at me to shut *up* even though I hadn't said anything, but I heard tears in his voice. He wouldn't cry if this really was Hell, honestly might keep hitting me if it were but not crying about it.

I was alive and it was even worse than before, it was some new Hellish version of life where Peter hated me now too, just like my Mom did, because he would never forgive me and that was my fault and I'd never be able to take it back. I deserved it.

Mostly because, even then, I was still tired.

Back in the interrogation room I slumped over halfway to my knees, my hair tickling my nose. I knew what they were fishing for, and if they were fishing it was because my brother had already told them himself. "He hit me," I couldn't let it seem like I was protecting him, "twice." Stupid to put so much focus on such a small detail. Like with gifts, it had been the thought behind it that really mattered. I sat up to stare Lucass in the face. "And I deserved it and more." I said it like I meant it, and I tried to. I also gulped and wanted to vomit.

But it was true, because as he carried me away my only worry was that by screwing up my death, I had screwed up my life, too. If I had only moved faster, or cut deeper, I would be where I was supposed to right now, floating in the warm gray for good.

Shut up was the second to last thing I would hear from my brother for a while, which is what makes it as easy to remember as the very last one.

I hit the bed hard enough to bounce into the air, then stay as

I've been dropped. The burning in my muscles is now an ache set-tling throughout my body, concentrating in my head and wrists. I am motionless, soaking my sheets while Peter rummages through my dresser, pretending I am dead, wishing I was. I'm stuck on *shouldn't* for a while—I shouldn't have been found for at least another half hour; I shouldn't have to feel this throbbing pain in my temples; I shouldn't be alarmed at how heavy, how weak I am feeling. In the water, I was weightless.

There is the sound of cloth hitting carpet, then I think I'm turning upside down, but it's the opposite, I'm yanked into a sitting position. I try to hold still—I don't pull away, but my stomach tightens painfully and swallowing a whimper causes another spasm in my throat—I still don't fully understand what happened in the bathroom, but I don't want to make him madder. Mad again. I don't know or want to. He yanks my sodden shirt halfway up, then carefully pulls each arm through, like I was a baby. I can do that myself, I think but am too smart, scared, or senseless to say, and then he yanks again, pulling it over my head, and I'm too busy not yelping to care.

A towel is draped over my shoulders a second later, and Peter is doing something with the ruined shirt. I can't read his posture but don't have to, to know; I start to fall back but am just as quickly sitting again, looking down at the carpet over the edge of the bed and trying not to even breathe.

Next time I leave you, he says and I deliberately do not flinch at what I hear in his voice. *Killing, even killing yourself, isn't just wrong, it's weak, a coward's way out, and I would never have wasted a second of my life on you if I'd thought that's who you are when things get hard.*

He waits, presumably letting his words sink in, then starts using strips he has torn off the wet shirt to bandage my wrists. He has to use more to wrap the one I did correctly—it doesn't occur to me to think of it any other way.

And then he starts in on my hair, scouring with the end of the towel so hard I'm forced to support myself on my aching hands. My head pounds in time and my hair will be in evil knots for days but I submit to it, let him torture me because I'm sorry not to be sorry and I don't know any other way to apologize. And because he's distracted enough now not to notice if my shoulders are shaking a little, if I sniff once or twice and blink a couple of tears onto my lap, where they won't be noticed.

"Miss Wilder? Did you understand the question?"

What question? I shook my head and mumbled "Sorry."

Lucass tried again. "I asked what he hit you with. Can you remember?"

For a brief moment I stared at him, incredulous. But, of course, he was not in my head—what was the last thing he'd heard? With a whoop like the swallow of air before a sob, I focused. "A fist, I guess. Somewhere on my head." I held my own hand to my face to demonstrate. *But you don't get it.*

That wasn't the important thing, and Peter had been wrong about this—I *had* learned something. I don't think he ever intended to watch me die if I'd tried killing myself again, but I do believe everything else he said was sincere. So what I learned was that there was a limit to my brother's tolerance of me. (Love)

Until then, I'd simply assumed it was unconditional. I could forgive him his occasional shortfalls because it was obvious, even to me, that of the two of us I was the real screw-up, not him, and he always forgave me. Well, he spelled it out for me *that day*: he would not tolerate me being weak.

(Love me if I were)

The thing is, even then, even as close as we were, there were so few people in my life who'd been able to stand me for long. My father had only put up with me for a few years before he took off, never to be seen again. My mother, obviously, had never wanted me much in the first place. I'd never been able to make friends last for longer than it took to learn my name. My teachers and principal referred to me as *a problem* when they thought I was out of earshot—even the doctors I knew at the hospital seemed to get annoyed when they saw me come in. It was pragmatic, then, to try my best to hold on to the person who had tolerated me longest. Because if I wasn't worth a second of *his* life, and nobody else really cared if I was alive . . .

I couldn't be weak. Which was fine—he'd already told me plenty of times how brave he thought I was. So if strong was what it took, what I had to be, okay. I would be it.

(And of course it stood to reason that if I *were* ever weak, it would probably be better not to let him find out.)

(Good Girl.)

chapter 31.

PETER was staring at the bottom of the top bunk again. Still. He could only be conscious of only one thing at a time tonight, and the options were limited, apparently, to either what he could see or how he felt. The bunk was crisscrossed by little interlinked pieces of black metal, and he felt nothing. A small girl coughed up lungfuls of bloody water— and there was no bunk anymore.

They hadn't spoken since this afternoon—Al had taken off for parts unknown hours ago and had seemingly elected to stay there, which could be good or bad news considering the night he was having. He was lonely for a moment . . . and then the floor came into view. It was dingy white. He felt nothing.

All he needed right now was a bottle of watered-down tequila and he could be his mother. A case of beer and he'd be his father. About ten of the pills that started this whole thing and he'd be no one at all.

There was a tiny prickling at the back of his neck, a second's warning before he heard it. It was muted back here in the sealed cell corridor meant to contain the sounds of a score of raucous prisoners (like himself). Still, he recognized the screaming as soon as he heard it, and either thought or yelled a few choice words before he was leaning into the bars and adding his own voice to the noise.

"*Don't touch her! Don't touch her!*" He roared at no one for either a few long seconds or a few very short minutes, shaking the heavy bars until the door rattled.

Finally there were two *bangs* at the end of the hall, and—of course—a disheveled Detective Lucass appeared in front of him. One hand held his keys at the ready, but Lucass hung back wearing a measured, crafty expression. "What's wrong with her?"

"Let me out."

"Daniels was only trying to wake her up."

"Let me out *now*."

"Tell me how to calm her down."

"I *am*."

"I'd have to cuff you."

Peter paused, but not for long. "Fine."

Lucass held on to the keys and the crafty look for a while longer, then unlocked the door and threw it open. "Problem is, I left them in my back pocket again," he drawled in a familiar, lazy voice. "Always takes a second to get them out." And he twisted around, groping backward as though he wasn't quite sure where his pocket was.

Peter didn't need a neon sign: he bolted. Beyond the heavy door the sound was louder and he followed it, less tense than he should be as he stretched his legs at last.

Finally he reached a doorway surrounded by a small horde and edged through, briefly questioning his sister's decision to spend the night in what looked like a storeroom.

Officers Vargas and Daniels, the older woman who never spoke to Peter and the man who still bore the marks of Alana's wrath, stood near a cot, while much of the other staff pressed around the doorway, staring in. Alana sat at its top, flattened against the wall. She was looking around, able to see their faces but unfocused, not sure who they were. She always came out of the nightmare like this, and then gave Peter that hateful look when he refused to let her go until she was fully awake. The frenzy was still in full swing even though he hadn't heard her pause for air yet; more than one of the onlookers' hands were over their ears.

"Get out!" He shouted at the two inside—Daniels especially. Both looked back at him, surprised.

"*Out*," he hissed again as he drew nearer. To his credit, Daniels did take the few steps required to bring him right to the threshold.

Peter sat on the cot by Al, still wild-eyed and shrieking and half-asleep. She struck at him, missed, tried to back away, couldn't. Screamed louder. He had never seen it get this bad before. He tried using her name, one of Di's tips that, this time, didn't work—Alana was making too much noise to hear it. He grabbed one of her hands and she ripped it away, lashing out with the opposing foot.

Peter recoiled hard as she narrowly missed his ribcage, but there was no time to dwell. His head start was expiring and his ears were ringing. Not bothering to think this time, he leaned in and seized her shoulders. "*Enough!*"

If he was not normally given to yelling, maybe he should be—it was working in his favor tonight. Al finally quieted a little, but didn't stop trying to break away.

Now he could talk her down. Before, it wouldn't have gone this far. And there certainly would have been no room of strange faces when she opened her eyes. If he had caught it then by now Al would have been in bed, asking him to tell her something about Jack, or Di's boys, and back to sleep in minutes.

But here, once she'd come around enough to understand what must have happened, when she looked past him to the doorway and noticed the spectators gaping through, her face twisted so, for a moment, Peter was sure she was going to cry. Then she turned back, buried her face in his chest, and screamed again—words this time. Distorted and muffled ones, but he thought he understood. "I hate this, I hate this, I hate this . . ."

Peter threw an arm around her head and rested his chin in her sleep-tangled nest of hair. He was starting to sigh that he did, too, when a flamboyantly out-of-breath Lucass lurched into the cramped space. At last, the eyes turned away. "He got past . . ." Lucass started to pant, but then, realizing the performance was unnecessary, turned to Peter. "You have five minutes, son."

That isn't enough time. And I wish you would stop calling me son. There was something uncomfortable about the title; it drew his attention too completely, made him want a closer look at the man who said it.

Lucass was nothing at all like David. With his graying five-o'clock shadow and stolid, sharp gaze, Detective Lucass was a completely different kind of contradiction. Peter and Alana's father had generally been a well put-together man. But he'd never quite been able to hide behind his eyes the way he could looks or lies. They were always just a little . . . lacking, too empty despite his best efforts.

Well, mostly. They did come to life sometimes, though, didn't they?

Peter's jaw ached and he relaxed it. He wondered, vaguely, whether Al's nightmares had anything to do with her father. It didn't seem likely—she never had them before he left, and he couldn't imagine she remembered David well enough by now to dream about him.

But why else would she refuse to tell him about them? He had spent so much time teaching her not to talk about David; perhaps she had learned too well.

I should ask her. He wanted to, but now was not the right moment. She was only just beginning to calm down, and if he had not trusted her answers before, she wouldn't be any more honest with the crowd eavesdropping outside.

Not much time left, anyway. He would have to try again next time. *Only . . .*

Suddenly, it occurred to him that this could very well be the last time she had one of these nightmares before he lost her. Even if it wasn't to Mom, if he went to prison—which it seemed like a lot of people wanted, and for a very long time at that—then Di would look after her, make sure she was safe, but still she would be gone.

He kept trying to convince himself it would be okay. But hope had an annoying habit of being trumped by what actually came to be.

Lucass clapped his hands. "Time's up."

girl.

chapter 32.

THE morning was long. To put it mildly. And it was my fault, which made it worse. Peter and Detective Solomon Lucass looked like they hadn't slept at all, or like they'd gotten as little sleep as I had, or like I felt. Whichever. Bad Cop didn't reappear until afternoon, and then seemed to be avoiding me, which he hadn't even done after I'd hit him with a chair and stolen his keys. It was like I had traumatized him.

And I felt bad. For making *Bad Cop* feel bad.

It was a weird day.

Still, Baby Face hadn't been there to witness my humiliating performance, and Lucass must have been especially curious, because here we were, sitting on either side of this sturdy, wide, oddly comfortable-looking table . . .

Baby Face looked at us oddly. Maybe I wasn't the only one giving the table greedy looks. "Should we reschedule for a bit later?"

"Aren't we such an official little group," I sniped.

Peter, who was far closer to his comfort zone (and who probably *hadn't* spent the latter half of the night standing in a corner, willing himself awake in case one blink was all it took to wake up staring a strange man in the face again), gave me a look.

I gave him one of my own. "Well I don't know about you, but I'm booked solid until Tuesday afternoon."

One of the officers gave a little snorting laugh, and Peter reached over and tugged at my sleep-matted hair. The door opened while I was grabbing for a lock of his, which was growing far too long; someone called "Sol," and Lucass walked out.

McCowan looked bored. He was a little put out, I guess, at being out of the loop. No one was talking about last night—not even my brother had brought up my not-so-minor freakout yet, even if basically everyone in the building had enjoyed the free show. It wouldn't last, but was fine for now, and whenever the taboo expired it would be that much easier to pretend I didn't remember what had happened before I came fully awake.

I wasn't the only one playing secrets, either. Detective Lucass ("Sol," apparently) was clearly keeping his mouth shut about something, and Peter, too.

I gave my brother a sideways glance. *You should probably say thank you or something.* I decided against it, though. I didn't want to bring it up if I didn't have to. *Still . . .* Peter's eyes were red-rimmed and closed, and he was drawing slow breaths. He had been there for me last night. *How many times have you* not *been there for him?* I made a mental note to ask Officer Friendly (ironically) about getting Peter outside sometime. These long days indoors weren't doing him any favors, and though I probably owed "Sol" a little, too, he was the most likely to understand. *Maybe.*

He was maybe the most likely to understand. And speaking of Lucass, I could hear him approaching from the hall. He sounded like he was saying something to someone—I couldn't understand what—and now they were getting closer and the other person was yelling back-

I sat up. Next to me, Peter did the same.

There was no mistaking that voice. It was the only one I knew better than my own; the one that carried more undercurrents than anyone else's. I could never *not* know it.

My mind should have been racing but couldn't, kept stumbling over small decisions instead—should I stand or keep sitting? Move away or closer? Did I go back to telling all the right lies when my mother was here and when she left . . . would she leave? If she did, where would she go? And would I be expected to go with her?

If so, she'll win. I knew it, though I didn't know how. It would only take a few hours alone with her, and this would all end, fast, miles back from where it started. This was the first thing I could be sure of since we'd been arrested, and to know it—know *anything*—was actually a huge relief.

No! Not a relief, it couldn't be that. I glanced over at McCowan, then Peter, apprehensive, and when I felt what I thought was a sigh starting in my chest I sucked in a deeper breath and held it until my heart pounded the way it should have been pounding all along.

I'd felt crazy before, but this new insanity confirmed it.

My mind was going slowly still, more and more quiet the louder the voice outside became. She was taking over, I may have thought, or maybe she did. The door opened.

I couldn't tell if "My *baby!*" was the end of a sentence or one on its own. What I did notice was the way my mother screamed the first syllable of the word, the second nearly swallowed up by it. By the time I finished noticing this and looked up, however, she was looking at me, *right at* me, and I realized I should have stood and moved closer to the door. That's what a good daughter would do. It was what a child who was happy to see her own mother would have done. It had been less than ten seconds, and I'd already screwed up.

I started to look away, then realized that was no better and settled for as ecstatic a "Hi, Mom!" as I could muster, idiotic silly-putty grin included.

Still got it, don't you? Hell if you aren't just as well-trained as a freaking circus poodle! But she smiled back as she started forward, lifting her arms at me.

Peter, ever the actually good son, met her halfway. "Hi . . ." he half-whispered and, incredibly, smiled. It had been so long since he had last seen our mom and, regardless of how scared he probably was, I obviously wasn't the only one with complicated feelings. I wished his back was to me; I didn't like seeing him this way. I tended to start thinking things I would never say—like *are you delusional?* or *wipe that dumbass smile off your face,* or *this is why people think you're fucking insane* . . . Less often it made me think about my father, how ridiculous it would be if I ever saw him again and started acting that way.

A few feet away Peter stopped. Mom had been heading over to hug me (there must be some curious eyes to satisfy), and her arms were still raised. Peter awkwardly lifted his, too, starting to say more.

She closed the distance in two steps and slapped him, hard. He reeled backward and I winced and turned away—to hide the look on my face, and so I wouldn't have to see the one on his. My chest tightened and I started, then stopped, rocking in my chair. Right on time, my right hand convulsed. *There's a joke in that somewhere,* part of my mind mused.

I didn't respond.

"How *dare* you, after all I did for you, after I tried to *help* you . . ." she actually started to cry, but slowed down to continue. "What have you done to my daughter?" she asked, tears still rimming her eyes.

It was a little much, honestly. Maybe my mother had spent too long preparing for today. Then again, maybe I was wrong—to those who didn't know her this melodrama might appear almost normal.

"*Answer me!*" She apparently wasn't finished. Peter had backed up, and Mom was advancing again. "Your own *sister.* What have you got her saying this time? Did I starve just her or both of you? Hook you up to a car battery? Feed you broken glass?" (No, she hadn't done those two things.) "They told me over and over to send you away, somewhere they could deal with you . . . I hoped you just needed time, but I should have seen you for what you were."

The tears made another guest appearance, and I could almost have believed her myself. Even lying through her teeth, the woman had this incredible ability to make me feel—well, *guilty*, but it was hard to say what for, exactly. For telling the truth? For leaving? For not missing her enough?

No idea, but . . . Apparently finished with Peter for the moment, my mother had left him to continue toward me. He stayed near the wall, but I still didn't really want to see him, so that was all I took in before standing, not sure if I meant to move toward her or away. I was afraid of what either direction would mean to McCowan, who was still in the room, to Peter, to my mother, to *me . . .*

She practically ran into me, wrapping her arms around me before I made a decision. "It's okay, baby, Mommy is here. Mommy's here." And I caught on at last, what she wanted was for me to break down and hug her back and cry like the nightmare was finally over. But it wasn't, it was far from over. The question was . . . what would *over* be?

Backing away, she held me at arm's length. I didn't know what to do with my hands. As she looked me over I realized something else, as well: she was only a couple of inches taller than me. Barely. In every memory from toddlerhood to the last time I'd seen her she towered overhead, bending almost double to look at me, talk to me. What else about her might my memories have exaggerated?

My mother told me to look her in the eye and when I did, I saw one more thing.

She did not look even the slightest bit anxious.

Which must have been what she wanted me to see, because the calm was well-hidden only a moment later. "You tell them what he did to you," she said sternly, with a small shake of my shoulders. "You be brave and tell them what he did. All of it."

While she spoke Peter had been very slowly inching back from his spot on the wall. Now he was a few feet to my left, his shoulder lined

up with mine. It was a kind gesture—*I'm still here*—but I was beginning to worry about how things he did might be interpreted by people
who believed what my Mom might—would—say about him. "I'll tell
the truth," I promised instead, almost silently. My mind dimmed and
brightened for a moment, shocked by a sudden flood of adrenaline,
but my eyes stayed firm.

Her mouth thinned a little. Compressed itself around the edges,
just for a fraction of a second. I was afraid she might smile.

"Good," she said. She smiled. She hugged me again.

Officer Lucass came back, and I was released. "You're the one I
spoke to on the phone." This accusation was immediately followed by
(probably genuinely) outraged demands to be told *why* exactly, despite her *very specific* warning, her daughter was in the same room as
him, after what he'd *done* . . .

I knew what he had done. Or, correction: I didn't know what she
would say he'd done, but I could guess. Didn't like it, but could. This
had never happened before—my word and Peter's against hers—but I
could be damn sure she had prepared for it after I went missing. She
would have come up with the story months ago. And, whatever else
she might be, my Mom was an amazing storyteller.

Still, it would take some serious creativity to pin everything she
would to try to on a quiet kid like my brother. With that much work
ahead of her it was strange she should only be *faking* distress, which
puzzled and weirdly almost impressed me a little.

I heard Lucass apologizing and looked up. *You better hope
he doesn't-*

My mind may have gone blank or it may have raced. I don't know.
I wasn't there; I had shied away from it. Oh, I was still in my body. I
was there, sunk down in it trapped screaming in it feeling something
suddenly give way and let go a little without even knowing what. I felt
a vibration somewhere, some low sound but could barely hear it, even

when a hand landed on me and it turned into a whimpering wordless shout and although I knew what it was I still twisted to get it off of me, sinking even further staggering back and away until it was gone, there was no hand anymore.

Now I understood why she'd smiled.

There was a face over Solomon Lucass' shoulder.

12,

SHE is doing dishes, thinking about nothing. Well, she's trying to think about nothing, she tries to all the time but she isn't very good at it so she pretends instead, which makes it easier to lie about.

Not that anyone ever exactly asks what she's thinking, but sometimes she sort of asks herself, in her head. Mentally. You ask mentally. Use the right word.

The dry dishes have spots on them. She picks up a glass and starts to polish it but is bored before long and thinking hard about trying not to think.

She's starting to hate summer. It used to be the best season of the year, even better than Christmas because there was more time to enjoy not having homework, especially when Mom would leave and it was just her and her brother . . .

She puts the glass away and picks up another. Where are they going to live after he comes to get her? She's a little optimistic maybe but not dumb; at the same time, she thinks, maybe a bit anxious but not worried.

Is that even possible? Maybe.

Most likely wherever it was, it wouldn't be very big. Maybe not very comfortable either, bugs coming out of the walls or something. She puts this one away and starts on the plates. That actually might *be okay. Honestly, maybe she should let some bugs in here too, so at least there'd be someone to talk to.*

She laughs. A car rumbles into the driveway and she stops to listen. Dying engine . . . slamming car door, then . . . another one? Mom's voice starts, gets closer . . . and then there's another one.

Crap. The girl is not unaccustomed to strange men staying in the house, but dealing with them is just another part of her new-found solitude that she has yet to figure out. The boy had made sure she didn't see them much before. He even locked her into her own room sometimes when he couldn't stay with her. She hadn't understood why, and she had joked once that if one of these men might be her new daddy one day, shouldn't she get to know them a little?

Only once. That had not turned out to be a good day.

Anyway, she thinks she kind of understands now. And even if she didn't, he thought there was danger, and she made a promise to be safe that she has been trying her absolute hardest to keep. So she starts on the next plate before this one is done, being careful but going much faster.

The lock clicks and the front door swings open. Mom asks something to the man and then she is standing here, watching the girl polish the second-to-last plate. "My friend wants a sandwich," is all she says, and then she's gone.

Is he going to make it himself? *The girl really, really wants to ask, but she needs to hurry and get back upstairs, even if she can't lock herself in, so she finishes polishing as fast as she can and is pulling the bread down when she feels someone watching her and realizes the man is in the entryway to the kitchen.*

"Hey, what's your name?"

She ignores him, finds some sliced ham and mustard and starts throwing them together.

"No name? Just a girl today. Well, girl," he says, moving a hand up quickly—the girl is proud of herself for not looking like she flinched— "I'd like to make a substitution."

Something lands on the countertop next to her, a loaf of rye bread that has been on the refrigerator for days and is probably going stale by now. The girl stares at it for a moment until she realizes what it means and re-closes the bread she'd grabbed first. This is weird, but not in the way she expected it to be, and she wonders if maybe she cares more than she thought that Mom has not been talking to her much lately.

Not important, *she reminds herself.* Go faster.

"Pretty outside," the man goes and sits at the table, looking out of the window. She can't decide if he's Mom's age or a little younger, but the plain shirt and jeans might make him look younger than he actually is because it's a pretty normal thing to wear. "I like fall better, though. The weather, apples . . ."

The girl agrees but doesn't say anything at first. The problem is, the sentence just hangs there for such a long time. She's not like the boy was. She is used to talking to people, and summer's almost over, which means it has been months since she's been able to—not that anyone really talks to her in school, either . . .

"Leaves," she answers, quietly.

He doesn't say anything right away, but the girl refuses to look up. Finished, finally, she is putting everything away when he speaks again. "You know, I know your name. I was only trying to make conversation, but I didn't know how."

He doesn't quite talk like an adult, either. He actually sounds a little sad she didn't answer him. Adults probably get lonely, too. That's never occurred to her before.

Well, he'll have to make friends his own age. *Sure. But . . . he sounded so sad. And it was such a little thing—maybe just once. Putting the mustard away, she gets up the courage to be a bit louder.* "Well, I don't know your name."

"You don't? Really?" He pauses, thinking. She puts the sandwich on a napkin, sets it on the very edge of the table and takes a big step back. "What kind of bread is this?"

The girl is startled and immediately a mix of suspicious and nervous. She feels her stomach tighten and takes another step. "The kind you said. Rye."

The man looks up and smiles, kind of a nice, small smile. "Then that's what you can call me."

"That's not a name," the girl blurts before she can think. Now she's glad she didn't tell him her name, even if he does already know it. "It's a food."

"Lots of people have food names," he replies, not missing a beat. They kind of talk the same way, the girl thinks. Still smiling, he continues. "Tell you what. You can call me Rye, or . . . Hamburger. The choice is yours."

She smiles back a bit. "Fine. Bye, Hamburger," she shoots back, unable to resist, as she turns and finally heads for the stairs.

If anyone asked, she would definitely say she's grateful for the company. Over the past couple of weeks the two of them have become great friends, and now when her mother brings him over—and he's here pretty often—the girl is usually happy to see him.

He even stays with her sometimes when Mom leaves to take a nap in her room or run out to get something. The moment she's gone he comes and finds the girl right away, almost always in the kitchen (she's started saving kitchen chores for when he's there). Sometimes he even brings her stuff, like a donut or cookies, and once a book he said he had liked when he read it. She started it, but a lot of the scenes were obviously for adults only and she just pretended to have read the rest.

Of course, it would be nice if he would help or something while she's doing her chores. But it isn't his house, so the girl guesses *he doesn't have to. He kind of sits there and talks with her most of the time, about anything. She likes that. What she doesn't like as much is when he gets quiet, because then she can't tell what he's thinking.*

He hasn't said anything for a while now. All he's doing is sitting there watching her clean, and she wishes for the hundredth time that she could tell him to get off his lazy butt and be helpful. But then he might not talk to her at all anymore.

"Hey, Girl." He still calls her Girl, even though he knows her name. She hasn't told him she doesn't actually like nicknames. Anyway, she calls him Rye, and she's sure that isn't his real name either.

"Hey, Rye," she replies, mocking his tone—weird, quiet and smooth. He can be such a dork.

"Hey Girl, I'm curious." The girl almost asks why but he doesn't give her a chance. "When you go to school, do you have a special boy you like to be with?"

The girl is caught off-guard, but keeps scrubbing the stove-top. "Huh?"

"You know, like a boyfriend?"

She isn't sure where this came from. He's never said anything about boys before. They do talk about all kinds of things, though, seasons and favorite foods and books and even school. Maybe it just never came up.

Still, she lies without a second thought, and without a clue why she's doing it. "Yep, Conor," she says cheerfully, making up a name on the spot.

Rye goes quiet again. Eventually she turns to look at him, just for a second. He is staring out the window rather than at her, which is what she prefers. Still, there is something weird about how he's sitting, and though the girl might be wrong, she thinks he looks angry. She's starting to think she made a mistake.

She turns back to her task quickly. But in a moment he has an-other question. "Does he touch you?"

Okay, she definitely *said something wrong. But what is he talking about now?* "Does . . . what?"

"You heard me." *His voice is different. Usually he sounds casual but a little sarcastic—kind of like her.* "Do you let him put his filthy little hands all over you?" *Now he sounds totally different, fast, low, quiet. Like a cat about to pounce.*

The girl swallows hard. It's okay, you're tough, remember? *She is, and she wouldn't normally let anyone talk to her like that. But she is also bored, and lonely, and Rye is the only friend she's got right now, even if she doesn't know his real name and he won't use hers. Even if he does read weird books. Even if, tough as she is, he is scaring her just the smallest bit right now.*

Maybe it's fair, though. She did lie to him, which she shouldn't have done. Anyway, she isn't sure how he meant but she's pretty sure no *boy had ever put his hands all over since she was a baby in diapers, and that isn't even what he asked about. So* no *is the truth no matter what, and she says it.*

"Good," *Rye says back. His voice is getting closer to normal again.* "Don't you ever let him. You're a good girl. You don't need to get attention by being a little slut."

"I know," *she replies, subdued. She knows that name, from her mom and from school, but it was the kind of thing where if she called herself that her brother would get mad. The girl wonders whether what he said means Rye thinks she is one or not.*

They're quiet for a long time. A weirdly long time, and it seems to keep getting quieter. She starts chewing on her lip; all of a sudden, her stomach aches. Great. *She tries to ignore it, rocking a tiny bit on her heels. She shouldn't have lied. If she'd told the truth, that she doesn't spend much time with any of the kids in her school, much less the boys, he wouldn't have said those things. He might even have been proud of her. Now she purposely refuses to look over, even though she's sure—positive—he's thinking something at her, and she really wants to know what.*

No you don't. No—it's probably nothing good anyway. And if this is the kind of thing he's going to think about her, how he's going to talk *about her, maybe she should go ahead and stop being friends with him altogether. Who wanted a friend that called them a slut?*

Not her. The girl keeps working until she can be finished, forcing herself to keep saying it in her head. Who wants a friend like that? Not me.

She's barely past the threshold when he speaks up. "I didn't mean to hurt your feelings," he says, and he sounds so pathetic she starts to feel bad for him all over again. Maybe he does the thing she does, where he says something he doesn't mean before thinking, and then feels so bad about it that he can't figure out how to take it back.

She still doesn't look at him, and he keeps sounding pitiful. "I'm sorry. You really are my good Girl," he tries hopefully.

Well, that's slightly better. "Except I'm not actually your *girl at all." Plus, sorry or not, he still hasn't taken it back. So she doesn't have to forgive him, and she doesn't—serves him right, maybe he won't be such a jerk next time.*

So she just walks away and misses the look on his face.

chapter 33.

SHE was older. This had been the first thought to strike Peter, and it hadn't gone away.

But it was a shock how *different* she looked after all this time. During his early childhood he remembered her (or *chose* to remember her) with an ever-present tired smile, golden hair that curled gently at her shoulders, and brown eyes sparkling with a harmless kind of mischief. Even later, once David was gone, Mom had still looked more or less like herself. She'd changed her hair now and then, gotten a tattoo or two; the smile had gone for good. Maybe, toward the end, she had started to look more tired.

But now the gold hair was heavily streaked with gray, clumped together, cropped much shorter than it used to be. Her mouth sagged at the corners, the teeth yellowed. The black and white sweater she wore was, though clean, nearly as faded as she looked—and Peter found himself hoping she had chosen it for the effect.

Of course, she hadn't looked much better the day he left, less than a week after the long night in the garage. For days afterward there had been moments when Peter convinced himself she had played a trick on him, or that he'd misunderstood or even dreamed the whole thing. But there were other times, times he caught her watching him with the same gentle, hungry look she'd given the handgun when she had not-quite-told him how she planned to use it . . .

Once, she had been holding the gun. That was the night he'd told Al he was leaving.

This day, though, Mom had come home late. Well, early. Like she sometimes did when she was especially "tired," she had torn through the house in a rage, yelling slurred obscenities at whatever lay in her path. In the end she half-fell onto the couch and vomited over it, then gripped its back like she might fall if she let go and stared at the mess. And when Peter had peeked in, investigating the sudden quiet rather than the noise, she muttered something about "all fucking day" and he started, then heaved a mental sigh and began cleaning up after her.

"Thank you," she'd said, and with effort launched herself toward her bedroom.

It might have been sarcastic, or perhaps she hadn't known she was saying it at all, but for the first time in years she had thanked him. And he had figured this might be his last chance to get out on a good note.

Thinking about her a few minutes ago, he realized something else: his Mom had looked smaller, too.

It was no surprise when Al appeared in the middle of the night, quietly unlocking his cell. He was staring at the wall and heard silence for a moment, then a small clang as the door slid shut again. Then more silence.

Peter glanced over his shoulder by way of greeting. She slept here often enough, and he'd especially been expecting her tonight, though she really shouldn't have come.

Actually, he had meant to tell her that—she shouldn't be here, better to head back to her room for the night. But she looked tense. Then again, why shouldn't she be? If he was worried about ending up in prison, she would be worrying about it, too. Plus what would happen to *her*. And maybe also looking for someone to blame for the trouble— hopefully not herself.

She shouldn't bother worrying, Peter thought bitterly. Sometimes it seemed like he was adjusting to life in a multitude of small rooms and hallways; at least the panic attacks were getting less intense.

Or else he was just forgetting what it was like to be out in the open. *It's okay, that'll come in handy in prison.*

"Can I sleep down here?"

He squinted. She always took the top bunk. "Why?"

She stood there for another long moment. Then, like a statue coming to life, her hands clenched and unclenched once at her sides and she tried again. "Just . . . can I?" She almost spat the question, but she didn't seem angry.

"No, Al. Sleep where you always do." He started to turn over again.

"Please?" He thought he heard her voice crack.

He swung his feet to the floor, looking her in the eye. "Why?"

She said nothing.

He stared harder, tried to wait her out, but she didn't notice. She had frozen into a statue once more.

He considered asking again, refusing again, then decided against both and pushed off of the thin mattress to stand aside. She scrambled in right away and stared back at him. The light from the hall reflected eerily in her eyes, made them glitter like a trapped animal's. He shook his head, muttering "Good night," as he started to climb the protesting metal scaffolding.

"*NO!*" she yelled.

There usually wasn't anyone around to listen in—the holding cells were all empty—but preservation of the near-silence had long since become one of their many unspoken rules. So that single syllable jolted through Peter like electricity, and he leapt away from the bedrails to meet his sister's gaze again, making frantic *be quiet* gestures although she hadn't said anything else.

Alana stared at him with the same caged-animal look and waited for his hands to stop waving. Then, in a new voice stretched taut, almost too thin to hear, "You, too?"

Peter's heart was pounding, but it looked like she was breathing almost as hard as he was. "What? Why?"

She stared back.

"Look, both of us will not fit on that bed. Okay? So I'm sleeping up there."

She sat forward, the animalistic look intensifying.

Please don't start yelling again. "I'll be right over your head, all you have to do is call me and I'll come right down . . ." At the same time he was thinking maybe he *should* be thinking she was right, maybe a few feet *was* too far.

Or maybe her odd behavior was making him paranoid, too.

She was shaking her head violently, the bed clanking tiny metallic echoes of her not-yelling-but-still-too-loud voice. "No, no, no, no, no, you have to stay here."

"I'm not going anywhere."

"*Peter.*"

She was getting louder. "Shut *up*," he hissed. She did, but the frantic look didn't go anywhere.

They had almost never slept in the same bed. As a little girl, Al was not the type to have nightmares or see sinister things in the dark, so she rarely left her own room at night. And if she did, she usually preferred to camp out in his closet.

There was only one exception, when he'd had pneumonia and coughed for days until he thought his ribs would break, then wheezed horribly when he lay down, and she'd spent every night next to him, one arm thrown across his chest so she would know if it ever stopped moving.

His practical side was in favor of holding firm, but Peter had been a brother for longer than he had been practical. And she would do it for him.

Plus, I won't get the chance to make it up to her from prison.

She opened her mouth—no doubt to yell something else at him—but he cut her off. "Okay, okay." He dragged the blanket and pillow from the top bunk and threw them to one end of the bottom one, indicating that the pillow, at least, should stay there, then climbed into the cramped space. Al took the side closest to the wall.

"Thank you," she muttered, throwing the extra blanket over herself, her feet by Peter's head.

He found himself strangely bothered by that for a moment, then remembered why and chose not to dwell on it. Instead he did something he hadn't done in a while. After she had settled in, he reached over and laid one hand on Al's head. "It'll be okay." He started to smooth the hair, realigning it so it wouldn't tangle while she slept.

Al ducked away. "Sure." She pulled the blanket over her head and was still.

Peter tried not to take it personally and failed. Sitting back against the frame, he let his head sink down until his chin rested on his chest and stared into the blanket until his eyelids began to droop.

This was not sleep, it wasn't even close; despite how miserably taxing this day had been emotionally, he was not tired at all. So instead began the frustrating cycle of trying to will his brain to rest while his body refused, grew bored and compelled his brain to make up something entertaining—which, with a *just let me die* groan, it always did.

He tried to focus on the coarse dark-green fabric of the sweater he had on over his t-shirt. He had come here with only the clothes he'd salvaged when the Drophouse burned, and it must have been unusual to have a visitor to the holding cells for this long, because after a few days there was the sweater, appearing like second-hand magic on his bunk while he was taking a welcome, if chilly, shower in the officers' facilities.

He had asked himself, when the sweater (probably a lost-and-found or charity item) appeared, why they had not simply provided him with one of the fluorescent orange jumpsuits he'd been expecting. The theme du jour gave him his answer, of course.

There are no jumpsuits where no one is meant to stay for more than a couple of days. Those are for more permanent tenants. At your next stop. And you know where that is, right?

He did, though he wished like hell he could stop thinking about it. Not until Mom arrived had it occurred to him so vividly, and so often, that he might be forced to spend much of the rest of his life trapped behind bars.

Maybe he hadn't wanted to think about it before. He didn't now, either, but the thoughts, like his mother, were here. And they were not letting up.

At least now they knew she hadn't been taking her time because she did not care, as Al sarcastically said. In fact, Mom had been up to nothing less than what she always did, the thing she was best at. She'd been planning.

The man who ambled in after Jacqueline had not been a pleasant sight; few faces from his childhood were. But this one . . . well, the memories associated with the face of his former "psychiatrist"— Peter's face twisted into an involuntary mask of distaste—gave "unpleasant" a completely different meaning.

Giving him too much credit. Maybe.

But here's a thought: if someone, a kid, had to go through, say, seven years of terror, bullying, mockery, welts, bruises, even gashes his mother would say he had given to himself, if he was constantly dodging special education classes for fear of "embarrassing" her? What about if the kid had to take every day of those seven years in near-total isolation? In silence? All because of one thoughtless moron who couldn't be bothered to do more than stare at the clock, his clipboard, then the clock again, for forty-five minutes every second Monday for seven years?

Just an idea: that moron might actually deserve some credit. And a lot of blame.

He shook his head, remembering. He had survived that time with only a small girl's help—and even then he was certain part of him had not survived it at all. Peter would not forgive the doctor's utter failure to recognize what was right in front of him.

Except there wasn't only one person. There was also the kid who wouldn't speak up for himself.

That wasn't fair. What could a kid do? Doctor Pollock was the adult, or should have been. He could have done something. Yet all he was ever interested in doing was doling out more pills, more diagnoses.

So what? He's an idiot. This was no revelation. And he was the perfect witness, one who would support Jacqueline Wilder's version of her "dangerous" son.

His mother had reinforcements. But by now Di would know what had happened—he should have met up with her long ago. He shifted, trying to get comfortable on his narrow perch. He had reinforcements of his own.

By the time it actually woke him up, it seemed Peter had been hearing the sound of quiet swearing for a long time, encountering and dismissing it in a distant and not entirely uncomfortable way until, at last, a tendril of awareness crept in.

"Hey."

A flashlight beam sliced across his eyes and he shied away. "What time is-"

"Get over here."

He couldn't get comfortable. It was too early for this—what did they want?

"Now."

Is something wrong? He started to ask but there was the answer, sitting up against the wall beside him. Exactly where she wasn't supposed to be.

Staring, he willed Al to say something, because he couldn't.

She leaned over, somehow looking both crazier and more coherent than Peter felt. "This is my fault. I can-"

But she was too late, because now there were more people in the cell and everyone seemed to be yelling. People often made too much noise, even though all it did was cause more confusion, he thought as they tried to push him through the wide doorway. They couldn't, not with Al hanging on, and when they pried her off and shoved him out into the hall he looked back and nodded, once, thinking that if everyone would just *shut up* for a second maybe they could think more clearly, maybe they would all calm down.

chapter 34.

THERE were maybe ninety tiles on the wall. It was hard to count them—the solid, windowless, endless walls seemed to become animated if he stared too long.

Weeks of being indoors, and he was not adjusting. The small station's equivalent of solitary offered only lying down and counting tiles for entertainment, but it was roomy; when the boredom got to be too much, he could take a leisurely twelve-inch stroll to the center for a change in perspective.

Sometimes it seemed he had never been out of this room. Of course that wasn't true. Every day he went upstairs and talked to his lawyer, (a bespectacled, too-young woman who was too unsure to be reassuring and appeared only to own one brown suit) or talked to one of the police officers while the lawyer squinted and cocked her head at them. Sometimes he talked to his mother, with his lawyer perched twitching beside him. Sometimes Mom didn't bring her lawyer, or maybe he was watching through the one-way glass.

The novice attorney *had* succeeded in making an addition to the routine, a short constitutional after each meeting before he returned to this cell. Sure, it was still indoors, but it was upstairs. There were windows there.

He spent some time talking to Detective Lucass, too. Solomon. Who had let him explain when everyone had lost their minds, after hours of him sitting paralyzed and unable to make himself say a word.

Sol had waited for him to talk, and listened, and then simply said they would have to start doing things the way they should have from the start. No more joint interviews. "Your mother didn't like it. And it's time we got you some counsel in the room anyway," he'd drawled dispassionately.

When Peter started to sputter a few promising consonants, Lucass cut him off. "Ah, no one was surprised she found her way over there. That girl breaks every rule she gets her hands on," here he leveled a warning gaze at Peter, as if blaming him for his sister's delinquency. "But we did not know she could get in. Made us all look like fools—or worse." No need to say more.

That night had not been the final stitch in the orange jumpsuit he was still certain awaited him. Still, it had changed things. He had an attorney. He had not seen his sister in a month (a *month*, shit), but had seen both his mother and former psychiatrist, and he'd been moved to the solitary cell in the basement, because it had only one key.

And no windows. And was even smaller than the last one.

Technically, there was *one* window. It was on the door, a narrow but very tall glass and mesh slab (Peter had not yet tried to count the small diamonds) whose shutter was always left open from the outside. He hated the shutter, the miniscule second door that anyone could close at any time. But all he could do was ignore it—even if it did not always cooperate.

Peter . . .

He pretended to be asleep.

Hey, Peter, over here, look . . .

He covered his ears. Damn it, he *hated* that door.

"Look, I don't have long, please pay attention."

Wait. Either the shutter was learning to do impressions, or this was a familiar voice. He played it safe. "Ma'am?"

"Ouch. Didn't anyone teach you never to call a woman that?"

Slowly rolling from the bed, he stood but stayed well away from the door. There she was, same hair, same old-fashioned glasses—the only thing missing was the lab coat. *And, more importantly, company.* At least she seemed to be alone. *Still, careful.* "I guess not. Sorry."

Doc looked disappointed by the cold welcome. "Now, come on, you remember my name," she cajoled, dropping a hint and playing along at the same time.

Peter wished he could be more sincere; unfortunately, even though she was alone he could not be sure there weren't cameras to catch the two of them acting like more than mere acquaintances. Anyway, his mind was racing: she said she didn't have much time, but Doc had answers—and he had so many questions. He nodded, apologetic. "Of course, Doctor Deleon. It hasn't been that long."

"Good." Doc dropped the coy act quickly and completely, suddenly curt as always. "What do you need to know?"

Strangely, he found himself taking a step back from this version of her—too much time with Mom did wonders for the nerves. From a distance, though, he took up his old part again. "When did you get in?"

"Three days ago, three and a half."

Peter was confused for a moment to be seeing her only now, but caught on. "So then, the obvious first?"

Evidently she'd hoped he would not ask. "The fact is, dear, it's not good news. I barely had a chance to talk to her, but . . ." It was unlike Doc to hesitate.

Peter looked down, shuffling his feet, and asked her to go on.

The pause lasted a while longer nonetheless. "I wasn't here yet. As a matter of fact, so you know, by the time I got here the whole thing was basically over. But at some point, someone suggested your sister should be examined. For . . ." Doc paused again, uncomfortable, but eventually allowed her training to take over. "For signs of sexual abuse, or sexual activity. Like I said, I was not here when the decision was made. I would have tried to stop them. She wasn't up for it. I'm sorry.

"And I don't think anyone asked her feelings on the subject either—I wish I had been there. I'm so sorry, I may not know her well, but maybe she would have *talked* to me."

Peter looked up then. "Why do you keep apologizing?"

Slowly, she ventured, "Well, she could have told someone she didn't want to, that's all. Instead, she went along with it—she didn't even give anyone a chance to help, and I just think, if I were here-"

He was standing still. They were speaking so calmly. So why was the ground slanting under his feet? "We don't have much time, Doc. What are you trying not to say?"

She hesitated again. This was not the Doc he knew; by the time she spoke again Peter had half-convinced himself to tell her he didn't want to know after all. "Ah, well. Ah. Your mother went to speak to the doctor, and then they went to get her for the appointment. She knew when it was, they'd told her what time to be ready. They think it's what she was waiting for.

"She's okay. I should have said that first, she is okay. But when they found her—I am so sorry," she briefly pressed a hand across her mouth, "She must have taken a pair of scissors when no one was watching. Apparently the timing was just slightly off . . ."

Peter froze, his heart heavy and hard as he regarded his friend. Doc didn't know Alana had done this before. He'd never told anyone, sure they would somehow use the information against her. "She cut her wrists."

Doc blinked uneasily. "Just one. She was interrupted."

Peter tasted blood.

"But they did find her, before—she's okay now. And . . . I'm sorry again, but your mother is spinning it against *you*. Not everyone is listening, but it's not good."

No, it wasn't. But he would have to worry about it later. "Where is she?"

"They moved her out of the station—she's in a foster home but still comes in for a while most days. She's usually in one of the cells. It isn't locked," Doc added hurriedly. "I only saw her for a minute and she didn't say much, only that she hadn't forgotten my name—thank you for telling her by the way—and she felt fine. "

Peter nodded, hardly listening. He was thinking, harder than he had in weeks. Finally he blinked. "You're welcome," he muttered belatedly, then added, "'Lita. What are you doing tomorrow?"

She considered. "Interviews, back-to-back. For a couple of hours."

"Good. Can you be . . . entertaining? Keep people busy for a while?"

"You know, I bet I could, if I put my mind to it."

"Great. And if you don't mind, there are some other things I could use."

"Shoot."

Tell me again about how this makes you feel safer.

Bang.

Slow down, you're going to run into something.

I shook my head, rubbing a spot above my eye. Fine, maybe sneaking around like this wasn't quite safe, but it was better than being alone in that cell.

A shadow of movement from the corner of my eye made me swing around and flatten against the wall. But the culprit continued to attack, buzzing formidably around my ear. I swatted it away. A louder noise followed; I ducked (barely). Someone near the front of the police station answered the phone, and quiet returned. It was a while before I started moving again.

I didn't do this every day.

I'd been under constant supervision now for days, though, up from the "constant" supervision Mom had demanded since she got here— all because of one dumb thing I'd said last week. Now everyone kept following or leading me around like a dog on a leash-

That isn't fair. If the cops weren't around, you'd be too scared even to leave your cell and cringe around like this.

I rolled my eyes. *More like if it wasn't for them, I wouldn't need to.* And anyway, I was not cringing. Just alert.

Normally, the lunch hour put a real damper on my sneaking-around time, but today there was some big argument about trials and state- ments or something up front—Doc/Adelita was yelling the loudest— and everyone seemed to have two cents to contribute.

I passed a couple more doors and peered at one, then felt my arm snared a moment before I spun backwards into darkness. Too sur- prised to make a sound, I let myself fly back into the wall, arms up and fists covering my face.

Now I was cringing.

Of course, that wasn't what I was thinking at the moment. What was going on in my head went more like *God, no, not again, not again-*

"Glad I caught you."

I ducked down even more at first, then lowered my arms. Mostly.

"Get it?" he said, but my brother wasn't smiling.

It was a while since I'd seen him, so I decided I did. At least, my face twisted itself into a multitude of shapes involving my mouth, one of which I *think* may have been a sort of smile. "Funny."

"Good. We have to talk."

"You're not breaking up with me, are you?" I tried to joke, but it sounded more serious than I'd meant to be. He seemed all right, and it was good to see him. But he was ruining it by not even trying to seem happy to see *me*, and I started to say so.

Then he moved closer and I turned away, trying to keep him to one side.

Peter was lurking in a janitor's closet even smaller than my first room. The only piece of furniture was a tallish wooden chair, which sat directly under the single yellow lightbulb.

I practically lived in a police station—I knew how to spot an interrogation. "Talk about what."

He stared at me like I had already done something wrong. "I spoke to Doc."

I don't think I winced. But I did take one step down the wall, just a little further away.

He followed, gripping my shoulder and lifting the wrong hand. I pulled away. "Stop it."

It sounded like he was watching me. "What were you thinking, Alana."

It didn't sound like he really wanted to know.

"*How* could you-"

"I didn't-"

He held up a hand. *Stop.* "You said you wouldn't do this again. You *promised*, Alana."

I decided the chair looked comfortable. But as I brushed past my brother I couldn't help myself.

I muttered, "I never promised that."

You'd think I, at least, wouldn't be surprised at some of the dumb shit I say.

I slammed back into the wall again, my shoulder in a vise-grip. My stomach and jaw clenched but I stared straight through Peter, whose face was inches from mine. "What did you say?"

I would have killed for a bathroom break right then. I sighed and looked away.

"Maybe not." He spoke through gritted teeth. "Maybe I imagined it. Maybe I thought you not trying to *end your life* again went without saying. But I still think you owe me an explanation, Alana."

I scrutinized the cracks in the far wall, the uneven gray paint on the ceiling. No way I was about to start swapping stories, not when I'd already said more than I was comfortable with. I could feel the pulse in my arm, but couldn't tell if it was fast or not.

He traced the adhesive edge of the bandage pasted across my left wrist. I could tell now. "Stop it."

"Start talking."

I might rip off my bandage if I tried to pull away so I didn't, just held still and—too late—kept quiet.

"Why did you do this?" There was real fear in those words. Weirdly, I actually felt guilt stirring in the pit of my stomach.

"Answer me, Alana—you have done some pretty bad things, but this was selfish even by your standards."

My hand was numb, arm throbbing, and suddenly I felt a lot less guilty. "I didn't-" *Shut up!*

He let go to point a finger in my face, but all I saw was the movement and, with a wordless shout, my good hand—I was running out of "good" hands—came up to stop it. I caught his arm the same second I realized the blow wasn't coming and dropped it the next, red-faced and fuming. Heading for the chair again, I clamped my twitchy hand under my cut one. It twitched anyway.

Now Peter was leaning down to my seated level. *Just go away,* I thought, and I was (more than) a little ashamed to realize I meant it. "I don't want excuses, Alana. I want to know why my little sister tried to kill herself again-" his voice broke- "and why she thought it was worth it to let everyone think it was because of something I'd done to her."

My eyes slid down until I gaped sadly at the floor. *He really thinks it's that simple.*

And if I told him, he might (*might*) understand. But all I could remember right now was why that was something I couldn't do.

The problem is, I don't really like to lie. Most of the time it doesn't do any good, or you're too afraid of getting caught to enjoy it anyway.

And like it or not, I've never been very *good* at lying, so I had to be careful.

So, choking back bile, I made myself annoyed again. "It's my choice, not yours. You can't make me tell you anything."

Which rang true, when I said it.

Then Peter laughed strangely.

I swallowed nothing. "I want to leave." This went without saying. I had heard that sound only once before, and it did not come from my peace-mongering, nervous brother. The nails of my left hand started to bite into the other arm, working their way up to my shoulder.

He was still in front of me, still smiling a little. "You can leave as soon as we're done talking." This person was a stranger, and I didn't think I liked him very much. So why was I asking for permission?

I tried again. "I'm leaving now."

The smile became a wider but even more humorless grimace. "Okay, maybe I'll just tell you what I think, then. I think it is unnatural for you to be so quiet. I think you're starting to dig your nails into your shoulder. And I think there is only one other thing I've seen make you do that."

I met his gaze with a hard warning glare, borrowing his own language for a moment with a slight tilt of my head. *Enough. No more questions.* I meant it so emphatically I had forgotten to be worried. *This is not something you can be part of.*

He responded in kind, matching my gaze for intensity but setting his mouth in a thin line. Slowly, he shook his head. Twice. *I don't understand,* the gesture said, or *I'm sorry, but you're wrong.*

12,

IT'S hard not to be lonely when you're alone all the time, she thinks. And loneliness feels horrible, like being hollow inside her chest. But she can't think about it too much, or it gets worse and she ends up with her head on her knees like she has a stomachache.

Only a little while since summer vacation ended, and she's already forgetting why she'd ever wanted to go back to school. Monday's homework is already done, but until then . . .

Until then it's getting late. And I'm getting hungry. *It's best to be in her room exactly when the sun goes down, but it's still out a little, just enough that the sky is pale and blue. And the girl can't hear anyone moving around downstairs. So now's the perfect time to grab dinner. She slips almost silently through the door and down the stairs, like a jaguar hunting its meal.* Please. You're more like a raccoon. Or opossum.

She smiles at her own joke, finishes making her way down to the kitchen, and peeks around the corner—though she already knows what she'll see.

"What's so funny, Girl?"

She jumps about a foot into the air, but doesn't yell or anything. Before, Rye popping up like this would barely even have surprised her. But he had kept getting weirder after that day when he called her a slut. Not all the time; sometimes he would be normal for days before getting strange again.

But the last visit was one of the weird times, and it's not exactly like she can tell, but it doesn't look like he's quite back to being normal yet.

"I was starting to think I wouldn't get to see my Girl tonight." Rye smiles at her, his usual kind of shy smile, and she relaxes just a little. "I have a present for you." He had a coffee mug on the table, pushed over close to her.

That makes the girl a little curious, a little hopeful, but not either enough to step all the way into the kitchen. She hadn't realized how much she'd looked forward to Rye's gifts until the past couple of days, when he hadn't been around to bring them. It's part of why she's been so lonely, though she's not going to tell Rye that. She has most of all missed the cookies, the brownies, the milkshakes.

Her stomach makes a noise and she steps forward—but only a little. "Soup?"

Rye grins at her but slyly now, not shyly. "Oh no. Better. Nectar of the gods."

The girl is disappointed but tries not to show it. She can't steal food now, because if he's here then her Mom probably isn't too far away, and her only friend hasn't brought her any—just something to drink. Still, his gift is probably better than nothing. "What's in it?" She asks, edging closer.

Rye pushes the cup toward her more. "Nectar. Of. The. Gods," is all he says, but he says it nicely.

She doesn't know what that is but she won't bother trying to make him explain if he doesn't want to. Finally going up to the table, she grabs the cup, careful not to spill. "Thanks," she says quickly, then turns and heads for her room before her mother can catch them.

Her growling stomach is making it hard to sleep. She almost groans in frustration, punching her fist down into the bed next to her face *a few times, but that doesn't help either so she just stares at the door instead.*

She almost regrets throwing out the nectar of the gods Rye had given her, she's so hungry. Because he wouldn't tell her what was in it she had given it a couple sniffs before tasting, and she was glad she did, since apparently the gods really liked whiskey. There was some other stuff in there, too, because it was all fizzy and even when she blew away the foamy part she couldn't see to the bottom of the mug, but there was definitely whiskey in there.

The girl has tasted plenty of alcohol drinks before and they all *taste gross. Plus she knows she hates when her head is all dim and fuzzy. Her brother used to drink a lot, though. He says alcohol is poison. That's why it's good for first aid, because it kills germs—but it kills people, too, just slower. So, with a* No thank you very much, *she had poured Rye's whole gift out of the window.*

The quiet is making her edgy, but maybe it only seems quiet because there had been all the yelling before, until the door downstairs slammed. She turns over and watches the tree tap at the window, glad for even a little noise, and at some point she must fall asleep because the sound of the door opening sort of wakes her up. The footsteps are what finish the job, though, and although force of habit tells her to pretend she's still asleep she wants to jump up because he's here! *After practically a whole year, her brother kept his promise and now he's back and this time when he leaves he'll take her with him and maybe he'll take her for dinner, and she can ask him if there are bugs where they're going-*

The bed dents so she almost rolls backward and then something is in it behind her. Then it moves, so it's not a something, *it's a* someone. *Did he get in bed with her? Why? She still doesn't move, but now that's mostly because she's confused and not sure if her brother is all right.* "Hey," *she starts, meaning to ask him.*

"Hey there," is the response and now the girl is way *more confused,*

because that is not her brother's voice, not even close. Did Rye get lost? Maybe he's been drinking some of his own nectar.

Either way, he needs to go. "This isn-"

"Shhh," he says over her, stroking her hair.

She thinks two things at once. The first thing is that no one has done that in a long time. This first thought kind of gets tangled up with a bunch of memories, and then it's hard to make any real sense of.

The second thing is . . . this might be Bad. To be honest, she isn't positive about this either, but she's a big reader and this past year she's been starting to put some things together on her own. So even though she doesn't know exactly how, she is starting to realize there are even more ways to hurt a person than she ever knew.

But then a third thing pops into her head, some rules she suddenly remembers from forever ago, and so she doesn't act too quickly, doesn't make noise or try to make him panic. Instead, real slowly, she starts to scoot forward, chewing her lip as she tries to inch out of bed. If she can get just a little space, maybe it will help her figure out which one of her thoughts to listen to . . .

She doesn't make it. Just as quietly Rye snakes out an arm and wraps it around her belly, pulling her backwards and holding her against him. She is worried enough now that she forgets to breathe for a moment, and Rye starts rubbing her back, ignoring her when she tries to duck away from him.

This seems like not the best time to be optimistic, but he doesn't do anything else the whole night, and this reminds her of another time, she can't remember how long ago, in winter. Mom had locked him out in the snow, and it had been so cold that the girl had taken a blanket and climbed down the tree to go looking for him. He was lucky, the Nguyens down the street had left their shed unlocked and she found him inside. But he wasn't moving. Suddenly the blanket didn't seem like enough, so she had climbed under it beside her brother and fallen asleep, and when she'd woken up later he was rubbing her back, hard, awake but worried, and he'd walked her back home.

Not that she thinks that makes it okay, but when she wakes up the next morning Rye is gone, which definitely isn't all bad, right?

She has always known she's a fast learner, and the last time . . . well anyway, sometimes things just aren't okay, no matter how much you try to pretend they are. This can't keep happening. No. You can't *let* it.

Right. But she hopes maybe she can do it on her own—she's strong, she doesn't need anyone's help—so she's trying something.

She knows his footsteps now. She can hear them, not as fast as hers or Moms, but heavier. And getting louder. She holds her breath for no reason as the footsteps fade: he has gone past her brother's old room and is in hers now. The girl closes her eyes and prays, I'll sleep here for the rest of my life, I promise, and I won't ever complain. Not once. Just make him give up.

Stupid, of course he doesn't. People are like that—they never give up on things they shouldn't be doing. For the next hundred years, she listens to the footsteps moving, quieter and then louder, sounding like they're everywhere all at once.

The boy's room is the second one he tries.

Now she's holding her breath on purpose. She expects him to call her or something but he doesn't say anything at all until he opens the closet door, moves aside the pile of clothes and sees her. Then, it's just "There's my Girl."

"Not-" she starts to say but then he picks her up off the floor and starts carrying her back to her room, and when he puts her back into her bed and he gets in with her with one arm around her stomach it's time to admit it. She is flat-out scared. More scared than her stupid stranger-rules are ever going to help her with.

He moves right up behind her, kneading at her neck and her throat. She thinks he might stop if she can shut herself up, but she can't stop making this creepy humming sound. Seriously, she tries to, but she can't. It doesn't matter. *She knows. It's always the same.*

He uses that arm to make sure she can't get away, partly. But mostly he just does this weird think where he curls up, and when she's this close it ends up making her do the same thing, like she's sitting on his lap, so she can't straighten out if she tries. She tried last time. That's how she knows better than to try again. She didn't like the noises he made.

Finally she can't hold them back anymore and two sobs kind of fall out. They have words; he ignores them so she tries to forget she said anything. That's basically the only time the hand leaves her body, coming up to cover her mouth instead. She gets herself back under control immediately and glares at the nothing in front of her, because she won't *let him see her cry, she* won't, will not *do it, and not because he's telling her a good Girl doesn't talk like that.*

She finds herself wishing a lot that she could go to sleep. It's because she tries so much not to, not unless she's sure he isn't coming. It's hard—harder than she ever would have thought, because Mom is around all the time now and she can't sleep in the daytime either, and she's not supposed to at school, and she has to do this every night. Letting herself sleep would be so much easier, but she has this feeling she can only protect herself when she's awake, if she can protect herself at all.

Then there's a night that proves her right.

It's a night when she isn't hiding because she hates being carried around, and she hates him, and she hates it when he touches her ever . . . when anyone does. She doesn't even want to touch herself anymore. She doesn't shower now because she can't, and even if she could she thinks she might have to use a scouring pad, or steel wool, and if she starts she'll just keep scrubbing and scrubbing and won't be able to stop until she's only a pile of bones and organs on the bottom of the tub.

He wouldn't like her then. Maybe he won't now, either, because she doesn't exactly smell great and Mom says she doesn't look great either. So maybe he'll stay away. She hopes, but it's not much of a hope, not the kind that can fool her into thinking it could be true.

She almost moves but doesn't and her back and shoulders still throb, painful and hot. It's been a rough day.

But rough days make for rough nights, so, yeah, he comes. And she's so busy trying not to notice anything (or cry) that she doesn't try to get away, not really.

Quit it. It was stupid to think he'd go away before, and it's stupid to be all whiny about it now.

She isn't stupid. It was just nice hoping.

Anyway at this point she isn't sure if what's making her almost cry is how tired, how so so tired she is, or how much she hates herself for lying all still and not doing anything like this—like . . .

Like what? Like a good Girl? What's so wrong with that, at least he's not calling you a slut anymore. Even if now it's way more true.

Where is this coming from? "Stop it, stop, shut up, shut-" she gets cut off yelling at herself when Rye covers her mouth up, and then she's surprised. For once she had almost forgotten he was there.

"That doesn't sound like my Girl, does it?" He likes to ask her questions when she can't answer them. "You shouldn't tell your friends what to do."

His hand starts to move down again and she doesn't know she's going to talk, but she's so relieved when she does. "I'll tell on you. I'll tell my mother. And the police. And my principal," she lets the words come out in a loud rush. Maybe they'll scare him away.

She's not surprised this time when he makes her be quiet, but then he doesn't say anything either for a really long time, and right as soon as she's starting to hate herself again because she still doesn't dare move he starts talking. "Is that the new game my Girl wants to play?" Now she moves her head some because she hates them both the most when he's making fun of her, but he ignores her. "Okay, Girl. Okay, then I have something to show you."

The hand around her waist lets go a little and she thinks about getting away, but then it wraps around again, only around her arms, too. There is almost time to worry about that, but then the hand on her mouth creeps up over her nose, and she thinks maybe he's trying to scare her. Maybe he'll stop if she shows that it's working, he's winning, she's scared now, so she twists around a little to show it, and when the hand doesn't move tries to pull it off, but she forgot her arms are stuck and that's when something drains out of the world in front of her and she's looking around at a grayish version of it and now she starts to really fight, bucking and rolling around as much and as fast as she can while the gray thickens at the edges.

She died one other time, she remembers. It didn't feel like this.

It's kind of nice, but even more sad that she thinks it's because this time she wants to live.

But then she gets too tired to fight anymore and the gray is everywhere.

chapter 35.

IT was not especially dark. Not bright, certainly, but the lone dangling bulb cast almost enough light to read by—if people did much reading in closets in their spare time.

The light was brightest in the center of the room, falling in a golden, smudgy and limply circular shape onto the wobbly old chair in its center. It had already been there, precisely in the center of that splotch of light, when he came upon this innocent-looking room on this innocent-looking hallway (with a little help from an innocent-looking doctor), and it seemed oddly fitting. So he hadn't moved the chair. Al would obviously find it hilarious, too, and they would probably share a much-needed laugh.

They hadn't, yet. But there was enough light to see her fingering the same spot on her arm that she scratched bloody during her nightmares. He'd only made a wild guess, but her reaction told him everything he needed to know.

"Alana."

She's stalling.

She was. She'd gone silent and blank, her eyes roaming the room vaguely, appearing disinterested as she tried to wait him out.

Not only was she stalling, but she had borrowed his trick, which was not just irritating because she was performing it poorly.

Once his Mom had forbidden him from speaking, it hadn't been long before she took it even further. Though at first she only wanted to control his psychiatrist's perception of him, over time she began watching him even more closely, cracking down until eventually any form of communication—real or perceived—was punished.

It was a self-fulfilling prophecy in the end, though; being so completely cut off from the world is what drove him to create and teach his sister some of the minute coded gestures that kept him from truly losing his mind over those seven years. Because if not talking had been hard, his Mom's preferred level of isolation was Hell itself.

And he would not allow his sister to imitate it because she was afraid.

That had to be it. Over the years he had become well acquainted with silence. He knew it as a friend and an enemy, a shelter and a prison. He knew what it looked like, how it tasted, what it liked and was afraid of, where it went when it was gone and exactly how fast it travelled when it fell. He hated it, but often missed it when it was away for too long.

For all his sister seemed to know of silence, she might have brushed past it on a bus, once.

Until now. And she was not incredibly familiar with fear, either—she was the most fearless person he knew. So the math was fairly simple.

"Answer me." She didn't.

A little clock in his head chimed *no time, no time*. He had to try something else, this was just exhausting and upsetting them both. "Al, I am your big brother. That means something to me, even if it doesn't to you."

Silence. Peter ran a hand over his face and answered what she hadn't asked. "It means you should trust me. I can understand why you might not want to," he was practically pleading at this point. He didn't mean to be, but couldn't seem to control it. "But if it was worth doing this to yourself," his eyes drifted down again and he grimaced, "don't you think it's worth talking about?"

"I didn't-" He glanced up but she cut herself off, looking away just before he caught her eye. This time without announcement, she sighed and started for the door.

Peter moved to stop her. Paused. How was he supposed to do that, exactly—stand in front of the door? Why? What was the point?

He followed her instead. "Fine. Go. I give up." The words had a life of their own, somehow; with each one he felt a little more like he actually meant what he was saying.

"You want to be alone in this? Then be alone. But from now on, why don't you—*whatever* your problem is—leave me out of it. Obviously the world revolves around you, and I am sick of people thinking the shit you do is my fault."

Alana stopped. Her hand was outstretched, reaching for the door, but she spun around instead and lunged, shoving him hard. "It *is* your fault," she whispered, not to him but to the floor between them, but just as suddenly met his eyes again with what, if he didn't know better, he would say was a look of pure, patent hate and shoved him again. He was too caught off-guard by that bright blue rage to know how to respond until she tried to shove him again, and he caught her arm, and she exploded.

"Your *fault*! It *was* your fault! It was *your* fault!" Her fists landed on herself and grazed him; like her words, they seemed to be aimed both nowhere and everywhere.

A dust mop clattered off the rusted nail that held it to its spot on the wall, threatening its neighbors on the way. Alana's already-injured arm flew past his face toward the nail, the abruptly grim cast to her glare saying she meant to do damage.

That was what it took for Peter to finally react, and he did so almost instinctively: he pushed her, roughly, enough to make her lose her balance. She staggered and he grabbed one flailing hand, caught the other when it followed. Then he negotiated his grip, crossed one leg in front of hers and sat down, hard.

Now he just needed to wait. Her energy only *seemed* limitless. She couldn't keep this up forever—though, for a moment, she seemed determined to try. She continued to thrash in what space she had, while his muscles burned from the effort to hold her.

After a long while she relaxed, limp, gasping softly.

Still Peter hung on, stunned. The diversion would not last much longer, and the one thing worse than a premature end to his escape was Doc's being connected to it.

But he had done this before, held her like this before. Only once. She'd only been this angry at him one other time.

Of course, she had every right to be angry; he had made his peace with that a long time ago. He thought it was working, though, these past months of trying to show her he was the same person he'd been before, assuring her he was not going to leave again. He hadn't realized *how* angry she was, though, and "before" was starting to seem so remote he could barely remember it anymore.

He felt a tremor and steeled himself for another round, but nothing happened.

Easily, if not fondly, he remembered telling her he was leaving, several nights before he'd finally gathered up the courage to go. It had happened in stages: she'd laughed, at first, waiting for the rest of the joke; asked what she should bring; backed away from him like he was on fire; tried to shout him down and then, like now, attacked as if demon-possessed. That time she'd split his lip before he managed to catch hold of her, and hadn't calmed down again for hours afterward.

If she ever had at all.

But for now, it seemed

safe enough. He loosened his grip.

"Your fault," she whispered. But he only heard what she'd said then. *Don't go.*

Suddenly he was re-writing his own story from the beginning, through strange eyes, starting years ago with a small girl who believed she could trust him. This wasn't that girl anymore.

He'd wasted so much time telling himself she hadn't changed. Well, he could wish all he wanted, but *he* had changed everything the moment he made the choice to leave, and he couldn't fix it.

So he ignored the ache and pulled her closer again, and even though she hadn't asked, he said, "I won't. I'm not going anywhere, I promise."

chapter 36.

IT was because you left me.

You left, and then he came.

I told you, I told you don't leave me, but you did.

The accusation swirled around and around in my head, breaking up and re-forming again as if one version would sound truer than the rest. *You'll just keep lying to yourself forever, won't you—first nothing happened at all, and now—what? He's supposed to believe you're happy to admit it, as long as you can force him to accept all of the blame?*

Maybe. And so what if I did?

Then it's perfect, I guess. Keeps him from placing it where it really belongs. Even though all you did—all you've ever done—is what you had to.

He thought he understood. But guessing a tiny part of a story isn't the same as knowing the whole thing, and I had no intention of bringing his focus back to the reason he'd started this in the first place.

Still, he was always so damned eager to take the blame for anything I did myself. Letting him do it was too easy to feel right. So

"I don't remember." It was a familiar, comfortable sound bite; I had to give it one more try.

"Yes, Ally. You do. And talking about it might help." It was almost funny—he sounded like he really believed that.

What the hell do you know. I shook my head. *Let go of me.*
"Please."

Honestly, I could almost sympathize. The way I had grown up (the way he'd raised me, when I thought about it, whether he'd meant to or not) the very definition of *secret* was something I only told my brother, and that he couldn't tell anyone else. It had never even occurred to me to keep anything important from him. It wasn't the kind of thing that went both ways, of course, not that I would ever bring that up; still, it must be hard for him, even more than me, to suddenly change the way things had always been.

Harder if he had truly believed I'd spent all that time simply playing alone in my room and we could pick up where we left off and after three and a half years nothing would have happened, nothing would have changed.

I said no. Let go of me. But I didn't say it.

I almost did. I wanted to go hide under a bed, behind a toilet, in a deep, black hole—curl up and pretend not to exist, pretend there had never been an Alana Evelyn Wilder, spend the next few days un-remembering my own reflection while in the outside world the voices calling out for her slowly faded away. The thought was soothing, and peaceful, and if he had let go it's what I would have done.

The reason I did not tell him to let me go is because he might. Whether it was wrong or not, and whether he ended up with the blame or I did, if I didn't give him some sort of answer now he would never forgive me.

I was damned either way, though. Because if I told him the truth— well, then he would let go of me anyway.

Rye had said he would. And one of Rye's many terrifying habits was often being right about things like this.

Rome fell three times during this silence, and with each sacking it got more obvious that, eventually, I would have to say *something*.

But . . . what, exactly? I couldn't lie again; it obviously wasn't working anymore.

I could start from the beginning—okay, no I couldn't. I couldn't do that. And not just because every alarm bell in my body went berserk at the idea.

My stomach twisted. I swallowed. I was probably about to throw up, which seemed about right, so I tried to fight the reflex with a few deep breaths—as deep as possible—as I strained for something to

"There was one night," I said quietly, but at once the alarms (not so much bells as sirens) and the gagging intensified, my vision tunneled, and in the midst of the chaos in my head I momentarily forgot to breathe. But just as quickly as it started it fell silent again, all of my adrenaline completely spent on four words I already regretted. What was left of my mind split in two: one part pretending to pretend, spinning history like fiction as if that made it easier; the other desperately trying to rebuild walls around something that refused to stay forgotten. Both were failing. I was incapable of stopping either. So it continued, "when I woke up in his car."

They started to rebuild Rome again. "Ha-had . . . did you f-fall asleep there?"

Something cool and sickly was creeping up my spine. "No" wasn't a good enough answer, but when I tried to say more my arm moved on its own, lashing out at something I couldn't see but suddenly felt was very real and now I was fighting to free myself, and I had no idea why, what I was trying to escape from, reality or fiction or present or past. But I couldn't get away, *tried* and couldn't and fought for my life as the world started to turn fuzzy at the edges and I waited for it to disappear completely into gray.

I got tired first, though, and the world was still there. Fractured as it was, my self got control of my body again and, as the two of them stopped fighting, I heard a voice promising no more questions and saying it would be quiet. Half of me heard the voice while the other half remembered that time coming out of the gray, and thinking at first that I was going to be sick because the world felt like it was moving.

My head aches; maybe it's hurt. But when I reach for it my arm is tangled up in the blanket and it doesn't take long to figure out my legs are too. Puzzled, I try harder.

There's my Girl.

I jump and then I freeze, remembering all at once the last moment before everything went away. I can't see but I don't think I'm blind. And if I'm not blind and I can get out of the blanket I can run away, or possibly fight. Mom won't like it but if I scream loud enough she might come, maybe.

The car stops. I haven't even moved, but only because I didn't know. I didn't know I wasn't at home, and now I can't even scream for my mother. My back hurts, my head feels like it's exploding and now my heart starts hammering, too.

Something lands on my shoulder and creeps up the side of my neck and I want to roll away from it but can't. Then the blanket gets pulled off of my face and I'm blinking at streetlights, breathing fresher-but-stale car air and looking hard for anyone I can run to if I get out. Even if it's just a stranger, maybe they'll take me to a phone or at least scare him into not following me right away. That would be good enough. But there is no one out there, and I look more and realize I don't know where I am. If I run, how will I get home?

The car turns off. But that hand stays on my neck and I don't want to feel like I'm giving up, so I'll still fight if I have to. I try even harder this time to get out of the blanket even though the seatbelt is holding me in.

Hey, hey. Come on little Girl, what's your rush?

I hear a low, deep chuckle. I tell myself *don't* look, but I never listen so, for a second, I do. What I see is night lights shining off of eyes and teeth, making them all sharp.

Where you going? I know, you want to get back home to your

Mommy. Well I'll tell you what, that's okay with me. How about we can just put you . . . back to sleep again, and by the time you wake up we'll be back home in bed?

No. I say it too fast and want to slap myself a moment later, when I realize that's exactly what he wanted, but it's what I want, too. I can't protect myself when I'm not awake. And I don't know where I am.

That's my Girl. I took you out tonight for a reason—there's something I wanted to show you. So just sit back and be good, and we can both enjoy our little trip before it's time to go home.

All of a sudden I want anything in the word but to go back home. Anyway, if I stop moving around he might take his hand off me. I try to look like I'm sitting back; he puts his hand on my chest and pushes so my back is pressed up against the seat. I close my eyes tight and try to figure out what that meant, took me out. It might mean like when you go on a date, or else like you take something out of the fridge, when you want it for now and you'll put it away again when you're done. And then, when it's all used up, throw it out for good.

Much better. Here's what I want to show you.

I try to make myself feel better by pretending I don't think it's either one.

Are you looking? I can't show you if you don't look.

I feel a hand touch my face, pull away hard.

Now you're going to start making me angry.

I should be the angry one, but I try and it's like I'm going to be sick all over again. It's quiet for a minute. *I'm sorry*. I don't like that I say it but I'm pretty sure I have to.

Then look.

I gulp and look up, right in front of me. I try to act bored, like I don't care if he gets mad or not, *At what?* There's nothing out there, just streets and buildings and alleys, dirty-looking in the dark.

Rye points at one of the buildings and I turn toward it so he won't touch me again.

That's my house. Not the one I live in, the one everybody knows about, it's a special one. A secret place for only me and a few close friends. He looks at me to make sure I'm listening. Then he points again. And that is your room.

I keep breathing. I won't cry. Not here. This time when he lifts my chin so I'm looking where he points, I don't pull away. Instead, I bite down into my tongue.

See? It's around the corner but you can see it from here. That one is just for you. The walls in it are so thick, you can't hear through them. The window, too, and it has big bars over it. And there are books in there, you like to read. A special room for a special Girl.

He makes me look at him.

You can be in a special room like that for a long time without ever coming out.

From the corner of my eye the house that was just a building before suddenly seems to take a step toward us and I glance at it to make sure it stays back.

Of course, I'd never be too busy to come and visit. And I've got lots of friends who'd be dying to meet my Girl.

He keeps looking me right in the face while he talks and now I can't look away.

And if you start trying to get me in trouble . . . then I guess you won't leave me much of a choice, will you?

I keep staring.

Will you?

Yes.

What?

He lets go and I shrink up as small as I can on the other side of the car. I think I've probably made him mad by now, but I need to say it. *You could just go away.* I'm not crying, it only sounds like I am.

It gets quiet again. I'm looking at a small corner of window facing the alley. Can I see bars on it? Rye sighs and reaches for me and I try to get even further away, thinking he's decided it's time to go back home again. He pats my leg.

No, I couldn't do that. I wouldn't just go and leave you behind, I'd miss you too much. That's why I have this place.

I look out of the window again, but not at anything. There still isn't anyone there. I think one of us must be insane, and if it's me maybe I'm dreaming this whole thing. I hope to God I'm insane.

So you'll always be my Girl.

But I'm not. I belong with my family. Rye laughs.

Little Girl, what family? You've barely got any left—and I bet they'd be happy if they knew I actually wanted you.

"You didn't believe that, did you?" Peter asked.

I wish I could tell Rye he's wrong, but I know better now.

If this were yesterday then I could just tell him I didn't care, that I would tell my mother anyway and she would never let him take me away.

But I've been *so* exhausted, and I'm trying to keep myself safe, and I figured maybe now it was time to get some help, so actually when he'd left just this morning I'd finally tried to be brave. I'd crept downstairs without permission and, watching the floor carefully, I'd told my mother about us.

I wasn't sure what to expect, but when she said take my shirt off I'd been stupid enough to almost be grateful, thinking there must be a mark or something she could see, or look for, that proved what I told her was true. Then my head banged against the wall and she left me there to wait, with no time even to say this wasn't right, I needed her to help me, that I didn't do anything wrong, not this time.

Sometimes you only figure out what you've done by what happens to you. And this morning, apparently, liars got the belt.

That's how I learned that he's her friend, not mine, and little whores need to keep away from what doesn't belong to them. At first I flinched, and she switched to the end with the buckle and hit harder. So then I just stood there, waiting for it to be over so I could start my chores, and I think that's why I don't cry now, with Rye, because I figured something out then. I don't even remember exactly what it was, but even though I know Rye is probably right I don't see much point in crying anymore.

"Ally? You didn't actually believe him?" Peter thought I hadn't heard. He let go.

I didn't care, at all. It was out there. He knew what he wanted, and more than he needed, to know—the blame part was up to him.

What he couldn't know about were all those nights after Rye had put me away again that first time—the ones I spent worrying he would find out I'd already told. Constantly imagining night after night the terror of waking up in a tiny bare room, miles away from anywhere I knew, with locked doors and bars on the windows and never being able to get home and his *friends* that were like him, probably just like him or even *worse* . . .

Night after night, until I finally solved my problem myself.

. . . or tried to.

12,

WHEN she wakes up a squirrel is staring through the window at her, like she's an animal in the zoo. At first she ignores it and doesn't move but it doesn't either, watching until she gets so uncomfortable that she lifts her head and tells it to go fuck itself. Then the squirrel gives her a hurt look and bounds out of sight.

She thinks she might feel bad, if she ever felt anything anymore. But it's been a while.

She wishes a little that she hadn't used up all of her feelings already. Anger, mostly, because it's the only thing she even really wants and now there isn't any left. The rest of the feelings can stay away. All she needs now is whatever wits she has about her, the ones that keep her doing all the things she has to so she can stay alive—like now they're telling her to get her ass out of bed before Mom does it for her.

It hasn't been long since the night in the car, but it feels like months. She doesn't remember the last time she got one whole day right, and since Mom has apparently not forgiven her yet for what she said—what she already thinks of as her lie—she's not cutting any slack about it. Everything hurts.

But it isn't all Mom's fault. Some of it is her own. Her tongue hurts because she's bitten it; her shoulders have all these little scabs from *where her fingernails dug in. She is getting good at using just the right amount of pain to keep awake for a whole night. So good, in fact, that now even her eyes hurt.*

Congratulations.

She would never dare fall asleep anymore. She can't know, but does know, that something terrible is going to happen if she ever falls asleep while he's there. She sees it as clearly now as she didn't before. She had been so optimistic then. Stupid. It's only going to get worse from here.

At first that was hard to imagine, but lately there's been a lot of extra time to think. One new thing she's learned: you don't have to be asleep to have dreams. Or nightmares. Sometimes the ones when she's awake are even worse, because when she pinches or scratches or bites herself to wake up they won't go away.

When it doesn't go away even when you pinch yourself, doesn't that mean it's not a nightmare? Then it's just real.

The girl laughs, not that she knows why.

Before starting on chores, she sneaks downstairs to steal a little breakfast. There is no one here yet and she's relieved. She can hardly believe she ever felt lonely before; now all she wants is to be by herself forever.

She toys for a minute with the idea of not doing any chores, since there's no one to make her. It is a fun thought, and so for a minute she sits down at the bottom of the stairs, right in front of the door, watching it, daring it to open. It doesn't last long—the thing is, keeping her skin in one piece is pretty fun, too—so she heads upstairs to start on the bathroom.

Now would be the perfect time, if you were going to go. *She thinks about leaving sometimes, climbing out the window and down her tree and never coming back. What could possibly be out there that's any worse than in here, right?*

The mirror is her new enemy. She doesn't like looking at it, wants to not be able to recognize her face. If she doesn't then she can imagine she's not really here, that nothing is really happening to her, the real her. It might all be happening to some girl who doesn't even exist, like a character in a just-okay book who she can feel kind of bad for and then forget about. She's here though, stooped over like she hasn't slept in days because she hasn't, tangled, greasy hair looking like it hasn't been washed in weeks because it hasn't, but she can see herself in her red-rimmed eyes and when the mirror-her starts to curl its lip she turns away because she's disgusted and because she doesn't want to see it looking at her with disgust.

She could *leave, but it also* could *be worse. She wouldn't know anyone out there, would be stuck eating out of dumpsters like she used to sometimes on trips downtown only always. And what would she say if someone asked where she lived, if someone asked any-*thing? *She would never even try telling the truth; she already knows no one would believe her.*

And she did make a promise, the kind that it's really import-ant to keep.

Avoiding the mirror means she finishes the rest of the bathroom in record time. Mom still isn't home, though, and all of the silence is starting to remind her of how much she hasn't been sleeping. Actually, it's dozing off and nearly falling face-first into the toilet that reminds her. Blinking around to be sure she really has finished, she starts to think she might have saved herself enough time for a quick nap. Which is when she sees the closet.

It's weird that she doesn't usually "see" the closet, it's not like it isn't always there. But it isn't a real closet, exactly, it's tiny and only has a couple of big metal things inside so no one ever bothers to open it.

So probably she won't get caught napping there now, if she can even fit inside. Bracing herself for dust or a lot of tiny legs brushing against her, she twists the doorknob and slides inside, fitting herself into the narrow space on the floor.

Not bad. *The girl thinks she might stash a blanket and nap here all the time. The floor isn't too dusty, and the dark feels good on her eyes. Her hand slides across the floor, measuring between it and the big metal box. A piece of piping is loose, and she absently pushes at it to see where it's supposed to fit. But instead it slides easily, clicking over the tiles. It isn't attached to anything.*

She wrestles the thing out from under the box and picks it up. She can't see and doesn't want to open the door so she wraps her hand around it, trying to figure out what it is by touch.

"Ouch!" *She covers her mouth like she can shove the sound back in.* That is definitely not a pipe. *It's a* knife.

There is a little sliver of light coming from under the door, and she holds the knife to it carefully. No way.

The blade is spotted with something the girl cannot scratch off, and the handle is splintery and has black stuff down one whole side of it, but this is definitely familiar. No Way.

She has always just assumed it was thrown away after the last time she'd used it. Whoever did it, all the sharp knives had suddenly gone missing from the kitchen back then and hadn't come back for months, and even then the girl could never get up the nerve to ask about the missing one. Until now it has never occurred to her that she was the only one who would even know where to look for it.

Now that she knows what it is, she pulls the knife back up to her chest and (carefully) wraps her arms around it, hugging it awkwardly. She is happy to find it but kind of wishes she hadn't, like seeing someone after a long time but you still aren't sure whether you're friends. Finding this has changed something. She can feel it.

The first thought is obvious: to just let the knife finish what she used it to start before. This knife is different, not really even a kitchen knife at all anymore, almost like a living thing. It's a special knife for a special type of job, and maybe it came back to her so it could help her again—not that it exactly helped the last time.

That's right, last time it just made everything worse.

Except Mom never made me take them again after, did she?

The girl has to think about that one for a moment.

Well . . . even so. It's like letting him win if she . . . does that again. And anyway, she was a little kid back then, only nine. And not thinking straight.

That's true. *She lets out a silent sigh of relief; she was actually starting to worry herself for a second.*

And plus, there's more than one way to use a knife.

She sucks the sigh back in, clenching her hands into fists. She doesn't like that any better.

Still, maybe if she hides it in her room she won't really have to use it. She can act. She imagines it—the knife is safely hidden under her mattress, or no, the pillow so she can reach it easier, and when he comes in she can just real quietly, warn him to leave her alone. And when he doesn't then pull out the knife and show it to him like, I *said* leave me alone! *And then he gets so scared he runs away—no, that's not enough. He* pees *himself and runs away, and Mom sees him coming out of her room and realizes she was wrong! And then— then she . . .*

Then she buys you a kitten, and you all go to a parade, and Santa Claus comes early and tells you he's your real father?

Although if even one of those things happened it would be the best day of her life, that isn't how things really work. Santa Claus doesn't exist and, if she wants this nightmare with Rye to end, she'll have to be ready to use the knife.

It's almost like he knows. He comes almost every night, but not this one. Not when she's finally ready.

Maybe he found out, and he's never coming back, she thinks. Anyway she falls asleep with her hand under the pillow.

She's been so anxious all day that, messed up as it is, she's actually happy when she hears the door creak. No, that is not good, she knows. But this has been hard.

Planning how to kill someone is hard.

The bed sags in behind her and she bites her tongue out of habit.

What if it doesn't work? What if it's like before, or he snatches it away, or laughs at you? *Worse—what if she loses her nerve? What if she gets partway and gets too scared and just gives up? That would be even worse than doing nothing at all.*

She could still change her mind. Honestly, she could—mom doesn't believe her and she never told anyone else. Maybe she should wait and talk to someone at school. Possibly she's overreacting, and they'll tell her to see it his way—he meets her and sees she's sad, he's nice to her even though he doesn't have to be and doesn't ask for almost anything in return, so maybe she should understand why he gets so mad when she won't just be . . .

Go on, say it.

She isn't talking.

Think it, then. You might as well. Because face it, if you don't do it tonight you never will, and then that's exactly what you'll be forever, right? His Girl. And you'll keep "not feeling anything" and pretending you're being safe by letting him do whatever he wants to you forever until eventually he stops pretending to be nice and it's too late to stop him, or he'll take you away anyway and then it doesn't even matter what he does because once he takes you no one will ever see you—alive—again.

Yeah, yeah, she gets it. She kicks one leg out, hard, shaking the whole bed.

Almost at the same time Rye's free hand is there, rubbing her leg up and down, up and down, higher up each time.

"Quit it," she says. This is part of it—she has to give him a chance to do the right thing first, so she memorized this part. Even what happens next. He's shushing her again, and she repeats herself a little louder, hoping he can't hear in her voice how many times she's practiced.

"I know my Girl doesn't really want that." It's good he's still talking—she wasn't sure he would. If he's talking then maybe she really can solve this without the knife.

Kitten, parade, Santa Claus.

"Yes, I do. I want you to quit now, or . . ."

"Or what?" He's smiling, she can hear it in his voice. She might be smiling right now, too. But this part is important.

"Stop it right now. I can hurt you. Bad." Can't spill the beans about the knife, and she doesn't but her hand still curls around it protectively.

He's quiet at first, and his hand lifts from her leg. This time the girl does a better job of not hoping too hard, so she's not even surprised when it reappears on her face, pulling the hair back from her ear. Instead she's remembering what she's supposed to say next. "I know my Girl wouldn't do anything to hurt me. Even if she could."

A heavy ball is forming in the pit of her stomach, but her mouth responds before she has to worry about her nerve. "I am-"

And then his hand is over her mouth. And like before, it starts to creep up toward her nose. She was hoping he wouldn't do this.

But he did. *And she knows what comes next—he'll pin her arms. Which she can't let happen. She's waited too long already, if she doesn't want to have to do this again she's going to have to do it now. Ready?*

No.

Go.

She pulls the knife from under the pillow, just like she practiced, angles it right, just like she practiced, and, shutting her eyes tight, yanks it down as hard as she possibly can.

She expected it to feel like cutting raw meat. Instead all she feels is that he gasps, his arms get looser, and then he starts bleeding on her.

She practiced a little yesterday and a lot today, but now she realizes there are things she couldn't practice for. She'd thought, without really thinking, that she only needed to get up her nerve for this one cut and then it would be over. He would let go of her and be gone, die or run away, just like that. But now she is thinking getting stabbed usually hurts, and she forgot that people sometimes make a lot of noise when they get hurt. How loud can he yell? What if someone hears? Will Mom call the police? Will she come at all?

Luckily Rye has spent so much time trying to keep her quiet he must be taking his own advice, because he doesn't make much noise after that first little sound. But he doesn't exactly let go, either. If he had run away or died, either way she'd be free. But he doesn't seem to be leaving and he doesn't seem to be dead.

Somehow, until the moment his arm tightens around her again this still doesn't feel real. It's like a plan still, a thing she was thinking of trying out but if it doesn't work, she can just come up with a better one instead. But she never planned for him to be so alive *still, so when he grabs her so tight she* shouts *she pulls the knife out and stabs him again in the same place, and he just grunts again and grabs her throat and pushes her up against the wall while he tries to pull himself up, too.*

What is happening? *The girl is almost, almost too confused to be scared and she just sits there staring, mouth open and both hands clutching the slippery knife to her. She stabbed him.* Twice. *How can he still be moving? She's more awake than ever now, she can hear, see and feel everything as clearly as an animal in the darkness—there is blood everywhere, the grunting and gasping getting faster and faster. Is this how long it takes to die? Or is he just not doing it right?*

He is finally upright and staring back at her. She feels like she has turned to stone, or maybe ice; everything is slowing down inside of her and she can't move, like she is the one dying even though she's killing him.

The grunting is almost words now. "M-. Mah." He is trying to accuse her, but it's like he can't quite believe what he's seeing, what is happening.

She can't either, but she has more air than he does. So she goes back to what she was going to say at first. "Not," she says, shaky but clear, "yours."

And at that moment she sees so much fury in his eyes that she knows he's going to try and take the knife.

He lifts his other hand fast, smashing it into her head so it cracks against the wall and her super-awakeness briefly dims. Then his hand is on hers, on the knife, twisting and prying and trying to break her grip, and he's still holding her throat and banging her head against the wall, trying to take it away.

But she has both hands locked around the knife for dear life, and she does not let go, although the back of her head feels all warm and soft and she thinks she might be crying. She can't let go, because her plan is about to turn into the way she dies and she doesn't want losing the knife to be the last thing she ever does. So he stops trying to take it and turns it instead, aiming at her and slashing like a crazy person, trying to stab it into her chest.

All she can do is push back, make it harder for him so the knife goes in all the wrong places and not too deep, but after a second it gets easier to do. He's stopped bashing her into the wall and he's leaning on her instead, weighing on her chest hard so she has to struggle for breath. He's panting harder, still holding the knife and twisting it, but now he can't cut at all. This is a chance to do something, if she can figure out what.

Coughing a little, she draws up one leg she can't see and drives a foot she can't see into a place she can't see. She gets lucky; he groans and falls into her, and she can control the knife again. He's not done fighting, though, because his fingers—on both hands this time—are tightening around her neck while she rips the knife free and plunges it down into his back one, two, three times.

The second time he makes a sound she has never heard before, like a drowning man sighing. He keeps squeezing her throat for a couple more seconds and then Rye's hands, like the last leftover piece of the world's longest bad dream, fall away.

She squeezes out from under the body and leaves it there. Then, because she can't think what else to do, she climbs outside and digs a hole with the knife. She buries it in silence, feeling like a traitor for making it dig its own grave after it saved her. Obviously that's silly, but it's how she feels.

You feel silly. You just killed someone, and you feel *silly*.

She had to.

I know. It's only . . .

She nods and stands up. It starts catching up with her then—pain, dizziness, followed closely by panic. She starts a blind, slanted walk through the woods, not sure where she's going, not sure where she can go but knowing she must keep moving. She thinks she has a concussion, and if you have a concussion you have to stay awake or you might never wake up. If she stops, she might fall asleep. And after all that happened tonight, just falling asleep forever would be the stupidest thing imaginable.

In one clear moment, the girl understands it's over, really over.

And not because someone bailed her out, or helped her because she was too weak to do it. She did it; she saved herself. Maybe she really is brave, like her brother always . . .

And suddenly the misery of just a little while ago has all come back, but now, in addition to stumbling around through the woods at night with no shoes and clothes all ripped and covered with blood, some of which is still leaking out of her, she is remembering maybe the last promise she ever made, and thinking of all the ways that she might have just broken it.

The thing is, it was two. She made a promise to keep herself safe, sure—but she also promised to keep out of trouble. If she had let herself get taken, or hurt, or even killed, she most definitely would not be safe. That's what he wanted. Her to be safe, so she'd still be here.

She doesn't know if that means here home—or here alive.

But she killed Rye, and she doesn't know how to hide him, and when someone eventually finds him they'll know it was her. She'll be a killer. A murderer. Which could land her in the kind of capital T Trouble that doesn't let you stay here home—murderers go to jail. Or worse. Do they execute kid murderers too?

And anyway, even if she is here, what will he do once he knows? A moment ago she thought killing someone was something a brave person would do, but she doesn't know anymore. He promised to come back and get her, but that was then, back when she had never thought of killing someone, even someone she wanted to hurt, even someone she hated.

Mostly.

"Next time I leave you."

Her face twists and it hurts her head. No, she wasn't a coward, she isn't weak, she had to, he might have killed her!

Maybe, but only because of what you did to him first.

He never would never have done what she had.

Any of it. She only had to kill someone because she let him get close enough to hurt her, maybe even more than she knew, maybe after he trapped her in that gray...

The boy would have ignored him, gone to his room and not come out until Rye gave up. She wishes she could go back and never have laughed at his dumb joke and called him Hamburger. She was so stupid then, acting like a little baby because she was bored and by herself—better to be alone than this. And now, whether she goes home just to be taken away by someone else, or left behind again, or just stays out here to die, she'll be alone again anyway.

She was weak, letting herself think of Rye as a friend. And killing is a coward's way out, so she's that as well.

She sits down in a pile of pine needles and leaves, past worrying about falling asleep. So she was weak, yes. And she not only did she not keep herself safe, but now she's about to be in more trouble than ever.

She can't stop thinking about what Rye said. "I actually want you." Will he be right about the boy like he was with Mom?

"I would never have wasted a second of my life on you if I'd thought that's who you were when things get hard."

And is that a chance she can afford to take?

Feeling very sick still but now also very determined, she shoves herself up onto her knees, then her feet and starts back. She's a murderer—she'll have to live with that. But there is one way to go back and not be put in jail for it. One way to make all of the questions still buzzing around in her head go away.

They won't need to be answered if no one ever finds out.

When she returns, sweating, panting, and bleeding, through her window, the room looks like a horror movie—blood on the walls, the floor, the nightstand. In the moonlight it looks like the whole room is splashed in dark paint, especially the bed.

Especially the spot where Rye's body had been lying when she left it.

"No," she thinks she says, suddenly finding herself leaning over the windowsill, squinting at the ground below. Maybe she has been here for a while and forgot. Is he already down there?

She looks harder and harder, trying to force herself to have memories of how heavy he was when she first tried to lift him, how hard it was to move him across the floor, how she finally managed to heave his body through the window and the sound it made when it hit the ground below. Like a sack of potatoes. She remembers. She does.

But no matter how much she makes herself remember, the body does not appear. Horrified, she turns around again, practically expecting to see the room white and clean in the pale light, proving the whole thing was just a dream, and maybe there wasn't ever a Rye in the first place. People imagine all sorts of things. Not normal people, but people.

The room still looks like the world's scariest splatter-paint picture. The blood was real. She touches her head, and it burns and throbs. It was all real. She really did kill someone in this room tonight . . . but where is he?

Mechanically, trying to feel the same resolve she had in the woods a little while ago, she keeps moving. It's a good thing his body's gone; obviously she wasn't strong enough to move it far alone. And anyway she has a lot more to do.

She staggers away, the black and white smears blurring past her. Her eyes avoid the mirror in the bright bathroom light. It won't be so scary once she gets all of this blood off. Then she can start on the mess in the bedroom. Since she won't be sleeping, she has plenty of time.

Maybe he wasn't dead yet when she left, but he definitely is by now. That's a bizarre idea, but it does make her feel a little more focused again. Most likely he crawled away down the stairs, not far, and she can probably roll him outside from there.

She's halfway into the shower when a thought hits her. Hamburger's dead. *It hits so hard it sticks and she can't shake it away, though she does try, and before she knows it she's shaking her head around and trying not to fall and holding in her laughter because* Hamburger's dead, Hamburger's dead, *and that's just too funny to be appropriate right now.*

The room agrees—it starts to race around and around her just as a shadow sprints out of nowhere and pounces, so fast that she can't even catch her breath to scream.

When she wakes up, the shadow slides away just as quickly and her only hint that she is still alive is the nurse turning down the bright light as she explains to the girl that it's okay, she doesn't have to say anything, her Mommy has already told them the whole story.

risk.

chapter 37.

OFFICIALLY, I have no idea what really happened the night I am told I snuck outside without permission and was attacked by a man wandering our neighborhood, who it would have been too hard to see clearly. *I don't remember.* It was all I ever had to say, and it was easy. So easy, in fact, that I started saying it to myself, too.

There is so much comfort in forgetting, as long as you're careful not to accidentally remember anything you're trying to forget. So, eventually, I lost even more. Days, weeks faded into thin air as though they never existed at all, and in time it only took a shake of the head, and before it could even start the memory would fall away and I could honestly ask myself *memory of what?*

It made sense, then, that I wouldn't want to face the things I *couldn't* choose to forget. Like what happened that one night, during the gray (minutes? hours?) times between blacking out and waking up.

So sure, I might have freaked out when they'd asked about the exam, because after all the things he took from me, nothing could have been more unfair than having to find out the answer to a question I didn't want asked at the same time as everyone else crowding a tiny, sterile room, to have it put on record and possibly used against me.

Looked at this way, it was almost noble—like I had finally taken back control over one horrible thing I hadn't been able to stop years ago. At the very least, that angle was better than anything I would have been able to come up with.

"Couldn't you have told them that instead?" Peter slumped down nearby.

I shook my head.

There was a moment of silence. "Okay. But you can still do it now, right? I mean, it's the sort of thing-"

I covered my ears. "No," I said, and covered them tighter.

"Why not? You could-"

"*No.* I don't even know his real name, and . . ." Yes, it would help our case. But they would probably want to hear more than I wanted to—or could—tell them. The whole story, for instance. The worst part. The end. What was I supposed to say to someone who asked me how it all ended? They wouldn't believe he'd just walked away, because he *didn't.* But I also couldn't let them find out what I'd let exhaustion and fear and stupidity turn me into.

Sure. Wouldn't want "them" to find out.

I know what I meant. Anyway, it was better to let Peter think— as he undoubtedly would now—that in my nightmares I was reliving all of those other nights, not just the last one. What other choice was there? *And so now, you know, I sometimes have these extremely realistic nightmares about killing—and nearly being killed by—someone who clearly isn't dead. But it's not for lack of trying, I can promise you that . . .*

Which was another interesting point. It was my word against his, probably Mom's too . . . how could I be sure talking wouldn't just get me locked up somewhere else?

So here was a lie I could see a reason for. I caught myself breathing hard, panting like I might run out of air any second. *Maybe more than one reason.*

My mother was mad enough when I'd only told her; what would

happen if they made me go back, and I'd told *everyone else* what she had let her "friend" do?

And Rye. Don't forget about him. Had I ever?

"And I don't want you to tell them either." Lie or not, I needed him to go along with this. "I don't want them to think I'm weak."

Okay, that part might have been a little true.

"Alana-"

"*Alana!*"

I ducked pointlessly and grimaced at the crack of light under the door, suddenly and fully part of the real world again. No matter how lax my "guards" were, of course they would have checked on me before they switched with the later shift. I should have been back in bed by now, ready to feign annoyance if they disturbed me.

"Crap." I got to my feet quietly, jumping at the intermittent calls. I wasn't as worried as I tried to look—the voices didn't seem to be too close—but I wasn't about to waste the perfect excuse to end this guilt trip masquerading as a two-way conversation.

Thinking fast (otherwise known as barely thinking at all) I approached the door and turned the knob. Holding it, I looked back to my brother, who stood to lose a lot more than I did if anyone noticed him missing—and whose cell would be the first place they'd look for me—expecting full-blown panic.

But he was still staring at me from the floor of the janitor's closet, obviously trying to decide whether he was willing to let this end. What I'd told him must have troubled him more than the possibility of being caught.

There was no time to dwell on what that might mean, so I ground my teeth on the thought and waited.

He couldn't hold out long. The next time someone called—"Miss Wilder" this time, adding some much-appreciated variety—he was up and we were out in the bright hall again, blinking at each other, in both directions, at each other again. Peter reached out and squeezed my arm once (which was reassuring, or a lie) and started for the basement stairs. *Interesting.* So that's where he'd gone when they hid him from me.

He couldn't go there, though—by now they'd already know he was missing. For a split second I didn't know what to do and just stood there being generally useless. I hated this. Of course, he was older and not by a little, and he assigned himself the job of looking after me before I was old enough to explain that it wasn't fair. He never got anything out of it in return, I was always a kid compared to him and all I was good at was getting us both into trouble and then sitting back while he took the fall, and if he left me alone for even a little while I'd just make even more trouble and then blame him for not being there to protect me and meanwhile Peter is stuck somewhere underground and hasn't seen the sun in weeks–

I lunged forward and grabbed his shoulder. Startled, Peter turned around and shook my hand off. With a small jerk of the head I glanced behind me, backing away. *Come on.*

He watched me like I'd said his cruise ship was leaving without him. Then he nodded twice and took two backward steps himself, turning away again. *Sorry. I have to go.*

I jumped at him again and yanked his arm twice, hard. This time I held on and dragged him a few steps, grinning forcefully, maniacally. *NO. I need you to trust me.*

The next call came from the basement stairs.

Peter gave me another are-you-crazy look, but this time when I let go he followed. Soon we were moving quickly through the hall of doors that felt even more like a minefield than before, under the shadowless fluorescent lights. I had only been this way a few times, and not recently, so I was close to losing faith in my mental map when the double door appeared up ahead.

"Miss Wilder?" It was around the corner, still not close but I could hear footsteps. The door looked a mile away and the footsteps were getting louder-

I collided with it and pushed it open, letting in a blast of chill air, plus a few dry leaves and a little real sunlight for good measure.

Maybe it was kind of cold out, but *out* was the important thing—what I knew my brother needed more than anything else right now, and one of the many things he wouldn't ask for. To his credit Peter almost hesitated, for about half of a second, just enough to make the flat-out sprint that followed even more conspicuous. Once he cleared the doorway (he actually jumped, like a dog vaulting a wireless fence) he slowed, moving down the concrete steps and forward as though he couldn't stop himself, and I sat on the flat ledge next to them, hugging my knees against the cold.

The loading area, or parking lot or whatever it was, was enclosed, walled in on two sides and gated on the other with those oh-so-cozy barbed wire rolls on top of all three, the police station itself forming the last barrier. It would be pretty hard for anyone to say we were trying to escape from here.

Although Peter looked like he might try. He kept going, and with each step my chest constricted a little more. He didn't seem to feel the cold, which was strange; I felt colder than it could possibly be.

At least I'd managed to distract him.

Yeah, by giving him a way out.

I hugged myself tighter. That wasn't fair. He'd said he wouldn't leave again; I should give him more credit.

And he should have given you less. Why should he deal with the fallout of you not being able to take care of yourself? Promise or no, you couldn't blame him if he left.

It wouldn't be fair to, no. But still, I would. Even if it was my own fault, I would blame him. And I felt sorry for him because of that, and I didn't understand why.

Maybe because it wasn't his fault. Although it wasn't yours either.

I snorted. It was a good moral for a fairytale, and from what I'd heard at school this was usually the line they fed people to make them feel better. But I didn't need to feel better, and anyway I've never really seen the point of lying.

Peter circled the lot twice, then went to the center and stood there looking at the sky for so long he appeared to be trying levitation. Instead he took a deep breath and turned back to me.

My stomach dropped—apparently I hadn't quite distracted him enough.

The door behind me banged open.

It was almost funny. Because we knew they were coming, Peter and I didn't move a muscle as policemen streamed into the lot and "surrounded" us.

One of my guards had been visiting from some other station; apparently my brother was such a security risk that reinforcements were needed. The loaner inched up behind me on the wall. "Miss Wilder-"

He was going to ask if I was okay, I knew it. He was going to escort me back to an unlocked cell on a quiet, empty hallway and leave me there, pretending to "watch" me a little closer from now on, and to add insult to injury he was going to ask me the one question I couldn't answer either way without lying.

Of course I'm fine; don't you see who I'm with?

Of course I'm not; don't you see who I *am*?

I cut him off with a big smile. "Sorry sir, but," I gestured with my head, turning away, "he hasn't been outdoors in weeks. And I was just so *bored*."

"Miss-"

"If it helps, he did try to talk me out of it."

No chair feels especially comfortable when you're just sitting and waiting to get in trouble.

I was waiting to get in trouble. Again. To know what lucky number I was up to I'd have had to start counting before I could count. Still, the waiting never seemed to get any easier.

I smacked my head down on the table and then lifted it into my hands, wrist twinging uncomfortably. I should have just taken a damned nap like I was supposed to.

"-can't imagine how this keeps happening if you are taking such *good* care of her." Mom always seemed to be talking before she entered a room. I wiped my face clean of expression and willed her to shut up. "I must have warned you a thousand times about letting him near her, and first you find them in *bed* together, and now this!" She was shouting, outraged.

I had almost forgotten what Peter had said they thought about him (because of me), and my head snapped up, mouth open, ready to defend. But I froze, awkward, blinking crazily, and when no words came gulped and hung my head again slowly, ragged fingernails eating into my palms. Lucky for me, I guess, no one had noticed, and my Mom carried on. "And then she tries to kill herself! *Again!* She is obviously unstable, and you're oh so *happy* to take her yourself, letting her rot in a foster home instead of sending her to a facility where she can get the help she *needs*, not letting her own mother be with her when your people interrogate her-"

Officer Lucass, who must have at first thought it best (or even possible) to let this tirade end on its own, finally cleared his throat. "Mrs. Wilder, we have already explained this to you. Your daughter is old enough to have a say in where she stays. She has expressed a desire to be placed in a foster home rather than go to a psychiatric facility,"—the nicest way of saying *nearly pissed herself when we tried it* that I'd ever heard—"and it was her decision to make that my home, as well." Not quite; my decision was to stay here, but my jailers weren't as accommodating this time and I'd been forced to compromise.

"And as for her being interviewed without a parent present, in custody cases like yours, you know it can't be allowed." *Cases like yours.* He said it so calmly. I was impressed.

My mother snorted. "Cases like *yours.* That's the problem here, that's exactly it. You take the word of a sick person like *him,* ignore the obvious hold he has over *her,* and suddenly you're looking at me like I'm some . . . some *abuser,* while you can't even protect the one child I have left."

I glared at my hands, very nearly dared to look up. *That "sick" person is your child,* I thought at her.

Lucass looked impatient, but ignored the rant. "And as for this particular incident, your daughter has confessed to organizing the whole thing. Is that right, Miss Wilder?"

Since all they knew about was the going-outside part, it was. I started to nod.

"Or is it just what you were told to say?" Mom cut in, using a tone that said very clearly to shut my mouth now if I planned to see tomorrow.

This was one of the worst parts of being arrested—how all of a sudden it was just as likely someone was making me recite words like a puppet as it was that, I don't know, I had thoughts of my own or something. Because Solomon Lucass did squint at me for a second, like he was waiting for me to change my story.

"It was my idea," I mumbled to the table.

Lucass nodded and turned back to my mother, who took a break from slicing me up with her eyes to meet his. "Mrs. Wilder, I think you told me you wanted to make sure your daughter was all right, didn't you? Because if so, I believe we've accomplished that."

My mother started to snap something back, but Lucass was through being patient and cut her off. "And now I need to ask her a few questions, if you don't mind."

"You know I mind. I mind very much." But she did leave us

alone—though not without first giving me an eyeless half-smile that left me wondering exactly how I would have to pay for this.

Lucass sat down. I tried not to look guilty, but my eyes kept sliding away; in the end, I gave up and stared into the table, swallowing an apology. Sometimes Officer Lucass actually seemed to kind of be on our side, and we could use allies. Even allies who'd threatened my brother with a gun once. I hadn't let that go. But Peter apparently had, and since Lucass was almost the only person here who didn't seem to hate my brother, even if he didn't exactly trust him, I figured I should try to make him . . . not-hate me, too.

I wasn't doing a great job.

I counted the small white hairs stuck to his pant leg. Without looking down I knew I would find the same ones caught in the dark lining of my jacket. Now that it was just the two of us, I snorted. It smelled in here. How hadn't I noticed the reek of dog rolling off him before?

His wife thought I was afraid of them. She was a *nice* lady, weirdly attentive, almost too considerate. I'd always figured someone must be kind of stupid, to be like that, but she wasn't. If anything she was sharper than her husband, noticing right away that it was best not to bother me about little things, like eating or taking showers.

And there was the sweater she'd given Peter, unearthed from her own closet long before anyone here had given him a second thought. I could have excused any level of stupidity for that one act of kindness alone, so her mistaken belief that their three molting, drooling dogs were anything but annoying to me was no big deal.

Then there was Lucass. He was strangely formal and awkward—if anything he dreaded the forty or so overlong minutes we spent in the car alone each day even more than I did. I had returned to my initial approach of saying nothing, also. Which couldn't be helping.

He breathed loudly, like the effort of dealing with me was starting to wear him down. "Alana-"

"It *was* my idea." It came out louder than I'd meant it to, and I glanced up to see what he would do.

He cocked an eyebrow. "Really? Not your brother's at all? I know how persuasive he can be."

I narrowed my eyes at him, but his expression didn't change. Sometimes he seemed to toy with me, saying things that might have been jokes, then going back to being serious and official a moment later. I couldn't decide what to make of it. So I shook my head.

"Miss Wilder, you have to know this can't keep happening." Serious again.

I know. I know plenty. Too bad you can't say the same. Not that I was going to tell him. That I only had one friend in the world, and I might be about to lose him for close to forever. That it felt strange to me, too, treating each meeting like it might be our last, but I just hadn't been able to leave this one with him mad at me. That Mom did get one thing right: he couldn't protect me, and while everyone was busy keeping an eye on her, there was no one watching her friend, who had already tried to kill me once.

chapter 38.

BACK in this windowless, subterranean bank of walls there was little to do other than notice. So he was noticing. Not how much better he'd felt out of this tomb of looming rigid heavy white walls. Not the stale basement miasma again after feeling fresh air in his lungs for the first time in weeks.

What he was noticing was how supremely stupid he had been. Still was.

His thoughts rolled, tumbled, boiled; now and then one bobbed up, hovering near the surface. And it was always the same: *You* knew *you shouldn't leave her alone. You* knew.

But he thought he'd taught her to be careful.

You knew.

He thought once he was gone, Mom might be less angry.

You knew.

He thought maybe she would take care of Al a little more, now that no one else was doing it for her.

And you left a little girl to test the theory for you? Alone, with no clue whether you were ever coming back, and you didn't think *that might not be worth the risk?*

I didn't . . .

He'd always felt like leaving was the wrong thing to do. But . . . he also thought there was no *right* thing.

Stupid.

I didn't. He was worse than her, making excuses, pretending there *were* excuses, for what he'd done. But maybe it wasn't too late.

It wouldn't be easy. He'd have to find the poor excuse for a man first and Al said she didn't even know his real name, he made her call him Rye. She also didn't want anyone else to find out—but she was on edge, not thinking clearly. Eventually she would calm down, and then she might be willing to speak to someone. Dr. Pollock roiled through his mind as a possibility but was quickly disregarded. She wouldn't want to talk to him once she found out how he knew Peter. Maybe Lucass? If not, at least the detective could recommend someone—Pollock popped up again and was, again, immediately pushed aside—the important thing was for her to talk about it. About what she'd been through, because of him.

I didn't . . . It was only one small piece of such a colossal conversation. Sure he was angry at her for making excuses, but did he deserve to be? He cleared her voice from his mind as well, blinking with the effort, not noticing his thumb tracing a line down the center of his own wrist.

Either way, he'd have to save his energy for now. It would be hard enough convincing her it was worth discussing at all.

So it was odd when, seconds later, he again found himself thinking about Dr. Pollock. He would certainly not be Peter's choice—and he was sure Al would agree wholeheartedly.

He closed his eyes briefly, yawning, trying to relax, failing. His finger again outlined a vague path down his arm; he had a vision of red water and shuddered, moving it away.

How could you?

I didn't*!*

His eyes flew open.

But that . . . it made no sense. The proof was right there, plain as day. It had *happened*. And if she had not done it herself, why tell that story explaining her reason? Why confess?

Mom was the obvious answer. But she couldn't have—Doc had told him as much. She hadn't even been at the station. Lucass, or one of the other detectives? An accident? Why would she bother keeping it a secret?

As for the story, might she have only said what he'd expected to hear? It was risky, but genius—telling a lie big enough to distract from an even worse truth—except for one thing.

Alana was a risk taker, definitely. Sometimes, she could be genius. But he was certain she hadn't lied.

This time when Pollock came back he was accompanied by vague, gnawing significance. Peter wondered why. Which was the worst possible thing because of course, then the question had to be answered.

But not quickly. His thoughts fragmented. Pieces rushed ahead, scattering bits and images like a trail for the rest to follow. And follow they did, slowly, reluctant.

But still following.

Al had only met Pollock once. It was the end of yet another fruitless "session," and Mom had brought her along to pick him up, and Pollock said she was a very pretty girl. Then Mom had shooed them away to talk to "Ryland" alone, using his first name in the conspiratory way she did when she wanted something.

That was it. Al had barely even noticed he was there, and had never seen him again.

But . . .

Peter remembered the night she was nearly taken, snatching her from the empty-eyed man and dragging her to the bus stop amid a hail of questions: *What's wrong? Who was that? Why are we leaving? Did you know him? Will you* answer *me?*

She hadn't asked who the man was who came with Mom. Hadn't asked anything about him.

(Can I sleep here?)

Peter found himself leaning against something he couldn't identify.

Al wasn't his patient, so there was no reason they should have met. But she had met him. She even knew his first name. *Rye.*

And who else could have introduced them?

But there's no way—even Mom wouldn't have . . .

He leaned on the thing harder.

"She wouldn't," he croaked.

Leaned.

She did. And she brought him here.

How could you?

I didn't.

He *did.*

Leaned.

You knew.

"I didn't-"

Crash.

chapter 39.

THE difference between the sullen Alana he had met weeks ago and the quiet, agreeable one he'd just spoken with was astounding. He'd even deliberately goaded her today, speaking to her like she was a child of many fewer years and scolding her about her latest escapade.

And all she'd done was sit, staring at the table, fingers drumming absently on her shoulder. Impassive, still, and clearly lost in her own thoughts. Eventually he'd left her with another officer, instructing them both to high-tail it back to her room, no detours.

Maybe Ashley was right about most things, but even she had to get it wrong now and again. In that case, bringing the stray girl home to sit on their couch and watch television into the wee hours while they were trying to sleep was one of her worst bungles yet. She'd hoped Sol would be able to convince the girl to open up a little more outside of the station—no dice, she was tense as ever, if not more so.

Still, it was the best of a bad situation. Even if he didn't particularly enjoy the girl's company, whenever he pictured her sitting tight-lipped, stiff, and pretending to pay attention to the box in some total stranger's living room, his heartstrings pulled all by themselves. At least with him she had Ashley to fuss over her—she didn't mind that Alana came with all the technical requirements of a high-level, intensive case. And the dogs were enthusiastic about their new foster sibling, except the oldest, Rosie, who seemed pretty impartial. Not that she would tell him why.

With the first trial days away, all those little bent rules—and the not-so-little ones too—were coming back to bite him, and he was getting almost no help from the higher-ups, but he'd find a way around it. He had to, much as he wasn't supposed to try, because poor house guest or not he believed what those kids were saying—for the most part—and he didn't want to do more harm than good trying to help them.

Ashley thought it was fine he wasn't always as impartial as he was supposed to be—she said those cases let her know what kind of man he was. But he couldn't afford any more mistakes. They'd be calling him up on the stand, probing and poking for signs he'd taken sides. Anything other than regulation quoting and frank descriptions of what he'd seen and the lawyers on both sides'd have his number real quick, plus his badge if they could get it.

Sol started downstairs. The trials couldn't last forever. With any luck, things would calm down soon.

Either that, or he'd see if any of Ashley's friends were up for another impromptu trip.

"All right—guess it's your turn, son," he said, pulling the door open, ready to rehash his conversation with Alana. But he stopped short just inside.

The sparse cell was completely destroyed. The metal bed frame stood slanted into the opposite wall, legs buckled like it had been wedged, even stomped, into place, peppered with white snags of the same fibrous fluff that covered the floor ankle-deep. A wadded mass of blue-gray fabric hulked gutlessly in the nearest corner. Sol spun in shock, wondering how he hadn't noticed the door's window panel had cracked along the inside. And throughout the room, drops of blood stood out boldly against the mess.

Peter Wilder sat beside the mangled bedframe, absently sucking on a cut at the edge of his palm. He didn't look up at first; when he did, he gave Sol a welcoming grin and held up the injured hand in a strange, informal gesture.

"It doesn't seem too bad, but still I think I'd better see my doctor." He didn't stutter at all.

Bunk beds weren't for everyone. All I had was the cot from the room-closet, which was small enough to make the empty cell feel practically spacious by comparison. Spacious, but a boring place to spend the day. I fell onto the cot and groaned.

They hadn't tripled security on me or anything yet—for some reason—but as a favor to Lucass I'd already gone a record thirty-something(ish) hours without slipping past my guard, starting any fights *or* setting anything on fire.

Someone has a gold star coming her way.

"There she is." Rye was at the door, grinning in at me.

I sat up, eyes flying up and down the hall behind him. *Stupid. No one's coming.* He wouldn't be here if anyone had seen him.

For a second I felt surprisingly calm. Then I realized I would have been hyperventilating, if I'd been breathing at all. I stopped rolling my eyes like a fucking puppet and tried to actually *be* calm, but when he put his hand on the door I took in barely enough air to say

"They locked it."

"What a shame," Rye said, pushing the door open slightly. He faked surprise. "Looks like we got lucky, G-"

I cut him off; I couldn't hear him call me that. "It doesn't matter. They come check on me every five minutes." Another lie. Just like no one liked locking me in (even though I'd heard them calling me "High Risk" when they thought I wasn't listening), they rarely checked on me and it was never anything like predictable.

Rye smiled. "Well good thing I don't need five minutes," he said, playful, easing the door open a bit more. Two times now, for two wrong answers.

I knew he didn't need five minutes. If this time was anything like the others, he would scarcely need two. In one hundred and twenty seconds he'd be gone, long before anyone came to look in on me, and I'd consider it a win if I had managed to keep him from touching me.

If we were counting, I wasn't scoring well so far.

Of course it was optimistic to assume this was just a normal visit. I had assumed it before, with the scissors, when I thought he'd gotten carried away and finally made a mistake. Then, I was wrong on both accounts.

One hundred and nine seconds left, then, if I was lucky. I didn't want to even think—if my head was suddenly filled with that screaming sound he might be able to read it on my face—but I had to try. I had to so I could feel in control of myself, even if for one hundred and six seconds I had very little control over anything.

"Your mother and I have been talking a lot lately, you know," Rye began. I tried to imagine a railroad spike was being driven into my head. "I mean, she was so broken up after you disappeared. She was worried—she missed you." Sometimes he sounded a little different from how I remembered him, gravelly, hoarser. But he still changed his voice for different effects; this one was low, riddled with dramatic pauses. "I know a little something about that."

And that *is your room.*

Projectile entering the top of my skull: senselessness, instant cool as the blood stopped in my veins. Limbs—lead-heavy, frozen. Even my eyes were still, fixed on the wall, lids drooping. Barely breathing. Numb.

"She was scared she'd never find her little girl again, and we started spending so much time together, who knows? You might be seeing a lot of me after you come home."

Slow, shallow breaths. I was in a coma. I tasted blood, but it meant nothing. I was being *calm.*

This time the silence lasted longer. All of my energy went into not letting it show, but I was vibrating inside, every muscle straining, hoping I was at least fooling one of us. "They said they want to ask me a few questions at the trial. I have plenty to say, I don't mind at all."

I very carefully did not sneer at him. Of course he didn't mind. He could probably make up hundreds of lies about me, and Mom would go along with all of it. Hell, she'd probably author some herself.

He repeated himself and then asked, "But what about you?"

That's what these "visits" were really about—making sure I wasn't a threat to him, that I was still scared enough to keep *our* secret. It's why, after the Scissors Incident, once he'd slipped away to let me be "discovered" trying not to bleed out on the floor, his had been the first subtle voice to suggest that, perhaps, this proved I wasn't quite up to testifying in court.

No one had agreed, although now when I did speak they might not believe me no matter what I chose to say. Fortunately for him, though, while I wasn't very brave right now, I also wasn't stupid—and I wanted him *gone.*

So, "No." It was an easy answer, and a true one—or at least one with an acceptable number of collateral lies—and I gave it with the ease of a child who had been keeping secrets since before she could talk.

But somehow it was still the wrong answer, because Rye pushed the door open wider and walked in. I was on my feet in a second, but he stayed just inside the door and I ended up edging farther into the cell instead, fully aware it was a Bad choice. "Really? Nothing at all?"

I tried to think but the thoughts were blurry, swirling too fast to sort out. The only one I could decipher kept saying that I could *fix* this if I just knew what I'd said *wrong.* Clenching and opening my hands, I swallowed. I felt years younger, and when I blinked I could actually smell the warm, slightly sweet tang of the pillow under my head, see the silhouette of my tree outside.

Feel the slick knife twisting in my hands-

He was still advancing, and I took another step back. His eyes moved down. I suddenly felt like I would choke on my own saliva if I didn't swallow—and like he would be on me in a second if I dared to. "You've been so confused since your accident. Your mom told me about some stories you made up a long time ago—I was worried, but not just about me."

He was near the middle of the cell. I bolted for the door, too early; he grabbed my arm and dragged me back. *Point Rye.* He chuckled as if he'd heard me, shoving me against the wall. "This has already been so hard for you," he leaned closer, pressed a thumb gently against the dressing on my wrist like he was looking for a pulse, "and a trial would be even worse. In this state, Girl—you might not survive it."

I wasn't listening. There was an arm holding me, *to make sure I couldn't get away.* I couldn't tell if it was happening now, or then— but it must be happening because when I tried to move I couldn't, couldn't pry it away-

Rye looked me up and down. "Your mom and I can stop them asking you so many questions," he whispered. "We can help you. I just need to know I can still trust my Girl."

Trying to hold onto the knife when it's slippery and warm and still cutting into me, but it keeps coming and I'm just barely strong enough to control it, too small to do anything more than-

When I laughed—a sharp, bark-like sound—I startled myself. How long had I been staring, or did I only now look up? "What do you mean, *still*? If I remember correctly-" a crazy grin was stretching my lips as I stared into the face of my own personal bogeyman, "last time you *trusted* me didn't exactly go well for you."

The smug expression froze on Rye's face and his grip tightened painfully, trying to regain control. But it was too late; I read undercurrents well. And right then, on his face and in his hand, I read that Rye didn't like to take risks. He liked control, he liked ownership, yes, but only when he was all-but-guaranteed to get what he wanted.

And I read that what Rye wanted was a Girl who was too scared and confused to fight back.

She had almost been me, once. I'd been small, kid enough to believe anything, naïve enough to let fear overwhelm my anger for far too long. And then, worse, I'd been too distracted by guilt to remember that, whatever else I'd done, being *angry* hadn't been a mistake.

But I didn't have to be her anymore. There had been one time I had fought back, made myself a risk. I could do—be—that again.

"You remember, right?" I half-whispered, needing to say something else, *anything* else before he interrupted me. It felt good to be the one doing the talking—I felt surer of myself, and I couldn't afford anything less right now. "Tell me if this brings back any memories." I drew one knee in, then kicked out as hard as I could.

Rye reeled backward but he hadn't let go of my arm so when he punched me he had a lot more leverage than I liked.

There's this thing—I've read it over and over—where people act like it's exciting, or like there's some sort of dignity, to being hit.

There isn't. Rye punched me, and I found myself wondering not for the first time if my stomach could snag and tear open against my spine, and I wanted to vomit and to cry, and my lungs wouldn't work right anymore, and I was terrified he was going to hit me again.

Seriously. Whatever dignity I may still have very much aside, I could have done whatever it took in that moment for him not to hit me again.

But it passed, like always, and I looked up again. I couldn't think of much to say. Spitting, however, was easy.

Our staring contest entered its second round. Rye put a hand to his face and then mine, smearing my saliva back onto me. I felt myself shaking and realized with surprise—and a little pride—that I was laughing, with no air and no sound. He may have had the advantage years ago, but in this new place I'd already survived his worst, and we were both starting to understand it.

"I think you have the wrong idea, Girl. You may have had your little tantrum, but I know there won't be any more *mistakes* like that one." The threat came out syrupy, like it would stick to my fingers. "I know I can still trust you. Because if I didn't . . . well, I have my backup plan, my friends. You remember now."

I wasn't laughing any more. But I also wasn't done. "You've never been anything, have you." I could make a question into a statement, too. "Nothing but a sad little shit who wanted control, but the only thing you could feel in control of was a little girl you thought couldn't fight back." Funny—it felt right, but I'd never considered how little I actually knew about Rye.

Whatever. It didn't matter if what I said was true. I just needed to say it.

I almost started to grin again, didn't. "And you even managed to screw that up."

Rye was still staring at me. His hand slid down to my wrist. "I guess I have my answer. As for control—I have a feeling we'll see about that."

I glared. Time apparently up, he turned to leave. But as he was sliding the door closed, he looked in at me. And something had returned in his eyes.

"See you again real soon."

I dare you.

I *really* hope I said that out loud.

chapter 40.

MOST rituals for good luck seem to involve food. Not that Di minded much, but days of eating black eyed peas and pomegranates started to make you feel like a witch casting spells after a while—and not very good ones! Not to mention, her boys were starting to look at her as though she were senile before her time, which was too offensive to bear.

So it was time to stop hoping for luck and start making it.

Di sat on the topmost step of the courthouse, stockinged legs crossed at the ankles, scanning the entrance in the aloof manner she had learned as a little girl watching her father work. Her ability to be professional in any situation was hard-won and honed, something to be proud of. Though she was having a hard time smiling about it right now.

That sudden dash from the room when Di had called her pretty. The seemingly unprovoked outburst in the courtyard. Di had tried to fool herself into thinking it was normal behavior for an angry girl. She didn't like compliments, fine. She was trying to chase Di away—that didn't have to be so strange, considering. But in her line of business, Di had learned more than she ever wanted to know about people and the scars they left on others. She only wished her typically oh-so-clearheaded friend had heard what she was sure Alana had been saying for a long time.

Maybe he had, deep down. But shock could do strange things to a clear head.

Wasn't it happening to her as well? The collection of habits and trinkets for good luck had been growing since she heard about the arrest. And she still spent most of her time worrying, living her lackluster day-to-day as Elizabeth, pulling strings from a distance when she preferred to participate firsthand. It was frustrating, not least because being Elizabeth meant she could hardly acknowledge that she had met Peter at all. She was too well-known, her presence would prompt questions.

So Di stayed back as cavalry. If everything went well, she shouldn't be needed at all.

She turned to study the courthouse roof, folding her arms into the sleeves of her plain gray suit and pretending to enjoy the chilly wind that was picking up.

The trial started tomorrow. Only a few more days until they knew what would happen to her friend and quite literal partner in crime. And what about Alana?

She was just as worried for the girl. Being returned to her mother's home . . . Di didn't have to guess what could happen.

Scanning, she straightened her skirt and found herself thinking again of that awful first meeting. All her fault, of course. And Alana had made that clear enough! She smiled to herself, remembering the seemingly sweet girl's savage growl as she warned Di away from her brother.

Di had thought she was lovely. She still did, and so much more. Dedicated to protecting her brother, for one.

This was something Di could understand. One of the first things she had noticed about Peter was his openness, but too much openness could make you overoptimistic, naïve. Vulnerable. In his case, to grief and the guilt that accompanied it. Little wonder his sister hadn't wanted to tell him.

Of course, what looked like vulnerability did have a tendency to change in her friend where his baby sister was involved. According to Lita (who was just as valuable a friend in her own right) he hadn't said much. But then he never did. He knew very well how to use silences. In fact, he used them nearly as well as she used her connections.

This had been almost too easy to be fun. He'd been tracked down already, this one and his merry band of like-minded comrades (why did they always travel in packs—no—*rings*?), and the Feds, whose investigation was nearly two years old and speeding along on its own, would only need one more tiny push to spring shut like a steel trap around the bunch.

She had thought about it. But Di preferred to guarantee her own results.

Finally. Di leapt into action as she finally found the face she'd been watching for, skipping forward like a child.

"Doctor?"

The man stopped, confused. He registered her a moment later, an unfamiliar face speaking in a familiar tone, and clouded over more.

She laughed. "I am sorry; no, you don't know me. I was hoping to talk to you, just for a moment." She held out her hand. "You can call me Dottie."

He looked from the outstretched hand to her face once more, and then he took it.

Peter swallowed bile for what he idealistically hoped would be the last time. The handcuffs clanked jarringly against the chain fastened around his midsection. He found himself shaking his head again—trying to clear the fog from it—and was reminded why he'd promised to stop doing that when a new wave of nausea struck him. The room tilted, started to rotate.

They would take him inside soon. He glanced at his lawyer—fresh out of school, she seemed disturbingly uncomfortable with the idea of being inside of the courtroom. He was no better, obviously. But it seemed as if *one* of them should be ready for this. Shouldn't it be her?

There were whispers and murmurs traveling up and down the corridor—an extension of the commotion he'd heard back at the station while he was being cuffed, chained and led to the waiting car. One of the witnesses for the state had not been seen since yesterday, and they were beginning to worry as the start of the trial drew nearer.

Well, some were.

Peter swallowed nothing, hard.

He was still waiting to regret it, at least how he'd done it. Pollock would have been easier to get to in a couple of weeks, far away and of little interest to anyone, but when one of the few witnesses in a well-publicized trial went missing people looked. Maybe even hard enough to find him. And if they did . . .

Well, then Peter's lawyer would *really* have something to be uneasy about.

But he was starting to think he would never feel the way he should. The trial itself scared him out of his mind, sure—the doors banged against the wall, and he swallowed his heart again—but Pollock had disappeared. He had made someone disappear, seamlessly, untraceably. And he felt nothing.

He was still watching the courtroom's doors. For the first time he wondered if perhaps all of this was something other than a simple, catastrophic misunderstanding. Somewhere, between Mom and David and raising his little sister while still a child himself, between running away and being homeless and meeting Di—had he actually become the kind of person who belonged in there?

Al had stationed herself firmly against the wall beside him but was avoiding eye contact. Incredibly, she was relaxed, smiling. Maybe she should give his lawyer some pointers.

This could be his last chance to speak to her for a while, but he hadn't said anything yet. He wouldn't be a broken record—she knew he loved her already—but the doors would open again any moment, and with her smiling like she didn't have a care in the world he felt he had to say *something*. She still thought he didn't know. He couldn't just leave it that way.

He elbowed her in the side. "Sorry. For before."

It was less than half of an already disappointingly short sentence, but she jumped, wincing a little. Perhaps she was less calm than he'd thought. She scowled at the ground for a second before looking up with a single terse nod.

He stared for a minute, well aware it annoyed her but missing that, getting on her nerves and having her do the same to him. It was almost normal. He missed almost normal.

Of course, they had never been anything near truly normal. They probably never could be.

It would have been nice to have a chance, though.

He tried to smile. "You."

She didn't. "You."

No time! Gulping (again), Peter launched in. "So—can we talk? About before . . . who-"

Now she looked away, stopping him midsentence. "No, we can't."

"I'm serious, Al, and there's not a lot of time, so please-"

She pivoted on her heel and leaned close. "It is over, so drop it, *now*." She let the words sink in and then stepped back. A full minute of their remaining time together was wasted in silence, and when she finally spoke it was in their mother's voice, a rock-hard tone that left no room for objections. "It's over."

Peter knew that. What did *she* mean?

He wanted to ask, nearly did ask, but all of a sudden it just . . . didn't feel worth it. She had barely looked him in the eye since their last "conversation." Now, in the squat, vaultlike hall of the courthouse, seconds before his trial, he didn't want to ruin anything else. The door opened again, the entire building started to bend and stretch, and Peter let the strange declaration go.

"It's going to be okay."

His eyes slid closed but he nodded. *I truly hope you think so.*

His lawyer was suddenly at his side, fidgeting with her pantsuit, nervous as only he had the right to be. *But I'm not so sure,* he thought, rounding off the conversation he had not been having with his sister.

EXCERPT FROM TRANSCRIPT

THE COURT: Have you found your first witness yet,
prosecution?
MR. EAGAN: No, your Honor. We are—we have no idea
what's happened.
THE COURT: Are you prepared to call your next wit-
ness instead?
MR. JOHNS: No, not at this time, your Honor.
THE COURT: Then you are allowing the defense to
testify first?
JOHNS: Yes, the defense can start us off.
THE COURT: Then defense may call its first witness.
MS. DADE: Thank you, your Honor. May it please
the court?
THE COURT: I just told you it did, counselor.
DADE: Yes, I--yes, thank you, your Honor. Defense
calls the defendant, Peter Wilder, as its first witness.
BAILIFF: Do you swear that the testimony you are
about to give is the truth and nothing but the truth, so
help you God?
WITNESS: Yes.
DADE: Your honor, I thought we agreed the wit-
ness was to be treated as unavailable due to the
circumstances?
JOHNS: Objection. What criteria does the defendant
meet for unavailability?
DADE: Defendant is unable to testify due to an ex-
isting condition, your Honor.
JOHNS: Yet the defendant is testifying today.
DADE: My client will be reading from a deposition
taken in the course of this proceeding, entered as defense exhibit 4. The deposition was already sworn.
THE COURT: The defendant wants to take the stand,
and we would need two people to read his deposition

either way, so in the interest of minimalizing prejudi-
cial effect the objection is overruled. The deposition
was--you provided it to both sides?

DADE: Yes, your Honor.

THE COURT: Go ahead then.

DADE: The following passages were selected for
relevance.

Q: Please state your full name for the record, Mr.
Wilder. Mr. Wilder. Your Honor, could we take a short
break? Five--ten minutes?

THE COURT: Let's take a ten minute recess.

Recess taken.

THE COURT: And we're back on record. Go ahead.

The defendant, PETER WILDER, read passages from his
sworn deposition as follows:

Q: All right. Please state your full name for
the record.

A: Peter Cole Wilder.

Q: You know what we are doing right now, correct?
Can you tell me?

A: Prerecording my testimony in case I need to read
it back at trial.

Q: And whose idea was that?

A: Yours. I mean, you--you came up with it but
mine--I agreed. That it was a good idea.

Q: Why is it a good idea?

A: Because--because, it--sorry. Because I'm not
very good at public speaking.

Q: You understand you will still read this
aloud at trial.

A: Yes.

Q: Mr. Wilder, do you have any family?

A: My--my mother Jacqueline and sister--and sister, Alana.

Q: How old is your sister?

A: Fifteen.

Q: And who does she live with?

A: Me.

Q: How did she come to live with you?

A: I went home in the middle of the night and asked if she would leave with me, and she did.

Q: Was she threatened or forced into leaving with you?

A: No, no.

Q: And have you threatened or coerced her into giving false testimony at trial?

A: No.

DADE: Moving on to passage two.

Q: How old were you when you left your mother's home?

A: Seventeen.

Q: That young? You were still a child. So why did you leave? Mr. Wilder, can--will you tell me why you left? For instance were you were kicked out, or something else?

A: Not kicked out, but--well she said she--said-- she was going to kill me with a gun.

Q: Who is the she you're talking about?

A: My mother.

Q: And had this sort of thing happened before?

A: No, others. Other things. Other things had--had happened. But this was the first time actually--she mentioned actually wanting to kill me.

Q: And how old was your sister then, was Alana?

A: Eleven.

Q: And did, and was it easy for you, leaving your little sister behind? Remember you need to answer out loud for the record.

A: No. I had to, but I was scared, for her.

Q: Scared? Why?

A: Because a lot of the time, it wasn't
safe with her.

Q: With who?

A: With my mother.

DADE: Finally, we'll read passage three.

Q: Earlier we agreed that we were doing this because you thought you might not be able to handle speaking in court. Why is that?

A: I--I do not speak well in front of strangers.

Q: What do you mean, you don't speak well?

A: Either I can't at all, or I kind--tend to stutter. Badly.

Q: Has that always been the case for you?

A: No, there was a long time--there were a lot
of years when actually--when I was not--when I wasn't
allowed to.

Q: To stutter?

A: Speak.

Q: To speak at all? Why not?

A: Yes. Sorry.

Q: Why not? Why were you not, Mr. Wilder?

A: It was just to people outside the family.

Q: But why?

A: (inaudible)

Q: Could you speak up, please?

A: My, I had a--a psychiatrist. She told him
what was wrong, he wrote prescriptions, but I never
took them.

Q: Are you saying that your mother used you to create fake illnesses just so she could get the medications
for herself? Will you--or, alright. Did she take them?
The medicines?

A: I didn't--I'm sorry, I don't know. I
don't, sorry.

DADE: No further questions for this witness,
your Honor.

JOHNS: I don't know how to proceed here. Am I going to be, do I get to cross-examine the defendant or is he still considered absent?

THE COURT: Defense, your client has been found competent to stand trial. If he began testifying now, he'd have to be sworn in and will not have the option of reading any pre-recorded answers. Do you--is your client prepared to undergo cross examination?

DADE: Permission to confer with my client, your Honor.

THE COURT: Granted.

[Defense counsel approached the witness stand.]

[Defense counsel was seated.]

DADE: My client will try--will do his best to go forward with cross. Your--your Honor.

THE COURT: Ms. Dade, I think that's probably enough your Honor for now. Let's continue.

PETER WILDER, defendant, having been duly sworn according to law, was CROSS-EXAMINED and testified as follows:

Q: So you testified that your mother, here, took the time to get you to a child psychiatrist for over five years not--according to you, not because she was trying to help you but in--but because she wanted to use you as an easy source of prescription pills? You are aware that you must answer these questions?

(Gallery interrupted)

THE COURT: There will be order in my courtroom, Miss, or you can wait outside. I don't expect any more outbursts, and I expect all counsel to instruct your witnesses accordingly.

JOHNS: Understood. Please answer the question aloud, if you can.

A: I--guess that is--yes. Sir.

Q: Well, that is something. Mr. Wilder, is it true you have been hospitalized for injuries you inflicted on

yourself--on your own--by hitting your head repeatedly
against a wall?

A: No.

Q: All right. Permission to approach the witness,
your Honor.

THE COURT: Why?

Q: To refresh his memory.

THE COURT: Approach, then.

Q: I am showing you what has been marked State's
Exhibit 6. Could you read this and then answer--

A: I--you don't, sorry, I already know what it
says. It was your--the question was wrong, sorry, it
wasn't injuries. It--that only happened once, one time.

Q: Only once? Because in this file there are several
other instances. Are you aware of any of those?

A: I never--none of them--I didn't talk. Those
didn't come from me.

Q: So your mother relayed these stories for you.

A: Yes.

Q: And one of them happens to be true, but the rest
are all fant--falsifications?

A: They--I--

Q: That would certainly be convenient, wouldn't it?

DADE: Objection--

Q: I'll withdraw. It's just, well some of these records say some things that, if true, would conflict a bit
with your, ah, ersatz testimony.

DADE: Objection.

THE COURT: Is there a question in the making
somewhere?

Q: Of course. Mr. Wilder, you are at least admitting here that some of these records are correct?

A: Yes, but--

Q: For instance, your name is mentioned in this record of an attack that injured Alana so badly that she
was rushed to the hospital in shock, and remained in a

medically induced coma for days afterward. Or is that
fantasy also?

A: I, no--no, it--

Q: You know?

A: No. No. No, I did not--

Q: So this incident was fake also.

A: Probably not, but I wasn't even--

Q: Yes, your mother had threatened by then that
if you stayed in her home, she would kill you. You
did--technically, you no longer lived there. This attack
occurred within a year of your disappearance. Your sister, she would have been a preteen, right?

A: Yes--sorry, yes.

Q: Do you have any idea why, out of the blue, your
mother would suddenly do something so—-would actually go
so far as to threaten your life?

A: Don't know if it was really out of--

Q: Please answer.

A: Not really.

Q: Ah. It's just that in this file there are multiple mentions of the possibility that the attack was a
failed sexual assault--

(Gallery Interruption)

DADE: Objection! Relevance?

THE COURT: Order. There will be no further warn-
ings. Mr. Johns?

Q: The circumstances behind both instances giving rise to our--the medical records are admissible
to prove character, your honor, as--and those giving rise to Mr. Wilder's running away were brought up
in direct.

THE COURT: I will overrule as far as both questions
being relevant, defense. You may continue.

Q: So, Mr. Wilder, is it possible that when you
ran away--as you admit you did because your mother es-
sentially forced you to leave—-is it possible that you

remained close by in order to, as it were, stay close to your family?

A: No. I did not. I wouldn't have even been in the same state.

Q: Despite the overwhelming concern for your sister's safety that you mentioned.

A: (inaudible)

THE COURT: You'll need to speak louder for the record.

A: I was, I also worried about mine.

Q: Mr. Wilder, after you ran away, or were chased away, you communicated with your mother through letters for some time, didn't you?

A: Yeah, yes.

Q: And, in one of these letters, you expressed I guess, what looked like concern? Saying your mother was not making adequate use of her daughter, and then--then you offered to, to purchase the child for the sum of five thousand dollars? Mr. Wilder, who are you looking at? Please answer the question.

A: Not--

Q: No? Permission to approach?

THE COURT: Go ahead.

Q: I am showing you what's been marked State's exhibit 4. This is a letter you wrote to your mother, isn't it? Please answer.

A: Yes.

Q: I am going to read a portion of this letter. Will you follow along to verify that I read correctly?

What do you even have to lose? You've got no real use for her anyway.

And skipping down,

You would get five thousand and she'd be my problem, not yours. It's a good deal. Think about it.

Is that accurate? I'm sorry, what did you say?

A: Nothing.

Q: All right, then could you answer please.

A: That--yes, it does say that but-

Q: Thank you, Mr. Wilder. One more thing and I'll let you go. You've said you were worried for Miss Wilder's safety, you've told the police some stories that can only be described as horrific. But you have not offered any proof, have you, beyond your word and that of the girl you admittedly took from her home under cover of night and kept hidden for almost half a year, whose life you once valued at--I'm sorry--five thousand dollars? You've offered no proof that it was your mother who committed these heinous acts of abuse?

A: I, I could--

Q: Yes or no is fine.

Mr. Wilder? Have you offered any such proof?

A: Well--

Q: That's because there isn't any, is there? Because it wasn't your mother who hurt your sister. Because it was you.

A: That is not true.

DADE: Objection!

THE COURT: Sustained. The State's last remark will be stricken from the record and not considered by the jury. Ask your next question.

Q: Nothing further, Your Honor.

THE COURT: Re-direct?

DADE: Just a few questions. Mr. Wilder, is this the same letter we just heard from?

A: Okay. Yes.

Q: Do you think you could read the first paragraph, the one highlighted?

A: I, ah. I don't, I--I don't know.

Q: Or maybe you could tell me if what I've read is correct after I read it aloud?

I don't know what you mean by hurt, Mom. Will you please tell me just this once if she is okay? You said

she had really done it this time. What did she do? Is
she alright?

    Is that correct?

    A: Yes--yes it--yes.

chapter 41.

WEIRD; it hadn't been that long but it felt like forever. Winters were different here, slower, and it screwed with my sense of time. So each still-not-bare tree always seemed like it was from somewhere else a long time ago, until I remembered what season it should be. And then I would be surprised for a moment, but I wouldn't show it. I'd just keep staring outside until the next tree.

I didn't want to talk.

There had been so much talking lately. I was enjoying the near silence, with only the rush of wind and other cars on the road going by.

Maybe I should be thinking of something more important than trees. Probably, I don't know, something wise, like how different everything would be from now on, or how dark it could get before dawn. I wasn't sure I could do wisdom, but stranger things had happened.

I tried to think something wise. But before I even decided what to be wise about I was already exhausted and annoyed by the effort. I masked a groan with a yawn and kept staring. Maybe at least I could *look* wise. Even though I still felt exactly as nerve-wracked and pissed off as every second since the trial began. My staring contest with the landscape started to tinge red.

It was like being on stage, or in front of a camera. We, Sol and Peter and his lawyer and I, had all agreed it would be best for me to tell the story—although only two of us knew exactly how much of it was *only* a story—technically meaning I was the one responsible for deciding how the jury saw my brother. So after Doc did her part, re-laying a doctored (ha) version of her first encounter with Peter and me, I was paraded out to the witness stand. They said to get comfortable, as if I could. The chair was too *public*, my mother staring me down from behind the table on the left and my brother from the right. Just my job to make up everyone's minds for them. No pressure at all.

But when they asked me to tell them what I remembered I had been a little trooper, barely stumbling over our somewhat sanitized version of the story even when Peter's annoying lawyer kept interrupting me to "clarify."

Well, okay, until then.

Wait, did you mean . . . If I may interrupt, when you said that, would you say you thought . . . ? So at this point, would you say . . . ? Thank you, now please continue.

I'm trying, but you keep stopping me and it's taking forever.

Someone chuckled.

I'm sorry, I'll stop interrupting you.

It was a pretty boring report after that, almost entirely fabricated, featuring the doting older brother and endearing-if-needy little sister, their pact to run away from home, and just enough detail to make someone think we really might have been squatting barely a state away for half a year. If they wanted to go and find where we'd really been, let them try.

It actually turned out a lot more like the version I'd imagined at first, before I gave up, when I was still a dumb and (relatively) optimistic little kid. The telling only got awkward when I had to deal with those annoying little nuggets of truth that kept popping up. That damned back of the truck thing I had been so amused to share, for one. I covered it up well enough—although I went with my brother willingly (I even said it without rolling my eyes!)—we got in a fight on the way to the car, leading to a few bruised ribs for Peter and a coach ticket for me.

I probably could have done better. I definitely could have after she started asking questions again.

It was obvious, what she'd want to talk about next, but as soon as she started to change the subject I looked over to the other side of the room. Like an idiot.

And she wasn't even doing anything, except smiling. I don't know, I figured she might glare threats, or look bored, like she had nothing to worry about. But she was smiling, which I didn't know if I'd ever really seen before, because she looked, honestly, just like Peter, or Peter looked exactly like her when he did that. I didn't know she could look that way.

So even though the attorney only asked me if I thought my brother took good care of me, here I am staring at my Mom all sad and sorry, and she's looking back like she's encouraging me and I'm thinking we're family, me, her and Peter, we might be the absolute worst kind but we're *family*, like we look alike and everything, and wondering suddenly if I ever look this much like her, and the lawyer hasn't even asked the big question yet.

Eventually I came back to the world, but not in a good way. I answered the question already tensed up for the next one, every muscle shouting that I was a *liar*. I looked guilty, I had lied before, and what reason did anyone have to believe me? Right then, I wasn't even sure if I believed *myself*; sure, I didn't get along with her, but . . .

She'd said I was uncontrollable, oppositional and defiant. Prone to violent rages when I didn't get my way. A self-injurer, and not quite a habitual liar, nothing like that, of course, just unable to understand the real consequences of my words sometimes. She mostly blamed my behavior on leaving me alone so much with Peter, whose list of phony diagnoses she'd only gotten about halfway through before the judge got bored. (On the bright side, I had apparently improved drastically with him gone.)

She was wrong about him, lying. Fine. But I *had* paralyzed a boy once. Attacked a police officer. I'd tried to kill myself over taking medicine once, and I came close to killing my brother, back in the Drophouse. I had lied about being-

No, I reminded myself. That was the truth.

Right. Right? Could I be so sure, after forcing myself to forget for so long? Could I really say she wasn't right to be angry back then? That there wasn't some truth to everything she said?

And if she was wrong, did it excuse any of those things I'd done? Did it make it okay that I'd almost killed a man in my bed one night?

So who would you say takes better care of you, your brother or your Mom?

I couldn't think straight. I didn't want to answer, didn't want to talk. I wanted to go home. I wanted a home so I could go back to it and not have to be here anymore.

I'd been warned against looking at my brother while I was answering questions. It looked bad, and looking bad was Bad; so I was on my own, fighting to make myself brave enough to do this. Even though my lungs had lost their ability to function automatically and my eyes felt dry, like they had been open too long.

He does.

It came out sounding wrong, all shriveled and sad and so not like me. But no one (else) seemed to notice. Not that I'd have known—after making such a squeaky, pathetic noise, no way was I looking up again. For once I did what I was supposed to, sat and answered questions, even when the other lawyer started in on me. When they asked me to explain, I (sort of) did. When they asked me to give examples I clammed up, and would only talk again if they either brought out the records or changed the subject.

Yes, I think I was in danger at home, no, things did not get better after Peter left, yes, they got worse.

No, I will not tell you how.

Yes, that is from a long time ago, yes, I remember how it happened, no, it was not an accident.

Yes, I attacked Officer Daniels, yes, I will tell you why, yes—no, I wouldn't do it again.

Like it was the easiest thing in the world, begging for my brother's life like that. Like it wasn't fucking terrifying, begging for mine.

I wanted to be dramatic. Wanted to leave the whole room in tears, clamoring for the judge to end this *now*, release these poor kids. Let them alone to go about their lives, maybe even apologize, especially to the girl, it was her who showed us all the error of our ways, after all.

I'd planned to tell them they couldn't send me back or she would kill me. Kind of over-the-top, but not untrue. I wasn't stupid, I knew what I was trying to do and I would say anything I needed them to hear—it being the truth was nothing more than a bonus.

But of course I didn't say any of it. Drama's great in theory, but when it could have actually helped, I lost my nerve. The judge finally asked who I'd rather stay with, I whined out some crappy two-word answer and stopped talking, and eventually they told me I could go. The only thing I did right was not looking at Peter. At all, really.

Somebody should've warned me there were still things I didn't know. I could have prepared if I knew I had something to prepare for. Maybe I couldn't have prepared enough . . . okay, definitely not, but at least it wouldn't have been so fucking *unfair*.

Even now, watching trees, it was hard to imagine Peter writing back and forth with my Mom all these years, chatting like old buddies while I was still wondering if he was even alive. Yeah, they wrote about me, sure, but . . . it wasn't good enough to make up for him not telling me.

I mean how could he, for all this time, the *whole* time, have been not-exactly-lying to me, to my *face*, like he'd missed me so much, when he could have talked to me any time he wanted? He could have, because it was my house too—*damn it, I was there too*—but it was like I didn't exist at all.

You can't be serious.

Oh, shut up. I always did this, interrupted myself right when I was getting worked up into a good old-fashioned sulk.

No. You have no right to be angry at him for trying to solve things peacefully. The right way.

But that was just it! He was trying to make peace with Mom as always, trying to negotiate over me like *I* was the problem. Like he always did.

Bullshit.

Then why didn't he ever talk to me?

Why do you assume he never tried? How many of those letters do you think had your name on them?

He could do better than letters.

Except that eventually he did do better. And look where it got him.

Whose side are you even on? I held in a sigh and closed my eyes, blacking the trees from view.

Okay, fine, the letters were more surprising than really bad. But I'd carried that envelope around for months not knowing I was actually preserving the last shards of Mom's and my brother's relationship, which had always been so much more of one than hers and mine. She wouldn't even let him talk most of the time, but when she did she *listened*, cared what he said. At least, that's how I always felt, and it was not a feeling I missed.

But the letters were nothing compared to the missing witness.

I didn't even know what to call him anymore—Rye? Dr. Pollock? The psychiatrist who helped make my brother's life hell for eight years? The one who personally made mine hell for . . .

Well, I couldn't use the last one; I wasn't sure how long, yet.

It had taken a while to figure this part out, but once I'd finally picked up that only one witness was missing, it clunked horribly into place that the psychiatrist and my mom's "moral support" were actually the same person.

I couldn't say how I reacted to the realization. I don't think I'll ever be done reacting.

I do know that at first when it hit me there was a surge, a jolt of shock like a gun had been pressed to my spine, like a held-in gasp. And then it had seemed like I might be crying, but looking around had told me I must not be. Crying would be noticed. Which made me paranoid that I *might* cry, so I tried to clear the idea from my mind.

I still had a sort of wall up around those memories. It took physical effort to dwell on that particular chapter of the past (seriously, I had to catch my breath sometimes), but even if it did take years I'd finally gotten rid of him, and even though technically I had already done it before this time I did it the right way. By being ready to tell the truth— and letting him see it.

I was so used to telling myself I hated to lie. But at some point, up there on the stand with all of those people staring at me, I'd realized that simply wasn't true. Lying was complicated, yes, and when done for the wrong reason, it was outright stupid. Except that I lied all the time—it was what I knew. I'd simply made some imaginary distinction in my mind: the Right Kind and the Wrong Kind of lies. The wrong lies were pointless, disruptive, ludicrous, but the right lies protected me, and if they kept me safe they could hardly be bad, could they?

I was so wrong about myself. I *loved* lying, as long as it was lying the right way. Like I had about Rye.

I hadn't told my brother the truth about him. Maybe I never would, now that I didn't need to. But if it could have helped, this time . . .

He always said how brave I was. He was wrong; infected was more like it. I'm infected by my family's violence. I was willing to kill— and hide it—to hold on to my brother, not to lose him, *years* before it occurred to me that I could trust him with the truth. Because the lie was safe, and telling the truth would have actually meant risking something of mine. Not some symbolic, single thing, like my life, which I didn't have to worry about after it was gone. Something I'd have to live with, that only came into existence when people found out the things only you were supposed to know about yourself.

This time, if it could have saved my brother, I would have been willing to risk the truth. Rye had seen that, and it had done what even a knife hadn't been able to. He was gone.

A dead deer was lying on the side of the road—I watched it fly by.

chapter 42.

HE'D seen the once-black three on the way in, but still Peter gauged the placement of his seat and swept the tabletop like a blind man. There it was. That little groove left behind by someone in this same place who had taken their frustrations out on the table with a key or, more likely, handcuffs. Peter understood; this room may have been dedicated to conversations, but he'd experienced plenty of physical self-expression here as well.

He didn't have to do this, of course. He'd been told as much. There was no need, not if it would be too hard. Odd, how people suddenly cared what might be difficult for him.

Peter wiped a hand across the corner of his mouth, using the other to trace the gouge in the table. He was rehearsing his lines, bracing himself. Pretending he knew what he was doing.

And to his credit, though all of his preparations slunk out right by Jacqueline as she opened the door—*Oh, I think someone's calling me out there*—his unease did not stop him from standing to greet her, or betray itself in his voice. "Are they listening?"

All right, so he didn't exactly *project*, but she did hear him.

"Of course not. You're free as a little *bird* now, aren't you? The whole world just loves you *so* much, all they want is in the world is to see your mother hanged! Why bother listening in when all of them would believe anything you say?"

That's a lot of bait for one hook. Peter sensibly ignored it, instead noting from his Mom's open (and loud) hostility that she must be telling the truth. It was strange not to be under surveillance.

"All right. Why did you want to talk?" He asked slowly. The most important thing was to sound confident.

He fell just shy.

If Sol was to be believed, it was not surprising that the jury had dropped the kidnapping charge. But logical or lucky, he'd dodged the orange jumpsuit. He *was* free.

Free-ish. There was more, a kind of fail-safe—something called custodial interference—and "sympathy" had done him less good there. Though it could have been worse, probation did not quite leave him as *free as a bird.*

Now there was only the small hearing, in a different room of the same courthouse, with a different judge who probably golfed with the first one on sunny mornings. If there was no decision today they would want to put her in a foster home, and then it would be much harder to get her back. Worse if it was only for a short while, because then . . .

Well, then he might actually have to give them time to decide.

His mother stabbed a finger at him. "I am here to *tell* you," the tangible force behind the word briefly caused Peter to break eye contact, "that I want my child back, and I am going to *get* her back because she is mine. *Mine*, not yours."

He backed away. For once, though, he didn't back down. "Your what? Your daughter? When has that ever-"

"You really have lost your mind, talking to me like that," Jacqueline's voice quaked, her eyes drilled into him, but she didn't advance.

She may be right. She'd called this meeting to intimidate him, and he was just as surprised as she was at how it was going instead. But the more he remembered that terrified look on his reckless comic-strip superhero sister's face, the more he understood this needed to be said.

"Maybe. But *she* gave you a chance once, didn't she? And what did you do? When Alana told you what—what your *boyfriend* was doing, she was asking you, for *once*, to be her mother. What happened instead? What did you *do*?" His voice rose but he didn't much care, about his tone or the betrayal of his sister's confidence (he could worry about that later).

Jacqueline darkened, actually appeared to fall into shadow. She snorted. "So she fed you that one too." Her eyes stopped stabbing at him to gaze into the distance. "Liar; she'll ruin anything she can't have." She seemed surprised and only mildly defensive, as if a teacher had dared to question her parenting. "I couldn't just allow that."

Peter shook his head, but didn't ask again. He knew very well what happened to liars. "So she came to you for help, and you *beat* her into keeping quiet about it and let-"

His mother came back to herself fast. "What is so hard for you to understand? She was *lying*," she spat. "I asked him about it, obviously. I did what I was supposed to. And Ryland told me what really happened—how she made a move on *him*, and tried to use me to get back at him when he turned her down. *He* was mine, too, but the little bitch just did what she always does, saw something she wanted and tried to snatch it away."

Now he was confused. "I don't understand. M-mom," his voice tried to break but he wouldn't—could *not*—let it, "she wouldn't-"

She continued as if she hadn't heard. "I tried to raise that girl, tried to teach her better, but it was David all over again."

Peter was sure he should say something, but he wasn't ready. Something was wrong with what he was hearing; something was not making sense.

Because something *was* making sense.

Jacqueline was glaring again, not at him but *into* him. "You remember what she was like with him. What they were like *together*," she hissed.

Of course he did. He remembered everything.

A colicky baby who'd turned more difficult by the day into toddler-hood, Al had always been starved for attention—and frequently got it through wordless screaming and violence. It was frustrating for Mom (or who she used to be), and a nuisance to Peter, who found excuses to keep his distance and encouraged her to keep hers as well.

But David was different. Probably because he saw so much of himself in his daughter he eventually overcame his contempt for her, and she adored him in return. Enough that she was all too quick to forgive when his attention invariably turned from doting to violent. In their family, it must have seemed perfectly normal.

Not that Al would remember any of those "good" times now. When he left them she had been devastated far past what her brother could understand, let alone tolerate, and so he had done the best he could think to when suddenly he found himself taking care of her all over again: he told her what he knew. The truth. And in telling her the truth about her father, he had changed the way she remembered him, turned all of her happy memories into hazy childhood fictions.

He might have felt bad. But had he really done anything wrong? Coward or not, Peter had watched everything, and what little he hadn't seen he'd heard instead, sometimes through the walls or sometimes across the kitchen table from David himself.

They all turn. Even a sweet little girl like that, you don't give them a firm hand and in a few years she'll just be another high and mighty bitch.

Can't let that happen.

The woman he was looking at now was unbalanced, dangerous. But she was merely a host—if any real evil was in her it was because she was possessed by the devil that walked away a long time ago.

Something in the re-telling of David had changed him, too, though, because even at such a young age he must have realized on some level what he had taken from her. It was too soon—Al was too young to cope with the truth and he was too angry to communicate it, so instead of making her informed what he'd actually done was make her *alone*, expose a hole in her life she hadn't understood was there before.

And after years of being the disappointing son, all he could do to fix this was to learn, even if he'd never gotten it right, even if he never would, to try and be good enough for *her* instead of David, to give back some of what he'd taken away.

That obnoxious, difficult little girl had saved him from becoming his own version of what stood in front of him. Anything he'd done since was only returning the favor.

He wished he could tell the judge that. But it was better not said at all. Even if she could possibly understand, Al had been through more than enough for one lifetime because of David. It was a more fitting punishment for him—and easier for her—to simply let her father continue to fade out of her memory.

Forgetting the past decade for a moment, speaking to her as if she were the sensible person he had once believed she could become, Peter addressed his mother. "I remember him walking out on us, all of us, when she was a toddler. There wasn't time for them to be *like* much of anything."

Jacqueline bristled, immune to his calm. "Oh, there was plenty! There was so much time, it was *almost* enough. She almost did it."

Peter was utterly lost now. He stared. This apparently displeased his mother, who seemed to be waiting for a signal to continue. She snorted again, impatient, watching him closely. "He walked out on you," she stated in a cold, patient voice that stood the hairs on her son's neck at attention, "and he walked out on me."

Do you know what culling is?

The hard floor of the garage makes him shiver as he stares and stares at the gun, unable to get up, afraid to move . . .

The memory was strong but short-lived. The walls barely had time to warp before he realized what she'd told him and held his breath, not ready to know it even though there was no other choice. Had he thought she wouldn't have prepared something special for this meeting?

Jacqueline scrutinized, then smiled, pleased to see he understood. "Exactly. She did nothing but sit there sucking up all of his attention, the spoiled little shit. He didn't even *want* her to begin with, and he— he had the nerve, the *nerve* to say I couldn't raise her right by myself and he was taking her, leaving me with his *other* reject . . ." she trailed off, panting, flushed.

The walls held still, but the room felt unnaturally silent as it sunk in, as Peter sought out and failed to find the words to make her take it back. For one anachronistic moment he was truly terrified it would happen, when David went he really would take her with him, away, forever, and Peter would never get the chance to know his little sister, never even know what had happened to her.

But it *couldn't* happen, because it *hadn't* happened. Which raised a new question. "Then—wha-why-"

She interrupted him with disgust. "You always were so damn full of yourself. Always peeking around corners, spying on everybody like *you* were the one in charge. Exactly like him, but even more useless.

"I knew what he was. You may have thought you saw it, but I *knew*. It wasn't right to let him have her. Your *father* thought he had me beaten down, too scared to go against him, but I wasn't. All I had to do was tell him, say what I knew, and swear if he took her that soon enough the rest of the world would know, too. That's all it took for him to drop her like a sack of-" she broke off, chuckling, "like she was *you*.

"And I did that for her, even after that little whore destroyed my marriage. I could have let him have her, I could have gotten rid of you both and finally had my life back, but I did that—for *her*. You should have been grateful."

He didn't want to be hearing this. Sure, he'd wondered sometimes how his mother could be so openly hateful toward her own daughter, but he had expected-

Well, maybe not for it to make sense. But not this.

Certainly not that Jacqueline was *jealous* of her daughter. Definitely not for her to still, basically, have saved the girl—only to be disappointed when the act failed to transform her into the perfectly devoted child his Mom apparently believed she deserved.

But she couldn't be—which was the problem, wasn't it? Because Jacqueline didn't seem to understand the reality that lay in the way of her fantasies of hero-worship, even if Alana had known. No amount of gratitude would have been enough to fix what was really wrong.

It could never change the fact that even after, *especially* after everything he had put her through, David had chosen to leave her behind.

He walked out on me . . . His *other* reject . . . She'd said it all. There was some part of her that had *not* hated David the way he deserved. Like Peter, part of her still felt she had done something to deserve his mistreatment—and, in the end, his abandonment.

But Jacqueline had chosen to cope through revenge. First against their father, when she took Alana from him (because that was what she'd truly done, though Peter couldn't fault her for it). Then against them. Both of them. Simply because they were there—in the most literal sense—and so was she.

He used to think some word or act could fix his family, like magic. Naïve, yes, but he was only a kid, and one who'd spent years dementedly dreaming about what it would be like, when he found it. He felt the last of that dream draining away from him now. It had lasted too long anyway.

"May-maybe it, it might not be . . . too late," he tried.

Jacqueline glared.

"You could get your life back. And I would be grateful." There was a knack to not choking on the last words, but stuttering would have made her doubt him, so he managed it.

His mother had lost her sneer; she just looked grim now. "You're exactly like him," she said again, her voice matching her expression, "and she's worse than you both. You all ruined my life. You made *everyone* hate me. And now you want to walk away from me like I'm nothing."

As if you could ever *be nothing,* Peter thought tiredly.

She advanced again, steadily. "So I will make sure you never see me—or her—again," she drew her conclusion calmly, without a hint of malice.

For her, that was it. Peter could tell, and not just because she immediately turned to leave.

The threat was empty, of course.

Mostly.

He watched her go.

chapter 43.

THE trees were ugly, I decided. No snow to paint a background for the bare ones, and the green ones looked out of place by comparison. A fire could destroy the whole landscape out here and it might actually improve the place.

I scratched at my teeth with a fingernail, tried to clean my fingernails with a tooth. Leaned my head against the widow, pressing against the glass hard. It helped—I had absolutely no idea how to feel, and the grinding of the cold glass against my skull provided at least some distraction for my raw nerves.

I was just doing this, wasn't I? Sitting on my ass, on my way to who-knew-where, in absolutely no control of my life. Although things were a bit different this time.

I mean, I was happy. Of course I was happy, obviously I was. Honestly.

And maybe if I wasn't also about twenty *other* things, I could be *happy* about being happy. As it was, my stomach was leaping and tumbling at every small bump in the road, and I was a little too sick to dance with joy.

I thought about trying to be wise one more time and almost cracked a smile, it seemed so boring.

"Damn it Alana, will you say something?"

"Language," I muttered, not moving an inch.

"Everybody gets one," Peter said easily.

I rolled my eyes. "This is the first I'm hearing about that rule."

"Probably because you used up your 'one' before you can remember."

Very briefly I considered protesting, playing along. He was trying so hard to make conversation and failing so miserably. I watched him from the corner of one eye.

He didn't look much better than before the trial—still unsteady, as if he expected the world to whip around suddenly and throw him off—but he was starting to quiet down. I was relieved for him; I knew well how the sound of constant mental screaming could weigh on a person, but he didn't do a very good job hiding it. My mouth opened, for some reason, and before I could think I'd said

"What was my first word?"

And finally startled myself away from the window.

He was quiet for a minute. "I don't remember."

I nodded and resumed tree-watching. Odd—it seemed like the kind of thing he would know.

Another few minutes passed in silence—it was bound to happen, we'd been driving for a while—but suddenly the van slowed and Peter quietly told me to close my eyes. A glance later he was telling me to calm down, it wasn't important, never mind. Pulse still racing, I stared at him, daring him to ask again, which he didn't. He even had the decency to sheepishly avoid my eyes afterward.

What it meant was clear, though. You only close your eyes when you're almost there.

(Or sometimes when a deceptively terrifying cop is about to arrest you and put a gun to your brother's head, but whatever.)

Last time, I'd imagined the next step. Hiding out for a while longer, waiting for something to blow over that maybe never would, possibly packing up and moving on again if it made sense to. Relatively comfortable, sure, and together, but always on guard against what might happen next. Basically, more of the same.

But this time, there was an ending. And we were almost there.

My stomach lurched again, and I realized I was smiling. And then stopped smiling, because I had realized it. Smiled again. *Enough, already.*

"So now that we don't have to go to Di's will you finally tell me where we *are* headed, or did you not actually plan that far?" I prodded.

"No plan? You must have us confused," he countered, almost deadpan except for the cryptic smirk he couldn't quite suppress. It grew wider as he swung a hairpin turn down a street I hadn't noticed.

Sitting on my ass, on my way to who-knew-where. But not so much in no control, really, right? Because this was the end I would have chosen for myself. If I could go back in time and talk to myself months ago, back when I was still lost in a haze of fear and rage and grief and confusion, taking it out on myself or anything within reach, that's what I would have told me. *I know you can't say what's wrong, and maybe you never will. But there is an end, and it's the one you would have picked for yourself.*

Then the van turned again, I heard gravel crunch beneath the tires, and my stomach plummeted all over again as I realized I had to re-think my definition of "end."

I avoided the ugly trees this time and moved my eyes as quickly as I could, turning my full attention to the drivers' seat. I would look in a minute, or whenever the hell I actually felt ready to. Whichever came sooner.

My brother looked at me too, hard, almost comically serious. We matched stares for a minute; I saw something in his face and pulled a wry expression to evade the waterworks, and he grinned. It occurred to me there was something someone was supposed to say, but it took

me too long to figure out what it was and by the time I had it he'd
squeezed my arm and opened the door and I heard him say

"Welcome home."

11, 17

TWO times fast, then three times slowly. The girl squeezes her eyes shut and curls up tighter, wishing her door locked from the inside, wishing it had even two or three strong locks with keys and bolts she could twist to keep people out.

But it doesn't. It swings open and then the mattress sags in behind her. She won't move, though; even when she hears her name she holds still and tries to look asleep. If she doesn't pay attention to him, maybe he'll give up. Maybe he can still change his mind.

He shakes her shoulder, calling again. The boy knows she's awake and he doesn't have much time, but he still plays along for a little while. It gives him more time before he has to start pretending to know what he's doing again.

He keeps going over this in his mind, trying to find a way to change it or take it back. Sometimes it's almost like he's only missed something, like if he just thinks about it hard enough he can find a way not to leave her behind.

He can't, though. She's a tough little kid, sure, but not a very careful one, and he wouldn't be able to watch her all the time, and . . .

He shudders. No. She's safer here. Anyway, it's him Mom hates. He sits up, chewing his lip, tastes metal, and winces. He is probably doing the girl a favor by leaving, even if he has to do it without saying goodbye.

Perhaps reading his mind, she springs upright. "You can't go. I won't let you," she whispers first, and then, louder, "I'll yell. Mom will come." She could. If their mother found out what he was trying to do there's no telling what she'd do to him, but it would be his own fault. She already told him not to go, she told him over and over again, she's been telling him for days not to, this is a Bad idea. Running is not allowed. "If you do I will never forgive you. Ever."

Part of the girl, the part that was listening when he told her, knows why he's leaving and understands that he probably does have to go. The rest of her wants to hit him again, and scream and scream until her mother comes to stop him from doing this because even if he does have to it doesn't mean he can.

Her brother is looking at her still and waiting, and she feels hot, painful tears starting in her eyes again even though she doesn't want them to because she knows she isn't going to do anything. But she already knew she couldn't change his mind, she just doesn't know she knew until she feels something in her break apart and she's gulping and crying and trying to be quiet all at the same time.

The boy leans toward her and she isn't done wanting to hit him, so she does, but she's crying so hard she can't breathe right so he hugs her anyway and she hugs him back, hard. He says something but she doesn't listen and after a minute he moves back. She holds on tighter, panicked. How can he go if the last thing she did was threaten and hit him?

He doesn't let go either though, he drags her with him, then picks her up and carries her down the hall. The next moment the light blazes on and the girl and boy are blinking, squinting at each other in the bathroom mirror. She'd thought she was the only one crying.

For a minute they stare at themselves and each other—the girl keeps looking even when she gets pretty uncomfortable—then the boy takes a long, stuttering breath. "I need you to promise me something."

The girl's eyes narrow, but she looks more tired than hostile as she talks around her tears. "Why should I?"

He doesn't blame her, but the sound of his own blood rushing in his ears and the weight of the bag on his back are reminding him that this night is far from over, and if he does not want to do this all over again some other night he needs to get out, and soon. "I need you to promise to keep yourself out of trouble, and promise to play it safe— safer than you usually do—until I get back." He waits for as long as he can stand. "I just need to know you'll . . . still be here, okay? So promise. Now."

He doesn't know if it will matter even if she does promise, but something in the back of his mind is nagging at him and it won't feel right unless she does. "Now," he says again, turning away from the reflection to really look at her.

She's still crying, though not as hard as before, watching the mirror. And she doesn't say anything. Maybe she was right; he might not have the right to make her make promises anymore. So he won't. It won't change anything anyway—no matter what, she'll be fine and he'll be worried, right?

He tries to memorize this, the stubborn set of her small jaw, the tangled, stringy mess of hair. Not that he needs this moment to remember the girl like this—it's familiar enough. The only thing that's really changed is how heavy she's gotten.

She turns away from the mirror, but he doesn't want to remember her eyes this way. Instead he thinks, obviously there's something someone's supposed to say here. He knows what it is, but she doesn't want to hear it and he doesn't need to.

He carries her back down the hall and to her room, finally peeling her off of him, and gets her back into bed. She hides under the blanket and rolls away. He tries to tell himself again that she's strong and she'll be okay without him as he strokes the fabric over her head, but it's like the world has twisted around and suddenly he's not sure it is her he's really worrying about.

He looks over at the window—it gets smaller and wider and smaller again, like a chomping mouth, and for just a second he's the one who feels heavy.

So it has to be now, before it's too late. The girl is trying not to look like it, but she'll listen. "I'll be back before you know it, okay, I'll only be gone a little while. Promise."

The boy shifts the bag on his back, for something to do. Goes to the window but his hands aren't steady enough to open the latch at first.

She doesn't come out, doesn't move. She isn't going to while she's still crying like a little baby. But she won't just lie here and pout like one, either. "I promise too," she says from under the covers, trying to sound okay. He said a little while, and she can tell he meant it. So if that's all it takes to help make him keep his promise, then fine, she won't ruin it. "To be safe and out of trouble. I promise if you do." There's a pause and, she's pretty sure, a hand on her head. Then a rush of cold air and the sound of a shoe against bark. Then nothing. Then more nothing.

The window is still open, and it's getting colder. The girl stays buried under the blanket anyway and tucks her toes under her. She knows the world on the outside of it is doing things, moving, shifting, changing into something different, and she'll have to be strong when she comes out. But she can't yet because she's something else right now.

acknowledgments.

MY sincerest thanks to my best friend Ruqayyah, who encouraged me to take my bad habit public. The most vehement promise I made to myself when I put down the first word of Patchwork was that no other human being would ever lay eyes on it. Clearly, I was a liar.

My four-legged writing and editing buddy joined me halfway through the first draft. His constant staring and lively dreams have been wonderful companions, as has he. I apologize for my loud and dramatic dialogue reading, which he never quite got used to. He deserves all the strawberry tops in the world.

Thanks go also to my parents and sister, for being decidedly NOT the inspiration for this book. Actually, maybe that's not exactly true. I have grown to appreciate their humor, honesty, and loyalty more and more, and the sheer number of ways we have come apart and back together over the years have truly made me a believer in the importance of family itself.

Someday I should really tell them I wrote this book.

I would thank God, but frankly I'm not sure I'm ready to bring it up with Him either.

Finally, if you suspect a child is being abused or neglected, please do your best to take action. A good place to start in the USA is the Childhelp National Abuse Hotline at 800-422-4453. And if you can do nothing else, it takes strength to be kind. Everyone has their own struggle.

L.

Made in United States
North Haven, CT
20 May 2023

36772847R00243